Praise for Jack Cady

"A fine, fabulous fable packed with marvelous events and wonders."

—Gahan Wilson

"A consummate yarn, told with many digressions and anecdotes that combine with folksy humor to create a tall tale suffused with pathos and melancholy."

—*Seattle Times*

"Without a doubt Cady's funniest, weirdest, most original, and—literally—spookiest novel yet."

—Peter S. Beagle

"A pungent mix of Tom Robbins, Ray Bradbury, and Charles G. Finney—but pure Cady, and it's glorious."

—Greg Bear

"Jack Cady's knack for golden sentences is an alchemy any other writer has to admire. "

—Ivan Doig

"Jack Cady is above all, a writer of great, unmistakable integrity and profound feeling. He never fakes it or coasts, and behind every one of his sentences is an emotional freight that bends it both outward, toward the reader, and inward, back to the source."

—Peter Straub

"A writer whose words reverberate with human insight."

—*Publishers Weekly*

"His structural control and the laconic richness of his style establish Cady in the front ranks of contemporary writers."

—*Library Journal*

"When Cady settles into yarn-spinning, his stories have the humor and comfortable mastery of Faulkner or Steinbeck."

—*National Review*

THE CADY COLLECTION

NOVELS

The Hauntings of Hood Canal
Inagehi
The Jonah Watch
McDowell's Ghost
The Man Who Could Make Things Vanish
The Off Season
Singleton
Street

Dark Dreaming [with Carol Orlock, as Pat Franklin]
Embrace of the Wolf [with Carol Orlock, as Pat Franklin]

OTHER WRITINGS

Phantoms
Fathoms
Ephemera
The American Writer

The Off Season

The Off Season

A Victorian Sequel

Jack Cady

Underland Press

Copyright © 2015 the Estate of Jack Cady
Introduction © 2015 Gordon Van Gelder

This is U018, and it has an ISBN of 978-1-63023-010-4.

This book was printed in the United States of America, and it is published by Underland Press, an imprint of Resurrection House (Puyallup, WA).

Obed began to dance . . .

Cover Design by Jennifer Tough
Book Design by Aaron Leis
Collection Editorial Direction by Mark Teppo

The first edition of this novel was released by St. Martin's Press in 1995. "On Writing the Ghost Story" first appeared in *Ghosts of Yesterday*, a collection published by Night Shade Books in 2003 and is © the Estate of Jack Cady.

First Underland Press edition: June 2015.

www.resurrectionhouse.com

For Carol

Contents

Introduction

Gordon Van Gelder

I HAVE NOT READ ALL OF JACK CADY'S NOVELS (ONE IS SOCKED AWAY in a cache of books meant for a time when I can enjoy more leisure reading), but I've read most of them and *The Off Season* is my favorite.

One reason is because I edited the book and twenty years later, I have only good memories of the experience. Perhaps the file for the book, somewhere in the basement of the Flatiron building in Manhattan, is full of contentious correspondence, but if so, those memories are buried deeper than that basement. I don't remember any difficult negotiations, no spats over editing the book or the cover design. *The Off Season* was not a book that made anybody rich, but the experience of publishing it was one of many small joys.

(I do, by the way, remember a wonderfully cranky letter Jack sent me concerning copyediting. He said something to the effect of, "I've gone on the record of saying how much I hate the city of Chicago. Hate the weather, hate the architecture. When I was driving, I'd go miles out of my way to avoid that city. But my feelings for Chicago pale in comparison with my hatred for *The Chicago Manual of Style*." I'm pretty sure, however, that Jack sent me that letter in regard to another work.)

There are other reasons why *The Off Season* is my favorite, but first, let me tell you a bit about Jack.

=

When I first met him in the early 1990s, Jack Cady was in his early 60s, a tall man with a craggy face and a full head of dark hair (gray around the edges) and a beard he would stroke enthusiastically—not as urbane intellectuals in movies do, but more like a little kid playing with a toy. I happened to see the 1948 film *Brute Force* recently and it occurred to me that Charles Bickford (Gallagher in the movie) would have made a good choice to play Jack on the big screen. Aside from the physical resemblance—both of them big guys with bushy hair and gruff voices who were clearly not afraid of physical labor—Bickford could have captured the sincerity, wisdom, and generosity of spirit that Jack exuded.

Jack worked a lot of blue-collar jobs: truck driver, tree high-climber, auctioneer. I'm pretty sure he met his friend Frank Herbert (author of *Dune*) when he was doing landscaping work on the Herberts' property in Port Townsend. Jack's appreciation of laborers shows in most of his fiction; Steinbeck's influence on Cady is strong.

Jack wound up teaching at the university level, including thirteen years at Pacific Lutheran. He told me that in his first year, a student asked him: "Do you think I can make it as a writer?"

As Jack told me, "The guy was writing the most godawful stuff—cutesy and clever and just bad. But I said to him, 'Sure, why not?' and damned if he hasn't gone on to have himself a respectable career."

I did mention Jack's generosity of spirit, didn't I?

=

In the summer of 1997, Jack hosted me and my wife as we were took off a week after a convention in Seattle. As I recall, Jack and his dog Molly had just returned from a trip to a jazz festival in Montana, but he made us feel welcome right away. His house in Port Townsend was full of good, solid wood furniture and the kitchen bookshelves overflowed with fiction rescued from thrift stores. (I particularly remember seeing Hervey Allen's work there. Was he reading *Anthony Adverse* at the time? I think so.) There was no television in the house that I saw.

Part of my reason for visiting Jack was because I wanted to visit Port Townsend—which brings me to another reason why *The Off Season* is a favorite of mine. I'm not giving away much when I say that the town where Jack lived for thirty years served as the model for Point Vestal; I found the information online after eighteen seconds of searching.* *[If you're curious, it turns up in the *Publishers Weekly* review for *The Off Season* and in the *Peninsula Daily News* obituary for Jack, both of which are online.] Jack was not one to let the sins of the past go unremembered and Port Townsend had plenty of such for the remembering.

While we were in town, Jack took us to the old jailhouse that has been converted to a museum and I spent a few minutes in a cell. Jack took us to the fort. Did he show us staircase like the one in the novel? Memory fails me. I know he pointed out some mansions as we drove, but I can't remember if he indicated that any of them modeled for the Starling House or the Parsonage. I do know for certain that we saw none of the strange doings that you'll encounter in *The Off Season*. Fiction did not become fact.

But I did get a feeling that Jack captured some of the town's essence in his novel. Look on the pages—in between the words—and you'll find the spirit of the place.

=

No one acquainted with Jack Cady's fiction should be surprised to know that his works are grounded in their settings, rooted to the land. Like the American writers he surveyed in his book on the subject, he was aware of the history, the traditions, and the terrain of his stories' locales. When he wrote about the homeless in Seattle, he knew the streets in question. When he wrote about the North Carolina wilderness in *Inagehi* or the highways of the United States in *Singleton*, the reality of the locales are there—they get under your fingernails, they lodge in your head.

I love *The Off Season* because there are spirits in the Pacific air of Port Townsend and they mixed perfectly with the magic in Jack Cady's fiction. This novel blends the past and the present, the darkness and the light, the weight of our sins and the joy of being alive, and damn if it doesn't get that blend just right.

And I didn't even mention the cats.

—Gordon Van Gelder
March 2015

Author's Note

THE AUTHOR'S IMAGINATION, BEING SUFFICIENTLY SARDONIC, FOUND no reason to fashion any character in this book after anyone living or dead. Resemblances between the town of Point Vestal and the city of Port Townsend, Washington, are, however, purely intentional. I am real proud of tatting together the histories of both places, and of capturing their essential charms. I'd be equally proud if I could take credit for the occasional snatches of Victorian poetry appearing here and there. Except for one sachet by Poe, however, they are quoted from *Poetry of the Pacific*, May Wentworth, editor (San Francisco: Pacific Publishing Company, 1867). The poets are Edward Pollock, W. A. Kendall, B. F. Washington, and Emilie Lawson.

Ever since I was a pup, I've been enamored with the works of Mark Twain. The book that follows is not an attempt to emulate the master, because that would be a surefire failure, a real dumb thing to do; and I am not a masochist. I had one thing foremost in mind when I wrote *The Off Season*. I wanted to write a book that would gladden the hearts of readers, but also a book that, if possible from the land of wit and poetry where all great writers surely go, my hero Mark Twain would enjoy reading.

The Off Season

. . . which showed me plainly that, so far from his imagining that there was anything ridiculous or funny about his story, he regarded it as a really important matter, and admired his two heroes as men of transcendent genius in finesse.

—Mark Twain,
"The Notorious Jumping Frog of Calaveras County"

Chapter 1

Tides along Point Vestal rise dramatic, like the ghosts who sometimes run this town. Tides lift boats to the level of the only road, and from the boat basin spectators peer through mist toward voices of the dead. People who work and live on the boats gaze downward toward the road. They step from high decks to worn concrete sidewalks stamped with emblems of the New Deal and the Public Works Administration, sidewalks carrying dates reading 1937, sometimes 1938.

Some of us were children when those sidewalks were poured. Some were adults. Our people are more than simply long-lived, for the town cares nothing about casting us into the mists of death. Tourists often look surprised to learn our oldest citizen carries 113 years, and is only in competition. The oldest person in Point Vestal history was/is 120, or 119; records remain unclear.

The New Deal's sidewalks line the downtown business district, its nineteenth-century brick raising Victorian facades four and five stories above the Strait of Juan de Fuca. The New Deal's 307-step concrete stairway runs a thin line up the hill beside the bluff. That stairway with its many small steps links downtown and uptown, although a couple of streets also lead up the hill. Everything on the bluff is uptown, where polite haunts echo.

Along uptown streets Victorian mansions congregate like parishioners sitting through an eternal sermon of rain and mist. Wet streets reflect stained glass windows, tall turrets, wrought iron fences. The houses bear creaking joints and windswept roofs; and people in those houses dwell comfortably beside a hundred years' worth of ghosts.

In the Starling House, a four-story mansion, a drawing room held one of many legends haunting this town. It is a Victorian tale, and we still think of the story in Victorian terms. In October 1888, when the Starling House stood brand-new and smelling of fresh paint, August Starling was discovered in full evening dress, dancing to the tinkle-bell music of an Austrian music box. His partner wore a plain but lovely long gown, which was not shocking, nor reason for fear. But some people were distressed, others thrilled, because she was dead. Starling danced with a corpse. Even more shocking, the corpse was not his wife.

Chapter 2

WE MUST TELL OUR READER HOW THIS BOOK IS GETTING WRITTEN. Five of us work on it: Bev from the bookstore, Frank, who tends bar at Janie's Tavern, Collette, who runs the antique store, Samuel, a retired pastor, and Jerome, who edits the newspaper. At first we thought we would each write separate chapters, but Bev said, "If we do that the book will sound like a combination of William Morris, John Ruskin, and the confessions of Amy Lowell."

"Around this town," one of us said, "that would make it a bestseller. What's wrong with that?"

"Nothing," Bev said, "but don't expect people in Seattle to read it."

As to why we write: every town has an official history. In Point Vestal, an official history is easy come by, but a *true* history is not. Around here history is not over just because an activity passes. We write an absolutely true history, one uncloyed with romance. We include our own awful mistakes because each of us played a part. The book reveals pretty horrid events that happened some years ago. In fact, since those events, our tourist industry has fallen off. We want to explain what happened, and we want to state for the benefit of tourists that the town is fully reconstructed.

Our problem in writing a true history is: at some time or other, strange forces got loose in this town. They probably arrived early on. When the first whites moved here, they asked the Indians where to settle. The Indians pointed to the site of Point Vestal and said, "Take that. We don't want it. It is cursed."

7

That was 130 years ago. Our founders, mostly from Puritan New England, came to this frontier coast and built big houses. Gloom and mist, eternal rain, criminality went into building the town—smuggling, prostitution, Chinese bond slaves—and caused the builders to feel depressed and guilty. Recall, also, their frontier isolation. The green forest pressed close, as it does today. The sea crashed down the Strait and battered beaches.

Our founders answered back by building an exaggeration of Victorian society. They were ultimate Victorians. If August Starling danced with a corpse, it was no more than many Victorians did symbolically. Combine Victorian firmness with a definite strain of East Coast Puritanism—add strange forces already running—you have a small town where history is active as the present.

=

It has taken a while to figure history out. We had to factor in men named Kune and Joel-Andrew, together with a multilingual cat named Obed. Those three supplied their own forces during the early 1970s.

These days we meet at The Fisherman's Café two mornings a week for coffee (except Frank drinks tea from his mustache cup). Everybody talks about how to get the history set down. Then we go home and write our parts. Then Jerome, our newspaperman, takes the parts and fits them together. He cuts and pastes, trying to make it sound like the same person is telling it all. We make jokes about who writes this book, and we call ourselves The Committee on Specters, which is, as Bev points out, a good way to write about this town. Point Vestal has manifested so many ghosts that only a committee would be ignorant enough to think it possible to handle all of them.

Meetings happen this way, more or less.

We arrive at the warm café about 7:00 AM. Outside, tide beats against rocks, and, if there is a wind, spray rises like gray fingers and blows across Main Street to hit the front of Janie's Tavern. Wind pries at the bookstore's cracked window. It blows salt spray against Mikey Daniels's milk truck, always moseying by about this time. At 7:00 AM nothing else moves out there except wind in the trees. Point Vestal's morning going-to-work traffic is composed of that milk truck.

At sixty-seven, Bev is our group leader. She is even taller than her mother, in her mother's prime. (Bev's mother is ninety-six.) Bev looks like Dorothy Lamour, except with silver hair. She is able-tongued, quick, and makes Frank twitch because she is so beautiful and Frank is such a bachelor. We suspect Bev is the smartest person in town, and know she is the kindest. Bev sits next to Samuel, our retired Methodist minister. Samuel is eighty-seven, looks no more than seventy, and also looks like an ancient dockworker. He stands tall, wide-shouldered, dressed in black broadcloth. He still owns some muscle, plus all his teeth. Samuel would impress a Jehovah's Witness.

We soon settle, breathe deep sighs, and it seems we go through a little stage play. It looks and sounds something like this:

BEV (*pushes long hair back with worldly gesture, smiles widely so her worldly gesture looks friendly and hometown*): We've got to put Kune in the book. No way out of it. Kune killed that woman in Seattle. Should we put that in? I worried about Kune, even after I got all the facts. Or, maybe, especially then.

SAMUEL (*steeples hands as if in prayer, gives Bev a look more seductive than preacherly*): If we tell, the Seattle police will come over and arrest Kune. If Kune gets arrested, he can't walk through the streets all night. If he doesn't walk through the streets all night, there will be no witness to all the carryings-on. That could cause a crime wave.

FRANK: And you a minister of the Bible.

Frank appears built around his beard, but Frank is smart for his age. He is fifty-seven, his beard getting gray, and he looks like John Ruskin. He even *dresses* like John Ruskin. Without the beard and his little potbelly, Frank would weigh 120 soaking wet. Younger people consider him a greedy little bartending priss, but most people think him sensible.

> FRANK (*pulls at mustache, looking more ministerial than Samuel*): A minister of the Bible is supposed to be straightforward. Especially if that minister is a Methodist.

> SAMUEL: Kune was well intended, and he was once a man of medicine. A real doctor. Let's have a little professional courtesy.

> COLLETE (*tries to look like Irish enchantress. Almost succeeds*): You can't prove Kune is alive, anyway.

Whereas Bev is beautiful, Collette is pretty. She is forty-one, but educated, and knows more about history than any other person in town. She is short, slender, dark-haired, blue eyed. If she had brown eyes, she would look like a gypsy.

> FRANK: I vote Kune's alive. We've found out the hard way that ghosts are not real consistent. Kune is consistent.

> JEROME: I vote Kune's dead. I vote the corpse who washed up on North Beach eight years ago was Kune. I wrote it that way in the paper, and I stick by my story.

> BEV: You can't just vote on this. Kune is either alive or dead. We'd better find out which.

> FRANK: We could ask him.

> JEROME (*peers from beneath green eyeshade with steely journalistic gaze*): Kune equivocates. He would not understand the question. Besides, how can you ask him anything when he is moving all the time?

That is the kind of question Jerome would ask because Jerome is 60 and so methodical he could tizzy watching a sailboat race. He thinks of himself as a literary gentleman and a closet humorist. We must constantly watch his editing because he keeps slipping in things he believes are funny. Jerome is bald and chubby. He wears a green eyeshade when he edits, wears a double-ender Sherlock Holmes hat when he does not. Jerome has steered the local newspaper for thirty-five years. He still hand-sets the headline type.

COLLETTE: Have Gerald ask Kune if he's still alive. Kune will still talk to Gerald.

Gerald is our town policeman. He raised forty kinds of almighty sand with Kune after Kune killed the woman in Seattle.

=

There's more to explain about our working methods, but at this point, Jerome says we'd better stop just telling things and start apologizing. Otherwise the reader will think we make bad jokes.

So, we offer apologies. We can't help it if history is alive in Point Vestal. We can't help it if no one knows whether Kune is dead. We can't help it if one of our most famous houses, The Parsonage, moves around town with a mind of its own. We can't help it if the ghost of Joel-Andrew prophesies along beaches, portraying images of seven golden chalices, of seven fatted cattle, of seven bronze trumpets blaring into raging wind. We also can't help it if people in Seattle do not want to read the book. Seattle people probably think they are modern and safe . . . although—to tell the truth—few of us know much about Seattle. Seattle people visit with red license plates, and green and blue and orange license plates, and spinner hubcaps. We know Seattle is sort of like the sky—not up or out, but around. As the crow flies, Seattle is circular: no way out of it except Point Vestal.

In Point Vestal, we may not be sophisticated, but we are not modern and we sure-God know we are not safe. We know about Indian uprisings and ghostly uprisings and earthquakes.

Finally, we feel the force of rain. Point Vestal sits north and west of Puget Sound. A little farther west lies rainforest. East lie the San Juan Islands.

This is the land of sea and fog and rain a Greek liar carrying the Spanish name of Juan de Fuca claimed to discover back in 1592; the land explored by George Vancouver and a raft of others through the seventeenth and eighteenth centuries. Explorers figured nobody could live here except Indians, who seemed half sea otter, half human. To be blunt, this place is gray and wet and haunted. And windy. Always has been.

Chapter 3

JEROME SAYS WE HAVE ONE LAST TASK BEFORE TELLING ABOUT KUNF and August Starling and Joel-Andrew and The Parsonage. Jerome points out that in Point Vestal everybody knows about Victorians and about Queen Victoria. We are so smug in our knowledge we might miss telling the reader about Victorians. We know all about Victorians, so we naturally assume everyone else does.

Queen Victoria ruled England from 1837 to 1901. According to the encyclopedia at the library, she was a good queen. Of course, the encyclopedia is a Britannica, so you can assume a Brit wrote it.

Queen Victoria set an elegant style with roots in what Englishers and English teachers call "the Romantic period." When Victoria ran England, the Romantic period changed into the Victorian. In the United States, people settled the frontier and had a Civil War, so heaps paid no attention. In Point Vestal, though, the Victorian period played to a full house.

Victorians carried style, and not the cheap kind bought at a blue jeans store. They believed in duty. In 1854, for instance, the charge of the Light Brigade happened in the Crimean War. Six hundred and seventy three horsemen charged through a valley toward Russian cannon, with Russian cannon enfilading from both hillsides. Fewer than 200 survived, fewer horses.

"Just remember," Collette cautions, "Victorians sometimes defined duty in narrow and selfish ways. They were authors of a lot of human misery."

"They built railroads," Frank reminds her.

Younger people in Point Vestal—kids at the high school—complain that Victorians were starchy. Our young people believe sex wasn't important to Victorians. Our young people are wrong. Young people often are.

We must be tolerant, Bev kindly points out, because after you've been *doing it* for forty-five years, you gain perspective. You forget a nineteen-year-old is most likely interested in being more liberal. Around here, "liberal" means Edwardian.

Sex talk shocks Frank, a man given to wearing morning coat and spats. Frank is so proper, he rarely gets crumbs on his Ruskinish beard when he eats doughnuts.

The Victorians were more than simply interested in sex, they were obsessed. Their obsession ran so deep, they managed to conceal it from themselves. A proper Victorian figured sex was—more or less—the unpleasant (and occasional) physical duty accompanying great and romantic love. A joke current in this town, after a hundred years, describes a Victorian gentleman the morning after his wedding night. He tells his wife: "I do hope you are with child, my dear. One would hate to think of going through that again."

Collette tells the joke best, since she runs the antique store and has time to study history. Collette claims not to be repressed, and she says Victorians repressed sex so much that they found other outlets. They found fascinations with romance and death and progress.

To which the literary Jerome adds: "Look at their writers. Look at Edgar Allan Poe." Jerome explains that nothing moved Poe to greater ecstasy than the death of a beautiful but consumptive virgin. "Because," Jerome explains, "Poe had to make a living, and that's the sort of thing everybody was reading."

To which the cultured Frank adds: "Look at their lace, their gimcracks, their sugar-candy facades on houses. Look at decorations swirling around like convoluted valentines. Look at sculptors like Rodin; romance on the hoof." Frank pauses, adds dreamily: "If they were stylistic, is that so bad? It is certainly no worse than those magazines under the counter at the drugstore."

Collette giggles. She had no idea Frank even knew about those magazines at the drugstore.

To which Bev adds sensibly, "Victorians were more complicated than you let on. Some were foolish and stupid; some were intelligent and great. They prided themselves on preparedness. They were usually overprepared. For almost anything."

"They believed in progress," Frank says. "Never forget that. It was their best feature."

"They liked windswept moors and heaths," Samuel says, and brushes his ministerial broadcloth. "They liked stormy beaches. They especially liked beaches where ships had wrecked." Samuel sighs. "It was a difficult time for Methodists. Methodists are realists."

Chapter 4

JEROME SAYS WE HAVE DONE PRETTY WELL INTRODUCING OUR history. It is time to tell the story. We start with 1973 (the year Joel-Andrew came to town) and 1893 (the year August Starling was released from the madhouse), because that is the logical year(s) to start.

Samuel says Joel-Andrew arrived in the clerical collar of an Episcopalian, while wearing the heart of a Baptist, and spouting the theology of a Moravian; which is not exactly correct—but—no one understood that at the time. As the tale begins, it is both 1893 and 1973, the month of October. Joel-Andrew is on his way to Point Vestal. He's been coming in this direction for quite some little while.

=

The road from San Francisco was long and worth celebrating. It ran through farmland, through hilly country where rivers flowed as rivulets in the sun-seared autumn. It ran beneath giant sequoia trees, so the clarion sun was pushed farther back in the sky. North of the Oregon border, rains coasted from the Pacific on a weather system gray-bearded and timeless. Dark greens of cedar, fir and hemlock contrasted with yellowing leaves of alder and the psychedelic red bark of madrona.

Joel-Andrew celebrated each step reverently, and took his ministry to each town or city along the route. He was small, lightly built with sandy hair going gray, sandy beard, and musician's fingers. He carried a violin case on a strap over his shoulder. When he played his hands looked like clever spiders, and even secular music sounded reverent. When he saved souls, his face glowed tranquil with gratitude to the Lord. He had an Episcopal nose, an Episcopal collar, faded jeans, sandals, plus well-groomed nails and gray-green eyes. In San Francisco freaks thought he looked suspiciously healthy.

From San Francisco to Point Vestal was a thousand miles give or take. Joel-Andrew had been walking four years. He sometimes caught a ride, but the trip took a long time because he occasionally got busted. Busts were for vagrancy, for violin playing, for impersonating a priest, for celebrating the Eucharist on street corners, and for being a fruitcake.

Each bust was an opportunity. In Mendocino his cellmate was a realtor who repented. In Arcata an attorney became so swayed by the Word of the Lord he promised to quit fighting disbarment and run for public office. In Yreka an automobile dealer was overcome and honored a warranty. If, early in August, Joel-Andrew had not been busted along the Rogue River in Oregon, he might never have heard about Point Vestal. The Lord works in mysterious ways, but the bust on Rogue River was obvious, the kind of straightforward message a prophet expects.

"He's clean," a skinny cop explained to the desk sergeant when he hauled Joel-Andrew into the police station, "but he smells like a freak, he *looks* like a freak, and he's higher than a nineteen-foot sunflower." The skinny cop seemed awfully young to Joel-Andrew. The cop looked like he belonged in a high school band, like he should be chasing behind a clarinet and being chased by a tuba. The desk sergeant looked like a tuba. Joel-Andrew breathed a silent prayer, one that was kindly.

The desk sergeant blinked clear blue eyes, curled fat fingers, and carried the sincere gaze of a sociologist. "What are you on?"

"George Gershwin," Joel-Andrew said. "William James. Slim Pickens. Tallulah Bankhead. Mother Macree. The Founding Fathers and the Living God."

"That ain't acid talking," the young cop said. "That's magic mushrooms."

The police desk sat in a room barely three-dimensional. Brick walls were like untextured linoleum. Paint clung flat to the ceiling like it was afraid to peel. The young cop seemed daubed into his uniform. The blue-eyed sergeant looked like a third-grader's sketch of her father: flat circles with hair.

"Flood," Joel-Andrew said unhappily. "Swine and cattle, barns, houses—Jeep pickups and chain saws. The Rogue River will run torrentially. Devastation. This I must prophesy."

"It floods every spring," the sociologist cop said. "We deal with it." He looked at the clarinet cop. "Print him, run him. Find a cell until he comes off the high." To Joel-Andrew, he said, "I'm writing a paper on acidheads for a scholarly journal. Otherwise, we'd use brutality."

"I understand," Joel-Andrew said. "It would skew your observations. It would also be unkind."

"I am an educated man, gone to fat in a small town."

"Not a sparrow falls," Joel-Andrew pointed out.

"Around here we got Oregon juncos," the clarinet cop said, "Plus a select group of freaks from San Francisco."

For the next three days Joel-Andrew did missionary work in the holdover. He had done so much missionarying through the years that the tasks were simple. He played the violin, his spidery and clever fingers peopling the cells with music, with grace, with reverence. His slight form stood above other inhabitants of the cells, while his soul and heart reached toward his brethren.

"O, Lord," Joel-Andrew prayed, "may thy servant once more be the instrument of thy power." He felt the familiar energy, vast and loving, wash through him. He turned to the freaks.

There were three cells in the jail: one for holdover, one for women, and one for drunks. In the cell with Joel-Andrew were three freaks. One was huge and redheaded. He rolled around and screamed. One was skinny and he hummed. He held one hand in the air so butterflies would have a place to rest. The third was a tubby black dude stoned beyond recognition. Joel-Andrew touched the screaming man's hand. "You are well," Joel-Andrew said. "You've been visiting infinity, but now you are well." The power of the Lord surged in Joel-Andrew.

The screaming man stopped rolling around. He lay curled up, confused.

"Sheee-it," the black dude muttered.

The curled-up man's eyes closed, opened. Fear and paranoia, which had made his eyes like saucers, disappeared. "Man," he said, "like, wow."

"Lie there and think about it," Joel-Andrew said. "The Lord did that."

It was always like this with Joel-Andrew. He worked among freaks, among kids who dispossessed themselves so they could complain of dispossession. He worked with the ill, the ungainly, the addicts. At some point in his ministry, people began calling him the "hippie priest." At that point, the Episcopal church kicked him out. Gone was ritual, the celebrating pipe organs, the pomp, the robes. Gone were silent-gleaming and polished pews, sunlight through stained glass windows, and devout parishioners with sanitary smiles. Gone the respect given a man of the cloth. Joel-Andrew became a defrocked priest walking in the echo of St. Francis.

"Sheee-it," the black dude said again.

"Possess my body," a girl's voice moaned from the women's cage. "Like, I never seen nothin' like that before."

It was always this way. Always. He asked them to love each other, and all they could do with the information was hop in the sack with more frequency and less skill than rabbits. Joel-Andrew sighed, persisted, and the Lord renewed his strength.

During three days in the cell, Joel-Andrew took care of five bad trips, one bleeding ulcer, three cases of clap, one broken finger, various sores, a rampant case of d.t.'s, one Oedipal complex, and he also acquired an aging cat named Obed. None of the freaks turned to the Lord, but the black dude (whose name turned out to be Princeton) said he'd think about it. Joel-Andrew also had four interviews with the desk sergeant.

"You've been walking from San Francisco for four years," the desk sergeant said. "Interesting." He leaned back in his creaky chair. Waiting.

Joel-Andrew admitted nothing. A skinny cat hopped onto the desk. The cat was dark gray, nearly black, with golden eyes and a white tail. A cat so skinny could not be in good health. Joel-Andrew cured it of worms. The cat looked surprised. It curled on the desk and contemplated Joel-Andrew.

"And," the sergeant said, "you've turned those cells into the Peaceable Kingdom. I don't know what you're doing, but the freaks are coherent." The sergeant leaned forward, fiddled with a pencil. "Interesting. "

"You have a lovely jail," Joel-Andrew said without rancor. "Few better this side of Mexico."

"But your violin playing is marginal. With the pressures of your ministry, I suppose you have little time to practice." The sergeant leaned back, waiting.

Joel-Andrew admired the ploy. "Prepare for a storm," he said sadly. "It will rain buckets, and soon. This I prophesy."

"This is Oregon," the sergeant said. "It always rains buckets."

During the last interview, the one before the cops put him back on the street, Joel-Andrew relented.

"A prophet experiences things differently," Joel-Andrew said. "I was not high when you picked me up. I'm that way all the time."

The sergeant stopped leaning back and he stopped leaning forward. He made worry-noises. He took notes.

"I became tired," Joel-Andrew admitted. "The Lord set me on this wandering path for some purpose. I am not tired from a state of grace, but tired from too wide a ministry. Do sociologists ever study fatigue?"

"They study stress," the sergeant said. "They study group illness, pop culture, relationships, advertising, sentiment, war, mores. They study Marilyn Monroe, jazz, inner cities, mobs."

"Because," Joel-Andrew said, "I'm *supposed* to be a prophet, but the demands on me are medical."

"They study homosexuals," the sergeant said. "They study market trends, busted families, corrupt politicians, folk music in Appalachia, kinship systems among Indians."

"Because," Joel-Andrew said, "I'm wandering in a wilderness of the spirit. I privately long for a small haven of rest."

"I know the place," the sergeant said. "Just the place. If," he added, "you can put up with a preoccupation for tourists."

"Because it's all beginning to float," Joel-Andrew said. "A place of stability to restore the soul. Then I can return to these, my beloved . . ." He gestured toward the quiet cells.

"My hometown," the sergeant said. "I left there twenty years ago. Tourists drove me nuts. Let me tell you about Point Vestal."

"It must have changed in twenty years," Joel-Andrew said unhappily. "We are in a season of float—of flux—the center will not hold."

"That," said the desk sergeant, "is a bunch of horse pocky. It shows you've never been to Point Vestal."

=

It took the rest of August and all of September to reach Point Vestal. Obed, the dark gray cat with the golden eyes and white tail, loved the trip. Obed ate what Joel-Andrew ate: cheese and peanut butter and carrot cake. When darkness came and Joel-Andrew huddled sleeping in barns, Obed knocked the living stuffings out of God's creatures, mice, baby rabbits, shrews and varmints. During the whole trip he had only a few bad moments, and those came when he tried to mate with a raccoon. By the time Joel-Andrew reached the turnoff to Point Vestal, Obed weighed thirteen pounds and had learned to dance on his hind legs when Joel-Andrew played the violin.

The two stepped from a modern highway onto a road that ran in layers. A small wooden sign held an arrow pointing down a narrow dirt track. The sign said "Point Vestal." A modern highway sign said:

POINT VESTAL—18 MILES
A RADIANT FUTURE
WITH PRIDE IN HERITAGE

A scraggly-looking macadam two-lane ran beside the dirt track. Sometimes the two roads crossed. When they crossed Joel-Andrew heard a low cacophony of sound.

Joel-Andrew experimented. When he walked the dirt track, more noises came from the surrounding forest; the grunts of bear, the faraway cry of cougars, the drip-drip-dripping of water from the tops of giant trees. When he walked the macadam, the forest sported third-growth trees, and he heard far-off engines. The dirt track was muddy from constant rain, but air smelled sweeter. In boggy places the road was corduroy: logs laid end to end and sideways. It was shortly after crossing one of those bogs that Joel-Andrew heard the steady clop-clop of a horse behind him. Joel-Andrew turned. The horse clopped black and shiny in misting rain.

The man driving had the same slight build as Joel-Andrew. He wore an old-fashioned wool suit and vest, and his dark eyes glowed with romantic fervor. He wore a fine beaver hat, and a light cape. A fancy whip stood in the whip socket of the small buggy. The buggy gleamed glossy black with elaborate gold ornamentation. Black tassels hung along the sides. Joel-Andrew thought the high-wheeled buggy looked like a little square merry-go-round with a roof. The dark-haired man broadcast fervor like a dandelion broadcasts seeds. Joel-Andrew thought the man looked like a Missouri Synod preacher trying to pass at a party run by the Knights of Columbus. Joel-Andrew also figured the man was hitting dexedrine, but Joel-Andrew immediately loved him.

The man whoa-a-a-ed the buggy.

"By heaven," he said, "is it the elder Dick Whittington and his celebrated cat? Or," he added, "a wandering minstrel?"

"It's a wet prophet on a wet road," Joel-Andrew answered. "It is the celebrated minister of music, healer of souls; and it is the equally celebrated cat Obed who can purr seven languages including ancient Hebrew."

"Climb up," the stranger said. "Can your cat purr in French? The language of love." When the stranger smiled, he looked like a little kid figuring it was about to get spanked.

"French is the language of fornication," Joel-Andrew said. "Let's not get confused."

Eighteen miles on a mud track in a horse and buggy took slightly over five hours. The black hide of the horse shone in the gloom, seemed brilliant when the rig occasionally passed from tall trees into unobstructed daylight. Joel-Andrew viewed the buggy and its contents, impressed by the man's preparations. A wicker picnic basket held wine, food, tablecloth, and napkins. There was spare oil for the little carriage lamps. An old-fashioned carbine nestled behind a kit of tools for repairing harnesses. There were lap robes, plus binoculars, a shooting stick, matches in a waxed tube, some patent medicine, a small kit of personal items, extra clothing, and a book of poetry.

"One of our better modern poets," the stranger said. "Shall I read while you tend the reins?"

Joel-Andrew was as comfortable with horses as a Pietist in a steam bath. "I'll read," he said, and began:

> What are the long waves singing, so mournfully,
> > evermore?
> What are they singing so mournfully, as they weep on
> > the sandy shore?
> "Olivia, oh, Olivia!"—what else can it seem to be!
> "Olivia, lost Olivia"—what else can the sad song be?
> —"Weep and mourn, she will not return, she can not
> > return to thee!"

"Ye gads," said Joel-Andrew, "Is this early Allen Ginsberg?"

The stranger's eyes filled with tears he did not allow to fall. His jaw firmed, but his hands trembled holding the reins. The poem affected his very visage. Joel-Andrew guessed his age at thirty and saw a young man deeply troubled in spirit.

"What is it?" Joel-Andrew asked softly. "Women, drugs, or a career change?"

"Beauty," the young man said. "Also, I think, a little fear. Perhaps we could have some music?"

Obed, of the golden eyes and white tail, stood on the seat between them as Joel-Andrew unpacked his violin. As Joel-Andrew played a Gershwin medley, Obed swayed and purred in Portuguese. The violin sounded a small and civilized voice into a wilderness of wet forest.

The young man drove and listened. The horse went clop. The forest dripped. Obed switched to Arabic.

"When was that music written?" the young man asked when Joel-Andrew finished.

"In 1920, maybe. Maybe 1930."

"Oh, preserve me," the young man said prayerfully, "it's happening again." He looked at Joel-Andrew in supplication. "I've never heard of Allen Ginsberg. Tell me honestly, what is the date? Not the day, the year?"

"It's 1973," Joel-Andrew said. "At least it was when I got here."

"It's 1893," the young man said. "At least it was when I began this journey. It is always 1893 when I begin this journey."

Nothing pleased Joel-Andrew so much as powerful forces, and powerful forces must be operating. "We have time to talk at length," he said. "It looks like you've done this trip before."

"Any number of times. I almost always pick up strangers. They most always talk about 1950 or 1960. Now you talk about 1973."

"And then what happens?"

"We arrive in Point Vestal," the stranger said. "My passenger steps down where the road branches. I follow the branch to my house, and the road disappears. The next thing I know, I'm in front of the turnoff to Point Vestal, being pulled by this horse . . . I don't even know the horse's name . . . and I don't even know where the buggy came from . . . and it is always daytime and always raining . . . and there is another five-hour drive ahead of me . . . and all I want is to return home in 1893 and answer for my mistakes . . . and see my sweet wife . . ." He looked at Joel-Andrew. "You aren't even born yet. I'm dead by the time you are born."

"Don't bet on it," Joel-Andrew said, "I'm pushing forty-five." He ran a spidery and violin-playing finger around the inside of his clerical collar. "O, Lord," Joel-Andrew prayed silently, "may thy servant once more be the instrument of thy power." He felt the familiar energy, vast and loving, wash through him.

"The Lord is with you," he told the young stranger. "This time the road will not disappear."

The young man looked dubious but hopeful. "It will not disappear," Joel-Andrew repeated.

"You see," the young man said, "some people believe I am mad. I was beginning to think they are correct."

"Your wife?"

"In my whole life," the young man said, "I've only seen her for a little less than six months, and that seven years ago." The young man smiled tenderly. "We were married in Boston before I came west to make our fortune, and to build a house. I did both. Then I was shipped to an asylum." The young man's voice sounded sincere, and that troubled Joel-Andrew because the young man so obviously lied. The sincerity troubled Joel-Andrew. He had heard the same kind of rap from pawnbrokers.

When they arrived on the outskirts of Point Vestal, the road forked. The young man clucked at the horse.

"Will I see you again?" he asked, and his voice vibrated with hope. Joel-Andrew thought the man very, very young.

Joel-Andrew made his voice reassuring, the bearer of serene power. "Follow your road," he told the young man. "From what I've been told of Point Vestal, we may end up being neighbors."

The young man turned the buggy down the left fork. After the buggy traveled about fifty yards, the buggy and horse disappeared, but the young man did not. The young man stood in the middle of the muddy road. The road did not disappear. The young man smiled, then did a stiff little dance. He began walking the muddy road toward home.

"The Lord did that," Joel-Andrew called after him. "Be sure to think about it."

Chapter 5

OCTOBER IN POINT VESTAL IS GRAND BECAUSE OF MIST AND LIGHT, especially this October as we begin telling about Joel-Andrew and Kune and Obed the cat and The Parsonage. Fog wraps around steeples of our eighteen churches, and fog swirls about high gables where Victorian carvings seem natural nests for birds, or gargoyles.

As we, who write this history, walk early-morning streets to our meeting at The Fisherman's Café, it is possible to travel a couple of blocks without seeing a parked automobile. We may see Kune walking and disappearing rapidly into mist. We may hear the distant sound of Joel-Andrew's violin. The stern figure of The Parsonage may rise before us (and we'll explain about The Parsonage real soon, because Joel-Andrew and The Parsonage had close ties). Electric lights behind drawn curtains of houses are dim as kerosene lamps in the fog. We walk expecting to hear the whinny of a horse, the clop of hooves. A few people still keep horses. It is not always possible to tell whether the sounds come from the mouths and hooves of living horses, or echo from a livery stable turned into the town's movie theater back in 1923.

It is also in October that The Parsonage grows more restless.

The Parsonage was once used by Presbyterian ministers, and it sat in one place for decades. Then things were done which will have to be explained later on. From the time of those mistakes, The Parsonage has never fixed in one spot for more than a few months. In October—especially with the approach of Halloween—The

Parsonage gets skittish. When this happens, Presbyterians in town get mighty silent.

One of the town's main problems happens because each time The Parsonage moves, it takes its lot with it. The Parsonage sets its lot (150-foot front, 200-foot depth) and its trees (one maple, three apples, one pear, and two cherries) smack down between houses that have rested comfortably side by side for a century. The street plan of the whole town shifts maybe one-third of a degree. Any map of Point Vestal is slightly askew. It is a surveyor's nightmare.

We get werelight in November, but during October, sun pries at clouds and fog. An occasional beam illuminates a stained glass window or reaches the streets. The light comes through as copper, not gold, although sometimes in summer it is gold as the gold in the eyes of Obed the cat.

=

And we find this book is being written rather more slowly than we hoped. These days we meet in October, having spent the summer mostly talking. In October, windows of The Fisherman's Café are steamy.

"It was October of 1973," Frank points out as he sips from his mustache cup, "that August Starling appeared in the drawing room of the Starling House." Frank chuckles, then blanches slightly. "That brought a few gasps from a few high places. Even in Seattle."

"You have to wonder about Joel-Andrew's motives," Collette says. "Bringing August Starling back to town." Collette looks especially Irish this morning, her blue eyes a little misty. She probably read poems of Thomas Moore before bedtime. "Joel-Andrew was emotional."

"It was Joel-Andrew's way," Samuel explains. "He never thought of consequences. He just saw another person in trouble and tried to fix the trouble." Samuel brushes at his broadcloth suit. "Which is rare among Episcopals," Samuel adds, or rather, intones.

"The most unmethodical man I've ever met," Jerome says. "Him and his dancing cat."

"Samuel and I were fantasizing about the past on the day Joel-Andrew came to town. The town gossips had it that Samuel and I were in an affair, or at least an assignation." Bev is so straight-forward, sometimes shocking the bewhiskers off Samuel. "That was the time The Parsonage seemed almost suicidal. You'll remember it took up squatter's rights on the cliff beside the approach to town. Not even an outhouse could live for long on that cliff, what with the winds."

Samuel says nothing, but juts his jaw forward and tries to look imposing.

Frank blushes, and his beard trembles. Collette chortles. Jerome snuffles.

"We were bird watching," Samuel says.

It is always endearing to watch a Methodist trying to rig a jib sail in a heavy wind. "Bird watching in the fields of the Lord," Samuel adds, for no apparent reason, as we return to our history.

=

We were much younger in 1973. Bev was fifty-three, Samuel seventy-three (and still occasionally doing some preaching), Frank was forty-three, Jerome forty-six, and Collette was a twenty-seven-year-old kid.

Joel-Andrew was forty-five, and Obed the cat had one white whisker.

They were two small figures, a man and his cat, rounding the curve in the road that takes a three-mile sweep along the Strait, descending from cliffs into downtown Point Vestal. Clouds scudded in copper layers, and mist licked thickly along the road. The Parsonage stood halfway down the hill, its widow's walk looking toward Strait and sea. This late in the season, most of the apples were gone from trees that attend The Parsonage. The pear tree stood gnarled, cropped out; the cherries were losing their leaves. To Joel-Andrew, The Parsonage looked lonely. Joel-Andrew could not figure out why anyone would build a house in such an exposed and haunted looking place. No lights shone in The Parsonage. A thin trickle of smoke came from one of three chimneys.

A small sign hung nailed to an apple tee. The sign said: "Presbyterian Parsonage." Joel-Andrew gave a little shiver of excitement. The Parsonage certainly *looked* Presbyterian. It carried the severe lines of New England Puritanism, and (although technically Victorian) it carried no gewgaws or ornamentation to reduce its severe certainty. Stained glass ran like vestal ribbons bordering narrow, plain glass windows. One square tower rose at the front, like the bell tower of a church. A second, but octagonal tower, rose at the rear; and the octagonal tower actually carried some bells. Silhouetted in the gray sky, the front tower gazed all-seeing, 360 degrees into the forest, the Strait, the highway and byways. It was obvious to Joel-Andrew that the tower contained the minister's office and library. He wondered (with a thrill) at the thousands of sermons which must have issued from that tower.

"That police sergeant in Oregon gave motherly advice about Point Vestal," Joel-Andrew muttered to Obed. "At least as much as any sociologist can."

Obed expressed the opinion that Joel-Andrew might be a real mouse-chaser when it came to passing miracles, but was a lousy judge of character. Obed shivered in his damp fur. He huddled beneath a trellised rosebush, his white tail flipping like a windshield wiper in the fog.

There should have been a church nearby, but there was none. Joel-Andrew thought it curious business. He also thought a knock on The Parsonage's door would do no harm. Perhaps this town even had a ministerial association. When the door opened, Joel-Andrew was shocked.

Joel-Andrew could tell a Methodist a mile off, and to find a Methodist in a Presbyterian parsonage was like finding an Anabaptist with a vow of silence. Joel-Andrew backed up a rapid and hysterical step, like a man going to the can and mistakenly entering the ladies' room.

The tall man who faced him carried a weatherworn and hawkish face. Heavy brows ran above stern eyes. High cheeks sported a network of wrinkles. Thick hair that was gray, and a short beard, made the man (who wore a frock coat) look like a 19th-century whaling captain.

"You are wet, poor fellow," Samuel said. He eyed Joel-Andrew's clerical collar. He turned, speaking to a woman. "My dear, we have an itinerant." He motioned Joel-Andrew inside. Obed, having mercy on himself, was already inside and licking his coat by the fireplace.

In its stern way, the room glowed. Joel-Andrew thought it fitting surroundings for an even lovelier woman. When Samuel introduced Bev, Joel-Andrew thought briefly of Dorothy Lamour. Then he reminded himself that he was in Point Vestal. Joel-Andrew was fascinated with this new version of reality. The year 1888 seemed to spread in front of him. The parlor was well illuminated by light from the fireplace.

Ornate Victorian chairs, ribbon-backed and rose-backed, sat like dancing partners in a quiet minuet. Samuel's formal coat was a complement to Bev's long and vaguely antique dress. The dress flowed elegantly, like poured cream decorated with pearls. Her hair piled high, woven with gorgeous ivory combs. Gold-leaf frames surrounded hanging portraits of Presbyterians, so walls were disapproving; but the rest of the room—with pristine white wallpaper and twelve-foot ceilings—felt light and airy. Crystal, and other glass, reflected firelight. Floors snuggled beneath Oriental rugs.

To Joel-Andrew, freshly come from soggy upstairs rooms above Haight Street, the purity and elegance of the scene were like strains of chamber music. Then his heart broke with happiness, with incredible love for Samuel and Bev.

"Bedad," Samuel said, "I do believe that cat is purring in Greek."

"Yes," Bev said, "it is Greek."

Obed shifted to Latin. Obed showed off, and Joel-Andrew thought it in poor taste.

"Latin," Samuel said.

"Yes," Bev said, "but it isn't as good as his Greek."

Joel-Andrew, who had spent his last several years among kids whose vocabulary consisted of "Wow," felt such a spirit of camaraderie that he unpacked his violin. If Obed wanted to show off; well, then.

The dancing which followed—as Bev remembers—as Samuel remembers—was a performance of delicacy that could be accomplished only by a cat; even though the cat scaled slightly overweight. It was an afternoon of entertainment in the best Victorian tradition, and ended in a triple flip with Obed standing on his front paws.

"Our practices must seem strange to you," Samuel said later over tea. "I assure you, Point Vestal is not so peculiar in every aspect. In many ways we are quite modern. In fact, we are a popular tourist town."

Joel-Andrew felt numb, felt he sat with Sterling Hayden and Dorothy Lamour somewhere off toward the end of the world.

"Samuel and I are getting older," Bev said. "I was born—well—some time ago. Samuel was born in 1900. We have seen a lot of change."

"And so," said Samuel, "instead of simply yearning for the past, we sometimes meet in this abandoned house and *live* the past. It is sad that the house is abandoned. There is a grim but presently unimportant tale behind the abandonment."

Joel-Andrew, who was celibate, told himself he had seen shack-ups, daisy chains, one-nighters, and a biker with three nuts. He had not for a long time seen genuine romance, a genuine love affair. He remembered his parents.

"And now," said Samuel, "you must entertain us with your own adventures."

Joel-Andrew told himself he was in for a total wipe-out. He could not tell about the Haight. He could tell about his excommunication, but it would make no sense unless he did tell about the Haight.

"I met a young man as Obed and I came to town," Joel-Andrew said. "A man by the name of August Starling."

"Yes," Samuel said.

"August," Bev said. "You came to a fork in the road and August disappeared."

"Because," Samuel said, "August—as he probably told you—did a session in the madhouse. He tried to return home and was prevented. He died in Seattle in 1922 of alcohol and madness. I was 22 on the day we heard the news, brought by a ferry-boat captain."

"It didn't quite happen that way," Joel-Andrew admitted, and suddenly knew that what he said would not be received as a simple and amusing story. "At least it didn't happen that way this time." He told his story. ". . . and then," Joel-Andrew concluded, "we came to the fork in the road. I stepped down and watched. August Starling drove down a muddy road. The horse and carriage disappeared, but Mr. Starling did not. When I last saw him, he was walking a back road leading to town."

"Oh, dear," Bev said when the story finished.

"Damn," said Samuel. "Blamit. Damn-blamit." Samuel lowered his head. "Let us pray," he said. "Fervently."

Chapter 6

"JOEL-ANDREW SAW A LOT OF THINGS THAT DAY," SAYS JEROME, "BUT still knew nothing of Point Vestal history." Jerome also says we have not yet given a true picture of Point Vestal. What we take for granted in the way of haunted houses would be considered remarkable elsewhere, even in Seattle.

So be it.

The road into Point Vestal curves from the cliff into town. On the left, as Joel-Andrew would discover, lies a saltwater swamp greatly beloved by ducks, grebes, Canada geese, mud hens, scoters, occasional auks and puffins; and where on dim days in 1973 a spectral rowboat plowed through reeds. The rowboat searched for bodies of three children who drowned in 1910. No one knows who actually piloted that boat, but we suppose it was the Christian Scientist teacher who took second-graders on a picnic and allowed them to roam.

On the right, behind a small hook of land augmented with boulders and fill, lies the boat basin. Beyond the hook lies the Strait of Juan de Fuca. The waters tumble furiously out there, but the basin is calm. Except for a few moorage spots for Seattle tourists, the moorage is composed of fishing vessels; trawlers, draggers, purse seiners, and long-liners. Crumbling concrete sidewalks run before the boat basin, and a variety of ghostly forms walk there. Like most fishermen, they are taciturn, and no one pays them much attention.

Traditionally, the only real excitement around the boat basin happens each Chinese New Year that celebrates the Year of the Tiger. People avoid the boat basin, because on that night drowned Chinese rise from the Strait and come ashore. Chinese can be pretty rowdy.

This brings us to a sore point. Frank does not like this, and the rest are not happy, but this is a true history and not an official one.

Point Vestal was founded and built by criminals. We suppose all towns are, but in Point Vestal you really know it.

This town rose in the 1860s and 1870s to handle the lumber trade. For a couple of decades, Point Vestal boomed. Our harbor held scores of masts, as ships waited to load.

In those days other profitable trade included opium, whiskey, guns, prostitution (for although the town was Victorian, the sailors on ships were not); and there was trade in Chinese bond slaves. Bond slaves were smuggled through the San Juan Islands, where the Strait nuzzles into Puget Sound.

And the San Juan Islands are a traditionally bloody place. They have always sheltered smugglers, even today. While our town has no drug problem, drug traffic comes through those islands, then through Point Vestal.

"Prove it," Jerome says.

"You are the newspaperman," Collette tells him. "You should have done an expose on the drug traffic ten years ago."

"And get my head blown off?" Jerome is methodical, but has a fair sense of melodrama. He knows if he did an exposé on the drug business, he would not be shot. The time-honored method is drowning.

When Frank gets mad, his beard twitters. Each little curling hair begins to snap and sparkle at the tip.

"The book is getting seedy," Frank says. "First it got pornographic because you insisted on telling things about Joel-Andrew. Now you rattle skeletons."

"If we are not truthful," Bev tells him, "I want none of this. I will not be a party to deception." Then she adds, "Oh dear, that sounded high-toned and phony."

"It accords with the facts," Samuel says. "Dearest lady," he says— sort of as an afterthought.

The darkest part of our history concerns murder and shang-haiing. Chinese bond slaves were illegal, and as immigration laws grew firm, and as other Chinese paid their ways in as illegal immigrants, dark practices arose. Smugglers came from the Orient, or from Canada. They transferred Chinese to small boats of local smugglers. When the police or Revenue Service got too close—and sometimes even when they did not—our local people tied weights on the Chinamen and dropped them overboard.

"We did none of that," Frank protests. "We fish, we timber. We chop wood and carry water. We raise daughters who are pure. We raise sons for the Army. Our bank is the oldest in the state."

"Uh-huh," says Collette, "Sure. And ducks don't whistle, 'cause ducks have got flap-yaps."

The point, as Bev explains it, is that people who are still alive remember those days. Everybody in town accepts past crimes without remorse. We live in the founders' houses. We brag about our past.

=

Let us try to see the town with Joel-Andrew's fresh view. He was bound to notice things we take for granted. He arrived in Point Vestal around 1:00 PM on an October Wednesday. He spent a couple of pleasant hours at The Parsonage with Bev and Samuel. It must have been around 3:00 PM when he left The Parsonage and headed into town.

Joel-Andrew passed the swamp and the boat basin. On his left, the bluff rose on a steep angle. The road ran so close to the bluff that he could not see great Victorian houses up there, facing the Strait like enormous galleons in dry dock. Before him the main and only downtown street stood flanked by four-story brick buildings. The buildings' ground floors were occupied by businesses, but upper stories stood empty. Along the sides and tops of the buildings, Victorian ornamentation curled, postured, frilled. The ornamentation might be snakes and cherubs—Oroboros—impressionist cat fights—phallic fire pokers. It might be calla lilies, roses, night-shade, parakeets. The brick and concrete showed rounded edges after a hundred years of mist and wind.

Obed owned a propensity for alleys, so was not impressed by a town with only one long street. Nor was he impressed when Joel-Andrew's voice sounded strange.

"Shapes of people move before those upstairs windows," Joel-Andrew observed. "They flicker a lot."

Obed expressed a typical cat opinion. In general, Obed felt, *people* flickered a lot.

"I think I understand," Joel-Andrew explained. "The people who *flicker* are ghosts, and the people who don't flicker are alive." Joel-Andrew did not know it at the time, but he had stumbled on the first principle which allows one to exist comfortably in Point Vestal.

"There are red lights up there," Joel-Andrew said, "and some of those flickers wear mighty revealing clothes. There is indelicate laughter." Joel-Andrew did not know that in Point Vestal everyone learns never to look higher than the first story of any downtown building.

October light faded toward night. Dusk rolled in, waving feathers of mist. On Joel-Andrew's right stood The Fisherman's Café, and on his left Janie's Tavern. When he looked over the swinging doors toward the bar, he saw a rotund gentleman with dark hair. The gentleman wore suit pants, a vest, a tie, a starchy white shirt. The gentleman was Frank. Two drunken Indians, seven drunken loggers, and three drunken fishermen sat along the bar. Conspicuous behind the bar lay a sawed-off pool cue, the cue beautifully carved with Victorian ornamentation. Frank runs a tight ship.

One of the Indians flickered. That was Maggie. She is real important in this history, and we'll tell a lot more about her later on.

Joel-Andrew was impressed. He turned away and continued his exploration. To his right stood the J. C. Penney store, the newspaper office, and the antique store. An absolutely fascinating dark-haired woman stood near the window of the antique store. She read a George Meredith novel. Joel-Andrew thought her little and cute, like a gypsy. Then he saw Collette's blue eyes and thought her Irish.

The bank stood on his right. It had stained glass windows shaded by enormous London plane trees. Old-fashioned lighting looked like intricately shaped kerosene lamps. Tellers moved with the grace of shadows, and gentlemen bankers wore suits. Lady bankers wore long dresses in pastel colors, the dresses buttoned beneath their chins. Joel-Andrew, in spite of his celibacy, momentarily stood in thrall. He had never seen anything so provocative in his life.

"Modesty," Joel-Andrew said. "Chastity. Dollars lubricated with classy morals."

Obed sneered.

Beyond the bank, bookstore windows displayed leather bound collections of Charles Dickens, and a sign read "Closed for the day." Joel-Andrew did not know it at the time, but the bookstore is the one Bev runs; and Bev was philandering with Samuel in The Parsonage.

Across the street a freak—at least a man Joel-Andrew thought was a freak—trudged. The freak's long blond hair flowed to his waist, and he walked with the methodical pace of pneumonia. He wore a lumberman's shirt, bleached cotton pants, sturdy walking shoes. He wore a wool sock hat, an open rain slicker and a ghastly smile. Joel-Andrew told himself that the worst of all drugs were memories of everything you ever did wrong in your life. That ghastly smile was in combat with memories.

"It is bad to be excommunicated," Joel-Andrew told Obed, who did not listen. "It is ugliness of the first order when you excommunicate yourself."

The blond-haired man kept pace with Joel-Andrew, but did not cross the street.

Along the sidewalks a few people passed, loggers and fishermen, ladies and gentlemen. They moved unhurried through the decaying afternoon. They stepped through doorways of a grocery store, a dry-goods store, a barbershop. They passed a few empty storefronts, a drugstore. The fishermen and loggers put a workmanlike smell into the mist, and the gentlemen and ladies wore perfume. They seemed preoccupied: because; when something terrible began to happen, the gentlemen and ladies paid no attention. None seemed to hear dying screams that began rising from the basement of City Hall.

Joel-Andrew reacted automatically. He thought, "bad trip," and began to run. Then he thought, "Hell's Angels," and ran faster.

Then he thought "National Guard," and his sandals pounded the sidewalk as smartly as rifle shots into a crowd.

The screams were faint, but were surely loud at the source because City Hall sat a block away. Screams lived in the mist, were blood-choked, then clear with horror, then blood-choked.

Someone—and that someone deep voiced—was dying, the death mean and cruel.

Joel-Andrew ran, praying for the man, praying for all men, praying no human would ever have a death so ugly. He stumbled as he ran, the pavement slicker than mist. Screams were no longer like layers in the mist, no longer the red of blood. They choked, the frothy pink of broken lungs. Chains rattled as though the dying man lay shackled and spasmodic. Obed's tail dropped and described a flat white line as he bounced all thirteen pounds in an attempt to keep up.

A sign on the locked doors of City Hall said, "Open Tuesdays." Joel-Andrew pounded on the doors, rattled the doors.

The screams ceased.

"Four PM." A gentleman stood before City Hall and spoke to a lady. The gentleman wore a full-breasted suit, an elegant raincoat, and carried a walking stick. He adjusted his elaborate gold pocket watch. Joel-Andrew rattled the door and called on the Lord.

"You can stop such conduct," the gentleman said to Joel-Andrew, his voice severe. "Are you drunk?" He turned to the lady. "I dread the day a bus line comes to this town. These Seattle people are impossible."

"That is not a local cat," the lady said. She was dressed modestly in a style of the late 1940s. Full skirts swirled across chubby calves. She wore an incongruous-looking sun hat freckled with mist. She had a Danish face with the serenity of a Baha'i. "I fancy I know Point Vestal cats, and that cat is an outlander."

"A man just died," Joel-Andrew said with desperation. "Or else he passed out and *is* dying."

"At 4:00 PM precisely, every Wednesday," the gentlemen said. "Been doing it since 1888. He is known as The Sailor. He was an English bo'sun, jailed for saying Queen Victoria had bowed legs." The gentleman blushed.

"I'm new here," Joel-Andrew admitted.

"That seems clear enough." The lady eyed Joel-Andrew's clerical collar. "Come, George," she said to her companion. "I fear this fellow is an Italian."

Joel-Andrew sat on the steps of City Hall and wept. He could not even be angry with the man and woman who were so indifferent. He thought he knew why he wept, but a part of his tears may have come from confusion, from isolation, rejection. Other ministers had sometimes accused Joel-Andrew of being too slow to anger. Such a thing flawed a prophet, yet he enjoyed no success at changing.

So he sat weeping for the man who died so horribly once a week. He thought of the number of years, then multiplied the number of weeks. In a hundred years, The Sailor had died five thousand and two hundred times.

In addition, there were theological problems. Joel-Andrew was a prophet. Prophets were notoriously putrid when it comes to theology. Second, he doubted if the library held the work of Thomas Aquinas. Joel-Andrew felt a deep need for that ancient theologian. He figured Aquinas worked this ghost business out for all eternity because, Joel-Andrew told himself, Aquinas worked everything else out.

His thoughts were interrupted. The blond man who had kept pace with him now sat beside him on the steps of City Hall. "Total nonsense," the man said, "and I am not a freak. Ghosts are pagan. No theologian would give 'em house space." The voice sounded subdued as sleeping sickness, withdrawn, but kind. "My name is Kune," he said, "and this town is no more crazy than Seattle, but it's alarming at first."

"You read minds," Joel-Andrew said. "You knew I thought of theology."

"I am a diagnostician," Kune told him. "I don't read minds. I read situations, symptoms, gross behavior, subtleties. I read signals of distress while using talent, intuition, scientific knowledge."

"I can call on the Lord," Joel-Andrew said. "The Lord could raise that man from the dead."

"It's a very fine idea," Kune said, "but let's go easy with it. By now The Sailor is used to dying horribly. You might not do him a favor."

Joel-Andrew recognized the red herring. Joel-Andrew remembered plenty of smackheads who shot up yogurt, dropped granola, and spoke of feeling fit. He looked at Kune. Kune's eyes were so light brown they were washed-out yellow. Kune's face held lines and traces of grief. People who feared change always came up with weak rationalizations.

"Besides," Kune said, "where do you stop with such things? The old jail is in the basement. It's more like a dungeon. The kinkos who ran that place killed off quite-a-many through the years."

"You stop at the end of it," Joel-Andrew said. "You stop when all the bad trips and all the trip-masters are whipped."

"You're setting yourself up quite a project," Kune told him. "In this town you'll have enough trouble just nailing all the Republicans."

Fog moved quietly into the streets, and as drapes of darkness descended over Point Vestal, a few streetlights became pale echoes of illumination. The red neon sign in front of Janie's Tavern flicked in the distance like the little demon on a can of deviled ham. On the Strait, a ship's whistle grunted, a bell buoy clinked, and a boat whistle shrilled like a child's scream.

"The key to Point Vestal," Kune said, "is that all the time is happening some of the time. At least that's the theory."

Obed once more purred in Portuguese. Obed was not confused.

"Portuguese," Kune said. "That lady and gentlemen who spoke to you about The Sailor live in a nice house on the hill. They are old now, but in the 1940s they were middle-aged. You just happened to meet them in 1947." Kune's yellow eyes looked momentarily cratered, as if with old scars of smallpox. "It's just a little jump in time," he said, "and it happens rarely."

"When time jumps occur," Joel-Andrew asked politely, "are the people alive or ghosts?"

"They are always alive," Kune said, "and I've never got this one quite puzzled out. We can get a time jump with live people—the kind that you just saw—and the only thing mixed up is the year. For instance, you can get a time jump and see a childhood friend running down the street. Or, you can get a time jump where a ghost pops in for a few moments, but the ghost doesn't flicker during a time jump. It is almost as if the ghost returns to life momentarily."

Lights in shop windows faded as storekeepers stepped to the sidewalk, locked doors, rattled knobs.

Joel-Andrew told himself he was no theologian, but he wasn't exactly an idiot. "That would mean," Joel-Andrew said, "you might walk around and someday meet yourself when you were younger. You could even tell yourself not to do something wrong, if you met yourself when you were younger. You could keep rewriting history."

"If only that were true," Kune said, "but it doesn't work that way. But, oh, if only that were true." He stood, turned, offered a hand to Joel-Andrew. "I'm headed up the hill to check a rumor. Some nut claims to have seen the ghost of August Starling in the drawing room of the Starling House."

Joel-Andrew thought it made elegant sense if he did not explain about August Starling. Still, if he did not tell, that would be a form of lying. "The rumor is true," he said. "I'm afraid I had a hand in it. I rode into town in a horse and buggy. The driver said he was August Starling."

"Then history around here is going to ring off the hook." Kune's washed-out yellow eyes stared into the golden eyes of Obed. "Can your cat speak Chinese? We're going to need someone who is fluent in Chinese."

Chapter 7

THE TWO MEN AND THE CAT PASSED QUIETLY THROUGH DARKNESS punctuated with the swizzle of small surf. They passed the little luminescence of a candle in the window of the Storefront Church, and the sweet and heavy smell of opium. The opium and swizzles flickered.

"It closed in 1901," Kune said about the opium den. "Now it's a haunted basement." Night mist clustered. The last time Joel-Andrew could remember such quickly gathering darkness came early in his San Francisco ministry. He stepped into an alley, saw a young girl . . . Joel-Andrew shook his head, rejecting the memory.

A 307-step concrete stairway climbed the hill.

"Put in by the New Deal," Kune said. "It drove the Public Works Administration into a feeding frenzy."

"The steps are teeny-tiny, like steps made for children."

"Made for ladies with long skirts and bustles," Kune told him. "Ladies would not have to show their ankles. Ankles were in during 1937, but not in Point Vestal. Be careful, at this time of evening there's always a body on the 188th step. Killed himself for love."

"In 1873," Joel-Andrew guessed.

"No, 1869," Kune told him. "Very early in the game. Poor chap never lived to see the twentieth century, but he's clung to the 188th step since 1937."

On the 200th step, mist thinned. Joel-Andrew could see the malarial look in Kune's eyes. By the 250th step, mist wrapped like gauze around Kune's face. By the 300th step, Joel-Andrew watched Kune move carefully, as if bound by arthritis. The sky cleared.

"It's most always this way," Kune explained. "Mist makes layers all through downtown, but up here it's mostly clear. I see we have a moon."

They paused at the top of the hill. Obed sat flipping his tail, winded, pretending not to snort oxygen.

For as far as Joel-Andrew could see, enormous houses stood on large lots. Moonlight lay saffron across roofs large as playing fields, although the roofs were not flat. They rose in moonlight beside high turrets, and above widow's walks. Joel-Andrew could imagine angels striding along the roofs in gigantic and godlike postures. Here and there, elaborate wrought iron railings, gewgaws, and wrought iron spires poked at the moon; while light through stained glass windows cast shades of red and yellow, purple and green across shrubbery and lawns. Joel-Andrew, accustomed to Victorian row houses of San Francisco, saw what a Victorian house could become when not squashed by neighbors.

"Meet some Victorians. That's the Tobias house." Kune pointed. "Haunted by Amy Tobias, who is mad. She shrieks from the left hand tower on Monday evenings." He stared at the left hand tower. "If I married the bull-pizzle who built that house, I'd have gone mad, too." He pointed another direction. "That's the Naavik house. Sven Naavik sobs in the basement. Except when he's crashed on laudanum." Kune pointed. "That's the Annie Wier house. Not all of these were built by men. Annie's a madam who ran a joint downtown. Now she does a number that is pale and wan—soft music among the shrubbery—delicate laughter—echoes of player pianos—stuff like that." Kune's voice tried to be funny, but carried too much sadness.

"I swear by Obed's white whisker I haven't the foggiest notion what all this means."

"It may mean suffering is eternal," Kune said. He slumped, pointing. "In that house a consumptive has choked for a hundred years. Next door a child falls into a blazing fireplace every Christmas Eve—in that house a guy collects feet; horses' hooves, dog paws—deer—raccoon . . ." He looked at Obed. "Don't go anywhere near that place. Pickled feet from mice, Indians, ducks, cougars, bears."

Joel-Andrew, accustomed to seeing only normal perversion, was appalled. He bent to stroke Obed's chin. Obed purred in patterns Joel-Andrew had never heard. Obed practiced rudimentary Chinese.

"That spire," said Kune, and pointed, "is the Lutheran church. That one over there is Baptist. That one is Methodist, and the one on the right is Presbyterian."

"And Episcopal?" Joel-Andrew asked.

"On a high hill beside the Catholics, toward the back of town. Also over there are Moravians, Mennonites, and a bunch of others." Kune pointed, and small surprise entered his voice. "And that's the old Presbyterian parsonage. It rarely locates in this section of town."

It was the same house Joel-Andrew had entered five hours before. It held the same stern lines, the same tower from which so many sermons must have poured. Its octagonal bell tower stood silent. Moonlight illuminated surrounding houses, but no moonlight touched The Parsonage. No smoke came from its chimneys. The Parsonage stood darkly, as if brooding on human depravity.

A thin scream sounded in the distance.

"It's 6:13," Kune said. "That was one of the Crocker twins jumping off the bluff. Prudence and Simplicity Crocker. Both fell in love with the same man. He was killed at Verdun. They take turns."

"I am not sure," Joel-Andrew said, looking seriously at The Parsonage, "that I'm going to cut it around here."

"It's no different from Seattle," Kune told him. "Seattle is just as Victorian as here. It is fascinated by sex and drugs and romance and money. It's only a question of style."

"Does it make you sad?" Joel-Andrew's gray-green eyes were moist. The awfulness of Point Vestal history seemed shrieking.

The Parsonage, which only hours before was such a welcoming place, now struck Joel-Andrew as the only sane place. The firm lines, the severity of the all-seeing tower, caused him to yearn for the warmth of that intelligent-seeming drawing room.

"I met two fine people earlier, but were they real?" Joel-Andrew asked. "Named Bev and Samuel. He's a Methodist. Can't be helped, I suppose."

"They are alive right now in Point Vestal, if that's what you mean," Kune said. "Yes, they're real. He's a preacher. Except for that, you can't fault him. No imagination, of course."

"I have discovered," Joel-Andrew said, "that imagination gets you excommunicated." Joel-Andrew pushed away memories. Excommunication was lonely, but it led him to addresses where he was needed.

Kune paused. "I try to live without any more imagination," he said.

"You can tell me." Joel-Andrew could not bear seeing someone in distress.

"Bev is the smart one." Kune spoke as if he had not heard. "If this business with August Starling gets out of hand we can count on Bev." Rustling sounds came from nearby shrubbery. Obed's white tail flashed beside a rhododendron. Obed tried to bust a field mouse.

"Because," Kune said, "the whole history of Point Vestal swings on August Starling. He was the biggest drug pusher, the biggest bond slave runner, the biggest whoremaster in Point Vestal history."

Joel-Andrew was appalled. August Starling had seemed a little weird, but Joel-Andrew put that down to Victorianism and lack of religious training. August Starling seemed so young, so romantic, so innocent. Then Joel-Andrew remembered how August Starling lied with complete sincerity.

"Maybe the history is wrong," Joel-Andrew said. "He was young, was he not?"

"He was a baby killer," Kune said. "Also a deacon."

"I'll deal with him," Joel-Andrew said, and the serenity of the Lord dwelt in him. "Prepare for miracles."

Kune stood erect as if stabbed. His eyes opened wider than nineteen yards of Benzedrine. Grief flowed over his face. His eyes stared, stared; then he slumped. "Please," he whispered, "if we are to be friends, never use that word again. You can speak of angels and demons and any other kind of critter. You can do what you wish with August Starling, but don't use that word *miracle* again."

"There will come winds of Heaven." Joel-Andrew found himself speaking with fervency that came only from the Lord. "There will come a mighty storm, and the trees will bend and the trees will break. The sea will run in the streets of the town, and across these fabled houses will flash the fires of the Holy Ghost; the fires of angels. This I prophesy."

"It storms up a racket around here most winters," Kune said, relieved to be back on conversational ground. "If anybody ever writes a history of this town, weather will play a big part. You can count on it."

Chapter 8

"I'VE NEVER HEARD OF A HOUSE THAT MOVED," JOEL-ANDREW SAID. "Plus, it's such a nice house." The two men stood beside The Parsonage as moonlight illuminated uptown streets.

"It is nice," Kune told him, "which makes it altogether different from the Starling House. A big part of town history is really a tale of two houses. This is the history:"

The Parsonage, Kune explained, was built in 1871, largely with money contributed by Janie, the owner of Janie's Tavern. Cussing was not allowed in her tavern. She was lightning and thunder when it came to overt whoring.

In 1871 the Presbyterians' barn-sized church ran in a high and almighty manner. Deacons stood at the helm of everything happening downtown. When threatened with loss of the best hell-and-brimstone preacher on the coast (because the preacher tired of living in the fifteen-square-foot sacristy with his wife and toddlers), Janie was elected a deacon. It was a Presbyterian first.

Janie—a red-haired Scot of medium height and more than medium temper—hired a builder, approved his plans, and built The Parsonage in three days. She enjoyed more help than was needed. It was a tour de force. She pressured every joint in town to cut off booze until The Parsonage stood complete. In Point Vestal history, the event is still remembered as "the dry spell"; it certainly impressed the Baptists.

Peace descended. The Parsonage sat beside the church through the nineteenth century, and through the first half of the twentieth. One hellfire-and-brimstone preacher followed another. The Parsonage felt happy, even content. Sermons issued from the all-seeing tower with regularity unknown since the days of Cotton Mather. Then the Presbyterians fell onto one of the seven deadly sins: the Presbyterians were racked with Pride.

In the 1950s Point Vestal went through a spasm of modernization. People felt compelled to pour concrete. There was talk of building an airport, of expanding the boat basin, of building a new City Hall. The bookstore sold collections of strange poetry. People bought three-toned automobiles fitted with air horns and spotlights; and the Presbyterians lusted for a place to park their three-toned cars.

They decided to put a parking lot beside the church and build a new parsonage. Their heritage was one of thrift. The Parsonage was a perfectly good house. In its way, it was even sanctified.

So the Presbyterians sold it to a Mormon.

The Mormon moved it to a nearby lot while The Parsonage reeled in a state of shock.

Awful theological confrontations went on in the mind of The Parsonage. Rain clouded the face of windows and ran from the eaves like tears. Wind moaned around the turret, and passersby heard congregated ministerial voices. Bells in the octagonal tower plinked like broken harp strings. Paint flaked from walls as shudders of grief racked The Parsonage. For eighty years it had issued declarations of Calvinist flame; now the poor thing looked at a Mormon.

Give The Parsonage credit. It analyzed differences and came to grudging admiration. The Mormon was monogamous. The Mormon was patriarchal. The Mormon's whiskers became heated when he argued for thrift and hearth and home. The Mormon was penurious, bigoted, and sometimes spoke well of Moses. The Parsonage, reconsidering, began to feel right at home. Things were turning out very well for The Parsonage.

Then something awful happened. To the horror of the whole town, the Mormon sold The Parsonage to a Quaker. That is when The Parsonage began its odyssey.

"I'm not a theologian," Kune murmured, "but The Parsonage is stern. Quakers are just blunt."

The two men and the cat stood looking at The Parsonage, at enormous houses on the hill, and at distant towers of the Starling House. A heavy scent of burning flesh lingered for a moment beneath glow of moon and scatter of stars. On wrought iron stakes of an elaborate fence, a ghostly gentleman hung impaled. A church bell clanked above Wednesday evening prayer meeting. A mutilated Indian led a limping horse, the two staggering toward downtown. A woman in a white Victorian gown emerged from mist as she reached the top of the 307 steps. Her dark eyes filled with fear. Her fingers fumbled at her purse. She breathed heavily, but marched past the men and the cat. The woman did not flicker, but she trembled. Joel-Andrew watched her, felt enormous pain, and remembered his excommunication. Frightened women always made him remember his excommunication.

"San Francisco," he told Kune. "I went in 1966 at the behest of the Lord."

"I've got to check out August Starling," Kune told him, but he mused. "San Francisco: That big suburb to the south." He walked slowly. "It is unbelievable the way Seattle has expanded."

"Before San Francisco I had a small congregation in Providence, Rhode Island." To Joel-Andrew, the memories of quiet days of study, of visiting infirm members of his church, of playing with children of the congregation were the warmest he owned. He had hoped for a wife, but the Lord willed him to be a prophet. Joel-Andrew could never remember having ever misunderstood about love. His father was a quiet minister; his mother cared only to teach, whether children or other small animals.

Rhode Island seemed long ago and far away. Joel-Andrew often wondered why the Lord picked someone so unsuitable.

"The Starling House can put on quite a show," Kune said. "In its way, it is as moody as The Parsonage." Kune stepped steadily, like one accustomed to walking all night. His yellow eyes were as remarkable in moonlight as were the golden eyes of Obed. He moved as routinely as measles.

"And because the Starling House is moody," Kune said, "you can never be exactly sure which year you'll hit when you go through the servants' entrance. The servants' entrance is a way of entering the past. If we go in the front door, it will be today, 1973." Unaccountably, Kune giggled. "This is not common knowledge. Even old folks in this town don't know about the servants' entrance." He paused. "How could they? All of them are decent. I may be the only one who has used the servants' entrance in the last five decades."

"You are a wonderful expert," Joel-Andrew assured him. "Perhaps no one living knows more about Point Vestal than you."

"No one living," Kune said, "except a young woman named Collette who runs the antique store. A few of the dead ones are simply gee-whiz-experts. There's an old Indian named Maggie who hangs out at Janie's Tavern . . ." He paused, his thoughts interrupted. A '66 Plymouth bearing high schoolers roared past. Beer cans popped like losing punches on a punchboard. A police car running on a single pinball light pursued the Plymouth. The police car was a '39 LaSalle, dark and flickering.

"Homecoming week," Kune explained.

"Tell me about August Starling." Joel-Andrew hoped the local football team would win. He was beginning to feel community spirit. He hoped the Plymouth would not get in a wreck, that people would not be killed . . . then told himself he did not know. Being killed in Point Vestal was not the same as being killed elsewhere. Then he told himself nope, naw, uh uh. A bad trip was a bad trip.

"l saw August Starling once," Kune said. "I walked into 1888, back when the house was just built."

"And Starling was going crazy," Joel-Andrew said. "Going crazy with guilt because of his sins."

"Nope," Kune told him. "He was going crazy because the house was being painted, and there was a lot of lead in the paint. It kind of snoozled his brain." Kune pointed to a massive house looming in the moonlit sky. Turrets and towers brooded in the night. Balustrades and porches and balconies stood deserted. The house seemed like a tomb.

Chapter 9

KUNE AND JOEL-ANDREW STOOD BEFORE THE STARLING HOUSE AS IT rose four stories into the night.

"We'll go inside in a few minutes," Kune said, "but before we do, I'll tell about August Starling. Can you pretend the year is 1888?"

"You got it," Joel-Andrew said.

"I am very good at making pictures with words," Kune murmured. "The year I'm going to show is 1888. We are presently standing uptown in 1973, but I am going to tell about 1888, and about downtown where the action started. It would have looked something like this."

=

Kune began by saying that gray skies drizzled mist on the muddy street, and buildings that were new in 1888 rose three and four stories. The buildings carried elaborate gewgaws splendid in pastel enamels. New brick on The Fisherman's Café shone beside stained glass windows, while carriages and lumber carts churned the muddy road surface bound together by wood chips, crushed rock, oyster shells, clam shells, twigs; and layered with horse poop.

Before Janie's Tavern stood two tough cops in boiler hats and cheap wool suits, while in the tavern a youthful August Starling sipped whiskey and blew kisses toward the street where an occasional madam passed with her bodyguards. An elaborately carved and beautifully painted wooden sign advertised the joint as a "discreet hostelry for gentlemen." A tidily rolled drunk lay wrapped around a hitching post.

One cop wore a bruise on his chin, a scar over one eye, and an Irish brogue. "We'll be carrying that one home," he said, and nodded over his shoulder toward August Starling. "I can't get over how he still looks like a youngster."

"He's a deacon," the second cop said. "You can get a deacon boiled out past 'halla-loo-yah' and he'll still walk." The second cop was skinny and morose. He slouched and chewed tobacco. He proved an accurate spitter.

"Steam," the first cop said. "Look at that precious darlin'."

In the harbor a two-stacker made anchor. It boiled coal smoke into the mist. Fresh paint on the iron hull shone red and black and white. Lumber barges were towed toward the ship by a steam tug, and beyond the ship six old clipper ships hung at anchor like wounded greyhounds. Clipper masts disappeared in low mist. Riding sails sagged yellow, stained like old parchment. Small waves breathed on the beach beside The Fisherman's Café.

"I worked in the engine room of a steamer once." The morose cop wrinkled his nose. "If you'd ever worked in the engine room, you'd be thinking it ain't so darlin'."

The drunk wrapped around the hitching post gave a small groan. He moved crabwise across a patch of mud and climbed onto the wooden sidewalk. Although a small man, his faulty movements still held hints of agility, echoes of squirrel-like scrambles along masts and yards. His hands were scarred and capable from fisting sails. He was too little to be a Swede, too blond to be anything else.

"Me lad," the Irish cop said, "you'd best get your bung back to your ship. There's a man in there"—and the cop motioned over his shoulder toward Janie's Tavern—"who eats sweet boys."

"Shanghai," the skinny cop said, "or cutting limestone in a pit alongside Chinamen. No floozies, no rum, for never—if Starling takes you on."

The Swede got to his knees, blue eyes staring. He struggled to stand, tipped over, began crawling down the sidewalk.

"He's got an hour of daylight," the skinny cop said. "If he crawls fast, he'll make it."

Across the street and half a block away, a four-story building seemed built to hold fancy decorations. A huge sign read 'De Fuca Trading Company and Chandlery—A. Starling, Esq. Prop.' On the wooden sidewalk stood wares: coils of manila, casks of salt pork, brass fixtures for ships and houses; one elaborate, gorgeous, waterproof ebony coffin. The coffin was big enough to hold a husband and wife, or a mother and child; the kind of Victorian chamber much favored when a family owned more than one corpse.

Sailors passed the coffin to enter through a red doorway and onto narrow stairs leading to upper rooms. Chinamen slouched quickly past wide front doors, while Indians sneered. Hitching posts displayed horses with buggies and wagons—while floozies, loggers, merchants, other riffraff strolled and gossiped, colorful beneath gray sky. Farther down the street a man either preached or politicked, his words smothered by mist.

"I reckon we had to have an occurrence," the skinny cop said. "Blamed if it isn't walking right at us." He reached in his pocket and concealed a two-shot derringer in his palm.

"Makes me weary." The Irish cop settled his right hand into a knuckle-duster. "It's like the old country, only more so."

The man approached with tight control, a heavyset farmer type wearing a horse pistol on his hip. He wore stained rubber boots, muddy overalls; his lips a tight line, his eyes so focused he did not see the cops. As he approached Janie's Tavern, he started to draw the horse pistol.

"Not a good idea," the Irish cop said in a loud voice. "Lad, what can ye be thinking?"

The skinny cop pointed the derringer. "We can shoot you to death or beat you to death. I recommend the first."

"Or you can walk up the hill and out of town."

The farmer stood and stared, disbelieving. "I have a woman missing. You know about that. I expect Starling has shanghaied her for his cathouse." The farmer's voice sounded flat, uncaring, ready to die, but not before doing a job. "He needs killing."

"Indeed he does," the Irish cop said. "And you may be the lad to do it, but not while we're on duty."

"Get a rifle," the skinny cop said, "and take him from afar. Where's your common sense?"

"I'd be obliged," the farmer said, "if you told me where she is. I want no trouble with you boys."

On the shaded side of the street, fancy oil lamps with stained glass shades shone in upstairs windows. Common oil lamps lighted the trading company. A small glow streaked illumination across the ebony coffin.

"We'll tell you true," the Irish cop said. "We don't know about any woman. If one is shanghaied, I'll *believe* Starling's behind it, but this is the first we've heard."

"We get off duty when we deliver Starling to his house," the skinny cop told the farmer. "After that he's on his own. Give me your gun. Walk away." The cop's voice, no longer sympathetic, was all cop.

The farmer paused. "You take it." He put his hands behind his back. "That way none of us makes mistakes."

The Irish cop pulled the horse pistol from the holster.

"Made before the Civil War. Junk. They sell better at the trading company."

"I was just stepping that way," the farmer said. "Got to price new harness." He turned and walked across the muddy street, his shoulders shaking with fear or fury.

"How much are you supposing?" the Irish cop asked.

"Starling's never been with a woman since his mommy dumped him off her lap." the skinny cop said, more morose than ever. "At least not with a live one—maybe a naked picture, maybe a woman cast in plaster. I'd bet a million."

"Still, a lass is missing."

"Probably shanghaied. Maybe dead. Maybe the hayseed will kill Starling, all to the good. But I'll lay odds Starling has never been with a living woman."

"He'd ought to do something about it abruptly." The Irishman grinned. "It looks like he's in for a short evening."

At the trading company, coils of line and the brass fittings were loaded aboard wagons bound for the city's wharf. A gaggle of Chinese came from the trading company. They surrounded the ebony coffin like lilliputian pallbearers setting out to inter an elephant. They wrestled the coffin onto a wagon, their golden skins wet, the wagon standing grayly, knowing, as it did, not a single word of Chinese.

"The press-gang stagecoach," the skinny cop said. "How long does Starling think he can smuggle shanghaied sailors past the customs in a coffin."

"As long as he pays off customs officers."

"At least," the skinny cop said mournfully, "he could use a different coffin once in a while. It's beginnin' to look familiar." The wagon squoozed along muddy streets as lamps burned bright in The Fisherman's Café. The Chinese pallbearers looked like mourning shadows.

A smelly logger flew through the doorway of Janie's Tavern, rolled between the cops, bounced off the hitching post, regained balance, and sat on the edge of the wooden sidewalk. He looked putrid, his color emerald. He looked like Paul Bunyan with a bald head, a shorn green ox.

The Irish cop tsked. "It's that last load of drippings," he said, "turns the customers mossy." He bent over the man. "What vile word did you say that got you thrown out?

"——," the man muttered.

"Shame be your lot," the cop said. "For Janie will ha' none of that."

"I can get drunker," the logger said with convincement. "I'll yard myself down to Annie Wier's cathouse."

"That's a good lad." The cop turned to his partner, looked through windows of Janie's Tavern. "Shall we persuade our man toward home? It's been just sip, sip, sip. And we linger here in mist and rain. 'Tis time to step inside."

Janie's Tavern, when the two cops entered, gave a homey feeling of nineteenth-century charm. Cut-glass chandeliers twinkled like fairies, or like elvish sparkles in the Irish cop's eyes. Gentlemen and harlots murmured, sitting at tables, elegantly tasting fine red whiskey. Large billiard tables were attended by a Chinaman who chalked cues for gentlemen, dusted tables, whisked small speckles of lint, cigar ash, and crud from wool suits. A poker game card-flapped quietly. At the bar August Starling whispered to a Chinese messenger.

The cops watched the messenger shadow his way past them. At the end of the bar an old Indian named Maggie muttered to herself.

"Maggie, me darlin'," the Irish cop said. "What can a lady such as yourself be doing here with chippies?"

"You're a sweet-speakin' Mick." Maggie smiled a toothless smile. Her face—at least when her mouth was closed—was as beautiful as an old book. "Thank God my mother never lived to meet the Irish." Wrinkles on Maggie's tan face showed as much intelligence as could be found in a whole library. She was a small woman, Skykomish tribe, and she knew about tides and winds and moon. Maggie knew nature so well she might have been nature's mother. She knew about medicines and the bark of trees, about child-birth and house cats and cougars. She knew about elk and halibut, homesteading, berry picking, how to strip cascara. She knew how to light fires by talking to the wood, and she knew what salmon gossiped about as they came upriver to spawn. She could not be sandbagged by poetic Irishmen.

"Yonder man"—and she nodded to August Starling— "is about to fold his hand." When Maggie made a prophecy, her prophecy always came true.

"Yes, indeed," the skinny cop muttered. "A hayseed is gonna shoot him."

"That ain't the way it's gonna happen," Maggie said. "Too easy."

"Welcome, officers." August Starling's voice bubbled approximately like champagne, and took the tone of one accustomed to being kind to servants. Starling's boylike face beamed cherubically in sparkling lamplight. His slight figure, dressed in wool suit and stock, stood dutifully erect. To the bartender he said, "A taste for these fine minions."

"Make it a water glass," the Irish cop said, "and wet a tad-bit more than the bottom."

At the far end of the bar, Janie talked to her bouncer. Janie was redheaded and was dressed in a purple gown. Her lips could press together in a ladylike pout, or open to raspiness. Janie was— according to sailor standards—"a gorgeous piece," but it never did any sailor any good to know that. Her bouncer looked like a tugboat with arms.

Large and polished mirrors behind the bar reflected dancing lights, and August Starling's eyes shone liquid with romance. Janie watched Starling, hid a snigger behind her hand, belched genteelly.

Starling turned from the bar and walked to the front window to look at his trading company.

The sidewalk in front of the building was empty, the coffin safely horsing somewhere through the mist. Starling turned, his face flushed with anticipation. "Everything comes to he who minds the main chance," he said to no one in particular.

"I wouldn't know," the skinny cop said dolefully. "I spend too much time mindin' my own business. That, and delivering gentlemen to safety."

"It is honorable employment."

"It's a job," the cop said. "Will we be leaving soon?"

"How long since the coffin left?"

"Fifteen minutes."

"Soon," August Starling said, "but first I wish to stand drinks for this establishment. Today is consequent. Darkness lifts. Sweet light of the celestial orb illuminates my passage as I don pure and flowing robes of domesticity. I drink to my new house." He turned, beckoned the bartender. "And now my dear wife can join me . . ."

"All the way from Boston," the Irish cop muttered. The cop looked helplessly to Maggie. "How flaming many times have we heard that? Suppose he breeds. All them little Starlings, flocks of 'em."

"He won't," Maggie said. "In the first place, he's a goner. In the second place, he ain't got a wife, except in his imagination."

"No wife?"

"No wife," Maggie said, and she was positive. "In the third place, you can't breed if you don't know where to put it. In the fourth . . ."

The Irish cop was mildly shocked. "Can this be Maggie talking?" He chided. "Shush, for if Janie hears such language—"

"There isn't a redheaded Presbyterian born that makes me fear," Maggie told him. "In the fourth place, if you lie about something long enough, you believe it yourself. Starling, he's a savage."

The Irish cop shook his head with admiration. "Maggie, Maggie, is there anything in the world you don't know?"

"I don't think so. I know the past, the future . . ." and Maggie grinned in a toothless way. "I know you are one year away from a shotgun marriage. You will have six children, twenty-seven grandchildren. One will be a girl named Collette."

"'Tis a sweet name," the Irish cop said, "and may what you say be true, for me bed is lonesome of late."

"Anyway," the morose cop said mournfully, "it won't make a bit of difference in a hundred years."

"Yes it will," Maggie told him. "In a hundred years there are going to be high times around here." She sipped her liquor, pointed toward The Fisherman's Café. "In a hundred years a red-hot preacher will be running around here together with a confused sawbones. Five people will sit yonder at The Fisherman's Café writing a book about all this. It will make a heap of difference."

"Not to me," the skinny cop said, his mournfulness a great contrast to the giddiness of August Starling. "I won't be here."

"I will," Maggie said. "I'll be here. I'm sticking around to see the fun, and to make sure those people get my name right in their book."

Chapter 10

"WHAT YEAR IS IT?" JOEL-ANDREW ASKED, AS HE AND KUNE ENTERED the Starling House. "I know you warned me about the servants' entrance. Plus, I don't see any electric lights."

"I'm afraid it's 1888," Kune told him. "It's 1888 again, oh, dear." He turned yellow eyes toward Joel-Andrew. "I do not want you confused," he said. "This is what has happened. I told you about 1888. As I told about 1888, we walked into the Starling House in 1973, but we came through the servants' entrance. The house likes to fool around. Maybe it even tries to please me. At any rate, we are now in the Starling House in the year 1888. The story I began telling you has stopped being a story. It is happening *right* now." Kune spoke with the mournful certainty of cholera.

Joel-Andrew, pleased with powerful forces, was also pleased with the brand-new Starling House. Walls shone pristine white, ceilings glowed with ormolu. Intricately carved banisters framed a curving staircase rising into night. No servants were present, but lamplight caressed crystal and lay warm across new and highly polished Victorian furniture.

Kune tried to settle a moral principle. "What happens next is not something a preacher ought to see. Let's get out and come back some other year."

"I've spent time in the Haight," Joel-Andrew said. "Nothing the nineteenth century shows is likely to do me in."

At Joel-Andrew's feet, Obed stirred, his ear cocked, as if trying to pick up diction of far-off Chinese whispers. At the same time, Obed seemed randy.

"If my theory is correct, all we do is look through windows of the tower to watch the story unfold." Kune climbed the curving staircase resolutely. "You'll remember," he said, "we left August Starling in the company of two cops. The cops were to escort him home. An ebony coffin already left Starling's place of business on a horse-drawn wagon. If we hurry, we may see the wagon arrive."

Joel-Andrew had known space travelers of many dimensions, including one freak who stirred mystical mileage from peyote buds by using a Waring blender. But this business about time was new. He climbed to the tower while Kune filled him in.

In 1888, while August Starling talked to the cops, the wagon bearing the enormous ebony coffin left the trading company and passed over the muddy street. The gaggle of Chinese murmured, at first in dismay, then chattered question marks as the wagon continued past wharves where it normally would have stopped. Chinese padded behind the wagon, shook their heads, argued, fell silent as the driver turned the horses onto the road leading uptown. The coffin jiggled. Chinese teeth chattered like bamboo chimes.

High on the hill, not far from the original site of The Parsonage, a church bell heralded Wednesday evening services. A clank from the belltower of The Parsonage answered. The black horses leaned into the harness. At a muddy spot the Chinese pushed the wagon. In a few minutes the wagon reached the top of the hill. The driver headed for the Starling House.

=

Kune and Joel-Andrew stood in one of the towers of the Starling House, staring into the night.

Somewhere a dog howled; a cat yowled. Obed tried to concentrate on his Chinese, but was losing it.

"I see a man with a rifle," Joel-Andrew said. He pointed where lamplight fell through the window of a nearby house. "Just crouching. That's the man you told me about."

"A farmer," Kune said. "In a few minutes, August Starling's press gang will get him. Back in the tavern, Starling spotted the farmer and sent a messenger. The farmer will be put on a ship called *Covenant*, will desert in Cuba, and make his way back to town by 1918. He will remarry. He is Bev's father, and she will be born in 1920."

"Can't we stop it?"

"Probably," Kune said, "but then he would not be shanghaied. He would stay here, maybe marry someone else. If he married someone else, then Bev would not get born."

"What about the Irish cop?" Joel-Andrew asked wistfully. "What about the morose cop? Did he ever find happiness?"

"The Irish cop became a medical mystery," Kune said. "He went on a bender and attained a condition we physicians describe as 'pickled.' Been pickled ever since. Frank keeps him in an old coffin in the back room of Janie's Tavern. Frank brings him out for display on Halloween."

"And the morose cop?"

"He never found happiness," Kune said shortly. "He got kicked in the head by a horse. His ghost manifested in the basement of City Hall. It is the morose cop who beats The Sailor to death every Wednesday at 4:00 PM."

"Oh, dear," Joel-Andrew said. "I'm not sure how much of this a man can bear." Joel-Andrew thought of ugly acts of evil. Then he smiled as he thought of plain, common, and pretty forces of the Lord.

The wagon came closer, and beneath a wan moon Kune and Joel-Andrew could distinguish the ebony coffin. There came a muffled shout: the sound of the farmer being clubbed by August Starling's press gang.

"The ship *Covenant* was a bucket," Kune said. "An old clipper redesigned to sail like a toad." He pointed toward the road leading up the hill. "If you look yonder, you can just make out August Starling. The two cops are seeing him home."

The wagon pulled up in front of the Starling House. It took nearly ten minutes for the Chinese to get the coffin up the broad front steps and into the house.

Obed's tail stood straight up, shivered, and he made faces. He sniffed the air, thinking naught of history, because Obed thought of jubilation. A cat yowled. Obed's tail shivered.

"Your cat is horny," Kune said with some dismay.

"He'll abide close by." Joel-Andrew was content that Episcopal discipline had persuaded Obed to a higher manner of life.

"You may know lots about a lot of things," Kune told him, "but you don't know *catnip* when it comes to cats."

There was scuffling, thumping, the hard breath of labor from downstairs as Chinese arranged the coffin on a low set of teak sawhorses. The front door slammed. The team of horses nickered, stomped. The wagon disappeared into mist as Chinese followed, fading like small and ancient echoes. August Starling's approaching voice sounded tinkling and gay. Then, in more somber tones, he quoted poetry:

> But ah! a cloud on swift wings passed,
> And all the sky was overcast,
> And then were wrecked, alas! too fast,
> My freighted treasures, Rosalie.
>
> I can not twine my fingers now
> In thy soft hair, nor kiss thy brow,
> Nor hear thy gentle accents flow . . . .

A bell clanked dully from The Parsonage. From the tower of the Starling House, Joel-Andrew saw three figures beneath night-shadow of Starling House turrets. The skinny cop trailed like a mourner behind the lightly built Starling and the husky Irishman.

"'Tis a nice lament " the Irish cop said about the poem, "but it has some whiskey in it."

"One of our better modern poets," August Starling said in his boyish voice. "You are a gentleman of culture."

"I own a sweet ear," the cop said, "and a thirsty feeling this night. Would that Janie ran a tab."

"It will be my pleasure," August Starling said. "You miscreants shall be rewarded with gold." He fumbled for his purse, tipped the two cops. The three men stood before the steps of the Starling House. "And now I enter my new house. My dear wife—"

"Will be coming from Boston," the morose cop said. "Sweet dreams." He shuffled away, followed by a thirsty Irishman.

"Now it starts," Kune whispered to Joel-Andrew. "If we creep downstairs and hide in the library, you can watch through a stained glass window. Some of these old houses are so fancy, they have stained glass in the doors between rooms. Keep that cat on a tight rein."

As they descended Joel-Andrew could hear only snatches of Kune's whispers. ". . . the farmer's wife . . . went to the trading company to price yard goods . . . Starling overdosed her with knockout drops . . . hid her in the coffin . . ."

"Murder."

"You bet it was murder," Kune whispered, "or maybe an accident. Maybe he only figured to knock her out."

"He really is insane," Joel-Andrew said. "The Lord must pity him, and so must we. That poor woman."

"He wasn't insane when he caused the murder of Chinese and sailors. That man saw at least thirty people under the sea or underground."

"He is very young," Joel-Andrew said. "I don't offer that as an excuse."

"He's as old as you are," Kune explained. "He's one of those fellows who never look like they age."

Obed's tail rattled. He purred in Italian argot. Ahead, disappearing into a pantry, a flashy and aristocratic white cat looked like a wanton spirit.

Joel-Andrew reached to reassure Obed. Obed went airborne, taking eighteen curving steps in a leap that—at one point—had him running along the wall; claw prints in wallpaper.

"I forgot about that house cat," Kune whispered. "Now we've bought a batch of trouble."

"He is a highly disciplined cat," Joel-Andrew explained. "He'll come to his senses." They entered the library.

The doors to the drawing room stood like little twin towers. Stained glass windows sat formed in reds and blues and purples; but with enough yellow glass, and enough clear etched glass, to allow the two men to see.

August Starling knelt before the coffin in an attitude of prayer. His lithe frame drooped, so his tailored wool suit seemed looking for a coat hanger. His arms raised against the coffin, his folded hands a steeple. Low sobs. A whisper: "Will you sometimes remember my trembling lips breathed / 'A life's dying blessing on thee'?"His steepled hands trembled in soft light cast by an oil lamp with a cranberry shade. Red light and dark shadow filled the room. Pure white wallpaper held streaks of red, pink, auburn; streaks of dusk, darkness, black. Louder sobs shook him. "Sainted presence," he murmured, "immaculate soul."

"He's flying," Joel-Andrew whispered. "I've seen it before. He's somewhere out around Mars. It's acid does it."

"It's 1888," Kune whispered, "so it isn't acid. It's romance."

> I think I see yet,
> Her sweet mouth in a pet,
> All puckered up with anger and persimmon;
> I tried to moralize—
> She scorned me with those eyes—
> Those eyes that made her peerless among women

"Good God," said Kune, "he's having a domestic quarrel. He's going for the whole nut."

"Blessed wife," August Starling murmured. He stood and slowly twisted brass handles to unseal the coffin. Two cats, a white shadow and a gray shadow entered the room from a door off the pantry. Obed rattled his tail and did back flips. Joel-Andrew thought the white house cat a beauty. Obed's white whisker twitched. He still purred in Italian, but now the Italian was operatic. The white cat was obviously experienced. She had Obed acting like a blind pup in a sausage factory.

As August Starling raised the coffin lid, the face of a young woman appeared, blue eyes staring in disbelief. The corpse wore her Sunday's best, going-to-town dress, a high-necked gown made of glossy blue stuff. Her remarkable eyes picked up the gown's reflection. Her eyes seemed momentarily alive.

Joel-Andrew started to open the doors. Kune stopped him. "There is nothing you can do," Kune whispered. "She's already dead. He's already insane."

"The Lord can do something," Joel-Andrew whispered. He found himself in a low-key wrestling match with Kune.

"That is the man you brought back to town," Kune whispered. "You are going to have to do something about it, but don't do it now. You'll blow Point Vestal to flinders if you play footsie with history."

Obed now sang in French, a light and giddy passage; perhaps from *La belle Helene*. Obed swept in a fine ballroom dance on his back legs. The white cat, born even before Fred Astaire, watched with grudging admiration.

August Starling bent over the coffin, snuffling and weeping. He raised one of the corpse's slender hands. The hand was work worn; a hand that canned garden sass, tussled with broody hens, shook out feather beds—a farmwoman's hand—now motionless. August Starling held the hand. With his other he drew forth a linen handkerchief. He wiped the woman's brow, whispered, blew his nose.

"It was a problem the Victorians had with all their weeping," Kune explained. "They never knew what to do with the snot." Kune's voice sounded bitter, angry, sad. "We got to remember," he said, "this is all history. This happened at least fifty-five years before either of us was born."

"It is happening now."

"Yes it is," Kune admitted. "Indeed it is."

Obed closed in. He gave the white cat a little lick behind the ear. The white cat purred.

> Some Deity see in stars, some in the moon,
> Some azure skies adore, or rising sun;
> But I, more infidel than these—or wise—
> Worship alone thy orient eyes.

"Worship alone thy orient eyes," Kune repeated after August Starling. "What in the name of all that's wonderful is he talking about? He's acting like she's Chinese."

August Starling snuffled. He raised the slender, work-worn hand to his lips. His kiss held for a long time. Red and auburn shadows flickered as draft passed through the great house. The eyes of the corpse lighted, dulled, lighted. Starling's free hand went to the corpse's hair and smoothed it. His hand stroked her cheek.

His tears fell on the rail of the ebony coffin, and the coffin turned glossy beneath red light.

Obed was making it. Obed was finally in. A celebratory yowl rose through the echoing house, and a cacophony of purrs sounded like the well-rounded notes of Caruso. Shadows of flipping tails wrote an ancient story on the walls. Obed looked only a little troubled, but it was obvious he had connected with a cutie pie who might be too hot to handle.

"Preacher man," Kune said, "what more do you know of hell than this?"

"Lots more," Joel-Andrew told him, sad beyond even his own belief. "I've never seen necrophilia before, but I've seen the Haight."

August Starling closed his eyes, reached for the corpse's left hand, and, deftly as a card dealer, removed the plain wedding ring. With his eyes still closed, he fumbled delicately, hands atremble, and hid the ring by inserting it between two buttons of the bodice. He opened his eyes, smiled, reached for his vest pocket. He drew forth a small box with an elegant and matching set of rings; the engagement ring a large diamond, the wedding band diamond studded. Red shadows and pink shadows flickered. August Starling knelt before the coffin and began to propose.

"He's got it bollixed beyond belief," Kune whispered. "First he thinks he's married, now he's getting around to the proposal."

"It is satanic," Joel-Andrew supposed. "Like the upsidedown cross, a reversal of symbols. The power of evil has him in thrall."

Obed was down to his last shot. He began to look hunted. He checked the room for exits. The white cat remained optimistic. The white cat was really getting into it.

August Starling placed the rings on the slender hand, kissed the rings. Lamplight lowered, dulled, and across the white walls shadows moved. Shadows were dancing figures not quite human.

"O Lord," Joel-Andrew prayed, "have mercy on each and all of us." Shadows moved with certainty; the darkness grew. The eyes of the corpse darkened.

Voices of men and women came distantly. People walked in the street.

"It won't be much longer," Kune whispered. "This is where he's interrupted. Folks come from Wednesday prayer meeting. They drop by to congratulate him on his new house."

Obed looked peeled. He lay flat, paws in the air, a goofy smirk on his face. His tail stretched along the floor like a usedup windshield wiper.

August Starling wound the handle of an Austrian music box. As the box tinkled, shadows on the wall assumed hellish shapes. Starling turned back to the corpse.

"This is the part I've never understood," Kune whispered.

A brief flash of exaltation stood in Starling's eyes as he bent over the coffin. Then he reached to lift the corpse. Starling gasped.

The white cat now licked Obed behind the ear. She tried to help Obed get it back up. Supine and operatic Obed twitched the tip of his tail, moaned.

Joel-Andrew could swear that the corpse actually moved. Either that, or August Starling was stronger than he looked. The corpse seemed to flow from the coffin, although the head drooped, the arms dangled. The music box tinkled, and August Starling began to dance as he clasped the corpse.

"We've got maybe one minute," Kune whispered. "The moment you hear a scream, rush into the room, grab your cat, and head for the servants' entrance. Hard to tell what will come from this night's work."

"Where will we go," Joel-Andrew asked.

"Back to 1973. Back to Janie's Tavern, to Samuel and Bev, and to Frank, who runs the tavern. Back to the future, because maybe you don't need a drink—but I do."

"Perhaps a little white wine," Joel-Andrew murmured.

Footsteps on the front porch announced the arrival of the church party. A door opened. A woman's voice tinkled. "Surprise, surprise, August!" the voice said. "There are beautiful thoughts in the daydreams of life / When youth and ambition join hands for strife . . ." Then the voice choked and a high scream rose through the massive halls of the Starling House.

Chapter 11

BEV AND SAMUEL USUALLY ARRIVE FIRST FOR OUR MEETINGS AT THE Fisherman's Café in this auctorial autumn. They meet at the top of the 307-step staircase. Samuel strides from his echoing old house on Jackson Street, Bev from her house on Blaine. They meet with a morning murmur, a touch of hands, and descend through mist. Behind them—or ahead sometimes—they hear Kune's muffled footsteps. On some fantastic mornings they hear Joel-Andrew's violin, the music thin and faraway; as though Joel-Andrew stands on the beach and plays the sun up.

Bev and Samuel's great friendship is of such long standing that it no longer amounts to gossip, even if it is cut with private grief. Samuel is a Methodist, Bev a Unitarian; and as anybody with a lick of sense knows, such a combination would never, never work.

They age in a town where only the old are valued, although it is not a town of the old. We wait for kids to age and assume their proper place. People here have seen generations become bearded. They have seen Seattle become youthful, pop mescaline, grow zits.

"Ours is a town," Bev explains, "where people cannot have an 'identity crisis.' The identity crisis is a modem luxury." She says this sort of thing to confuse Frank.

Perhaps she is correct. Not many people move here from Seattle, and when they do they change. Women stop having abortions and begin having babies. Men stop getting divorced while hungering for "meaningful relationships." The men and women buy worn Victorian houses and restore them. They dicker for five acres of timberland outside of town as a real estate investment. The only one who ever moved here and did not change was Joel-Andrew.

"I should have understood about Joel-Andrew that first night in 1973," Frank says, "back when Joel-Andrew and Kune came to the tavern after leaving the Starling House. But I was excited. The Loyal Order of Beagles pulled an upset over the Grand Army of the Republic." Frank looks a bit shy. "I try not to take sides in the pool tournaments," he admits with a blush, "but the Beagles look so *cute* in their little doggie hats with the red velvet tongues."

This morning the doughnuts are tawny yellow with speckles of light chocolate, like freckles on a Chinaman. We sit listening to the lap of waves on the rocky beach behind The Fisherman's Café. Mikey Daniels's milk truck piddles past.

"I should have known," Frank mourns, "because Joel-Andrew was almost in a state of shock. When prophets get that way, they either lay plans or call on the Lord. Then Maggie started talking to Joel-Andrew and Kune. Maggie hadn't said a dozen words in over twenty years. Suddenly she's a chatterbox."

"Was Maggie still drinking as much?" Collette asks with concern. Collette's grandfather is the Irish cop who saw August Starling home, the cop who got pickled and kept in the storeroom of Janie's Tavern.

"Maggie has always been a lady." Frank's tone closes the subject. Frank shoots his cuffs, raises his mustache cup, crooks his pinkie, and sips tea.

"And hummingbirds don't whistle," Collette says, "'cause hummingbirds have got sip-yips."

"Joel-Andrew had seen some of the town," Samuel sighs.

"But he met few people. It's sad he had to see everybody all at once."

"And at their worst," Bev says. "He handled it well."

"If only he had not spent time in the Haight," Collette says. "His slang and his sandals made folks suspicious."

"We'd better be getting on with this," Bev suggests. "Although all of us were there on pool-tournament night, Frank was first."

"For a while," Frank remembers dreamily, "even Janie showed up." He lowers his eyes and feigns modesty. "She complimented me on how well the tavern has been maintained in this century."

"Let's pick up Kune and Joel-Andrew when they left the Starling House," Collette says. "They left right after Starling danced with that poor woman." Collette shudders, looks slightly pale and un-lrish. She squares her shoulders. "This is the way it must have been."

=

Kune and Joel-Andrew emerged from the servants' entrance of the Starling House into a town that seemed unchanged, although it was about to change drastically. They stepped from 1888 to 1973, and the only differences were electric light and the ghostly shadow of a prowling 1939 LaSalle police car. Joel-Andrew carried Obed, all thirteen pounds minus a shot wad. Obed had a story to tell his male grandchildren, and that was fortunate. From in back of the Starling House, a white cat with a gray tail tip streaked, followed by a gray cat with a white tail tip. One of the cats had a leaning toward languages. It wailed in virulent Japanese. The other had a talent for seduction.

"You've changed the feline history of Point Vestal," Kune said to Obed. "Let this be a lesson."

Obed feebly flipped his tail. He smirked like a scoundrel.

"I'd make him walk," Kune said to Joel-Andrew. "Don't pamper a sinner."

"Stop for a moment," Joel-Andrew said. He put Obed down. Obed resembled a folded pizza. "We've just seen murder and madness." Joel-Andrew's voice filled with concern for Kune. "And you worry about the sins of a cat. Whenever something serious happens, you change the subject."

Kune's yellow eyes glazed with grief. His eyes shone luminous, owllike; his eyes beyond weeping, his soul wept dry.

"It's how we do it here," he said. "For that matter, it's how they do it in Seattle."

"It's how they do it in San Francisco," Joel-Andrew admitted. "But you'd be surprised how easy it is to be both tough and honest."

"I don't want to talk about it," Kune told him, "but I'll tell you this much. The reason I walk is because there's nothing better to do." Kune's smile was bitter as herbal medicine.

Joel-Andrew spotted the evasion. Joel-Andrew had brought acceptance of the Lord to pimps, automobile salesmen, TV newscasters and radio preachers. He had changed lives of call girls, collection agents, telephone solicitors, and people who peddled bankcards, angel dust, and motor scooters. He privately gave himself three days, four days at the outside, before Kune accepted the Lord's grace.

"After all," Kune said, "can you honestly say that even drug dealers don't do some good? Certain people are better off stoned."

Joel-Andrew had heard the argument too often on street corners and in upstairs rooms. "Perhaps you've had only a pinch of experience," he suggested to Kune.

"I was a doctor," Kune said. "Don't talk to me about experience." From the octagonal tower of The Parsonage, a single bell clanked a sarcastic comment. "No matter what a doctor does," Kune said, "everybody dies. August Starling is only another disease."

"I honestly don't know what Starling is," Joel-Andrew said. "He does not resemble the usual run of psychopaths."

"There are such things as comic diseases," Kune said. "Take my word."

"We'll get a glass of white wine." Joel-Andrew was filled with optimism. Kune was only a smidgen away from being hogtied in heavenly bands. A man did not get as bitter as Kune unless he had ideals.

"We'll work out this business with our unhappy Victorian friend." Joel-Andrew walked toward the 307-step staircase. "Shall we push you back through the servants' entrance?" he asked Obed. Obed struggled to his feet, snerkeled, and walked.

"Something most unusual is happening," Kune told Joel-Andrew as they reached the bottom of the steps. "There's more traffic than I've ever seen."

Murmurs, mutters, hushed little explosions of gossip sounded in the mist. A school bus passed filled with old people, silver haired and dressed as if for church. Three-toned cars passed, and a couple of Model As. A Hupmobile and a Terraplane cruised after them. The murmurs, the cars, the bus headed for Janie's Tavern.

"As long as the mayor doesn't hear about this," Kune muttered. "As long as city council remains ignorant. Maybe we'll scrape through."

Joel-Andrew did not understand that everyone headed for the town meeting. Joel-Andrew had never even seen a town meeting. At least one with any teeth.

"If only the press stays dumb," Kune said. Then he reconsidered. "Jerome is usually discreet."

As Kune and Joel-Andrew entered the tavern, the Beagles barked their fight song. Pool legends were being made, records set. Ollie Jones blushed plumpish and proud. He had just pulled a run on the stripes, then a two-rail kick-shot on the eight ball after being badly corner hooked. Ollie's face beamed red beneath his doggie hat. GAR players mopped their foreheads with little forage caps, put extra salt in their beer, suffered weight loss.

Joel-Andrew stood bemused. The room was not as big as warehouse, but the back bar seemed as long as a train headed out of Salt Lake City. Elaborate Victorian carving frame sparkling mirrors. The mirrors reflected red and doleful faces of the GAR, the doggie caps of the Beagles, the long and colorful dresses worn by the Beagle Auxiliary, and the colorful—and long—but not so lacy dresses of some wide-hipped and generous ladies. A jukebox played tunes from World War I. With the increasing crowd, Frank recruited help from his steady customers. Before long Frank had three more bartenders polishing glasses and tapping kegs.

"It is an awfully large bar," Joel-Andrew said.

"The town used to park the fire truck in back," Kune told him. "When the fire station was built in the 1950s, Frank added the gallery." Kune pointed to the gallery halfway filled with figures that flickered, and halfway filled with figures that did not. One flickering figure had red hair and wore a lovely purple gown. Another flickering figure looked like a tugboat with arms.

"Janie and her bouncer," Kune said. "My-oh-my."

A couple of Indians sat at the bar, and one Indian sat at a table. The one at the table flickered, diaphanous as sunlight through leaves.

"Kune," said Maggie. "You've come to see Maggie. You were always a dear man." Maggie had a table near the windows. She motioned to empty chairs. "Get a seat while you can." A potted plant beside Maggie shed flower petals.

The two men approached, sat, watched the flurry around the pool tables reflected in the elaborately mirrored ceiling. Antique neon competed with flashing modern beer signs. The old jukebox circled rainbows of color, and mirrors reflected bent heads of fishermen and loggers as they guzzled; the heads covered with watch caps, cowboy hats, ski and baseball caps. The Beagles barked, woofed, gamboled puplike.

"It's raining hard in Oregon," Maggie said to Joel-Andrew, "hard enough to wash the mud off a saint." Her voice held guarded admiration. "The Rogue River is taking houses and barns, Jeep pickups and chain saws. There's a cop down there who'd love to skin your dogma. You're a tidy little preacher."

"That big suburb of Seattle," Joel-Andrew tried to be kind.

"You already talk like someone from Point Vestal." Maggie's toothless mouth crinkled when she smiled, her eyes bright as liquid moonlight. "Even Kune, and he ought to know better."

Joel-Andrew decided one should always speak truth to power. "You seem to be flickering," he said to Maggie. "Are you well?"

"It's the twirly light from the jukebox," Kune told him. "You look a little flickery yourself." Kune's yellow eyes glowed.

Maggie looked at Obed and muttered something invisible. "And study your Chinese real hard," Maggie added. "Real hard." Obed stood, stretched, looked impressed, humble.

As old people entered and were seated by Frank, Joel-Andrew retreated further into contemplation of Maggie. Joel-Andrew knew a lot about the power of the Lord, and—because of the power of the Lord—was smart enough to know that other power existed. Kune became vibrant, looked speeding, then gradually became morose as pellagra. Kune watched as Frank—without once reaching for his sawed-off pool cue—arranged seating with the skill of a choreographer. One may say what he likes about Frank's morning coat and stuffiness, but when it comes to protocol one may look to Frank.

People over a hundred were seated front and center around the pool tables. Those in their nineties ranked behind. The sixty- and seventy-year-olds grouped around Samuel, who—because he was a preacher—came first in line after those in their eighties. Raw kids under fifty were tucked in here, there, everywhere; which accounts for Collette being seated beside Joel-Andrew. The pool tournament hit an ascending note, crescendo. Ollie Jones fought off the last charge of the GAR. Ollie was so hot, he could make three rails in the spittoon. Ollie sank them in every pocket not hanging from a pair of pants. As he dropped the last ball, the Beagles' fight song rose together with strident march music from the jukebox.

Eighteen men and a priest came through the doorway. "The ministerial association," Kune said to Joel-Andrew. "The methodical man with them is Jerome. Bev, sitting over there, you have met."

"I was well acquainted with your grandfather," Maggie mentioned to Collette. "He was a bonny man."

Collette, who held other opinions, let it pass. For one thing, Collette felt embarrassed because she knew that even then the pickled Irish cop, her grandfather, lay in the storeroom of the tavern. However, Collette knows how things are done in Point Vestal. She was not about to sass Maggie for at least another forty years.

With the pool game ended, Kune lost interest. He looked into red-glowing mist beneath the tavern's neon sign. From the Strait a foghorn sounded, and a strong smell of tide flats entered the room with each opening of the door.

"I've seen it all before," Kune told Joel-Andrew. "They'll jaw for two hours. The crux of the problem will be discovered somewhere in the 1920s because of the Suffragettes or the Industrial Workers of the World, the IWW. The 1920s were very hard on Victorians. Resolutions will be proposed. They will pick a scapegoat and censure him. When this town makes a scapegoat, matters get less than jovial." He smiled modestly. "That scapegoat will be either you or me. Time to take a walk." He stood. "Where are you crashing? Can't sleep in the rain."

Joel-Andrew sat bemused, watching Maggie. In the middle of gusting wind and rain, a warm little breeze came from beneath the door and swirled around their ankles.

"I sleep in the basement of The Parsonage," Kune said. "That is, I sleep there when I sleep at all."

"Mostly he walks," Collette told Joel-Andrew. "He's been doing it ever since he killed that woman in Seattle."

"Missy," Maggie said to Collette, "until you *know* what you're talking about, it's best to hold your tongue."

"That is," Kune said, "I sleep there when I can even *find* The Parsonage." Kune's yellow eyes blinked. He adjusted his watch cap, checked the ties on his walking shoes. "All this because some fool saw August Starling in the drawing room of the Starling House." He moved smoothly, quietly, was through the doorway and gone.

"Preacher man," Maggie said, "our Kune has given you his blessing."

Joel-Andrew sat confused, but reverent. He understood Kune's action. He had also just heard that Kune was a murderer. A slow realization about the roots of Kune's bitterness came to him. Joel-Andrew's compassion stretched toward Kune, and he prayed to the Lord for guidance.

"They're afraid," Maggie said about the crowd, "so they're going to pick a scapegoat. They don't have any usable Chinamen or Indians. Kune stepped out of here, so they would pick on him, not you."

Chapter 12

TALL. STAUNCH. PATRIARCHAL. SAMUEL FOUGHT THE GOOD FIGHT. HE thrust, parried, and tussled the ministerial association. Halos of bar light rode above heads of preachers and made Janie's Tavern a concordance of purity. Samuel's tall dockworker's frame and large dockworker's hands cast shadows across the walls. Shadows walked like eighteenth-century figures proclaiming The Rights of Man, proclaiming Revolution.

Samuel was backed by Suffragettes, the IWW, three Nam vets, a disgruntled Anabaptist, one old buster from Coxey's Army, a drinking Universalist, two Quilliute Indians, and a ninety-three-year-old spinster who was shirttail cousin to Eleanor Roosevelt. Samuel was also backed by Bev and the bouncer who looked like a tugboat with arms. Maggie stayed out of it.

The ministerial association was backed by the GAR, the Beagles, the Martha Washington Brigade, the Republicans, Democrats, Birchers, the Mothers Against Transgression and Sensuality (MATS), the Forest Service, Janie, and the WPA foreman who had installed the 307-step staircase.

It was not—everyone agreed—a problem of politics. It was a problem of morals. So—it was further agreed—the way to whip the problem was kick it softly with heavenly intervention. The question debated was: "Should we direct Gerald, our town policeman, to shoot Kune on sight?"

Joel-Andrew sat dismayed. Beyond the windows, darkness seemed even darker with Kune gone, like the darkness that once danced on red- and pink-toned walls of the Starling House. Somewhere in history August Starling still danced.

Joel-Andrew told himself anybody would shudder, even the Amish.

Bev's mother led the Suffragettes. She dressed in the same manner as when she wore the sash and carried the cause in 1919: straw hat, skirt six inches above the floor, patent leather boots with buckskin tops, petticoats without frills, tan stockings, envelope chemise. She orated, scraping the bark off Mothers Against Transgression and Sensuality. Joel-Andrew had known some tough old bats in his time, but this was the first ever who could take the snap out of a buggy whip.

How the question diverted from August Starling, to shooting Kune, Joel-Andrew could not say. He could say sensations of dark thrill, of expectancy and dread washed through the meeting as Starling's name was first mentioned—as if, Joel-Andrew thought—a cadaver were introduced as guest speaker.

A Victorian lady suddenly leveled a blast at the Suffragettes. Words were flung about "purity" and "unseemly showing of body parts." Bitter words; and the words had something to do with Freudian psychology, a Mademoiselle from Armentieres, Charles Darwin, the RKO movie company, the Teapot Dome, that trashy Wilson, and the sainted Warren Gamaliel Harding. Somebody named Robert Benchley came in for abuse, and all this somehow related to the rising sewage rates.

"When will they talk about August Starling?" Joel-Andrew asked Maggie and Collette. "August Starling is badly troubled." As he spoke, circling neon illuminated the stage onto which Janie stepped. Her red hair and purple gown glowed darkly. Janie spoke with warmth and with very few flickers—and at length—about the Red menace, the sainted cause of Presbyterianism, the curse of Prohibition, the Boston Police strike, and the Trotskyite mobsters of the IWW.

A member of the IWW said, "——." The bouncer threw him out.

Samuel spoke of Sacco and Vanzetti.

"They are not here to talk about August Starling, not exactly," Collette told Joel-Andrew. "They talk about the tourist business." Collette's blue eyes were more excited than when she found a rusty trivet for her antique store. She breathed reverently. "History. Perfect Americana."

"They're here because they're afraid," Maggie told Joel-Andrew. "August Starling is worse than anything out of a book. August Starling was the worst man in this town, because he actually *believed* what the town wanted to believe . . . only the town didn't have the innards to admit it." Maggie's voice sounded like a contained wind, one you hoped would not grow stronger.

"I don't know what that means," Joel-Andrew said helplessly. "These are good people, are they not?"

"Like horses with blinders," Maggie assured him. "August Starling did not have blinders. He cut through all the Victorian charm and became a *real* Victorian." Maggie belched discreetly, looked where Obed watched her with admiration. "It's no different in Seattle."

"Patchwork quilts," Collette breathed. "Ethan Allen, duck decoys, weathervanes. Revereware. The Democratic Process." Collette blinked back tears of passion. She fought to keep from hollering. "Iron skillets, copper wash boilers, sleigh bells, muskets, Dixie dollars, cider presses, Democracy in action."

Joel-Andrew looked around the tavern where Frank's pickup bartenders worked with the precision of a well-trained choir. Joel-Andrew saw faces; old ones, older ones. He saw starch and lace. Lights from beer signs twisted, glowed, blue, red, white. Faces of the ministerial association mingled among faces of shopkeepers. Janie's red hair flamed like battle-banners. Green covers of pool tables, the mirrored ceiling of the bar, the racks of shiny beer glasses, picked up light and cast it across Pilgrim brows of cow breeders, top fallers, bank tellers: and across the bald head of Jerome who took methodical notes. At Joel-Andrew's feet, Obed muttered something vaguely Oriental.

"Because," Maggie said, "Seattle is as Victorian as this town but Seattle don't know it."

"Our people are afraid," Collette explained. "If word gets out that August Starling is back, tourists will be scared to visit."

"Because August Starling is the very heart and gut of tradition." Maggie pointed to a group of elderly and distinguished gentlemen, only a few of whom flickered; gentlemen accompanied by ladies with rosy cheeks and flowing gowns. "No drug pusher or whore ever went hungry in Point Vestal."

Joel-Andrew figured he would get everything figured out once the meeting ended. The Lord brought August Starling back to town, and if The Lord did not want August Starling back in town then The Lord would not have opened the road. Joel-Andrew stood, ready to ask for the floor.

"Don't," Maggie said. Flickers of amusement crossed her old, old face—or possibly—her old, old face flickered with amusement. "They don't get to poot often, so they've got a few poots left."

"Because," Collette explained, "they are not really going to shoot Kune. I don't think Gerald owns a gun. They can't even ostracize Kune. He's already done that to himself."

Obed chewed indifferently on a fallen potato chip. Bev spoke, articulate, funny, angry. Her silver hair flowed as smoothly as her voice. She faced the Martha Washington Brigade, both the members who flickered and those who did not, and said something about "the pigs finally arriving in the pasture." The Martha Washington Brigade gasped, adjusted its collective skirt, crossed its collective ankles, assumed superior smiles. Bev humorously suggested that perhaps the Martha Washington Brigade was Irish.

"When it starts to get *that* dirty, it's hoot-and-holler time," Maggie explained. "You'll notice Frank just picked up his pool cue."

Cries of "Lucky Lindy Is Our Man" mixed with yells of "Fifty-four-forty or Fight"; the cries tangling with denunciations of Rudolph Valentino, Janis Joplin, John Foster Dulles, and Lawrence Welk. Pushing and shoving came from the gallery. The bouncer twirled a Pentecostal in one hand, a Nazarene in the other.

Frank rapped with his pool cue and quieted the mob. It became one of Frank's finest moments. He apologized for his comparative youth, hoped his experience with tourists counted for something. He admired the purity of Mothers Against Transgression and Sensuality, admired the cultivation of the Martha Washington Brigade. He said words in behalf of motherhood, Sunday school, Grover Cleveland, the White motorcar, the New Home sewing machine. He modestly admitted that he had made a study of tourists. "And," Frank said, "tourists are mad for novelty. When tourists hear of a black hearted creature like Starling, tourists will break the road apart getting into town."

"That just deflated hoot-and-holler time," Collette told Joel-Andrew. "Now we'll have a vote of confidence in August Starling, plus a resolution saying that Kune is depraved."

"August Starling . . ." Joel-Andrew stopped speaking, helpless.

"The plot unfolds," Maggie said. "August Starling now stands at the crossroads where you first left him when you came to town." Maggie's voice flickered like a school of silver minnows. "You'll remember the road divided. August Starling went along the dirt fork. His horse and buggy disappeared. He gave a little dance and headed home in 1893. You walked on down the hill into town."

"It *is* a very confusing town," Joel-Andrew admitted. "But I remember that much."

"When Starling got home, in 1893, he entered the drawing room. Then he got kicked out. While he was in the madhouse, his business friends stole his new house and his business.

August Starling now stands at the crossroads, twisting his hankie, and yelling, 'Dolor—dolor—oh, woe, oh, woe is me.'"

"Trust her," Collette said. "Maggie knows."

Someone announced a Beagle victory and a new pool hero. Ollie Jones grinned and blushed. Jerome snapped his notebook shut, looked benevolently at the crowd. Frank laid down his pool cue.

"Take a hike to the crossroads," Maggie told Joel-Andrew. "Kune will be there, along with August Starling."

Joel-Andrew wanted to explain the will of the Lord, but Maggie did not listen. Then Joel-Andrew thought he should explain the will of the Lord to everyone. He rose, his green eyes flashing with authority. "Understand the will of the Lord," he began in tones of power. He stopped before a rising murmur. A vote was taken. He was voted down 17-0 by the ministerial association, Samuel abstaining.

Chapter 13

THE NIGHT SEEMED DARKER THAN IT OUGHT AS JOEL-ANDREW headed for the crossroads. His violin case bounced on this back, and his sandals squished from fog and mist. Even his brain felt squishy. Were it not for the loving power of the Lord, Joel-Andrew might have despaired.

His methods used to work. Then he remembered a young girl standing in an alley in San Francisco, and tried to push the memory from his mind. From the moment he saw her, his methods changed. True, prophets had a long record of being ignored, but it seemed that the nice people of Point Vestal lived quiet lives and should be open to original messages. After all, this was hardly Seattle.

A woman passed on the other side of the street, hurrying and afraid. Walking through fog and mist, Joel-Andrew remembered events leading to his excommunication. The year had been 1966. He heard the clear voice of the Lord, saying, "Go to San Francisco."

So he stepped with regret, with hope, with fear from his small congregation in Providence. He rode a bus across landscapes of which he had never dreamed. He saw the Lord's Creation from windows of the bus, and again and again he hungered to step down, speak to folks, examine the Creation. Yet the voice mentioned no wayside shrines, no pause for devotion. The voice said, "Go to San Francisco."

The first night he walked along Broadway and hung a right onto Grant. He found himself in an Italian neighborhood—coffee shops, spaghetti stores, dago red, onions, garlic, hollers and heavy breathing, while a Caruso record played on a jukebox. Expressionist painters wore colorfully daubed jeans, and a poet stood on a mailbox and read. Three Jamaicans congregated in the middle of an intersection. They played a symphony for drums on upturned garbage cans. A police car cruised past, drove carefully around them, continued on. Joel-Andrew watched surprised and pleased. An entire life spent in Rhode Island prepared him for none of this.

The following morning he strolled in Golden Gate Park where he saw a man dressed in tuxedo, boiled shirt, tie; but who also walked on bare feet and sported a carrot in his lapel. Joel-Andrew listened to an impassioned harangue about *something* from a self-anointed spokesman, the harangue delivered by bullhorn operated from batteries in a grocery cart. Joel-Andrew fought feelings of distaste. No prophet he knew ever needed a bullhorn.

The park glowed. Bands of eucalyptus cast tall halos above grassy clearings where people walked wearing beads and sometimes clothes. Sunlight touched cherubic faces of abandoned babies, touched tangles of forsythia from which issued ejaculative groans. Hell's Angels rode swift and quirky bikes or swapped their women for motorcycle parts. The Hell's Angels were benevolent, protective, and warded off the police. They rarely chain-whipped ladies, or put the boots to children. Foggy San Francisco air pocketed beside lakes where all the ducks had been eaten, and where little piles of duck bones seemed monuments to an otherwise benevolent nature. People cavorted danced, played tunes on wooden flutes. Bells tinkled. Incense tickled noses, and in the distance hard-rocking music carried across the grass, played by an outfit called Moby, and the Self-Inflicted Injury.

Joel-Andrew was shocked, innocent, also very young. Pungent smoke wafted above beautifully trimmed lawns. Joel-Andrew knew enough about drugs to identify aspirin, so he did not know what he smelled. He discovered, walking through clouds of the stuff, that he emerged feeling far, far away from Providence, R.I.

The place was doomed Atlantis; beautiful and terrible, flower-filled and broken-spined. Or, Joel-Andrew thought, maybe it was only like ancient Rome. Maybe he could turn things around.

"This too shall pass," he prophesied, his thundering voice drowned beneath rock music. "As seasons change, drawing decay through freezing blasts of winter; as the world emerges to a new spring . . ."

"It never snows in San Francisco," a freak drawled. "Get it together, man."

Joel-Andrew walked on Haight Street. Starving dogs staggered past, wearing chains of woven daisies. Head shops—decorative, exotic, fascinating—reminded Joel-Andrew of the luminous and miraculous Orient. Strangers smiled, vomited in gutters, fell stoned and grinning from doorways. Pretty girls admired his clerical collar. Handsome young men viewed his clothing and called it "a good trip" or "a real gig." People told him he was relevant, while flowery painted buses passed and people overdosed in upstairs rooms. "O Lord," Joel-Andrew prayed, "I'm not the man You need. I'm not big enough to handle this."

Then he met the girl who began his true ministry. He found her in the entry to an alley, leaning against a wall. She was nearly naked, probably fourteen, a thin girl with long unbrushed hair and brown eyes. Smudges of dirt darkened her cheeks like a child who played with makeup. Her eyes closed, but her mouth trembled, and her eyelids fluttered in a terrible attempt to open. Her hands trembled. She raised her hands to her face, her fists digging into her eyes. Old bruises, dark and green, covered her small and used breasts.

Joel-Andrew had no more than an intellectual view of hell. Behind him, sitting on the sidewalk, someone chanted "om."

Softly, and with the love of the Lord in his voice, Joel-Andrew said exactly what he should never have said. "Can I help you?" he said. "I am here to help."

Her eyes opened. Joel-Andrew's intellectual view of hell vanished. Her eyes stared, stared, stared. Her eyes were greater than oceans stocked with sharks. Deep in those wells a mortal soul fled screaming.

Then her mind connected. The scream became a cry, a thin and improbable wail along the hollow alley. She turned, screamed louder, and fled—and—although Joel-Andrew knew he was a fool, he was not so great a fool that he chased her. He would drive her into the path of a bus or taxi. The drug was too deep. He knew he would never see her again.

He was wrong. He saw her again that same night.

=

Joel-Andrew fought his memory. There are things even a prophet's mind should not know twice. His violin bounced on his back. He slapped his cold cheeks to bring him back to the present. He had struggled in that vineyard of San Francisco, had made his mistakes, but now he worked in a new vineyard. In the cold fog and mist, he told himself to pay attention or he would make mistakes in Point Vestal.

Obed felt complainy, his white tail drooping like an ironed out question mark. As they passed the boat basin, figures of taciturn fishermen flickered. From the saltwater swamp, a thin Christian Scientist wail called the names of children. The road headed uphill. High schoolish chortles came from beneath shrubbery. A beer can arced onto the road. It tinkled in a tiny aluminum voice. A '66 Plymouth, parked by the roadside, rocked gently with giggles from the backseat.

"Homecoming week," Joel-Andrew told Obed. "Pom-poms, mums, marching bands. Letters on the sweaters. Football heroes. Young love."

And, Joel-Andrew had to admit, years of experience in the Haight gave no handle on August Starling, or even Kune. In comparison to the normal community behavior in Janie's Tavern, both Starling and Kune were sociopaths.

=

It took more than an hour to arrive at the top of the hill. Occasionally an old car roared past as people drove home from Janie's Tavern. Mist lightened as the road climbed. In deep silence Joel-Andrew could hear August Starling hollering, "Dolor—dolor—oh, woe, oh, woe is me." The quieter voice of Kune said, "You had it coming, creepo." A match flared. Kune lit a small campfire. Joel-Andrew shivered, moved forward.

Kune's yellow eyes shone sparkly, like the tiny saucers of a child's tea set. On some low level showed Kune was having a wonderful time. "Transmigration," Kune muttered. "Transmogrification, transmutation, transnatural." Kune giggled and pointed at August Starling. "That boy's sins have whelped."

> The tree thy axe cut from its native sod,
> And turns to useful things—go tell to fools,
> Was fashioned in the factory of God . . .

August Starling yelped, whined, lathered.

"What year is it?' Kune asked.

"It's 1973" Joel-Andrew said. "It was 1973 when I left Janie's Tavern, and there have been no changes."

"There has been one," Kune said. He leaned toward the campfire to warm his hands. "The fork in the road has disappeared." Kune again pointed at August Starling. "Our corpse molester can't go back in time. He's stuck here in 1973."

"He's got to go back," Joel-Andrew told Kune. "He just received a vote of confidence from the whole town."

> Farewell! through wastes of distance now
> I gaze with eyes astrain;
> O'er billowy years that ebb and flow
> Sweet voices of the Long Ago . . .

August Starling sounded awash in happy misery. At the same time, August Starling's voice gained a note of confidence. Obed flicked his tail, looked worried.

"Because," Kune said, "if he can't go back in time, he can't dink with Point Vestal history. We'll arrest him for murder, throw him in a cell with the ghost of The Sailor, let him simmer . . ." He turned to August Starling. "The town historians have a rap sheet. You make Al Capone look like an uncommon cold in a convent."

Campfire light flickered over Joel-Andrew's face, but August Starling did not flicker. As Joel-Andrew watched with interest, puzzlement, and then a touch of horror, a dried-out skull clacked its jaws beneath the young face of August Starling. Starling looked like one of the trick-pictures beloved by Victorians. If one viewed the picture from one angle, he saw beauty. From a different angle he saw death. The illusion faded.

"My clerical friend." August Starling's voice grew confident. "You witness great trial that a cold and inhospitable world has untimely thrust upon one of the most stalwart and dutiful of men."

"I've tried and tried," Kune mourned "Impossible to get this pinhead speaking anything resembling English."

"And who, pray tell, is Al Capone?" August Sterling's slim form stood erect. With his beautifully barbered hair and mustache, with his neat little beard, he might pass for a missionary, or possibly a door-to-door brush salesman.

"Submachine guns," Joel-Andrew said. "Rackets. Protection money. Guilds, associations, rotgut. Bribery, gambling, payoffs. Politics, St. Valentine's Day massacre . . ."

August Starling interrupted. "And what, pray tell, is a submachine gun?"

Kune turned to Joel-Andrew. "We got to set this guy on simmer. Not just in the jail. *Under* the jail." Kune had been temporarily happy that August Starling, trapped in the present, could not change the past. "It's a handheld Gatling gun." Kune explained submachine guns to August Starling.

"O brave new world that has such people in't!" August Starling stood above the fire and busily cast a shadow while admiring technology. August Starling had not yet seen hand grenades, automatic car washes and napalm. He carried no acquaintance with nerve gas, television sets, or mass-circulation magazines. It was love—Joel-Andrew had seen it before. He figured Starling would have his new world doped out within two days.

"All you're going to see," Kune said, his face grim, "is a nineteenth-century cell, in a nineteenth-century basement fulla dying ghosts and no heat." He turned to Joel-Andrew. "This little priss has thirty murder raps, drug running, extortion, slave labor, press gangs, death ships, bribery, cathouses, insurance scams; plus, of course, the import-export business."

"I see the problem," Joel-Andrew admitted. "It's all more-or-less legal in San Francisco, but the Lord doesn't like it. We'd better consult the Lord." He lowered his head. August Starling chortled lewdly. Obed snored. "O Lord," Joel-Andrew prayed, "deliver us from evil, and even into the hands of righteousness."

Normal pressures of sea and air and gravity churned like atmospheric butter. The barometer did a hop and skip. A gust of wind popped like a hiccup.

There came a whisper, a faint rushing, a confused zephyr. The landscape altered slightly. The campfire winked like a hot little coronary in the deep and awful night shadow of The Parsonage. The Parsonage had moved again, or else it came to answer Joel-Andrew's prayer. The all-seeing tower of The Parsonage rose above the campfire, while downhill, but visible in the thin mist, flicked the gumball light of a '39 LaSalle police car.

"It's a night for records." Kune was astonished. "Ollie Jones wins the pool championship. Now we've seen The Parsonage move. No one ever really *saw* it move before."

From far away, a ship's horn sounded on the Strait, low and mournful like an elegy for souls of dead sailors. High above, the all-seeing tower blanked a thin moon. A pencil of light shone through a window on the second floor of The Parsonage. The light extinguished.

Joel-Andrew and Kune did not know that, during Joel-Andrew's long walk up the hill, Bev and Samuel went directly to The Parsonage when leaving Janie's Tavern. Joel-Andrew and Kune did not know that Bev and Samuel sprawled on the second floor, experiencing dizziness. No one in Point Vestal had ever actually seen The Parsonage move, nor had anyone ever been in The Parsonage during one of its moves. Samuel and Bev dazedly discussed options. They peered from the second-floor window.

"Before we get absorbed in our troubles," Bev giggled, "we'd better count our blessings and admit it was a smashing ride. In the whole history of dalliance, no one ever saw a dallie like that."

Samuel peered from the window. "It's that imitation, itinerant Episcopal," he whispered. "He's with Kune and a vaguely familiar-looking stranger. Gerald is arriving in the police car." Samuel was old and getting wiser by the minute. He would not admit that his Methodist hanky-panky, framed in a parsonage, earned a lot of extra zip. In his quiet way, he sorted puzzle pieces of his problem, and blamed the whole thing on Presbyterians.

"We could just 'fess up," Bev giggled. "The whole town gives us credit for an affair, anyway." She brushed her long hair, put a blush of powder on her cheeks. "Besides," she said, "if we 'fess up, Gerald will give us a ride home."

"Confess to what," Samuel asked. "Bird-watching? Enumerating screech owls? All we were doing was enumerating screech owls."

"There was quite a bit of screeching going on." Bev felt even more giggly, irrepressible.

"In the fields of the Lord," Samuel added, and for no apparent reason. He stood at the deeply shadowed window, looking onto the scene. The vaguely familiar looking stranger, who—of course—was August Starling, asked questions about pinball, slot machines, arms budgets. Starling's voice sounded innocent, clear, and guileless as a child. Joel-Andrew answered politely. Kune glowered. Obed snoozed.

Night shadows of The Parsonage licked at edges of the campfire, cast darkness into the very heart of fire. From high in the all-seeing tower, low muttering echoed into hallways of The Parsonage, sounding like a tough-minded preacher musing as he wrote his fifteenth point into a sermon.

The 1939 LaSalle parked. "Oh, dear," Bev said, "Gerald looks ready to gnaw the hind end off a Sasquatch. I've never seen him look so mean."

"Homecoming week," Samuel whispered. "Homecoming week is very hard on Gerald."

Tall, lean, and sinewy, Gerald rarely flickers. Except for a few weeks off, he is the only policeman Point Vestal has had since 1932. Gerald does not like the New Deal, but does like J. Edgar Hoover—admires him, even—and Gerald is so tough, he could run the Democratic National Convention with a squirt gun. Young Dobermans have been known to follow him around, just to pick up a few tricks.

"Illegal campfire." Gerald hitched up his pants. "Trespassing on sanctified ground." Gerald tilted his hat. "That tomcat looks like a pork chop, and it has no pet license." Gerald looked at Kune. "You're a real disappointment, Doc. Bad enough you walk all night and all day; now you hang out with a known vagrant." To Joel-Andrew he said, "Impersonating a preacher, inciting to riot during town meeting, walking without a driver's license, no visible means of support, no credit card."

"I've made a citizen's arrest," Kune said to Gerald. "This is August Starling, and the charge is murder."

"We were here first," Joel-Andrew explained. "The Parsonage just arrived."

"Failure to yield to a haircut," Gerald said. "Disorderly conduct, possession of a violin, conspiracy to smuggle Bibles, aiding and abetting alcohol in the presence of an Indian—I mean Maggie—untrimmed toenails, and footwear unbecoming the propriety of Point Vestal." Gerald looked at Obed who was waking up. "Fornication, mouse-napping, harboring fleas . . ."

"That is August Starling," Kune said. "Prostitution, drugs, capital crimes."

"Almighty grace has brought you here," August Starling said to Gerald. "Midst greater woes than can be shown / with deeper sighs than can be known . . ."

"Button it," Gerald said. He turned to Kune. "Rules of evidence," he explained. "All you've got is history. The statute of limitations has run on a lot of it. You've got no bodies. They became skeletons ninety years ago, those he didn't drown. You got no proof."

"I own the honor of being a deacon," August Starling said, and set about proving he had never done a wrong thing in his life. He pointed out that the blessed land of America was the blessed land of freedom. Chinamen yearning to be free had every right to immigrate; and, in helping them, he, August Starling, was a patriot. Drowned Chinamen were not his doing, and that, as all positive-minded men would agree, each person had a right to the pursuit of happiness. If a man was locked up for smuggling Chinamen, Starling argued reasonably, that man could not pursue happiness. No blame could thus attach to his boat crews because they drowned Chinamen who tried to be free, while the boat crews were about to get caught by the Immigration Department, and thus jailed in violation of the Constitution. Perhaps, Starling argued, laws sometimes fell at cross-purposes, but he, Starling, had not written the laws. Starling's voice hummed innocence.

Gerald scratched his head. Kune moaned. Obed muttered an obscenity in Portuguese.

As for other charges, Starling argued with sweet reason, he had no dealings with prostitution, although as a loyal (and possibly noble) son of Point Vestal, he had provided lodging for homeless women. Certain drugs passed through his hands, but they were medicinal. Joel-Andrew listened to the childlike twitter of Starling. Starling actually believed what he said.

"There will be days of wrath," Joel-Andrew said. "Innocents will rise from the sea and walk. This I prophesy." The ground trembled. The campfire flickered.

"Impersonating a prophet," Gerald said. "Do it one more time, and you are busted seventeen ways from Sunday." He turned to August Starling. "Make one wrong move in Point Vestal, and I'll throw you in a cell with the ghost of The Sailor."

The ground trembled; the fire flicked like the nervous tip of Obed's tail. A bell clinked, another tinkled, a third bell clonked. From the all-seeing tower, orchestral murmuring swelled like congregated voices from generations of clergy. Obed purred in Latin, but his Latin was indifferent compared to his Greek. The personage of The Parsonage ignored him.

"That makes sense," Gerald said to The Parsonage. "If you think that's the way to go, I'll buy it."

"I didn't know Gerald could talk to The Parsonage," Bev whispered from her hiding place on the second floor.

"Gerald is a small-town cop," Samuel whispered unhappily. "There is very little a small-town cop does not know."

Gerald looked at Starling, Kune, Obed, Joel-Andrew. "You make a matched set," he told them, "and there's going to be no bust. I'm turning the four of you over to custody of The Parsonage. Douse the fire; sleep here tonight."

"In the basement," Kune said. "I always sleep in the basement."

Gerald looked toward the second-floor window, where Bev and Samuel believed themselves hidden cleverly. "That's a good idea, because we want to avoid complications." Gerald removed his cop's hat, rubbed his forehead. He stared at the second-floor window. "Homecoming week," he said. "The high school kids are pikers."

To which Bev murmured, "Oh dear," while Samuel gnashed his teeth and said something sounding more like a dockworker than a preacher.

"When those four get settled in," Bev said, "I'm going to sneak downstairs and listen."

Samuel replied that he could not care less about what went on between misfits.

"Because," Bev said, "I think some changes are about to happen in Point Vestal. We ought to gather facts, in case we ever have to testify in court, or write a book, or something of that sort."

Chapter 14

FROM THE FISHERMAN'S CAFÉ ON CLEAR DAYS WE SEE AN ENORMOUS skyline. The 8,000-foot Olympic mountain range rises to the west, the 8,000-foot Cascade range to the east. Dormant volcanoes Mount Adams and Mount Rainier tower above those ranges like ancient gods. Maggie knows all about such things, but these days Maggie speaks only to Kune.

And, on clear days, it is possible to see straw-yellow haze above suburbs of Seattle, like a road of celestial kitty litter. Seattle is too far off to see, but on the Strait its emissaries cruise back and forth; chubby nuclear subs, slim hunter-killer subs, destroyers, sub tenders, mine layers, aircraft carriers, coal barges, oil rigs built like little palaces. We see presidential and royal yachts, and ships of Panamanian registry carrying corned beef, cocaine, political defectors. Shiploads of Japanese cars, radios, toasters, computer chips, and tape decks pass with well-lubricated efficiency.

"I'm never sad when fog and rain return," Frank admits. "When you can't see Seattle things, you don't have to think about them." He stares into the wet and windy street where Mikey Daniels's milk truck staggers. Today the doughnuts are kelly green with sprinkles of red.

"Living here makes us simpleminded," Bev points out. "I know, because I know what went on that night at The Parsonage."

"Screech owls," Samuel says, "spotted owls, barn owls, great northern owls."

"August Starling mostly listened, while trying to steal things from The Parsonage," Bev reports. "He also filled gaps in his information. Joel-Andrew encouraged Kune in the direction the Lord. Obed snoozed. The Parsonage listened. The Parsonage began forming a great camaraderie with Joel-Andrew. Kune kind of spilled his guts. It went like this:

=

The '39 LaSalle disappeared down the hill. Three men and the cat stood beside the campfire, momentarily hesitant. Kune stamped out the fire. "You'll like this place," he told Joel-Andrew, as he headed for The Parsonage.

The basement lay dry, dusty, and warmer than upstairs rooms; certainly warmer than the all-seeing tower that rose toward heaven. The basement seemed like a cove on a stormy coast, or a nest for drunken janitors, fallen women, adventuresome schoolboys.

August Starling herked, snerked, sneezeled. Dust from old furniture clouded close-fitting air as Kune lit an oil lamp. The lamp illuminated unused rose-back and ribbon-back loveseats, sofas, armchairs, armoires, mirrored hall trees, portraits of preachers, and slop jars.

"It is awfully nice for Obed," Joel-Andrew explained. "We've been sleeping in barns." Joel-Andrew unslung his violin, wiped mist and fog from the case and looked inside. Glue had not melted. "Nice for the violin," he added. "This is a difficult climate for strings." Joel-Andrew felt pleased. He sat marooned in a small basement with two men who, for all he knew, were sociopathic killers; and with a cat whose Latin was deficient. Compared to Joel-Andrew's tenure in the Haight, this was a vacation.

Tiptoeing footsteps sounded above. August Starling gasped, then sought cover behind a Victorian wardrobe. Obed cruised stacks of furniture looking for mice. The footsteps sounded sneaky.

"It must be Bev," Kune said. "No one but Bev and Samuel ever come to The Parsonage. It can't be Samuel because Methodists always canter." Kune looked into shadows where August Starling's eyes were spotlights of terror.

"Uh-huh," Kune said. "Starling has no experience with ghosts. Most of the ghosts rose after his time."

August Starling cowered.

"Nothing is going to hurt you, dimbo." Kune's voice held amused contempt. "Most ghosts are in town, anyway. There might be a ghostly preacher or two rambling around upstairs."

"These ghosts," August Starling squeaked, "perchance some exercised prudent frugality during the course of their worldly span. Perchance in cloistered places they wisely, and in concealment placed certain saved bounty . . ."

"Starling is set to con some ghosts out of hidden money," Kune told Joel-Andrew. To Starling, he said, "Forget it, dingbat. Every hiding place in town got probed during the Great Depression."

Joel-Andrew feared for August Starling's future. Starling might be temporarily afraid of ghosts, but Starling was not so afraid he was unable to cut a deal with one.

"And speaking of Starling," Kune added, "something odd is going on. He went to the madhouse in '88 and died in Seattle in 1922 of madness and alcohol. However, you encountered him driving a buggy back to town in 1893, although it was 1973 for you. He had been doing that for quite a while. We have a mystery." Kune sat on a loveseat, pulled a pack of cigarettes from his shirt pocket, lit a smoke, and inhaled a nourishing drag. "Here's to the Surgeon General," he intoned, "and *up* the AMA."

Joel-Andrew knew there was no mystery. The Lord wanted August Starling alive in Point Vestal, or August Starling would not be alive in Point Vestal. Joel-Andrew figured the Lord wanted to give August Starling a second chance. Kune did not look at mystery, but a miracle. Since Kune could not stand to hear the word "miracle," Joel-Andrew changed the subject.

"It's cozy here," he murmured, "and it's pretty cold there."

Bev's footsteps neared the top of the stairs.

"If it were Samuel, I'd say let him freeze but since it's Bev . . ." Kune stood. He returned with Bev a little shivery, but looking more like Dorothy Lamour than ever. August Starling skipped from behind the wardrobe. He brushed his vest, adjusted his hair, his tie, his look of innocence. He chirped, "When the soul to new beauty and glory is born / There is life in its waters, and joy in its breeze . . ."

"Tuck it in your nose," Kune advised. To Bev, he said "The guy with the tweed underwear is August Starling."

"If you're trying to impress me," Bev told Kune, "you've done it."

Upstairs a door slammed. A Methodist cuss echoed and Methodist canter sounded. The ground trembled. The Parsonage settled onto its lot with satisfaction. The Parsonage was like a bouncer rubbing his hands after a particularly gratifying bounce.

"Oh, dear," Bev said, "The Parsonage gave Samuel the old heave-ho. It had to happen someday."

"It's a day for records," Kune muttered. "First Ollie Jones wins the pool championship . . ."

"Why has it never asked him to leave before?" Joel-Andrew did not realize that The Parsonage had roosted on the cliffs outside of town, almost as if it were waiting for him. Then The Parsonage appeared on top of the hill when Kune and Joel-Andrew visited the Starling House. Now The Parsonage moved to the outskirts of town when Joel-Andrew walked from Janie's Tavern to the crossroads.

"The Parsonage has been through a lot," Bev said. "I expect it's finally losing patience."

"I don't worry about August Starling," Kune said. "He can't fool with history, he's stony broke. Sooner or later he'll do something crooked, and Gerald will throw him in a cell with the ghost of The Sailor." Kune spoke as if Starling were not present.

August Starling said nothing. He was entranced with Bev, and with feeling behind pillows of sofas for dropped coins. From a Victorian loveseat he drew forth a one-dollar gold piece. His eyes lighted.

"That's worth quite a bit to a collector," Joel-Andrew said.

August Starling became feverish, fervorish, and obsessed with feeling. He felt every stick of furniture.

"I packed a picnic," Bev told the men. It occurred to Bev that she was alone with three men. Two had killed women, and all three were probably celibate. Bev was not sure what that said about modern society, but she secretly armed herself with a hatpin.

"Item one and item two," Kune said mournfully to Bev. "First, you needn't be afraid. I'm not that kind of killer. Second, why do you hang around with Samuel who is the world's leading hypocrite?" Kune sounded as tactless as a Holy Roller.

"I didn't know you read minds," Bev said.

"He's a diagnostician," Joel-Andrew explained. "Kune reads emotions, symptoms, situations." August Starling gave a happy chirp as he discovered a three-cent piece in the stuffings of a morris chair.

"Item one and item two," Bev said without friendliness. "First, I hang around with Samuel because he's a hypocrite only about sex and Presbyterians, which is a better score than any other man in town. Second, just what kind of killer are you?"

"A fair question." Joel-Andrew laid his violin aside. August Starling twittered. August Starling might have run press gangs, but he was not used to spending the night with a confessed killer. Obed yawned, stretched, made do with a piece of peanut butter-and-jelly sandwich. Lamplight cast dusty glows about the basement. Bev thought of windswept moors and heaths, of melancholia. Shutters rattled, walls creaked. Bev thought of gothic novels, colonial governors, ivory tusks, shipwrecks and gold.

"It's a fair question," Kune admitted, "and I suppose the truth is only slightly worse than folks imagine." Kune looked like a small and blotchy melanoma. "Imagine me as a younger man," he muttered. "Full of ideals. If you are a Point Vestal boy, you're going to be sort of romantic. It went this way."

=

The road through medical school was rigorous, and Kune, a boy from a hick town, carried no connections. He earned his grades because he could not afford to buy them with gifts of stock certificates or Mercedes-Benzes.

And yet, he loved the magic of endocrine glands, the nervous system, the structure of cells, the intricate chemistry drawn so systematically on thick and glossy pages of overpriced texts. He loved long and polished hospital corridors, the romance of medicine, illusions. Kune's yellowish eyes and nimble fingers eagerly dealt with tumors, fractures, samples of naughty blood. He peered up noses, down throats, into ears, vaginas, rectums. He listened to respiratory gasps, hearts whopping ragtime, the RPM of lungs, throats; his eyes watching telltale signs of drugs, booze, anxiety, fear, occasional relief. On the day he became a full-fledged doctor, he felt priestly; Kune felt ordained.

He wielded the Power and the Glory. He wielded miracles. All around him eyes were made to see, kidneys transplanted, hearts, lungs, gizzards. The dying rose from the dead. Given enough spare parts, he could cure anyone of anything. He was a miracle worker—he and his fellows—striding above ranks of the ill like Samaritan Angels. Their stainless steel machines were chariots riding high across the heavens registering brain waves, checking pee samples, flipping surgical lasers. He lost sleep, loving the work, loving the Power and Glory. The Pharmacopoeia was his Bible. He was indifferent to all but the laying on of healing hands.

The hard fact is, he did *everything* wrong. He regarded life as sacred. He thought of patients as almost human. He ignored the stock market. Kune walked the hospitals in his great contest to preserve life. He took refresher courses, refused to exploit lab people, janitors, dietitians. He failed to become arrogant, sometimes treating charity cases. He gave no kickbacks, padded no welfare bills. He refused to play golf, and drove a pink '59 Rambler. He insisted on sterile needles. There was no sin he did not commit.

Kune became a maverick. His colleagues stopped greeting him in the halls. Patients scorned him. Nurses regarded him as unmarriageable, unbeddable. The AMA decided Kune belonged among naturopaths, herbalists, witch doctors.

Through it all, he more or less kept his head. When banned from practice in all hospitals, he thought of returning to Point Vestal. The AMA moved rapidly. He was blacklisted in his hometown. On the flip side, though, he met a nurse and fell in love. Her name was Shirley.

Kune had dreamed of what the practice of medicine could be. The realities of medicine faded back into dreams when he met Shirley. She was compassionate, skilled. The dying loved her until their deaths. Infants added weight, stopped squalling in her presence. Shirley worked as hard at being a nurse as Kune worked at being a doctor.

In a small and run-down suburb of Seattle, Kune set up a neighborhood practice. Patients who came to his lightly decaying house were Eskimos driven south from the oil fields, blacks driven north from the oil fields, Okies driven west from the oil fields, and Asians driven ying-yang by gunboat diplomacy.

It was a quiet and rewarding life. The house had two stories and Kune lived on the second. The former living room became the waiting room, with flowered wallpaper, overpriced Salvation Army furniture, and pictures of heroic doctors; the pictures torn from calendars distributed by legalized drug dealers.

His lab sat beside the toaster in the kitchen. His two examination rooms, one a former bedroom, one a dining room he painted white. He was too absorbed to smell the smells of Seattle, to hear surprised little grunts of people stabbed while walking dark streets, to hear roaring traffic from a nearby freeway. He painted his bedroom rose and misty blue, anticipating carnal knowledge. Loving Shirley.

She was blond, statuesque, with maternal skills at nursing; small squeals of surprise when nuzzling. Shirley was voluptuous Norwegian, Lutheran, thus confused. She was not innovative but a good learner. When nursing, though, she was the teacher: Kune learned a lighter touch, learned a gentle smile. She taught him to be a better doctor. Kune and Shirley laughed, loved, practiced medicine, went to movies, zoos, bowling alleys. To Kune life could offer little more. In a few years, no doubt, there would be blond children. More medicine, more Shirley, a station wagon.

Then anguish stepped into the waiting room, quiet as an abashed thirteen-year-old sodomized by police. Shirley developed a little zit between her shoulders.

Kune rubbed it lovingly with alcohol. They went back to work. On the next day the zit became a large pimple and moved to the lumbar region. More alcohol. The pimple became a boil, moved to the inner wrist. The boil became two boils, then three. It developed symptoms, a harsh cough, wheezing, rapid pulse, diarrhea, cold sweats, dizzy spells, temporary blindness, numbness in toes, fingers, nose. It resembled typhus, plague, infantile paralysis, Legionnaires' disease, smallpox, premenstrual syndrome. It was all of these and none. Kune was temporarily affrighted. Shirley lay semiconscious. Kune entered the greatest battle of his career.

He fought symptoms. He diagnosed. He sat beside her rereading medical books, reading journals. He brought her some relief, but with each relief the disease changed. It was wanton, capricious. Kune closed his practice to devote every minute to Shirley. The disease went into a final change. It became a wasting affair of the kind beloved by pop medical magazines, quick and dirty researchers, fundraisers. It resembled Parkinson's, Crohn's, sullen varieties of cancer.

Kune called in every marker he owned, and they were few. He placed Shirley in a hospital, and because he was banned, ran tests under a false name. She was probed, X-rayed, transfused, scalpeled of spare parts, fed steroids, antibiotics, aspirin. Kune rifled the racks of home remedies, consulted colleagues. He drove at the disease with desperation, zeal. He fought malaria, psychosomatics, mumps, leprosy. She lost weight, developed tubercular sweats. The shiny machines buzzed, zapped, hiccupped, chuckled over salts, hissed oxygen, Ping-Ponged lasers.

He grieved, brought Shirley home; the home where the power of her own skill had healed so many. She lay in the upstairs bedroom—rose and misty blue—and, fresh from the hospital, begged Kune to love her. She was wraithlike, had but three toes, a facelift. Kune pumped away, tears flowing, but the life-making fluid was not life-giving fluid. Shirley lost more weight. From a solid 160, she declined to 85. The case was hopeless.

Still he fought. Alcohol rubs, massive shots of vitamin C; the Power and the Glory, failing, the miracles failing. Shirley wanted to die.

Still he fought. Day by weary day, night by weary night, he was, it seemed, inexhaustible. He was pernicious, omnipresent, omnipotent. He was Shirley's entire world. He owned her, possessed her, pilled her, filled her with shots. He did everything he could, and still she did not die. He longed for rest for her, himself. Still—no matter how hard he worked—he could get her to die.

He was the disease. He realized that the Power and the Glory, the miracles streaming from his standard were the great symbols of victory over life, not victory over death; and he, the disease, was a plague on his own house.

Kune withdrew treatment, allowed her to die. He howled with grief. He paid for a funeral.

Kune wandered through the house inexorable and insidious as any disease. He infected the waiting rooms, the toaster in the kitchen, the supply cabinets. He infected the toilet seat, the inner crannies of woodwork. He began to understand disease, to sympathize. He thought of wonderful ways to attack lymph nodes. He muttered to himself, to Shirley, to blond-but-unborn children. When he could bear his own presence no longer he lit a match. Flames rose around him; sterilizing and Inquisitorial. He stood in the fire and prayed for redemption in the cleansing flames. He passed out from smoke inhalation.

A courageous fireman dragged him away as the house broadcast fire against the neon-lighted firmament above Seattle.

Chapter 15

... IN THE DUSTY BASEMENT OF THE PARSONAGE: BEV SOBBING HER grief for Kune. Joel-Andrew in silent supplication for all of us, for those who are human, for those who are cats. Starling weeping Victorian tears for beauty, because Starling has never heard of anything so romantic in all his life or death.

And, high above them, the all-seeing tower gazes upon the town, the Strait, the surrounding forest, the sky; and the all-seeing tower looks into silent centers of minds, hearts, good intentions. Because not even Gerald, a small-town cop who knows most everything, can see as does the all-seeing tower.

Beneath the Strait a sudden churning, a ripple, a ground swell spreads against the outrunning tide. A covey of salmon, perhaps, a gaggle of halibut? The ground swell whispers, hisses, is contentious. Chinese voices gargle, choke, and sink beneath waves as they await Chinese New Year, in the Year of the Tiger.

In Point Vestal ghosts huddle in storefronts, cellars, attics. Ghosts strut like proprietors through morning streets where an occasional homeward-bound drunkard, clapped in an aura of booze, obtains random insights into the meanings of life, art, communication; insights that will be gone on the morrow as an aching head contemplates diarrhea, trembling hands, a bloody stool.

And there are marching ghosts and singing ghosts. Ghosts discuss chowder recipes, stove polish, butter churns, and ghosts in pink lace attend birthday parties. There are political ghosts, soldierly ghosts, ghostly schoolteachers, and ghosts impaled on picket fences. There are bankerish ghosts, and ghosts of Rosicrucians.

The all-seeing tower pauses momentarily to view third growth forests where ghostly Indians trade beads and slaves and wives. The all-seeing tower watches Gerald's 1939 LaSalle thread along dark streets.

The LaSalle runs like a busy needle stitching the patchwork that is Point Vestal. The LaSalle has been, was, is a street traveler, a *time* traveler, and Gerald notes the usual news that will not get into Jerome's newspaper. Cars are parked in wrong places, betraying who is shacked with whom, and faint glows of late-late-late televisions are watched by sleepless businessmen. Gerald sees the shadowy form of Samuel, as Samuel arrives home at an indignant canter.

The LaSalle passes Washington Street, where echoes of 1912 whisper about the fate of the *S.S. Titanic*; passes Lincoln Street, where echoes of 1914 grieve for the *S.S. Lusitania*; while a cobbler changes his name from Schmidt to Smith. The LaSalle idles along Grant, as Gerald hooks second gear to check a three-shack apartment of ill repute built in 1922. There are echoes of jazz, the surrealism of art nouveau. On Coolidge Street it is 1935. A man chokes from a noose—a suicide—as two children cry from hunger in the next room. The Great Depression. With the man dead, a foundling home must take his children.

The LaSalle gleams shiny, black, spectral. Gerald rolls along Jackson, where—at this time of night in 1942—a mob beats death into a Japanese gardener; while a smuggler uses the frenzy of the crowd as cover to transport counterfeit ration stamps.

On Garfield it is 1956; racial strikes in Montgomery, workers' strikes in Poland, general strikes in Hungary. A woman wearing a tight angora sweater parades large breasts as she examines the size of her new refrigerator. Gerald idles past darkened windows of Janie's Tavern—silent now—past darkened windows of The Fisherman's Café, and for a while it is 1965. From the boat haven swirls the heavy perfume of marijuana, grass, weed, Mary Jane. Elsewhere there is a blackout in Boston; Malcolm X is assassinated; the International Society for Krishna Consciousness is founded.

When Gerald and the black LaSalle drive the long road and arrive back at the outskirts, it is once more 1973.

Gerald, who has seen it all before, sits in the police car as pink sunrise lightens mist. He tells himself the new preacher is harmless, and Kune is just one more box of Cracker Jacks, but August Starling had better be watched. Gerald wonders idly how Bev is going to explain staying in a house all night with three men and a cat. Then he chuckles. The cat is the only make-out artist in the bunch.

Perhaps Gerald has been at the job too long, has fallen too deeply into routine. As the long years pass, perhaps Gerald has become a little deaf. From the town a congregated sigh rises as ghosts flicker in morning mist. Generally speaking, the sigh is not remarkable. Ghosts are experts at sighing. This sigh, however, might even impress Maggie, who snores in an upstairs room above Janie's Tavern. The sigh is filled with hope.

After all, the sigh seems to say, August Starling's return from the dead may be a sign. Will all of Point Vestal return from the dead? Because, the sigh says, a second chance would change this dull eternity. Because—hell is whatever place you are when you are tormented. In the dungeon below City Hall, The Sailor clanks his chains.

Gerald does not hear. He heads the LaSalle down the hill, into the sunrise, headed for the barn. He leaves the sleeping town to its daily tasks of selling things to each other, its rituals of multicolored sprinkles on vanilla doughnuts—like balloon at a children's party—and Gerald chuckles because he remembers Collette saying clams don't whistle, 'cause clams have got clack-yaks.

Chapter 16

OCTOBER OF 1973 PRODUCED HALLOWEEN, THEN FADED TO November. Werelight shone luminous above the Strait, and in Seattle they were having a splendid little war somewhere, battling well-oriented Orientals. Point Vestal loyally sent a few sons, and one became highly decorated. After his burial, the town installed a plaque on the windy bluff. Then everybody went about their business.

=

All of us have November tasks. Bev, wearing sturdy apron and slacks, looks like a movie star in a murder mystery. She climbs ladders to dust every bookstore shelf in anticipation of Thanksgiving. One show window displays Pilgrim Father coloring books. The other displays heavyweights: Cotton Mather, Perry Miller, Jonathan Edwards, and Jonathan Livingston Seagull. This confuses Samuel, who, back in 1973, still did some preaching.

During November and December, Samuel used to be an outrider, bringing the Word to scattered Indians with blood dulled by chill weather; Indians so forgetful they failed to hide in the forest. Samuel rode an old horse named Wesley around the circuit. Samuel rode valiant, and, wearing a frock coat, and with his gray beard pressed by the wind as the dark horse cantered, Samuel was imposing. One may say what one wishes about Samuel's notions of Presbyterians, but when a really good missionary preacher is needed, one may depend on Samuel.

In November Jerome must write his Turkey Day editorial praising the local high school football team, and advising us to patronize local merchants. Jerome wears his double-ender Sherlock Holmes hat to Friday night football games. At the newspaper office, lights burn late.

In October and November, Collette nearly has fits. Every brass spittoon, every piece of coin silver, plated silver, sterling silver, every pan, pot, skillet, trivet, turnip watch, wash boiler, moon-phase clock, and straight razor in her antique shop gets polished. Collette is little and cute, her dark curls sometimes tipped with silver polish.

But Frank is busiest. For a week Frank decorates Janie's Tavern with gold and black crepe paper, pumpkins, black cats, cutouts of witches, pictures of Point Vestal founders. He also uses real artifacts: dried-out skulls and crossbones, skeletons awry, a tacky old coffin complete with a pickled Irish cop dormant since 1913, gorgeous daguerreotypes of Victorian funerals showing young women, babies in lace, stalwart gentlemen—eyes closed—(serious and dutiful, but with lots of frills); and Frank decorates with symbols: crosses, totems, and Chinese signs left over from World War II. According to Obed, the signs above the restrooms read "Chinese relief." At the end of the bar, Maggie sits like a small and feisty volcano. Frank brushes his whiskers, twiddles his mustache, looks sorrowful. Frank must ignore Maggie because he engages in tradition.

It was onto this November stage in 1973 that drama entered. Lights. Camera. Action.

=

From the basement of The Parsonage, on that November morning, Joel-Andrew and Obed stepped into werelight. Joel-Andrew carried his violin because later in the day he would go to work. Kune muttered at their heels. Two weeks had passed since Bev, Kune, Joel-Andrew, Obed, and August Starling spent a night in custody of The Parsonage. Now August Starling lived in a modest downtown hotel. Since the town meeting at Janie's Tavern, Kune was censured, a scapegoat. Kune walked with the inexorable flow of contamination.

"I didn't think being a scapegoat would be this tough," Kune confided to Joel-Andrew. "I never used to talk to anyone but Gerald and Maggie and Bev, anyway. Now I feel just awful."

"When people do something bad," Joel-Andrew said, "you get the credit. They get the fun."

"That's why some kid picked his nose and then wiped me with the booger," Kune said reflectively.

"Some people care for you. Me, Bev, Maggie."

"It was different when the AMA banned me," Kune explained. "I hurt their feelings."

For two weeks Joel-Andrew and Obed drifted, as Joel-Andrew tried to enjoy his vacation. Joel-Andrew found that idle hands are not the Devil's workshop, only boring. Since Frank enjoyed the music of George Gershwin, Joel-Andrew daily entertained at Janie's Tavern before and during happy hour.

Joel-Andrew also enjoyed relaxed evenings with Kune, who came to The Parsonage each night like a laborer returning from work. The men spoke of weighty matters, drank red wine, ate onions, French bread, soft cheeses. The Parsonage listened, approved. Obed usually sat at Joel-Andrew's feet, although Obed was technically shacked up with a calico yum-yum on Madison Street.

"Something is different about the town this morning," Kune said. "Something awful."

Werelight glowed through patterns of mist: On this strangely lit morning, mist boiled, churned, sent little wind-devil tendrils. Mist formed vaguely Chinese-looking faces, plus the figures of tigers, rabbits, and oxen.

"I've seen it before," Kune explained to Obed. "You may have another white whisker before this day is past." Kune explained that when mist took shapes, one or more time jumps were likely.

"You'll recall when you first came to town," Kune reminded Joel-Andrew. "You met a middle-aged lady and gentleman outside City Hall, where you heard The Sailor dying. I explained they were actually old people who lived in a nice house on the hill, but you encountered them in 1947. We had a nice discussion."

Joel-Andrew remembered. He also remembered, after meeting the lady and gentleman, he and Kune had entered the servants' entrance of the Starling House. On that occasion they had shifted back to 1888.

Such things amazed him two weeks before; now they seemed common. Joel-Andrew had still not brought Kune to the Lord. Kune was not an infidel—that could be overcome—but Kune had learned not to believe in anything. Joel-Andrew was not discouraged. When The Lord wanted Kune, Kune could be netted like a guppy from a fish tank.

"August Starling," Kune said mournfully, "is noising it around that his wife will arrive from Boston the moment he restores his fortune."

Joel-Andrew was appalled. History would repeat. If August Starling kept conning himself about having a wife, August Starling might kill a woman once more.

"Starling is too blamed interested in Collette," Kune said. "Collette can't talk to me because I'm censured."

Joel-Andrew gasped. Collette, with her antique shop and her fascination with history, was a natural target.

It was time for the Lord to take a hand, although Joel-Andrew said nothing to Kune. Talk of the Lord, and talk of miracles, did more harm than good.

"Come to Janie's Tavern during happy hour," Joel-Andrew told Kune. "We'll talk this over with Maggie."

Kune pulled his watch cap to his blond eyebrows and checked the ties on his boots. "I'll leave you here," he said. "Time for a walk." He strode into the mist—promising nothing—walking pneumonia.

"You will probably be amazed," Joel-Andrew mentioned to Obed, "but it looks like I goofed. I thought Kune would be easy, and August Starling tough. Now it looks like a toss-up."

Obed was unamazed. Having coupled with the white cat back in 1888, Obed became the founder of a dynasty. No matter where they traveled in Point Vestal, they met white cats with gray tails and gray cats with white tails. Obed's white whisker twitched. He compared himself either to George Washington or King David.

The first jump in time happened as they passed the boat basin.
A great, shaggy man strode toward town. He sang a lewd ditty,
walked with a rolling gait, and wore a gold ring in his ear. The
Sailor headed ashore with a thirst, the thirst complicated with a
case of unrequited lust.

"We must warn him about Gerald," Joel-Andrew told Obed.
"Gerald will not allow bawdiness."

Obed objected, alarmed, proprietary. Obed wanted no one but
Obed to change Point Vestal history. Obed gave advice. By the time
the squabble with Obed ended, The Sailor disappeared.

Fog. Mist. Rain. Joel-Andrew loafed through the morning.

Bright lights of The Fisherman's Café drew him. He drank herb
tea, listening to the small lick and slurp of wavelets on the stone
beach behind the café. Important talk shifted between tables as fat
men and skinny men, bald men and barbered men spoke excitedly
of August Starling. They chatted about real estate, interest rates,
tourism. Visionaries spoke of ways to improve the town; a fertilizer
plant, a tannery, a pipeline to transport oil. The men were dutiful.

In the café and in the streets, Joel-Andrew saw renewed determination in squared shoulders and resolute eyes. He observed
humility, pride in right conduct, and sacrifice. Gold Star mothers,
proud wattles beneath firm chins, paraded like infantry. In the
streets talk was of duty, duty, duty. And progress. Proposals were
made to send missionaries to Seattle.

Joel-Andrew wanted to talk with Maggie. He showed up for
work an hour early.

Maggie momentarily looked like an abandoned bird's nest.
"Four-flushers," she said about the people in town. "Five-flushers,
even. Sheep. Now that Starling is loose this hick town will turn
dutiful as a steel engraving." Maggie belched, then viewed Janie's
tavern with native tranquility.

Along the bar, this early afternoon, sat five drunken fishermen,
two snoozled loggers, a World War I vet, and a couple of wide-
hipped ladies who were no better than they should be. Frank
arranged a bouquet of shamrocks at the feet of the pickled Irish
cop. Obed sauntered to the cop's coffin and saw a wizened but
still stocky figure smelling of mash. The cop's eyes squinched.
Nicely dusted with Frank's feather duster, the cop looked fresh

and lifelike. Obed seemed impressed by the pickling process. He muttered barely acceptable Chinese.

"August Starling has been doing his duty for two weeks," Maggie said. "He sold a bunch of old coins to Collette. He parlayed the money with a minor drug deal, a bigger drug deal, and then a really big drug deal. He researched the twentieth century by reading every *Life* magazine in the library. He contacted City Hall and the school board. He was introduced at a businessman's lunch, gave a talk about Victorians to the seventh grade. He is a town hero and welcome at the bank. August Starling is not yelling, 'Woe, oh woe is me.' He is too interested in the tourist industry."

The Lord was not going to like that. Joel-Andrew told himself he had best get busy, or Starling would moult all over his last chance. Joel-Andrew, who genuinely loved the sinner while despising the sin, watched Frank arrange the last of the shamrocks. The coffin was little more than an old packing box, but Frank thought it good enough for an Irishman.

"It has to be hard on Starling," Maggie said, "not that I care." She watched Frank put finishing touches on the coffin. "You showed up at an interesting time," she mentioned to Joel-Andrew. "In a few minutes, Frank will need splints for his his whiskers." Maggie's wise and wrinkled face hid behind a toothless grin. "Because," Maggie said about August Starling, "the Victorians didn't just have boffing on their brains. They did a balancing act with how they thought."

Joel-Andrew watched Obed, who sat on the end of the coffin watching Frank. The Irishman's face reflected in the mirrored ceiling and seemed to be watching all of them.

"The Victorians were crazy over sex," Maggie explained, "but they were crazy over religion, too. They tied their religion to what they called progress and duty." She sniffed. "That meant they had to lie and cheat and steal."

To Joel-Andrew it sounded just like San Francisco.

Maggie caught his drift. "It wasn't that plain to see," she told Joel-Andrew. "The way they talked up their big religious news made the difference. It was missionary. So they turned the screws on Indians, Chinese, and on their own people. Anybody who wasn't rich was dirt."

To Joel-Andrew it still sounded like San Francisco.

Maggie explained, "The difference was something called the white man's burden. They felt responsible for civilizing the people they walked on. They'd work a servant twelve hours a day while paying only room and board, get her pregnant, be starchy about her immorality, and ship her off to a home for wanton women. The point is, they had the dutiful foresight to build the home."

Joel-Andrew thought that was a little bit different from San Francisco.

Obed walked along the edge of the coffin. Obed wanted a closer look.

"Kune says Starling is interested in Collette." Joel-Andrew's gray-green eyes were attentive, and his thoughts tender as he recalled Collette's verve and vivacity.

"That missy better dig a foxhole," Maggie said, "or Starling will have her dancing like he danced the last one."

"O Lord," Joel-Andrew prayed, "Thy will be done. But Lord if it be Thy will, show Your humble servant a way to save Collette."

"It's about to start." Maggie giggled. "I've been waiting since 1913 for a look at what happens next."

A stirring of air in the tavern—a flicker of neon lights—a dust kitten rolled past, gave a little hop, mewed.

"By me sainted mither," a choked voice said from the coffin, "there's a *cat* on me face."

Obed startled. Obed bounded, hid behind a pool table. Obed sported *two* white whiskers.

The WWI vet turned slowly on his bar stool. The vet was varicose, liver spotted, shades of tan and purple; a good man with a beer glass, and no fool.

"Frank," the vet drawled, "you have a new customer." Then the vet yuk-yukked. "A renewed customer. An undisputed champion of the sauce." The vet raised his beer glass.

"Oh, dearie me," the Irish cop moaned, "to leave a man lie here with dry throat and scratchy eyelids . . ." He blinked, made a feeble motion to sit up. The cop's cheap wool suit, pressed in one position through many years, breathed crinkly. "I'm safe at Janie's," he said with satisfaction. "For I recognize the ceiling."

At the bar five drunken fishermen, two snoozled loggers, and two ladies who were no better than they should be turned in unison. Frank's back still pointed toward the bar as he froze. Frank stared in the mirror, stiffened, stared. His eyes became as round as his tummy. Frank's beard seemed to grow as the rest of him shrank. For this situation there was no protocol.

"I figured he was faking," one logger said to the other. "These Irishers are sneaky." Both loggers turned to the bar.

"There's *something* to it, I reckon," one of the drunken fishermen said, "but it ain't gonna bring sailing weather." He shoved his empty glass at Frank. "I'd better have another against the time the weather breaks."

"He's right about the weather," another fisherman said. "And if it breeds no break in weather, what good is it?" The other four fishermen turned back to the bar. Frank drew a beer, trembled. The two ladies headed for the women's can to put on lipstick.

"Saints surround me!" the Irish cop yelped. "'Tis a dreary coffin I'm in." The cop managed to sit up and look about. His square jaw trembled; his pug nose squinched. He rubbed eyes with the back of his fist and yawned. "Maggie, me darlin'," he whispered, "who did this wretched jest?" The cop saw Joel-Andrew's clerical collar. "Maggie," the cop said in amazement, "can this be so? Maggie consorting with an Episcopal?" Then the cop remembered he sat in a coffin. He crossed himself, eyed Joel-Andrew. "I've missed me own wake," he mourned. "What day is it?"

Frank had a problem. Bad enough to have a live Irishman on the premises, but this Irishman also broke tradition. Between Halloween and Thanksgiving, the pickled cop was *always* a fixture in the decorations. Frank had not been so disconcerted since the awful time a lady tourist entered the place wearing shorts and halter top. Some things are simply *not done* in Janie's Tavern.

Beneath his beard, Frank's lower lip quivered. He smoothed his vest, his sleeves, and donned his suit jacket. He arranged the hankie in the pocket. He picked up his pool cue, looked puzzled, laid it down. Large tears appeared in Frank's eyes. At that moment, Kune came through the doorway.

"You did this," Frank whispered hoarsely, and he looked at Kune.

Kune stood and dripped. He smiled a little, and his teeth showed even and white. His mouth held a hint of excitement. His long blond hair spread from under his watch cap all the way to his belt. Frank touched his pool cue, brushed at a dust mote on his sleeve.

"The conception which led to your birth was not immaculate," Kune remarked to Frank. "As a physician, I estimate the whole deal was strained through cheesecloth."

Kune seemed fairly happy, which meant he had no bleeding ulcer. "We just had a time jump," he reported to Maggie. "Three Chinese outside the bank. Gerald investigates."

Joel-Andrew sat giving thanks to the Lord for the Irishman's revival, but feeling guilty because Kune took the blame.

"Bring the poor man a drink," Maggie said to Frank, and embarked on her own ministry. "Matter of fact, bring several." Maggie's scorn washed over Frank like kelp over a clam.

Maggie looked at the Irish cop. "He's new around here." Maggie pointed toward Frank. "He's bright enough most of the time. This one," she explained about Joel-Andrew, "is like being around a cherub on a bender." She pointed to Kune, "And this one is a dose of salts on the hoof." To Kune she said, "Help the dear man outta the box." To Joel-Andrew she said, "Wipe Frank's nose."

Frank reached for a glass, dropped it, heard it shatter. Then all that is fine about Frank came to his rescue. Frank's upper lip stiffened; his eyes became dutiful, even steely. His shoulders squared. True Victorian gentlemen never show themselves disconcerted by a downward turn in fortune. He chose another glass. His hands did not tremble.

Kune pointed to the Irishman. "From a medical point of view, this is unlikely. Whatever in the world happened?"

"Time jump," Maggie said, and she mused; like wind over the tops of tall branches. Maggie's eyes warned Joel-Andrew from any explanation.

"That's reasonable," Kune said. "For a moment I was afraid it was one of those things I can't stand to hear about." Kune assisted the Irish cop from the coffin. The cop staggered as he gained the floor.

"Unlikely am I," the Irish cop muttered. "Me man, when I retrieve me strength, we'll find out who's unlikely." The cop was short but muscular. His eyes sparked blue as Collette's, and his sandy-colored hair tinged with orange . . . tinged with red, rather. He took a seat at Maggie's table. "It ought to be Sunday, for 'tis Saturday night we celebrated." He looked about the room, puzzled, having never before seen a jukebox. In the wet street, a Model T puttered past. The cop looked impressed. "It isn't Sunday," he said. "Maggie, tell me true . . ."

"This is gonna be a shock." Maggie spoke most kindly. "Rip Van Winkle slept for twenty years, but you've been pickled for sixty. There's been changes."

"Me partner," the cop asked, "what happened to me partner?" He remembered the skinny and morose cop who was once such a good spitter, the cop who helped escort August Starling home on the fateful night Starling danced with the corpse.

"He haunts the jail under City Hall," Maggie explained. "He beats The Sailor to death every Wednesday at exactly 4:00 PM. It's hard on The Sailor, but it's harder on your partner."

"Poor, dear man," the cop said. "Can naught be done about it?" The Irish cop downed two quick glasses, lingered over the third. "The news will surely be bad," he mourned. "Is anybody left from the auld gang?"

"A few," Maggie told him, "all of them on their last legs." Maggie paused. "Except for August Starling."

The cop yelled. Swore. Took hasty gulps.

Maggie looked at Kune and Joel-Andrew. "He is a sensitive man," she told them, "and his relatives have all moved away except for Collette. You boys can't help." To Joel-Andrew she said, "Play us a bit of Gershwin." To Kune she said, "Take a hike."

The Irish cop seemed ready to break into sobs, ready for another try at getting pickled.

"Old friend," Maggie said, "Maggie will explain and get you through your grief. This is what's been happening . . ."

Beyond the window Kune stepped into the rain. A time jump arced like chain lightning. The street, momentarily, lay choked with Chinamen.

Chapter 17

Novemer Proceeded apace. Werelight lay over ornate uptown houses and played on tumbling waters of the Strait. In that November, the Strait ran turbulent. Tide-fall and tide-rise confused fishermen, because tides did not follow instructions written in the tide tables. Water licked at tops of bulkheads behind The Fisherman's Café.

"Because," as Maggie told a fisherman on one weirdly lit day, "sometimes the wolves sit silent and the moon howls." Maggie did not explain, and Frank was too busy tending bar to ask.

Joel-Andrew played violin each afternoon at Janie's Tavern. His slight figure, clerical collar, sandy hair, and spidery fingers became familiar to happy-hour regulars. Among the riffraff of Point Vestal, Joel-Andrew gained acceptance as quirky but nice.

During long winter evenings in The Parsonage, Joel-Andrew made subtle suggestions to Kune about the validity of angels, of grace, of the peace which passes all understanding. Kune said that anything fascinating to a Baptist must have something wrong with it.

"Don't get your funk confused with 'funky,'" Joel-Andrew told him. "Even Baptists have moments." Joel-Andrew knew that if he opened enough interesting issues, enough possible visions, Kune's brain would jump into overdrive.

Samuel still rode circuit. He preached to Indians.

"We never see Samuel at his best," Joel-Andrew told Kune. "If we were on circuit, we would learn something." Joel-Andrew thought the missionary business not unlike the medical business; but in the missionary business, one hoped for permanent results.

Obed offered neither help nor hindrance. Obed was partly distracted by his shack job, partly because he studied Chinese.

Meanwhile, Maggie and the Irish cop spent long days in Janie's Tavern. The Irish cop turned into an interesting fellow—albeit fond of the old sauce—but an embarrassment to his grand-daughter Collette. She did not call on him.

Then our town policeman Gerald, and the Irish cop, spent time together. The cop began wearing Hawaiian shirts with purple flowers.

The newspaper reported the return of August Starling and the Irish cop as extended time jumps. It seemed the only possible explanation.

As November proceeded, it became obvious that the Irish cop and August Starling agreed on only two points. They each despised the other, and each did not appreciate all changes the twentieth century had brought to Point Vestal.

August Starling stood shocked and displeased by the absence of cathouses, and the corresponding presence of generous ladies no better than they should be. "Because," as he explained at a Chamber of Commerce luncheon, "the purity of Point Vestal women is the purity of the unblemished sun, the holy robes of their chastity shining fair light on those strong endeavors rising from our masculine and noble nature."

August Starling felt shocked and displeased because no Chinaman came anywhere near Point Vestal during the twentieth century. Plus, the IWW and the labor movement made him livid.

August Starling liked the new pavement. He liked the 307-step staircase. He thought well of automobiles, telephones, radar, speedboats and smuggling; but he struggled emotionally with the roughshod feminism of the Suffragettes . . . "clacking females subverting fair womanhood." Coeducation made him ill, though he admired cheerleaders. He shivered and tsked about the Miss America contest, was titillated by television commercials displaying crotches and armpits.

August Starling could be found simpering on the sidewalk outside Collette's antique store for a few minutes every day, but he also stayed busy. During the third and fourth week of November, Starling disappeared in the direction of Seattle.

"We can only hope," Kune said, "while Starling is checking out drugs, child porn, auto theft, and credit card fraud; we can only hope the mob kills him."

"We can only hope," Joel-Andrew replied with kindness, "that he will become astounded. He will look at depravity and do a one-eighty."

"And bears don't whistle," Kune quoted Collette, "'cause bears have got gruff snuffs."

Joel-Andrew remained serene. "I've seen some pretty hard cases turn it around. I'm not asking Starling be perfect. I would like to see him get at least as straight as the Irishman."

The Irishman was enchanted with ladies who were no better than they should be. He thought birth control a grand thing, though he looked over his shoulder toward Rome when the subject arose. He felt overjoyed that civilization had pushed wild cougars back into the Olympic Mountains. "For, they used to steal sheep, cattle, wee lads and lasses."

The Irishman abhorred Mikey Daniels's milk truck, "for it has none of the warmth of a cow," but spoke favorably of jukeboxes with Dennis Day records, of backhoes and bulldozers, dump trucks, forklifts . . . "Anything," he confided to Maggie, "that shoves the Irish into a higher line of endeavor." The Irishman enjoyed polyester shirts, electric beer signs—"'tis a fairyland, they are"—and was overjoyed because the street lay free of horses. "Nasty beasts. Just dumb enough to do what you say, just smart enough to resent it. And, oh, Maggie, do you recall the stink of the creatures?" The Irish cop could wax poetic about horse poop, street cleaners mostly Irish, and horse bite suffered by Irish hostlers.

And during November, werelight cast yellowish and grayish and bluish shadows in places where no objects existed to cause a shadow. Light curled thin and spooky. The newspaper reported an increased incidence of time jumps.

"Ghosts are skittish," Kune confided to Joel-Andrew. "I spoke to Bev only this afternoon. She feels the same." The two men enjoyed a relaxed evening in the basement. Obed visited his kitty-poo on

Monroe Street. The all-seeing tower was first to see the '39 LaSalle pulling off the roadway. Gerald and the Irish cop stepped from the La Salle.

"Bev is smart," Joel-Andrew admitted, before he heard footsteps above him. "We should invite Bev and Samuel to one of our evenings."

"Not Samuel," Kune noted. "You'll remember The Parsonage gave Samuel the old heave-ho." Kune's yellow eyes widened. "Someone is walking around upstairs."

When Gerald and the Irish cop entered the basement, Joel-Andrew resigned himself to bad news. He figured a bust, or else Obed made the slammer, maybe the hospital. Then Joel-Andrew saw trouble creasing Gerald's brow, and Joel-Andrew's heart went out to him.

"Ghosts are popping like popcorn," Gerald said. For a moment he blew his control, and flickered. Gerald shoved his cop's hat to the back of his head. He sat on the stairway beside the Irishman. "Boys," Gerald said, "there's stuff going on in town like you don't even see in a picture show." Gerald's face was hawkish, thin, a little lantern jawed. His grayish eyes were steely.

"You want to put August Starling on ice," Kune said, "and you're dead-ended. Starling's pulled a fast one, and you're trying to rake up a charge. You figure I can help."

"Kune is a diagnostician," Gerald explained to the Irish cop. "He reads situations, not minds."

A couple of mice peered from behind a sofa, discovered Obed's absence, trotted to the middle of the room. They cuddled against Joel-Andrew's left sandal. Joel-Andrew leaned forward, absent-mindedly rubbed them behind the ears.

"I ain't even going to try to explain the preacher," Gerald told the Irish cop. "His rap sheet says he's from Rhode Island."

"The more facts, the better the diagnosis." Kune looked pretty happy, which meant he did not suffer from elephantiasis. "What is Starling doing?"

"A couple of trucks are on a back road," Gerald said, "loaded with enough stuff to build a brewery—only it ain't brewery stuff. It's test tubes and chemical business. It's stuff for building August Starling's new pharmaceutical company."

Kune looked reflective, remembering his association with prescriptions. "It is a protected field," he told Gerald, "and Starling will not be allowed in. If Starling manufactures drugs, the drug companies will ice him for you."

"Plus a South American yacht carrying two speedboats moored in the boat basin. Eight or ten Cubans aboard," Gerald said, "but I can eat that many Cubans for breakfast."

"If Starling deals drugs on that level, the Cubans will ice him."

"Plus we've got two narcs in town," Gerald said. He eyed Joel-Andrew suspiciously. "Maybe three."

Joel-Andrew felt vaguely misunderstood.

"We needn't sweat that," Kune said, "because narcs are like the CIA. Meaningless, more or less."

Joel-Andrew saw Gerald's problem. Something awful threatened Point Vestal. August Starling imported the ways and values of Seattle. Metaphorically speaking, Mohammed was not going to the mountain, the mountain was coming to Mohammed.

"This is not a prophecy, only a prediction," Joel-Andrew told Gerald. "We may soon see a change in ideas about smuggling." Joel-Andrew rubbed the ears of the mice.

"Six Sicilians checked into the hotel," Gerald said. "They're armed with automatic weapons and drive a limo. They have two women. One woman is a stockbroker, the other talks real estate." Gerald's eyes pleaded for understanding. "Mind you," he said, "six men with machine guns are no problem. I can root 'em out easy as parsnips."

The Irish cop watched Joel-Andrew, watched Gerald, watched Kune. The Irish cop knew little about real estate and the stock market.

"Worst of all," Gerald said, "and only the Lord knows what to do with this one—there's another truck"—Gerald's voice broke—"and it's loaded with . . . it's loaded . . . it's . . ." Gerald's voice cracked like flaked ice.

Kune's yellow eyes reflected terror, a man knowing he would hear an ultimate horror, a blow so cruel it would swizzle the soul.

". . . and it's filled with stainless-steel kitchen stuff and a sign saying 'burgers' . . ." Gerald interrupted himself with a sound suspiciously like a sob.

Kune literally staggered, and that was not easy since he sat in a morris chair. Mice whimpered. Joel-Andrew, as an expert on the Lord, did not figure the Lord would help on this one. The Lord expected people to take some hand in their destinies.

"A burger franchise," Kune said, stunned. "Defiled. Perverse. Satanic. Doom." Kune turned to Joel-Andrew. "I told you," he whispered. "There's no hope, no hope for any of us. August Starling is a creature from hell."

Chapter 18

As the men sat in stunned silence interrupted only by chirps of terrified mice, the all-seeing tower looked into the heart of Point Vestal. Ghosts popped, as Gerald reported. Among more shallow ghosts, at least, the return of August Starling seemed the most important event in the past hundred years. Even wise ghosts were intrigued.

Because, as Maggie might point out, there is nothing fine about captivity. All very well, perhaps, to spend thirty or forty years sitting at the end of a bar. The Loyal Order of Beagles could tell us that. Bar talk being what it is, however, the joy of anchoring a bar fades as a century passes.

And proud duty, itself, is too stern for long wear. The ghostly Crocker twins, for instance, would have us ponder their careful question: How many times can you jump off a cliff and still put your heart in it? The Sailor, dying each Wednesday at 4:00 PM, would inquire: How many times can you die at 4:00 PM on Wednesday, and still have it *mean* anything?

Throughout Point Vestal, questions echoed. Over and over the ghosts had howled, tinkled, chimed, woo-wooed and woe-woed. They had rattled chains, sobbed, screamed, stomped, pattered, flowed, been ethereal. They had, on the whole, done a sturdy job; but the grim fact was, they were having a hard time going to work. A few managed to hold matters together for important dates,

Halloween or their birthdays; but starting in approximately 1950, ghosts began sloughing off.

Take The Sailor. He was to be chain-whipped by the morose cop. During the early years, The Sailor died miserably. During the rest of each week he suffered anxiety, depression, fear, regret; and even hoped for atonement from sins he might have committed and could not remember. During those early years The Sailor existed in a living purgatory as real as anything found on Her Majesty's ships.

It went equally hard for the skinny cop. In the early years he took some satisfaction in duty, although no joy. It was terrible to chain-whip a man, terrible to hear the screams, the choking; terrible to see last flickers of life depart from a horribly battered body. By 1950 the skinny cop figured something would have to be changed, or he would become a butcher; an Eichmann, or a Secretary of State.

A compromise developed. At first, the skinny cop went light on his blows. The Sailor exaggerated his screams. Years passed. A pattern emerged. By 1970 the skinny cop indifferently smacked chains against a wall. The Sailor, untouched, might have won an Emmy for screaming and choking. By 1973 they sometimes swapped. The Sailor beat on the wall; the skinny cop screamed and choked. No one in Point Vestal noticed, and so—as The Sailor put it—"If *they* don't give a bloody farthing, mate, why in the weeping world should we?"

Thus—except for Maggie, Gerald, and a few spectral preachers— every ghost in Point Vestal faked it—at least when Gerald was not around.

The all-seeing tower watched ghosts dropping all pretense toward duty in favor of dancing, singing, and skipping school. They could not bear their traditional work, and there was no other work they could do. A new purgatory rose. The ghosts despaired. The Parsonage did not favor what went on, but it said nothing to the men and mice who caucused in the basement.

"Starling brings in the stock market. Real estate. A burger franchise." Kune's voice broke. Tears dilated his yellow eyes. The morris chair creaked in sympathy. "Next there will be condos, subdivisions"—Kune's voice sank to a horrified whisper—"used car lots."

"Smuggling," Joel-Andrew said. "Murder. Mayhem."

"Smuggling is traditional," Gerald said. "We pretend we don't see it as long as the stuff goes through town and doesn't stay here. Our Founding Fathers . . ." Gerald removed his hat, bowed his head.

"I am not a contentious sort, but I am well acquainted with your Founding Fathers," the Irish cop muttered, "for I have scraped them out of many a gutter. Pig-slime."

Gerald put his hat on, assumed a cop-like demeanor.

"Dog-droppings," the Irish cop said. "Auld friend," he said to Gerald, "forgive it, but I know those men."

"We are in distress," Joel-Andrew said kindly, "and that makes us forget the main problem. The main problem is that Mr. Starling is so far astray from principled behavior . . ." Joel-Andrew heard his own words. They sounded like bird gravel on the floor of a birdcage. "Oh, dear, that sounded phony." He looked at Kune. "Whether it's hamburgers or real estate, we've got to turn this Starling cat around. Quit yelping and come up with something." The mice seemed impressed.

Gerald, unaccustomed to hearing that the founders of Point Vestal were scumbags, still looked at the Irish cop.

Joel-Andrew rubbed a mouse's ear, felt the tiny body shiver.

"Shoot him!" Kune said to Gerald, his voice savage. "Shoot Starling. He was supposed to be dead in 1922, anyway."

Joel-Andrew felt overwhelmed with sadness. It was always like this. He ministered to cops, solid citizens, professors of psychology; the shapers of society who preached the dignity of systems. Joel-Andrew asked them to love each other, and the most they could do was buy more guns.

It was always this way for Joel-Andrew, but Joel-Andrew was a child of the Lord. He played from a position of strength.

"Uh-huh," Gerald said to Kune, "shoot Starling. Yep. Sure. But there will have to be a town meeting at Janie's Tavern. I expect you've been at some town meetings?"

Kune twitched. He had attempted to suppress his feelings and imagination. Now, the first feeling he allowed himself was a recommendation for murder. Kune reflected on his own version of bird gravel.

The Irish cop watched Joel-Andrew. The Irish cop expected Joel-Andrew to come up with something—and it had better be fast—and it had better be right.

"At this I'm an expert," Joel-Andrew said with misery. "I think I know everything about evil." He nearly choked. The memory of a young girl standing in an alley nearly silenced him. "I know suffering. Even when suffering is necessary, all suffering is evil." He looked at Kune. "You know that. You remember Shirley's suffering, and your own. Makes no difference whether it's natural causes or induced, the result of suffering is a kind of death. When you kill a killer, it spreads the killing."

The love of the Lord filled the room. "For some of the awful things in this world," Joel-Andrew said, "there are cures. Mostly there are only treatments."

Above them, in the empty hallways of The Parsonage, echoes of ministerial voices held their breath. The screams of Point Vestal history paused momentarily. Suffering. The presence of evil twisted, whirled, churned like red shadows on the walls of the Starling House when August Starling danced with a corpse.

"I used to understand that." Kune's yellow eyes showed old pain. "I took the Hippocratic oath. These days I ain't much, but I'm still something."

"Suppose," Joel-Andrew said to Kune, "and just for the sake of argument—suppose the Lord is interested in this affair. How would He proceed?"

"Brimstone," the Irish cop said.

"That's church talk," Joel-Andrew murmured. "Not fit for the real life of the world." He looked at the Irish cop, Gerald, and Kune. "All the Lord has is *us*," he said. "Maybe that's quite a bit."

Above them The Parsonage approved silently, although The Parsonage would not swear to its reasons.

"We can't shoot August Starling," Kune said.

"And yet," the Irish cop said, "the monster must be abated."

"Have him committed," Kune said. "The modern nut ward is strikingly different from the Victorian madhouse. Everything is clean, and the food acceptable. Tortures are only chemical and electric, a few lobotomies."

"You can trump up anything to hold a guy, but a case needs evidence," Gerald said.

"Get ghosts to testify," the Irish cop said. "If some dear souls can be found unburdened by prejudice."

Gerald sat on the stair step, his face haunted by frustration. "It wouldn't stand up," he told the Irish cop. "It's called 'spectral evidence,' inadmissible since 1693."

The two mice chirped confidentially. Whispers gathered overhead. The Parsonage settled firmly on its foundation. From the all-seeing tower came echoes of ministerial voices. Lamplight flickered in the basement, and Kune's long yellow hair looked white. His eyebrows knitted a straight line as he diagnosed the situation.

"We don't try just one thing, we try several," Kune said. To Gerald, he said, "Watch Starling every minute. He isn't accustomed to the twentieth century. He may fail to pay his income tax."

Kune looked to Joel-Andrew. "You're pretty good at what you do," Kune admitted. "Take some heavenly shots. It is a fertile little situation because of Starling's associates. You get to take holy shots at gunmen, the Chamber of Commerce, drug runners, the city council . . . actually, the field seems unlimited."

Kune looked at the Irish cop, whose jaw would have jutted were he not slightly overweight. "You have the toughest job," Kune said. "Keep a constant eye on Collette."

"Starling is after Collette," Gerald explained. "Starling looks for a new dancing partner."

The cop's jaw stopped jutting. He sat silent, surprised; then, finally, unsurprised. He looked at Kune.

"If ye be expecting a scene," he said, "let the thought be leaving. Be ye thinkin' of drink and Irish curses, ye can forget it." The cop no longer sounded merry.

"Don't kill Starling," Gerald told him. "You know what our jail looks like."

"The dead d'na feel pain," the Irishman's voice became cop-like. "I will carry my end of this stick." The cop watched Kune. "What will you be about?"

"It's delicate," Kune told him. Kune looked worried, and also a little frightened. "I'll be drifting in and out of the servants' entrance at the Starling House. Sooner or later, at some place in history, there'll be a document or an action that will accuse Starling. Something must exist that puts him in jail or back in the nuthouse."

Chapter 19

AUGUST STARLING SLIPPED INTO TOWN THE LAST SUNDAY OF November. A couple of Seventh-day Adventists and a hungover fisherman saw him standing the deck of a rumrunner dating from the 1920s. The rumrunner was a sleek eighty-footer, painted as gray as the tumbling waters of the Strait.

August Starling stepped to the pier, looked at moored fishing boats, and at werelight above downtown buildings. He looked at the tall brick building he had just purchased, the same one that in 1888 had held his own trading company.

The rumrunner backed into the channel, spun its nose, headed to the Strait where a distant Panamanian freighter wallowed at three knots. August Starling watched, his smile tender, dutiful. Then he walked the deserted street. His boyish face was now smooth shaven. His Victorian wool had given way to a conservative business suit. He went directly to his room at the old hotel. August Starling knew the ways and customs of Point Vestal. Duty or not, nothing in the line of "progress" would happen on Sunday morning.

On Sunday morning, whether 1888, or 1973, or today, our churches steam along like a parade of hardworking tugboats. Church bells clink, dong, clank.

Some congregations talk about the holiness of labor, while others examine the sins of labor unions. At least a dozen diaper their children with dogma blaming nastiness on Eve; while more timid congregations discuss the economic ramifications of the theory of entropy. Here and there a congregation breaks silence to praise the responsibility of doing good, while ignoring thoughts of goodly being.

Ideas ebb, flow, return and then again return; a stern seventh wave rising from the restless tides of history. Puritan certainty overtakes the town. Mists of history murmur that Puritans had trouble with love, Victorians had trouble with sex—and the twentieth century has trouble with both—and mists murmur that each group solved (or solves) its troubles by wrapping itself in the comforting cloak of questionable duty.

August Starling experienced, with clinical detachment, the movings and murmurs, the flutters and outcries of a troubled civilization. It would soon develop that he had doped out every problem confronted by the twentieth century.

Imagine him, then, standing in his hotel room on Sunday morning, staring into gray and vacant streets while simpering toward the darkened windows of Collette's antique shop. Imagine his chuckles, his dream filled eyes as he ruffled his knowledge like a cardplayer shuffling eight aces. August Starling knew progress was a smoke screen. More importantly, he knew everyone in Point Vestal still believed in progress. In the name of progress, all criminal behavior was still possible.

He laid his plans that Sunday, and then, perhaps, he rested.

=

Starling appeared bright-eyed and chirpy when he entered Jerome's newspaper office the next day. The newspaper office was inky, smudged, capably lighted. In older days it served to warehouse furs of bear, cougar, beaver, and sea otter. Old perfumes still lingered in the bricks, mixing with scents of a hundred years of journalism. Over the lintels of doorways Jerome placed significant headlines from Point Vestal history. *T. Roosevelt Hunting Party Visits, Shoots Cow. Author Twain Addresses Sunday School, Superintendent Miffed. Explorer R. E. Byrd Recruits Local Samoyed for Dog Team.*

Jerome recalls seeing Starling arrive that day. Jerome tipped his green eyeshade upward in time to see a tiny sneer behind

August Starling's friendly smile. Jerome has reported war, plague, devastation. He covers visiting carnivals, snake oil salesmen, faith healers, revivalists. Jerome knows every grift, shill, con, scam, and lanternslide in the book. He would not be taken in by August Starling's medicine show.

=

"Because," Jerome explains, as we sit in The Fisherman's Café, "there are more things unreported in the newspaper, than are ever reported." He looks carefully at each of us: Samuel and Bev and Collette and Frank. "Because," he says, "back in 1973, an awful lot of information came across the desk. I would not print happenings until I had a handle on the facts."

=

This morning the doughnuts are blueberry, colored with lemony yellow sprinkles. The wind wangs and bangs something fierce. It is already January, and we have been writing this history for an awfully long time. The windows steam, so Mikey Daniels's milk truck is a vague blob moving thumpedly before the wind.

"... would blow a crab out of a crab pot," Samuel mutters about the weather. "I never thought writing a book would do such extraordinary things to a person's dreams."

"I always thought a book was about what *was*," Bev admits, "and now I find they are more likely to be about what *might* have been." She looks at Frank, and Frank is confused.

"It is a history," Bev explains, "but it's becoming *our* history, not just town history." Her smile is sad, but Bev is tough and brave. "We might have been better people."

"Not me," Frank tells her. "I behaved adequately, thank you." Frank leans over the warmth of his mustache cup. "Decorum," he says. "Protocol. Decent behavior."

"I was such a kid," Collette mourns. "It takes such a long, long time to grow up." She looks at Bev, a look asking for another woman's understanding. "Starling sent a dozen white roses every other day. You can see how a person's head would get turned around."

"None of us did our shining best," Bev tells Collette. "Kune and Joel-Andrew keep looking better, and we keep looking not so good."

Samuel looks patriarchal. Of course, at his age, Samuel *is* a patriarch. "A lot of information came across your desk," he says to Jerome. "What information?"

Jerome pulls a notebook from his jacket. We have always known Jerome as a good newsman. These voluminous notes prove it.

"Roses to Collette," Jerome says. He settles back. "Item one: The increase of time jumps grew larger than anyone except Gerald and I imagined. They were largely Chinese. However . . . Item two: A persistent time jump appeared in the vicinity of the Starling House." Jerome looks apologetic. "Perhaps I should have reported this one."

"Which was?"

"The woman Starling killed back in 1888," Jerome says. "She had never made a spectral appearance in Point Vestal history. In 1973 she began appearing. Her name, as you know, is Agatha."

"What manifestation?"

"She danced," Jerome says. "That, of course, is reasonable. The dance began slowly, slowly speeded up, and ended in fury. She caused a vortex in the mist."

"Scares me even now," Collette admits. "Maybe it's best you didn't report it."

"Item three," Jerome mutters. "Miscellaneous. Unexplained. Twenty dancing ducks performed on North Beach. The fishing vessel *Northern Lights* reported a talking porpoise. The porpoise said, 'Howdy.' Tone of voice, sarcastic. Mice began emigrating from downtown basements to uptown churches. A flight of ravens argued in iambs. Except for Maggie, every Indian left town to visit relatives."

"I expect those ducks were mergansers," Samuel says. "Mergansers have always struck me as imaginative."

"Mallard sports most likely," Frank mutters. "Mallards miscegenate with anything."

"Those ducks were muscovy," Jerome tells us, "but that may not be the point. The point may be that Nature smelled a rat."

"What else was happening," Bev whispers. She watches Samuel who watches her. "I'm beginning to form a notion," she says only to Samuel. "August Starling was the worst man of his century, Kune was one of the best of his. Joel-Andrew was timeless."

Samuel shudders, controls his pomposity, reaches to touch her hand. "Perhaps you are correct," he murmurs.

"Let us get along." Frank is stuffy, there being no protocol to handle tenderness. "You keep good notes," he tells Jerome.

"Item four." Jerome looks at us, and we do not know if he is defiant or apologetic. "You heard of a jailbreak. Rumor said The Sailor and the morose cop broke jail. People whispered that Gerald was beginning to slip."

"An unfair complaint," Samuel admits. "The only jailbreak Gerald had in over fifty years."

"It wasn't a jailbreak," Jerome admits. "It was undercover. Gerald deputized The Sailor, the morose cop, and the Irish cop. The Sailor and the morose cop moved in with the Irish cop. For a while all three lived in the basement of the bookstore." Jerome looks at Bev. "You never suspected?"

"Never," Bev says, "or I would have fixed the place up a bit."

"After a hundred years in the jail, The Sailor would have been happy living in a swamp," Jerome tells her.

"Gerald must have had a reason," Collette murmurs.

"He had several," Jerome answers. "In addition to deputizing those men, he asked Obed to go undercover. Cats get into places men cannot."

Samuel is impressed. "I had no idea the situation was so intricate."

We sit and remember ourselves in those younger days when the date was only 1973. We remember the years, the daily mist, innumerable winter storms. Time seems a roll of gray fabric that can be unwound, rewound, or wrapped, stitched, fashioned like the suits and dresses of our lives. Joel-Andrew is dead. Kune is either alive or dead, and we do not know which.

"August Starling visited the newspaper office the last week of November in 1973," Samuel says to Jerome. "Tell us about it."

"He ran a variety of cons," Jerome said. "He looked for free advertising. It went something like this:

=

When Starling arrived at the newspaper office, Jerome worked at a desk covered with photos of a tricycle wreck on Maple Street. One kid sported a bandaged pinkie, the other lost her television privileges for a month. It was not front-page stuff, but the photos were excellent, and it was a slow week. Jerome nearly did not recognize the boyish figure wearing a business suit. Without his whiskers, August Starling looked about nineteen years old.

"How gaily shines the morn," August Starling said, "when companions in the common weal their enterprise enjoin, and fairly sounds beloved and clarion cries—"

"I don't have all day," Jerome said.

"—of duty," Starling said.

"You want something," Jerome told him. "You probably can't have it, but I'll give you ten minutes."

"It concerns missionary efforts in the tourist industry."

"Twenty minutes," Jerome said, "and cut the posied speech." He removed his green eyeshade. "How did Victorians get any business transacted? It takes you an hour to say 'good morning.'"

August Starling's eyes reflected the happy realization that Jerome was an editorial man, one given to impassioned speeches— but short ones. "Excellent," August Starling said, "I shall be direct." He pointed into the empty street. "It is not crowded with tourists," he said mournfully.

"It's winter. It's the off season. Seattle is covered with snow and ice and probably polar bears." Jerome also looked at the empty street, and for a moment was saddened. "Not a blamed thing to be done," he advised Starling. "The Chamber of Commerce once tried a Fog and Mist Festival. The only tourists who showed up were three Sasquatch and a Greek Orthodox sponge diver named Absorba."

The '39 LaSalle cruised by, with Gerald attempting to look innocuous as he kept tabs on August Starling. The LaSalle looked like a car that had burned up three odometers, which, in fact, it had.

"New police cars are part of my plan," Starling confided to Jerome. "As a loyal son of Point Vestal, I wish to contribute two brand new police vehicles." August Starling blushed. "It is best to be prepared, even at the risk of being overprepared."

Jerome smelled a rat. Circa 1888, but a rat.

"Police cars cost a lot of money," he told Starling, "and I doubt if Gerald would take a fancy to 'em."

"A matter of progress," Starling murmured. "Gerald approaches retirement."

"Gerald hardly ever flickers. He's at least a century from retirement." Jerome studied Starling with a steely journalistic gaze that could drill holes in boilerplate. "Blow some more smoke," he advised Starling. "I'm beginning to enjoy this."

August Starling seemed clumsy with his twentieth-century knowledge. He shoved his hat back, turned a chair around and straddled it. Jerome had the impression of a chicken sitting on a pointed egg. "Ask yourself this," Starling said. "What do people fear most?"

"The IRS," Jerome told him. "Plus getting behind on house payments. They fear nuclear pop-offs, chemical fertilizer, catastrophic illness, higher sewage rates. They fear unwed mothers, feminism, recalls of manufactured goods. They fear Breathalyzers, venereal disease, food additives, and homosexuals. They are scared silly of having a pancreas, of meditating on the universe, of thinking about acid rain. They are frightened by Latins, Orientals, mysticism and Yiddish. There is nothin' they won't do to get away from—"

"A century of fear," August Starling interrupted in a low voice.

"—to get away from fish inoculated with mercury, bureaucrats inoculated with ego, and dogs without rabies shots. I'm a journalist. You can trust me." Jerome leaned back and began enumerating. "People are most afraid of—"

"Death," August Starling interrupted. "When you get right down to it, people are afraid only of dying." August Starling hugged the back of his chair and attempted to look wise. "If Point Vestal can find a way to make people comfortable with death, the tourist industry is assured."

Shocked and intrigued, Jerome reached for his note pad.

"They fear death so much," August Starling mourned, "a funeral is just no fun any more. Cremations. Plain old caskets. No photographers. Simple ceremonies."

Jerome pushed his pad away. "If you're thinking fancy funerals, think again."

"You underestimate me," August Starling pretended to be sad. "What I have in mind is rather elaborate. It begins with an old religious custom."

Jerome took copious notes. Years later, when he reviewed those notes while sitting at the table in The Fisherman's Café, all of us—Bev, Frank, Samuel and Collette—would be fascinated by Jerome's methodical entries. By that time, the yellow legal pads were fading, but Jerome's notes remained a telltale of emotions. Sometimes the writing is bold and firm. Sometimes it trembles, as if written by a ghostly hand.

Chapter 20

"AUGUST STARLING'S PLAN WAS GAUDY," JEROME TELLS US. "THE MAN had unerring instinct for euphemisms. He had 20/20 vision for troublemakers. That is why he wanted Gerald to retire."

"He could make money." Frank is not given to flattery, but his voice holds an edge of admiration. "August Starling took a handful of capital from coins sold to Collette. In less than a month, he controlled a young fortune."

"Dealing drugs," Collette and Bev say in chorus.

"Smuggling is traditional," Frank reminds them.

"An argument from 'tradition' no longer carries much weight in Point Vestal," Samuel reminds Frank.

"Certain people," Collette says, "will walk across corpses while sniffing from a perfumed hankie. At least they will when corpses turn a profit." She looks at Frank. "Do something to make me like you."

"Starling's reasoning went this way," Jerome says. "People are afraid of death. Point Vestal is filled with ghosts. Therefore, death is different in Point Vestal. While it is true that many of our ghosts develop flickers, none has flickered out completely. It follows that dying in Point Vestal is a very good deal. We might be witnessing a form of immortality."

"Yep," says Collette, "and elephants don't whistle, 'cause an elephant got a hose nose."

"It would be grim immortality, indeed," Samuel admits. "If you have nothing to look forward to except eternal grief or eternal birthday parties . . ." Samuel sees Frank's confusion. "You couldn't even teach Sunday school for all eternity without the conversation wearing thin."

"August Starling knew that," Jerome explains. "August Starling did not talk about what *is*. He talked about what *sells*."

"There is a difference," Frank points out to Bev.

"That was part of the plan," Jerome tells us. "There were other parts. First, this business of an old religious custom: Starling spoke warmly in behalf of indulgences. He pointed out that the world has run on the low side of the indulgence business for maybe four centuries, which is why things went downhill."

Samuel gasps and chokes.

"August Starling wanted the ministerial association to sell indulgences covering all sins committed in Point Vestal. It follows that if you sell forgiveness for sins, you must have a variety of sins from which the customer can choose. Remember, also, such sins must be consistent with the Victorian charm of the community. August Starling spoke of tasteful cathouses, beautifully furnished opium dens, ornate gambling parlors."

"It is all traditional," Frank says. "What's wrong with that?"

"The ministerial association wouldn't cooperate," Samuel says. "That's one thing wrong with it."

"As you recall, Starling had a contingency plan," Jerome says. "I'll get to that in a minute. Meanwhile, in addition to guilt-free sin, Starling planned the return of the Victorian funeral." Jerome consults his notes. "Rotating preachers, ebony hearses, black horses in spans of six, silent mourners hired like movie extras, gorgeous selections of coffins, fruit-flavored embalming fluid (raspberry, strawberry, grape), ten days lying in state, an abundance of photographs—pictures of the happy corpse, of the corpse and living friends, pictures making contrasting and noble statements—such as photos of beribboned babies regarding the remnants of old men."

Jerome glances again at his notes, gives a low whistle. "Starch and lace concessions," he murmurs, "a small fortune in starch and lace. In addition, money for barbers, dentists, suit and dressmakers, florists. Steady employment for chamber music groups, gardeners for the cemeteries (Starling planned a modest dozen cemeteries for a start), and jobs for masons who would build the mausoleums—"

"Dentists?" Collette is as confused as the rest of us.

"Standard maintenance," Jerome explains. "The Victorians owned a fascination with teeth. Starling thought it unkindly to inter a mossy bicuspid."

"Keep it up," Collette says, "and I am gonna urp." Even her blue eyes look pale.

"Equipment sales," Jerome says. "Backhoes for digging graves, plus sales of granite and marble. Stonecutting equipment, polishers, engraving tools. Employment for sculptors, artists, singers, writers, and other such trash. A large market for memorial souvenirs, dinner plates carrying sentimental quotes, Bibles held by the deceased, plaster sea gulls with drooping wings and mournful looks . . ."

"I get the picture," Frank says, not a little excited. Then Frank thinks of some problems. "Hard to sell," he says. "Seattle people are too afraid of dying."

"I am certain," Bev says, "that August Starling had a scam."

"Starling peddled immortality," Jerome tells us. "He would sell indulgences. Since the customer was free of sin, the customer would have a happy immortality. There was additional bait, plus a kicker."

"Bait?" We all breathe the word at the same time.

"With each funeral, Starling would issue coupons good toward eventual resurrection. After the funeral, the ghostly presence could earn additional coupons by playing ball with Starling. The ghost would give testimonials, serve as tour guide of cathouses, et cetera. Starling used his own resurrection, and that of the Irishman, to prove such a thing possible."

"Did Joel-Andrew know about this?" Bev is astounded. "If Joel-Andrew knew, he would have called down angels."

"Joel-Andrew did call down angels," Jerome reminds her, "but later. To answer your question: at the time, Joel-Andrew did not know. Obed probably knew, but Obed worked undercover for Gerald."

"What was the kicker?" Samuel's nostrils widen. He snorts, ready to canter into battle. Samuel has warred against evil all his life, but it has been mostly garden-variety evil. He rarely gets a shot at the mainliners.

"There were actually two kickers." Jerome consults his notes. "First: Only tourists were eligible, and they could buy insurance against the time they might die in some other place. The insurance paid for their funerals, plus transportation to Point Vestal from any point in Seattle." Jerome's hands tremble. He looks at Samuel, at Bev. "You are not going to like the second kicker."

"I didn't like the first one," Bev tells him, "but I'm not blaming you."

"The second kicker was the Messiah," Jerome says. "Starling interviewed several candidates—gurus—television preachers—football coaches—that sort. He would train his man, then stage the Second Coming—get the networks involved—use a stage filled with country singers, a dozen choirs, characters from the Disney Studios, testimonials by football players, politicians, aging comedians, other riffraff, as well as the chorus line from *Auntie Mame*. He would bring his Messiah to Point Vestal aboard a fancy tour ship. He planned flyovers by the Air Force stunt team, 'The Hallelujah Chorus' performed by the Marine Band, twenty-one-gun salutes, free balloons in mourning black for children . . ."

"It will work," Frank says dreamily. "By Gadfrey, this is the biggest thing since the Wright Brothers."

We sit stunned. We are stunned by the colossal ego of August Starling, by the Victorian tastelessness of August Starling, the arrogant certainty of August Starling . . . but mostly we are stunned because Frank is correct. In a few short weeks, back in 1973, August Starling had cased the entire twentieth century.

"Let me see if I've got it right," Collette muses. "Starling had it set up so the customer received all the drinking, gambling, and boffing he could handle; then all sins were forgiven. Buying a funeral, he gained immortality and the likelihood of resurrection. In addition, Heaven came to him in the form of the Messiah."

"That's basically it," Jerome assures her. "There were trimmings—vibrator beds, cathouses for nonsmokers—stuff like that."

Even the wind that woofs around The Fisherman's Café seems in mourning. It is easy to hear remembered echoes in that wind; the gabble of a Chinese mob, the desperate and persuasive voice of Obed. We hear Kune's drawn-out cries, and quiet echoes of Joel-Andrew's voice.

Of course, we also have things for which we may be glad. Collette is still alive. Joel-Andrew may be dead, but he has not deserted Point Vestal. Kune walks, walks; is a quiet witness reminding us to retain our senses.

"It must have been confusing for Joel-Andrew," Collette says. "It certainly confuses me." A scoop shovel of rain hits the windows, crash-splash. "Regretting but never forgetting the roses . . ." Collette whispers, and she is off in some field of memory.

"Joel-Andrew was unmethodical," Jerome says. "Him and his dancing cat. But Joel-Andrew was never confused. He was too innocent."

"Maybe less innocent and more methodical than we believe," Bev tells Jerome, "but his methods were different. He exerted an enormous influence on Kune. He brought The Parsonage to an understanding of the difference between works and faith."

"To get on . . ." Frank looks to Jerome "Resume our story before distractions overtake us."

"Let us pick up the story back in the second week of December 1973," Jerome says. "August Starling's burger franchise was sited beside the boat basin. The pharmaceutical company rose quickly on the cliff at the approach to town. Let us start with Joel-Andrew, who by then seemed to be having some influence on the all-seeing tower. That he influenced The Parsonage—and profoundly—is a matter of record."

Chapter 21

IN DECEMBER, AS JOEL-ANDREW DISCOVERED, WINDS CARRY HARD and slanting rain. Sometimes a cold front sags through, dropping south from polar regions of Seattle. The all-seeing tower sees snow. The snow never lasts, for in a day or two it will be driven seaward by rain. In early mornings people feed airtight stoves with fir, alder, madrona; and people, no less than ghosts, are loath to go to work. In October we get October light, in November we get werelight, and in December we get black light. Streets reflect a midnight mood.

Through more than a hundred years, the all-seeing tower had pretty much seen it all; but the all-seeing tower had never experienced Joel-Andrew, who, on the second Wednesday of December, viewed the black morning as one more opportunity to get August Starling bombed into a heavenly high. Joel-Andrew had already taken one shot. August Starling, preoccupied with what seemed sheets of notes about chemistry, had been polite, chirpy, distant. The conversation went nowhere. Joel-Andrew also took some shots at Kune.

Joel-Andrew sighed and remained hopeful. He waited for revelation.

"O Lord," Joel-Andrew prayed, "after what Solomon went through when he prayed for wisdom, I'm scared to death of saying this—but Lord, may Thy humble servant be granted wisdom by which he may work Thy love." Joel-Andrew raised his head, looked around the drawing room of The Parsonage, bowed his head in an afterthought. "And Lord" he added, "You may want to take a kindly look at Kune. Our boy is turning it around."

Joel-Andrew stood at a drawing room window and planned his day. A distant rattle of small-arms fire sounded not much louder than fleas playing hopscotch on a rug. The small-arms fire came from the boat basin. Gerald had waited until dawn to mount another assault on the eight or ten Cubans aboard the drug-running yacht. The Cubans proved tougher than Gerald expected.

Gerald had trouble—Joel-Andrew thought with kindliness—because Gerald tried to take the Cubans alive.

Joel-Andrew riffled through his obligations. He had an appointment with Obed at 9:30, an appointment with Bev at noon. He figured Bev felt lonesome because Samuel still did missionary work with Indians. Joel-Andrew thought of Bev and Samuel's long friendship, and it also made him lonely. He remembered his small congregation in Providence. Joel-Andrew was getting old enough to fear he might never have a family of his own.

At 2:00 Joel-Andrew would see Maggie and Kune. Between 4:00 and 6:00 he would play Gershwin at Janie's Tavern. Joel-Andrew thought momentarily about Kune. Kune's trips in and out of the Starling House asked a heavy price. Kune lost weight.

"This is a blessed and wonderful business we're in," Joel-Andrew muttered companionably to The Parsonage, "but it sure asks for sinew in our spirits. Otherwise, it's wipe-out city."

The Parsonage stood mute, but for a few moments the drawing room lighted with a spirit of calm affirmation. Portraits of Presbyterians stared disapprovingly. The Parsonage rattled its walls ever so slightly—the portraits swaying and shaking their heads—then The Parsonage bounced so the portraits rattled and nodded yes. The Parsonage had been gaining confidence ever since giving Samuel the old heave-ho.

"We have the Lord," Joel-Andrew said, "and we are the Lord's children. I expect some of us carry our home and family with us. Still, it's lonely." He placed a candle stub in his pocket. "I expect to be home this evening," Joel-Andrew told The Parsonage. "If it is convenient?"

The Parsonage sat solid, stolid, as though promising to remain in place. Then it shivered, as if giddy.

"Until then," Joel-Andrew muttered, and stepped into the black morning light. The all-seeing tower saw Joel-Andrew's departing back, the hump-lump of the violin across his shoulders; the flappity-floppity sandals.

Small-arms fire rose on the wind, crescendoed, then faded as cries rose from the boat basin. The all-seeing tower turned attention to Gerald's firefight with the Cubans; and the all-seeing tower felt gratified because Gerald carried the day.

Gerald—as Jerome later reported in the paper—pulled a coup. It was a mixed victory, but looked good at the time. In all fairness, Gerald did analyze his tactical situation. He even consulted with Obed. Gerald's reasoning went like this:

There were eight or ten Cuban smugglers in the boat basin. The smuggling angle was no problem, but Point Vestal had never had a Cuban and did not need any more. Add to this the fact that ghosts of Point Vestal were in sullen rebellion.

Thus, Gerald reasoned, there were two alternatives: knock some ghostly heads together, and kick everyone back in line—or, Gerald reasoned, make use of the discontent while helping the ghosts take an active part in community affairs. Thus, Gerald reasoned, it only made sense to use ghosts in an assault on the Cubans.

That happened as the all-seeing tower heard cries of the mob, diminishing gunfire of the Cubans, the hard-churning engines as the yacht backed from the boat basin. The attack force of ghosts hit the Cubans with a full arsenal. Cubans were strafed with birthday-party cupcakes, hit with lace hankies. The Cubans got their slats rattled as ghostly blood flowed in the firmament, as ghostly cries sounded above the hard snap of buggy whips. The Cubans recoiled before shouts of "Remember the *Maine*," and were knocked slaunchwise as a flying squad of flickering irregulars from the Martha Washington Brigade zapped them with corset stays. The whole affair so rattled the Cubans that they returned to Seattle where, it is said, they joined the House of David.

If matters had ended there, all would have been well. However, matters did not. Ghosts looked for other little tasks requiring attention. They muttered about "cleaning up Point Vestal." Those mutters began as the all-seeing tower watched Joel-Andrew, a small man humpbacked with a violin, a man headed for his appointment with a cat.

On Joel-Andrew's right, raw cuts in stone marked August Starling's pharmaceutical company. The new building, already three stories tall and rising upward, seemed a vaguely modernized design of downtown Victorian buildings. Curlicues went on first, the rest to be added later. A secret passage and secret elevator shaft tunneled down to sea level. Machine-gun ports mounted in the front and sides of the pharmaceutical company were framed ornately in gold leaf.

Joel-Andrew passed the saltwater swamp. No ghostly rowboat cruised; no ghostly Christian Scientist called the names of missing children. On Joel-Andrew's left, clusters of ghosts drifted through the dark morning. Ghosts chortled, slapped each other on the back, giggled: even staid and proper ghosts had attended the battle. Janie's red hair made a little smudge in the mist as she chatted with her bouncer. The morose cop, who had once been the Irish cop's partner, stood on a pier. He spat reflectively at an itinerant dogfish.

"There's nothing to compare with it," a ghostly voice said rising from weeds and sludge beside the roadway. "I've not 'ad so much bleeding fun since me mum give satisfaction to the vicar." The Sailor emerged from the weeds. The Sailor stood broad shouldered, narrow waisted; had huge hands, smallish feet. He looked designed to scramble across rigging. He brushed weed seeds from luxuriant black whiskers. The Sailor smiled, although he carried the slightly haunted look of a man who has been chain-whipped to death more than five thousand times. The Sailor looked at Joel-Andrew's clerical collar. He tsked, shook his burly head, tsked, tsked.

"Are you walking in my direction?" Joel-Andrew asked, his voice interested and kind. "I take it you've just engaged in a rout." Joel-Andrew heard the foolishness coming from his mouth. "They were drug smugglers," he murmured. "They had a bust coming."

"They were probably good enough lads," The Sailor said. "For papists." He motioned to August Starling's burger franchise. The walls were up, the design vaguely imitating the shape of modern banks. Stained plastic windows portrayed hamburgers and franchise cartoons. "Progress," The Sailor said. "I haven't had a proper tuck-in for a century."

Joel-Andrew, employed before and during happy hour, enjoyed the unfamiliar feel of coins in his pockets. "Walk with me to The Fisherman's Café. I'll spring for doughnuts. The doughnuts have little colored sprinkles," he told The Sailor. "The sprinkles are different every day."

"Can't be done, mate." The Sailor sighed. "I'm technically a bloody fugitive. It's said I busted gaol." The Sailor looked at giggling ghosts, celebratory ghosts. "This affair brings change. If I know this crowd they wait for Frank to open Janie's Tavern."

Joel-Andrew felt pleased. Maggie was morose of late. A visit from this huge crowd would surely cheer her.

"The last time there was a meeting at Janie's Tavern, August Starling received a vote of confidence. Did news of that reach you?" Joel-Andrew found himself attracted to The Sailor, who seemed straightforward.

"Bugger these townies. For that matter, bugger August Starling." The Sailor looked at the celebrating ghosts. "*They'll* give him a vote of confidence, lad. After a century, they might have learned something, but they haven't. Can they be blamed? Before Starling hove in 'ere a second time, this was a dreary port." He sighed, but did not hide his anger. "All their antics for a century used to entertain tourists?" The Sailor regarded Joel-Andrew with trust. "Being dead is not so bad," he said. "But dying is ruddy bad. I've done it times immemorial. A bit of an expert, I suppose."

"August Starling acts so young and innocent," Joel-Andrew said. "Your usual ragtag run of hypocrites act old and wise."

In the dark and misty day The Sailor's eyes reflected memories of a hundred ports of call, memories of keelhauling, tots of rum, ocean calms, fistfights, scurvy, the beckoning arms of bar women. The Sailor remembered drug running, gunrunning. He recalled doses of clap, vibrating and windblown halyards. "The slave ships became illegal in 1806," he said, "but the trade continued for many a year. I was but a lad . . ." The Sailor's eyes were haunted not with ghostliness, but with memories.

Joel-Andrew did not understand. "August Starling dealt in bond slaves, not in Africans. All of the bond slaves were men."

"A bit of an expert," The Sailor muttered. "And bond slave or Afric, there was no difference, except men were raped instead of women. I'm no fool when it comes to evil. I mention slavers only to say that I understand the subject. You clergical fellows only talk about evil, just natter, natter, natter."

Joel-Andrew told himself that it was not likely The Sailor knew more about evil than he. At least Joel-Andrew prayerfully hoped not. At the same time, he might learn something if he kept his mouth shut.

"Doubtless hell has a dark side and a darker side," The Sailor said. "August Starling comes from the darker side." He slowed his pace, stopped, looked at Joel-Andrew. "You clergical chaps speak of the creations of heaven. Do you think, then, there are no creations from hell?"

"It's a new idea," Joel-Andrew admitted. "At least it's new to me. I'm not a theologian." Joel-Andrew did not try to hide his puzzlement. If August Starling were evil incarnate—and that was what The Sailor seemed say—then why did the Lord bring August Starling back to Point Vestal?

"Many a tale is told before the mast," The Sailor said, his eyes as faded as the mist. "Decent folk think of seamen as innocent packs of rats, but there's some wisdom in the fo'c'sle. There are evil men, and there is evil which masquerades as men." The Sailor shrugged, looked toward the Strait, the masts of fishing boats in the basin, the masts of a few yachts. "There is also purgatory, and there are purgatories. This bloody town is not heaven nor hell, but purgatory. For which," he added, "there flaming well seems no end."

"Purgatory? That's a new idea."

"It *is* purgatory," the Sailor said. "You clerics use a name, then can't connect the name with what you see."

"I do not understand ghosts," Joel-Andrew said.

"Do ye believe a seaman *wants* to go into the slave trade? Ye believe a seaman is naturally interested in evil?" The Sailor's voice grew husky. "When a chap is starving and the prisons filled with yellow fever . . . and when the press gangs lay him aboard a vessel of the triangular trade . . ." The Sailor asked no sympathy, but asked Joel-Andrew's attention. "Point Vestal is a port for those unworthy of consignment to hell, and don't pull my beard about heaven. Whores, seamen, phony gentlefolk."

Black December light seemed a velvet cloth behind The Sailor. It made The Sailor appear showcased, solid flesh instead of ghostly. "I hope I understand," Joel-Andrew murmured.

"You don't," The Sailor said, "but you may come to it. The hell-born are not the whores and sailors. The hell-born are the manipulators. This purgatory of Point Vestal belongs to poor blokes who had things happen, or let things happen." The Sailor's eyes were momentarily hollow with death. He looked toward the boat basin, where the morose cop still stood. "I'll be leaving you here because the many years of my life and of my death weigh like old legs on a steep hill. I journey to the basement of the bookstore. A bit of rest . . ."

"Will I see you later?" Joel-Andrew did not understand all the sorrow he felt, but knew he must not insult The Sailor by acting helpful.

"My mates and I will be at Janie's further in the day."

"A glass of white wine," Joel-Andrew murmured.

"Drunk and puling and puking," The Sailor said. "Falling-on-your-face-in-it drunk. That's the only ticket, parson."

The Sailor turned away, and Joel-Andrew ruminated as he passed through the black morning and walked toward town. All about him stood signs and symbols of Point Vestal's renaissance. Discount-gasoline pumps stood like sentinels before the windows of converted service stations; the windows filled with skin magazines, hash pipes, leather, all displayed tastefully on backgrounds of black crape. August Starling's master plan was under way, although Jerome reported none of it in the newspaper. Funeral wreaths enclosed striking new innovations imported from Seattle: dildos, mass-circulation newspapers, love oils, pastel breakfast cereal. These combined with posters displaying breasts, autographed photos of presidents, revivalists, advice columnists, and with filmed documentaries of sex practices starring nine-year-olds.

Joel-Andrew shuddered and made his way to The Fisherman's Café. Even this early in December, a little Christmas tree decorated the café. The tree shone in black spray paint decorated with tiny ebony wreaths. The doughnuts were chocolate with licorice sprinkles.

Joel-Andrew sipped herb tea, listened to townsfolk enthusiastically discuss plans for the tourist industry. Fat men clucked and bald men chortled. Thoughtful men commented on the great changes brought through the efforts of August Starling. Two narcs spied on each other while a couple of fishermen informed the crowd around the coffeepot that August Starling was on another trip to Seattle. When the wall clock read 9:20, Joel-Andrew left for his appointment with Obed.

Chapter 22

THEY MET, THOSE TWO OLD FRIENDS, IN THE DOWNTOWN BASEMENT that was once an opium den. They met in secret because Gerald did not want Obed to blow his cover. They believed they met in private, but were in for a mild surprise.

Joel-Andrew's sandals tap-flapped on the concrete stair. He pushed the creaking door. Black December light gave way to basement darkness. Joel-Andrew struck a match, lit a fat nubbin of candle. Empty cartons, overturned tables, and high Victorian beds cast streaks of shadow. The beds belonged to ghosts who were supposed to haunt the basement, but who now celebrated victory over the Cubans. The basement seemed deserted. Every downtown rat, mouse, cricket, shrew, and garden snake had moved to uptown churches. A sweet smell of opium permeated the walls. It mixed with remembered scents of uncontrolled bladders, suppurating wounds, soy sauce.

Obed's shadow arrived before him. Obed attempted to look jaunty, but he now carried two white whiskers and his fur was ruffled. He brushed rain from behind his ears. Obed scaled a pound or two on the light side. His white tail slouched like an endangered species.

"Your lady friend," Joel-Andrew inquired.

He received no direct answer. Obed's affair was not going well. The undercover work kept him from home and hearth. He ate pickup meals and caught an occasional catnap. His throat felt scratchy, his singing rusted.

It was, Joel-Andrew realized, a lonesome situation. He sat cross legged on the floor, for all the world like a yogi with sprains. A man does not become deeply involved with a cat then dismiss the involvement lightly. Obed licked rain from his paws, purred in competent Chinese. Obed made a couple of moves to restrain himself—decided restraint could go to perdition—and hopped onto Joel-Andrew's right knee.

"It must be difficult for you," Joel-Andrew murmured. "I confess it is difficult for me."

Obed assured him that this, too, would pass. Warm evenings in The Parsonage's basement must still be in the future. Then Obed shivered, looked frightened momentarily, but resumed his oration. A job must be done. Obed's purr faltered. When he switched to Latin his syntax shattered like crumbled flakes of dried catnip.

They sat in silence, like old Shakers regarding God or furniture design. A distant honk sounded, either a Canada goose or a Pierce-Arrow; while faint and faraway, from a store upstairs, Jerome's voice solicited an ad for next week's paper.

Neither Joel-Andrew or Obed could say who first heard desperate and suppressed sobs coming from the back of the room. Someone hid in terror.

"I doubt it is a ghost," Joel-Andrew told Obed. "The ghosts are at the boat basin. They wait for Frank to open Janie's Tavern." Obed hopped from Joel-Andrew's knee and faced the door, prepared for sudden attack or defense.

"We are only a defrocked priest and a cat," Joel-Andrew murmured to the sobbing silence. "We will not harm you."

The sobs burbled.

"We want to help," Joel-Andrew whispered.

"Even"—a voice choked—"even if I'm Irish?"

"Look at it this way," Joel-Andrew said. "Things are not so bad. You *could* be Dutch."

"My hair is a mess." Collette crept from behind the bed. "Don't look at me. I've been hiding for two hours." Her dark hair looked limp in flickering candlelight.

Obed pointed out that his own fur was a mess, and that Joel-Andrew last had a haircut in 1966. Obed pointed out that Collette's problem—whatever it was—had little to do with good grooming.

Obed took a seat, and the three sat around the flickering candle like Campfire Girls telling ghost stories.

"It would help," Collette sniffed apologetically, "if I were not so awfully interested in history." She wadded a well-used hankie. Her blue eyes blinked pale, her dark hair tangled around a face Joel-Andrew thought as pretty as any he had ever seen. Collette's mouth was small though generous, but her cute little Irish chin trembled. The hankie looked exhausted.

"We'll start with the nose," Joel-Andrew told her. "Once the nose is fixed, the rest will get fixed." Joel-Andrew had not owned a handkerchief since he left Rhode Island, but his violin lay protected by remnants of an old bed sheet. He opened the case and passed the cloth to Collette. Obed lowered his gaze discreetly as Collette snerked and snorted. Joel-Andrew twanged a violin string, ran his finger along a string, and the violin sounded a little sneeze.

Collette snerked and giggled, then gave a sob. "It's time jumps," she said. "Worse than that, it's August Starling." The candle cast a golden glow like the gleam of Obed's eyes. "It isn't that I would not like a lover," she admitted, "but who needs it if you've got to be dead to get it?"

From outside the opium den came the chatter of ghosts headed for Janie's Tavern.

". . . so what will Gerald do?" a querulous and ghostly voice asked. "If we kick up a bit, what is he going to do? He can't put us all in the pokey?"

"Yep," answered the disconsolate voice of the morose cop. "He can."

"We must display our unbounded commitment to those bold and higher forms of duty," a Victorian voice said. "We must show truth's sacred flame to Gerald, and with unremitting purpose levy stern effort against the mobsters with the machine guns."

"That might do it," the morose cop said. "If you mean the mobsters who came to town with the real estate lady and that trollop who plays the stock market."

"For indeed," the Victorian voice said, "our efforts of the past century surely earn us some regard." The voice choked with romantic calm. "I have earned a pittance, just enough a pauper's end to save— /And have a spotless suit laid by, to clothe me for the grave . . ."

"That's so beautiful," Janie's voice said. "So sensitive." The ghostly voices and ghostly steps faded into mist and rain. Jerome's voice sounded from the store above. "Some news is about to happen. I'll drop back later about that ad."

"Oh, dear," Joel-Andrew said, "oh, dear, indeed." Then his normal optimism returned. "Perhaps Maggie will provide a calming influence."

Obed grunted. Obed sounded dubious.

"It began so well," Collette explained. "August Starling sent a dozen white roses every other day. I ran out of vases. This morning he sent another dozen . . ." Collette's voice choked.

Obed, with authority gained from working undercover, assured Collette that August Starling was out of town lining up a network of drug pushers.

"And this time," Collette told them, "the box was black, the tissue paper black, and the roses were tied with a black ribbon."

Obed shuddered in alarm. Joel-Andrew's face went white.

"And delivered by a Chinaman," Collette said. "There hasn't been a Chinaman in Point Vestal during the whole twentieth century."

"Time jump," Joel-Andrew guessed.

"Of course," Collette told him, "and if that were the only time jump, it still wouldn't be bearable. There's been others."

In the near distance, Gerald spoke to the Irish cop. The two men stood on the sidewalk above the opium den.

"My inclination," said Gerald, "is to go into Janie's and bang some skulls together. Bust the lot of them."

"Think it through completely," the Irish cop said. "They be good lads for the most part, 'tho the lasses be a bit dubious of virtue."

"Because," Gerald's calm voice said, "I figure *you* can handle Janie's bouncer, the one who looks like a tugboat with arms. I can handle the rest of 'em."

"I can surely drydock the gent," the Irish cop told Gerald. "But be askin' of yourself this, me man. Is it not better to leave 'em howl? Not a lad there has been on a binge in this century."

"They're not attending to business," Gerald ruminated. "Of course, they can't attend to much business if they're warming up the slammer."

"They carry resentments," the Irish cop said. "Give them a fine and skull-busting bout amongst the chippies. Encourage them to profligacy. Press them into becoming degenerate."

"Of course." Gerald's voice filled with admiration. "Being Victorian, they will go crazy; and, being Victorian, when they sober up, they'll have enough guilts to kick them right into line."

"The method has always worked for meself," the Irish cop assured him.

"I'll even stand for a round," Gerald said. "The town gives me a discretionary fund. I'll tell Frank to tap all the sauce that's wanted."

Silence descended, was uninterrupted until Joel-Andrew once more said, "Oh, dear," while Obed muttered something that began with "Oh," but ended elsewhere. Collette's teeth chattered.

"I wish Kune were here," Joel-Andrew confided to Obed. "Between your undercover work, and whatever Kune does at the Starling House, we might avert disaster."

Obed's words carried no encouragement. Obed revealed that Kune took a beating. Kune continually walked in and out of the servants' entrance searching for evidence that would jail August Starling, the search itself, like an intelligent force. Kune had little faith in anything, but he gained faith in himself. Obed's investigation followed similar lines, except that Obed traced Starling's current connections. Gerald and Obed figured Starling could no more stop from eventually ordering a murder than a Dunker could stay away from rivers.

"If evidence is what you need," Collette said between chattering teeth, "I already have it." Collette's pretty face was apologetic. "Because I'm too awfully interested in history. My parents and the PTA said it was a failing."

Obed looked cynical but hopeful.

"Some years ago," Collette explained, ". . . and I was very young at the time . . . I salvaged a carton of nautical charts from an attic . . . you know how kids are."

Obed was fascinated.

"They sat in back of the antique store for years. A week ago, I sorted through them." Collette looked like someone guilty of gossip. "Folded into one of the charts I found a deposition by August Starling's boat crew. It concerns Starling's orders for drowning Chinese. It is legally attested."

"They were copping a plea," Joel-Andrew murmured. "I wonder if it did that boat crew any good."

"It did not." Collette spoke with the certainty of an experienced historian who is frightened gaga. "August Starling bought the judge. That boat crew was ordered hanged in 1887. Starling saved their lives by shanghai to a clipper ship named *Spirit of John Knox*. August Starling made fifty dollars sterling from the deal."

"We must tell Kune immediately," Joel-Andrew said. "It will preserve him from further difficulty."

"Kune is censured," Collette said, "we can't talk to him."

Obed was dumbfounded. Obed started orating about reality. Obed pompously stated that an entire lifetime spent in Point Vestal would not resolve every mystery, or reveal every custom in the universe.

"I fear a connection," Joel-Andrew said. "Did you receive those black-boxed roses before or after the discovery?"

"After." Collette's puzzlement changed to fear. "There was no possible way August Starling could have known . . ."

"There was a way," Joel-Andrew said. "I don't know how, but he knew." Joel-Andrew turned to Obed. "Perhaps August Starling has someone working undercover?"

Obed pompously promised to work that angle.

"Because otherwise," Joel-Andrew said, "the man reads minds."

Analytic Obed supposed that the discovery of the deposition might have something to do with time jumps.

"Tell me about the time jumps," Joel-Andrew said. He was not in despair, but in a state of confusion very like despair.

"Indians," Collette said. "A lot of time jumps are Chinese, but most are Indians. They dress ceremonially. They wear paint and carry war clubs."

Obed pointed out that all living Indians had left Point Vestal to visit relatives.

"I have a theory," Collette explained. "In November, and sometimes in early December, Samuel canters around the circuit." Collette paused to tremble. "Samuel is a powerful preacher."

"You believe he incites the Indians?" Joel-Andrew knew as much about Indians as anyone from Rhode Island, which is to say he was baffled.

"Part of this town's history," Collette said, apologetic as she used the word "history"—"is this: when the first white settlers came, they asked the Indians where they might settle. The Indians pointed to the site of Point Vestal and said, 'Take that. It is cursed. We don't want it.' I think Samuel is being insensitive. He inflames Indian spirits. That, in combination with awful things planned by August Starling, is causing the curse to come alive." Collette's frightened face looked nonetheless thoughtful. Obed mentioned that the idea seemed farfetched.

"Why the curse," Joel-Andrew asked. "Whatever in the world happened?"

"The first explorers were enraptured with the Indians," Collette explained. "They kidnapped Indian women and children. The curse says if such a thing happens again, the sea will rise against the land." Collette's pale lips trembled. "That's not the worst of it. Once the curse begins, it must be contained rapidly. Otherwise it will spread as far as a man can go in a day and a half." Collette was brave and Collette was good, but Collette's shoulders shook with fear. "These days, you could probably go around the world in a day and a half."

"Are there other time jumps?" Joel-Andrew's quiet concern for Collette did not allay Collette's fear.

"Standard things," Collette told him. "Drowned seamen, mutilated Chinese, emaciated and dying children, raped women, battered animals . . . the regular Victorian hoopla." She paused. "A rumor says twenty dancing ducks were seen on North Beach. That's bound to scare anybody a bit."

"We must weave a scheme." Joel-Andrew took charge. "Collette should stay in hiding, but not in this smelly cellar. Obed should tell Gerald of the evidence Collette obtained. I see Kune and Maggie at 2:00. We will lay plans." He turned to Collette. "Hide in the basement of the bookstore. I doubt if even August Starling can make his way past the morose cop and The Sailor and the Irish cop, your grandfather."

"I haven't spoken to my grandfather." Collette was timid, but anger seemed just below the surface. Collette started to get her Irish up.

Obed stated that it was time for one member of their company to mature. Obed barely avoided sarcasm as he wished he had met Collette when she was a little older.

Collette remarked on the historical degeneracy of cats. Collette suggested cute ideas concerning cats and the fall of the Egyptian empire. Collette barely avoided sarcasm wondering if cats were reincarnated dung beetles.

"Your grandfather must feel lonely," Joel-Andrew suggested. "His friends are ghosts. A little kindness might persuade him from Janie's Tavern." Joel-Andrew did not tell Collette that the Irish cop stayed sober, or that he used the tavern as a base from which to watch August Starling.

"It's worth a try." Collette combed her hair with her fingers. Her eyes held a missionary look, dangerously apostolic. "I'll speak to him." She left the opium den and hummed with a touch of zeal.

The candle flickered, guttered, the nub nearly gone. Obed stretched and yawned. Darkness lay heavy with silence, and in the minds of both man and cat lay a dreadful premonition. It seemed to each that this might be their last time alone together. They would forever regret this moment if something were not said as a seal of friendship.

Joel-Andrew leaned down, picked up his violin, and began to play, almost timidly. Obed snuffled, sniffled, equally timid. As the music became firmer, and as the guttering candle faded into dark, Obed began to dance.

Chapter 23

BLACK LIGHT COVERED THE TOWN, AND DECEMBER CHILL SWEPT through grayly falling rain to lay skims of ice. Joel-Andrew headed for Bev's bookstore. The all-seeing tower shrugged at frost on its windows while it peered myopically into streets and minds and hearts of Point Vestal. Then it hesitated.

The all-seeing tower noted the arrival of a network news anchor. The news anchor looked nearly human, her form sylphlike. She slipped into a modest hotel accompanied by her cameraman who sported a forty-dollar haircut; and the bumpity ride into town had made the news anchor horny. No one, except the all-seeing tower, noticed as she undressed and slipped on—or rather, around—her cameraman: managed to salvage one whoop and one yip, then rose to clothe herself and inform the public. No one, except the all-seeing tower, knew of her cameraman's frustrated sobs as he trailed behind, unfulfilled; deserted; feeling himself a sensitive and caring person who had been used, a mere sexual object.

And certainly no one noticed Joel-Andrew, who stood in the bookstore holding earnest conversation with Bev.

"I don't worry about Samuel," Bev confided to Joel-Andrew. "Samuel is an old pro who has ridden circuit for years." Bev found it easy to confide in Joel-Andrew, because Joel-Andrew tended toward optimism. She thought Joel-Andrew slightly inexperienced. However," Bev said, "something is different this year. Samuel sends

155

letters by messenger. He describes wholesale converts. Samuel is also madder'n a Jesuit teaching kindergarten."

"Is he angry at Indians?"

"He is angry at this town," Bev said. "The town rallies behind August Starling who has some fool scheme. This town acts like cats chasing Mikey Daniels's milk truck."

"I figure," Joel-Andrew told Bev, "the ministerial association will sling brimstone against August Starling if a leader prods them. That leader will be Samuel."

"They'll come out in favor of motherhood," Bev said, "because they're realists. Be grateful that you are defrocked. You might have had a congregation in Point Vestal." Bev spoke kindly, and even looked kindly. She wore a conservative green dress of the same color as library book bindings. Her long hair was piled in a thick mass. She looked like Dorothy Lamour playing the role of a schoolteacher. "Point Vestal doesn't *want* a God."

"What would happen if the Lord showed up?"

"The Chamber of Commerce would advertise to tourists."

"The Lord is in the neighborhood," Joel-Andrew said confidently, "and that's not preacherly rhetoric."

"They'll endorse high principles," Bev said of the ministerial association. "Otherwise they'll get tangle-toed in dogma." Bev motioned to a shelf titled "Sermons." "The only way to keep a bookstore alive in this town is to stock what sells in off season," she murmured.

It was, as Joel-Andrew looked carefully, an elegant and unusual bookstore. It was not quite as large as Janie's Tavern, but walls were stacked to the fourteen-foot ceiling. Beside the wide section titled "Sermons" sat a thick section of theology. Beside that stood yards and yards of nineteenth-century histories; and next to the histories—and even mixed in with them—were hundreds of gothic romances. Further along stood leather-bound sets of presidential papers, the confessions of Lola Montez; and a section containing tales by Bill Nye, George Ade, and Josh Billings. Sinclair Lewis and Philip Wylie brooded above the peregrinations of Robert G. Ingersoll, while in the ladies' section, Dorothy Parker's work flashed flaming red beside blues and purples and blacks and grays of Austen, Lowell, Fuller, Dinesen.

"This is the finest collection of theology in the country. The other side of the store," Bev said, "is for tourists." She motioned toward cartoon books about clever cats, diet books, how-to books on sex and skin diving, guides to the ghosts of Point Vestal.

"Instead of denouncing August Starling, let the ministerial association promote kindliness," Joel-Andrew said. "It may run Starling out of town."

"You are a dear man," Bev told him, "but you've placed your brains where the sun is not exactly beam-y . . . I don't mean to be unkind." She was disconcerted. "Oh, my dear man, what do you *think* they've been doing all these years?"

Bev stood beside Joel-Andrew, and suddenly found herself supporting him as he slumped. Joel-Andrew's face drained of color, his gray-green eyes widened with shock. He faltered, stumbled. His violin case bumped a biography of Mary Baker Eddy, his elbow tapped sermons of George Whitefield. Joel-Andrew suffered a revelation, but Bev could not know that. Facts added up, and the scene shifted. Joel-Andrew slumped before the awful power of the Lord's message.

"You are ill," Bev said. "Are you getting enough to eat? Do you have a place to sleep? What in the world is wrong?" Bev, an unmarried woman, had little practice at being motherly. She steered Joel-Andrew to a chair, watched his face slowly regain color.

Joel-Andrew trembled. He finally understood why the Lord sent August Starling back to Point Vestal. August Starling was not a simple sinner. He really *was* a creature from hell.

"I thought August Starling was given a second chance," Joel-Andrew muttered to Bev, "but I'm wrong. *Point Vestal* is being given a second chance." Sounds from the street intruded on the quiet sanctity of the bookstore.

"Is there sex after death?" From the sidewalk an aggressive female voice spoke toward a TV camera. "In a new series titled *American Improbables*, our network brings this reporter to Point Vestal where a question of vital national importance may indeed find an answer . . ." The voice trailed as the news anchor stepped quickly down the sidewalk in search of a "ghost on the street" interview.

Joel-Andrew held the arms of the chair, then rose slowly to his feet. "I have to go to Janie's," he told Bev. Bev smiled cautiously, then patted Joel-Andrew on the head.

"An appointment with Maggie and Kune." Joel-Andrew was awed in the face of his realization. "O Lord," Joel-Andrew prayed silently, "you've got yourself a prophet, but Lord, I'm afraid you've got the wrong boy."

"You are not well." Bev simply could not figure what ailed Joel-Andrew. "However, your color is improving."

"I used to believe I was very good at what I do," Joel-Andrew explained to Bev, "but now I'm seriously afraid. The Lord has given Point Vestal a chance to repent. Otherwise it's Sodom all over again, it's Gomorrah."

"It isn't," Bev told him. Bev looked fondly at high walls filled with books. "When you run a bookstore," she said, "you have a lot of time to read. At least that is true in off season. I promise you it isn't Sodom, and it isn't Gomorrah."

Joel-Andrew stood thinking, his violin keeping its mouth shut as he pondered. He thought about Victorian pretentiousness. He thought of the tackiness of August Starling. "It's Nineveh," Joel-Andrew said finally, with relief. "It's just plain old seedy Nineveh. It can be turned around." Joel-Andrew felt strength returning. "O Lord," he prayed silently, "may Thy humble servant have Your helping hand. I'll try to be the boy You want, Lord."

"Nineveh," Bev agreed. "Samuel could have told you that years ago . . ." She paused. "I told that to Samuel years ago."

"The innocents will yet be spared," Joel-Andrew prophesied, "but move your wives and cattle, children and bookstores to high ground. The sea will storm and the sea will break. The sea will run in the streets of the town."

"It usually does in January," Bev assured him kindly. "When we get a good sou'wester, water blows all the way across the street. I've seen rivulets in the gutters."

"I'm talking about halibut munching sprinkled doughnuts at The Fisherman's Café," Joel-Andrew said. "I'm talking about ling cod admiring themselves in the mirrored ceiling of Janie's Tavern." He stood, sincere, earnest, his toes wiggling in his sandals.

"The least I can do," Bev said, pretending she was not trying to reassure a maniac, "is check the flood clause in my insurance." She touched Joel-Andrew's arm, fearful for him. "You must discuss this with Samuel," she murmured, "when he returns from riding circuit." She looked to the back of the bookstore where three Makah Indians and a Chinaman browsed among publications of the American Bible Society. The Chinaman wore a tunic, baggy drawers, ornately stitched slippers. The Makahs dressed in elaborately painted sealskin.

"Drat it," Bev said, "I don't mind the time jumps, but those Makahs always smudge the pages with their blasted whale oil."

Chapter 24

BLACK LIGHT GLISTENED ALONG BLACK SIDEWALKS AS JOEL-ANDREW headed for Janie's Tavern. His legs carried springiness he did not expect in a man of forty-five. After years of study, of strife; after missionary work in the Haight; after excommunication and fall from the world's grace, Joel-Andrew stood gifted with a situation needing a prophet. He walked thankfully before the Lord.

"One does not speak of such things in Point Vestal," a gentleman's firm voice said as a television camera buzzed. "I daresay such subjects are appropriate in Seattle. However, madam, you are not now in Seattle." The gentleman seemed vaguely familiar, and Joel-Andrew searched his memory. It was the same gentleman who set his watch when Joel-Andrew first heard dying screams from The Sailor.

"I notice a number of children," the news anchor said in a brittle voice. "It follows that sex is not unknown in Point Vestal." The news anchor stood tall, willowy, and manicured. She wore casual attire that did not conceal the fact she was a mammal, but the information seemed secondary to radiated hair spray, armpit sanitizers, breath mints, and foot powders to combat toe jam. The news anchor's hair glowed bluey-brown, her nose functional for prying. "What *does* one talk about in Point Vestal?"

"Coffins and tourists," the gentleman explained. "Point Vestal currently embarks on a renaissance. The first major shipment of coffins arrives within the hour." The gentleman checked his watch.

"I beg leave to be excused. I will add we are a well-known tourist town."

Black ice moved downward from high turrets. Thin rain dampened Joel-Andrew's sandals, and little flicks of frost edged his toenails. He walked quickly. Something exciting erupted from Janie's.

=

As Joel-Andrew arrived, the door slammed open. A drunken logger skidded across the sidewalk and wrapped tidily around a parking meter. The man's blond hair was long, his eyes blue and bloodshot, his blond brows thick. Against his red logging shirt he wore a necklace made from sharp parts of busted chain saws. Ornate Victorian impressions stood like roses on his face where he had connected with Frank's pool cue. He carried the slightly disconcerted look of a man who has been run over by a tugboat.

"Oh, dear," Joel-Andrew said, "whatever in the world did you do to get kicked out?"

"I say '——,'" the logger muttered. "By yumpin' yimminy. And I'd say him again."

"Frank will have none of that," Joel-Andrew explained. "Janie will not allow it."

The logger unwrapped himself from the parking meter. "I can, by gar, get better drunk than these. I'll yard myself 'round the back door. The boys can pass me jars of mousewash." The logger stood. He took off his necklace and wrapped it around his fist. "Missing dis a man just cannot do," he explained kindly to Joel-Andrew. "Dis here is a bigger show dan in d'whole north woods." He staggered around the corner of the building.

"You've come at an interesting time," Maggie told Joel-Andrew as he entered. "I've been waiting quite a few years to watch what happens next." She motioned him to her table, where Kune sat pensive between bruises. Kune looked like a surgical procedure for sleeplessness. Maggie sat serene as a robin on a nest.

"I have wonderful news," Joel-Andrew told them. "Collette has evidence to indict August Starling." Joel-Andrew reminded himself that when a prophet gets too eager, somebody usually ends up

161

eaten by bears. He forced himself to relax, as he stared fascinated at the mirrored ceiling that sparkled and displayed inhabitants of the tavern.

Seven drunken loggers, a dozen drunken fishermen, a large group of merchants drinking the businessman's lunch, one member of the IWW, and the World War I vet sat along the bar. As brightly turning beer signs flashed light and shade across introspective brows, Jerome sat in a corner taking methodical notes. At the far end of the bar a group of flickering ladies wore pastel Victorian gowns and giggled. One hussy in a greenish gown was slippered, her slippers askew. She nearly displayed a stockinged toe. The ladies stood in circles and chatted, but cast shy glances at fishermen and loggers. The fishermen and loggers gave manly belches.

"I have to reckon," a fisherman said studiously, "that all of this-here *means* something. Maybe a turn in the weather."

Victorian gentlemen flickered around pool tables. Victorian gentlemen chatted discreetly with wide-hipped and friendly ladies who were not flickering. The morose cop stood before the jukebox whispering to Janie's bouncer; while, beside her bouncer, Janie stood in silent contemplation of the tavern. A smile kept trying to bend her lips.

"The weather will certainly turn," the World War I vet predicted, giggling. "But not outdoors." The vet had seen bars explode from Hackensack to Marseilles.

The IWW man hummed about solidarity, while casting seductive looks at Victorian ladies. This particular IWW man was no older than ninety. In his day he enjoyed a good reputation as an organizer, a strike boss, a vocalist; although no champ on the picket lines. He was skinny, vibrant, and thought of himself as a good lay.

"I've nothing against ghosts, Indians, darkies, or Irishmen," a chubby merchant said. "Some of my best friends are ghosts."

"Still, they should stay in their place," another merchant pointed out. "If you let them get pushy . . ."

"They might miscegenate," the vet giggled. "Waters down the breeding stock. Mongrelizes the welfare system." The vet seemed happy, but looked for a safe place to hide.

"You got it right," the merchant agreed. "Breed a logger with a Victorian chippie and what's produced will have a tail. It will yodel and swing through trees."

"From a medical standpoint," Kune muttered, "what the gentleman suggests is unlikely." He shivered. "However, unlikely stuff keeps happening." He diagnosed the situation. "The lid will blow off in exactly ten-and-a-half minutes," he said. "The loggers and fishermen and merchants will be asked to leave. The wide-hipped ladies will be asked to stay. The trouble begins when one of the merchants puts a move on Janie." Kune turned away, bored.

"I'm worried," Joel-Andrew told Kune. "Obed says events are strange as you walk in and out of the Starling House. Plus, you have assorted bruises."

". . . got chastised by an irate husband in 1923," Kune said. "His poor wife was innocent, or at least I was. The Starling House dumped me into a bedroom when I walked through the servants' entrance." Kune drew designs in a little puddle of beer. He added up his adventures. ". . . got bitten on the shin by a three-year-old in 1899 . . . turned out to be the same guy who walloped me in '23. Molested by an old maid in '42, got rolled over with knockout drops in 1891—Chinaman sneaked that punch—in 1892 there was a cook at the Starling House who chased people with a meat cleaver. In '36 I intruded on a Communist cell meeting—no violence, but my head still buzzes with dialectics—and in '07 I was assaulted by two guys in drag, their long skirts tripped them up . . . Otherwise,"—Kune was displeased with history, but did not look discouraged—"I feel pretty guilty about causing that trouble in '23. That man's wife was only taking a nap."

"Best thing that could have happened to her," Maggie explained. "She left him, married a Ford salesman. Never regretted it. If that trouble hadn't happened, Frank would never have been born; because, in spite of evidence, Frank actually had a mother." Maggie belched genteelly. "History does not repeat itself," Maggie said, her wisdom unarguable. "But people repeat history." Maggie did not explain, and Kune was so deep in thought he forgot to ask.

". . . attacked by two poodles in '28, by a Great Dane in '61, and by a chow in 1889. Clawed by house cats in '33 and '41 . . . gray and white cats . . . bitten by a parrot in 1947. That place has been a historical zoo." Kune was apologetic. "I ran into August Starling twice. In 1926 he sold me a building lot. Turns out the lot is in a suburb named Miami. I can't figure it out, because he was supposed to be dead at the time. In 1891—when he was supposed to be in the madhouse—he conned me into buying stock in a railroad." Kune seemed perplexed. "I knew the history of that railroad," he muttered. "It was to run from here to Seattle. I knew it was never going to be built, but Starling convinced me."

Beyond the tavern, in the black and icy street, the news anchor and her cameraman entered The Fisherman's Café. The news anchor's face carried suppressed excitement. The cameraman glistened with ice.

"New people in town," Kune murmured.

"No one you want to meet." Joel-Andrew feared for Kune's sanity. If Kune could not bear a little thing like a burger franchise, he was not going to be able to handle television news.

"She's a news anchor." Kune seemed about to sob. "If you've seen one, you've seen 'em all."

"Perhaps," Joel-Andrew suggested delicately, "there will be no news."

"There will be news," Kune checked his watch. "In seven-and-a-half minutes, it explodes. What is this business about Collette obtaining evidence?"

Kune's eyes brightened as Joel-Andrew explained. "There's no statute of limitations on murder," Kune whispered. "Are the Chinamen listed by name?"

"I don't know."

"Maybe we can nail him for conspiracy," Kune said. "As Gerald points out, we have no actual corpses." Kune looked across the room, where Jerome made methodical notes. "There may be supporting evidence in the newspaper morgue." Kune straightened, looking mildly pleased. "I picked up a little something. Back in 1897. A journal in Starling's handwriting. The Victorians were absolutely mad about journals."

"It amounts to a signed confession," Maggie told Joel-Andrew. "In spite of the euphemisms." Maggie looked into the street where a huge truck tiptoed over black ice. The truck was painted ebony. Tasteful gold lettering announced that it belonged to the Laid in

Peace Coffin Company. "August Starling's first shipment of coffins." Maggie belched. "You ain't gonna like 'em, but they are a sight to see."

"If you knew about the journal," Kune said to Maggie, "why in the world didn't you tell me? It would have saved time."

"I know everything," Maggie said. "I know that come Chinese New Year, which is January 23, you will get to meet the very Chinamen who Starling drowned. You will meet Agatha, the woman who Starling killed and danced with. I know why volcanoes lose their tempers. I know cures for typhus, bubonic plague, how to worm kittens. I understand sunspots."

"You might have saved Kune some trouble," Joel-Andrew murmured. "Kune has gone through a lot."

"Don't talk to me about going through a lot," Maggie said. "Do you think it's all that great to know everything?"

"Do you know why science is a failure?" Kune asked. "Do you know why government and baseball are illusions? Can you actually say you understand why we should not give the boot to institutions, systems, legal codes?"

"Child of Grace," Maggie said, "I even know the meaning of life. But I won't tell you. You'd get too excited."

"I love bar talk," Kune confided to Joel-Andrew. Kune's eyes brightened, close to realizing some great principle. To Joel-Andrew, it was nothing new. He had known philosophy professors who discovered thought, and known pimps who came to understand dress codes.

"I see it, of course." Kune muttered, trying to downplay the thrill that pushed him. "Systems always fail because they are systems. Maybe though, within systems, there are people who do not fail." Kune tried to quench his excitement, but his eyes sparkled.

Joel-Andrew gave silent thanks to the Lord. Kune looked convalescent, like a man recovering from simple food poisoning.

A shadow fell across the table. The shadow had a tummy. "We will soon be having a touch of unpleasantness," Frank whispered. Frank stood above Kune, his beard cringing in distaste. "You are to blame," he told Kune. "Gerald will hear of it."

Kune no longer resembled an illness. He looked optimistic. "I have spent several intimate moments with your mother." He checked his watch. "Put that in your report to Gerald. And, you have exactly two minutes before this dump busts like a ruptured appendix."

"You see!" Frank huffed and puffed like a man inflating life rafts. "He knows. That means he's causing it." Frank's beard underwent convolutions.

The Sailor entered the tavern. "Better tend to your new customer," Maggie said. The Sailor brushed speckles of ice from his black beard. He sensed the tension in Janie's Tavern. The Sailor grinned.

"How could August Starling be at the Starling House during times when he was supposed to be dead or in the madhouse. That is one I really don't understand." Kune watched as Frank retreated to his position of power behind the bar.

"August Starling is unusual." Maggie belched, admired The Sailor. "I've had my share of men," she sighed, "but I wouldn't mind another share."

"Janie will not allow such talk," Joel-Andrew cautioned her. To Kune, he said, "August Starling really *is* hell-born. I was given a revelation. We may expect him to exhibit some strange powers."

"There isn't a redheaded Presbyterian, dead or alive," Maggie began. ". . . whoops!" she finished. "Play ball!"

Maggie quieted, then cheered, as she admired the flying figure of a merchant caroming off a beer sign, a chandelier, a pool table, and a spittoon before skidding to a stop beside the front door. The merchant was a portly fellow, but his tum-tum seemed made mostly of muscle. He contemplated his reflection in the spittoon, wrinkled his nose, adjusted his tie. He brushed back well groomed hair, and examined his nails. "OK, kiddies," he said to no one in particular, "we're playing hardball." He stood, bent over, began wrenching a barstool from its base.

"Drat it," Maggie said, "we got so busy talking, we missed the first pitch."

No bar fight is especially pretty, but one with ghosts is generally interesting. We may also remember that everyone was an old hand, experienced, wise as cats. The playing field cleared as wide-hipped and generous ladies dove for the women's can, where the WWI vet and the IWW man were already hiding. Jerome stuck a little "Pressbox" sign on his double-ender hat, and withdrew farther into his corner. Flickering Victorian ladies drifted gently upward to the balcony, a bleacher position favorable for delicate flinging of saltcellars, popcorn, beer pitchers, and furniture. Flickering Victorian gentlemen removed jackets, while smiling to each other with narrow and dutiful lips. They armed with pool cues, as Jamie's bouncer began festivities by taking first at bat. He tagged a bohunk logger for a three-bagger. The logger sailed in a little looper, getting down beneath Frank's nose, then skidding along the bar. Frank never got a glove on him. A Victorian gentleman stepped forward. He doubled a wop fisherman off the wall. The score stood 1 and 0 as the merchants came to bat.

"I deeply regret that the Irish cop is missing this," Maggie said, "the dear man will be all broken up." A Victorian gentleman flickered past. He woo-wooed and woe-woed and sailed over the jukebox. "They're going for the long ball," Maggie groaned. "Babe Ruth was the ruination of this game."

"So it follows," Kune said to Joel-Andrew, "that if all systems are certain to fail, a man must rise above systems."

"You got it," Joel-Andrew told him.

"Is that what you do?" Kune asked. "Do you try to rise above systems?"

"I follow the Lord," Joel-Andrew told him. "That can become a system, but when it does, it fails. That failure is why Point Vestal has eighteen churches, no God, and exports drugs."

"Tinker to Evers to Chance," Maggie said admiringly. "You don't see a play like that once every fifty years. I mean, you *hear* about them, but you don't actually *see* 'em."

The merchants were getting shut out. Janie's bouncer coldcocked them, fielded them to The Sailor who added finishing touches, then fielded them into the street. Joel-Andrew looked through the window. On the sidewalks the morose cop stacked merchants in a tidy and growing pile. The morose cop looked like a batboy sorting equipment.

"So it follows," Kune said, "that if a man can't function within a system, that does not mean the man is necessarily perverse or guilty or awful."

"It may mean just the opposite," Joel-Andrew assured him.

"I like feeling this way," Kune murmured. Kune no longer looked diseased. He did not carry the sickly pallor of a health freak, nor did he look organic.

". . . threw a bean ball," Maggie said. "That's what did it." Maggie looked toward the center of the bar, where the teams bashed each other with careful regard to good sportsmanship. The loggers bit ears, the fishermen gouged eyes, and the Victorians went for the groin. Janie's bouncer stood above the pile and chose his pitches carefully. It was obvious that the bouncer would go the whole nine innings. The Sailor yelled as loudly as the fans, and the pile on the sidewalk grew.

"I like the way Janie handles her cheering section," Maggie pointed out. "You'll notice not a single chippie has thrown hatpins or busted glass."

"Oh, dear," Joel-Andrew said, "we've made the evening news." The news anchor and her cameraman ran from The Fisherman's Café. The pile on the sidewalk rose. The morose cop proved good at stacking. From the balcony, cheering Victorian ladies lent an air of gaiety to the proceedings. The news anchor yammered into her mike. Her cameraman shot in color; and so soon all the world saw flickering pastel gowns, starchy white shirtfronts, random stacks of glittery teeth, a cacophony of bruises, bloodstains, limbs at peculiar angles. Joel-Andrew gasped as Frank flew by, and gasped again as Frank was added to the pile. Frank wore his morning coat and carried his ornately carved pool cue. His eyes fluttered as he sat confusedly on top of the pile. Frank tried to look dutiful.

"That's the old ball game," Maggie said. "What's really interesting is what happens next." She pointed to the back of the tavern, back toward the ladies' can where the IWW man emerged. The IWW man hollered that it was time to *organize*. It was time for the Victorian ghosts to hold a general strike.

Chapter 25

THE FIRST RUMBLINGS OF TROUBLE CAME ON HEELS OF THE EVENING news. The news anchor used sarcasm and jollity. Her cameraman recorded the pile of merchants, loggers and fishermen; but the news anchor did not point out that it was a carefully placed pile only little larger than a haystack. The camera caught Frank at a clear disadvantage (Frank is unaccustomed to looking goofy), and nasty editing attended footage shot at The Fisherman's Café.

The network played Point Vestal for laughs. With such terrible publicity, next year's tourist season seemed knocked into a cockaded hat. When the Victorians hoisted a big sign reading "Strike Headquarters" across the front of Janie's Tavern, the camera attended the festivity.

Our mayor and city council went into extraordinary session, and once again raised sewage rates. A town meeting took place at The Fisherman's Café. At Janie's Tavern a mob of celebrating ghosts got rid of a century's worth of frustrations. The wide-hipped and generous ladies certainly did not leave; nor did the WWI vet or the man from the IWW. There was not only a rift between the living and the dead of Point Vestal; there was a rift between some of the living and the living. When the Suffragettes, to a woman, marched into the tavern and joined the strike, the whole town reeled. When Bev crossed the street to join the strike, the town reeled further.

=

"Because," Bev explains, as she sits at the table in The Fisherman's Café while we discuss the writing of our history, "I had no one to consult." She touches Samuel's hand. "That was the second town meeting in less than three months. I wanted to stay sane."

Frank sniffs and snuzzles. Mikey Daniels's milk truck stumbles past. Today the doughnuts are yellow with little sprinkles of purple, like promises of springtime crocuses. The doughnuts do not cheer us. If this book gets all the way written, and we remain friends, we'll gain deeper understanding of the word "miracle."

"We have to be methodical," Jerome suggests. "We should specify, back there as the strike began, exactly what everyone did. Otherwise the situation gets confused."

"Makes sense," Frank says. "Samuel rode circuit, Bev whooped it up at the tavern with the Suffragettes—"

"I did not whoop, and I left for work on time the following morning." Bev avoids a scrap that looks like a sure thing, then continues, "Collette hid in the basement of the bookstore. The Irish cop remained on stakeout. Jerome dashed between town meeting and tavern, covering the story. Obed lurked undercover. He watched a crew unload the truck containing coffins. The Sailor kept order at the tavern. Maggie instructed The Sailor. Gerald brooded in the LaSalle. Gerald thought of busting the tavern, the town meeting, and the city council. Gerald about had a bellyfull of the whole business. Frank whimpered in the back of The Fisherman's Café—"

"I did *not* whimper," Frank says. "I may have trembled a bit, because I knew August Starling would hurry back to town after he saw that news broadcast."

Jerome consults his voluminous notes. "F. (whimpering)," he reads with satisfaction. He flips a page. "Joel-Andrew and Kune were busy getting kicked out of town meeting . . ."

Samuel hunches above his coffee cup and broods. His broadcloth suit sighs at the elbows. "I used to understand the nature of Evil," he mutters. "Before August Starling."

"I never believed it was showy or spectacular." Bev is broody as Samuel. "I figured Evil was the absence of Good."

"We're still missing something," Samuel mutters.

". . . in addition," Jerome continues, "the gunmen with the limo guarded the shipment of coffins. The real estate lady planned a tasteful series of condos. The condos were to be built on the saltwater swamp, as soon as the Department of Interior could eliminate the wildlife. The stock market lady put together a prospectus. She planned a development company that would eventually turn the entire county into a series of tasteful cemeteries." Jerome looks up from his pages. "That takes care of everyone in town."

Samuel gnashes his teeth. Bev sneers. Collette trembles.

"Let us resume," Jerome says, his voice morbid. "Let us pick up Joel-Andrew and Kune just after they got kicked out of town meeting."

=

As Joel-Andrew and Kune left Janie's Tavern after getting kicked out of town meeting, bright lights from The Fisherman's Café slid across black ice. Ice covered the street. Wind had turned to light breeze, but the breeze carried mist that rapidly froze on the men. Within two blocks, their clothes crackled. They stepped carefully over ice and prepared for the long walk back to the warm basement of The Parsonage. A frightened figure huddled in a doorway. It might have been a woman.

"In a way," Joel-Andrew said, "my task is easier. I no longer have to save August Starling, only defeat him. The force of Evil has picked the most evil man in Point Vestal history; and the man and force are becoming one. I don't think they have completely come together yet."

"You may enjoy some help in fighting," Kune muttered, then relapsed into thought.

"What I do not understand," Joel-Andrew said, "is why Starling acts infantile. Starling is very old. He is skilled in old, old knowledge."

From the darkness on the Strait a sea lion hiccupped. Muffled sounds of powerful engines whispered above the tide. A voice, faint above engines, chirped. A second voice intoned.

"August Starling, come back to town," Kune said. "I wonder who is with him." Kune paused, listened as the engines headed for the boat basin. "Starling has hired his own preacher," Kune diagnosed, "because the ministerial association is not about to start selling indulgences."

"And the customers are not about to start buying them. Not if I can help it." Joel-Andrew hitched his violin higher on his shoulder. "Nineveh," he said, but he was not talking to Kune.

"I don't know anything about Nineveh," Kune admitted "but I understand other things. My *world* may be banal, but *I* don't have to be." In the darkness Kune's footsteps sounded like scattered raindrops. ". . . don't give a popcorn poot for revolution," he confided secretly, "but rebellion suits me fine as fine." Scattered lights from the boat basin reached toward low overcast, but were dimmer than they should be. Kune stared. "The skyline changed," he said. "I can't quite say how. Maybe The Parsonage has moved."

Joel-Andrew understood that he was about to be confronted by Evil. "Lord," he prayed silently, "I have to make a start sometime. Be with me, Lord." He felt the energy of the Lord, vast and loving, surround him.

From the boat basin, red light lay like red fog. Joel-Andrew could see it and was surprised Kune could not. Then he told himself no—Kune could not see it because Kune did not expect to see it. The light was every bit as pervading as fog, but dark as night. The light, and the darkness from the Strait, meshed so completely that the unsuspecting mind would believe red was black, or black, red.

". . . unloading something," Kune muttered. "Can't be drugs—those go to Seattle. Can't be anything good. Maybe I'd better confront Starling." His voice sounded apologetic. "You seem a little bit innocent."

"You do not understand the reasons for innocence." Joel-Andrew knew it was useless to explain the situation, for it was really Kune who was innocent. Joel-Andrew nearly looked forward to a confrontation with August Starling. August Starling, who was the essence of true Evil, understood the conditions and terms, the jargon, the background, and the traditions of what was coming down. There were certain things Kune could not understand because Kune was a child of the twentieth century. He had the twentieth century's weird faith in logic and process.

Joel-Andrew held himself in careful control. If he exercised too much power, August Starling would simply flee. That would not turn Point Vestal around. "I'll start by giving Starling a mild burn," he said to Kune.

The red light faltered, ran through a spectrum of reds, pinks, auburns; then to purples and blues, finally to green, then blushed a tinge of peach, turned tangerine. The light blushed golden, then became silver as burnished hubcaps. As the light became contained but celestial, the red was defeated. August Starling and his hired preacher stood on the pier, overflooded with light, like actors caught between scenes.

"Fifteen-love," Kune whispered. "You've got him nailed. As long as we stand in this darkness, he can't tell who we are."

"He knows." Joel-Andrew watched Starling, and he watched the preacher who was Starling's hired gun. Celestial light framed Starling, handcuffed his movements, pinioned him like a black moth mounted against black ice on the pier. Starling's face—which might have reflected terror—was bland, even bored. Only the preacher registered surprise. Starling made an attempt to move. The light softened. Joel-Andrew released him.

"My clerical friend." August Starling chirped, and his hand covered his crotch. Red light seeped across the pier, but was shoved backward. August Starling looked wizened, old, bent. Then he looked a couple of years younger.

Cages stood stacked on the pier. They contained birds and beasts; rats, mice, crows, ravens, small dogs, cats, squirrels, rabbits. A goat stood tethered on the boat's deck. The creatures' eyes glowed redly. They scampered, snarled, moaned. August Starling's preacher did not look like Samuel, but looked like he was *trying* to look like Samuel. He stood tall, in broadcloth, and bearded. His eyes held no wisdom, although they were steady as sealed beams. His teeth gleamed large and regular. His face looked like the front end of a '47 Buick.

"Experimental lab?" Kune whispered. Kune was awestruck. "Those animals are scary."

A bird screamed, the scream mechanical, like a movie imitation of a lost soul. The bird perched ruffled, rumpled, black, with a blood-red bill and blood-red feet. A dark red squirrel foamed at the mouth, spit like a cat. The tethered goat nickered, and accomplished an obscene little dance.

"Give it up," Joel-Andrew said to August Starling. "Admit you are whipped. Save us all some trouble."

August Starling began to explain. As a loyal—possibly noble—son of Point Vestal, he cared about the amusement of children. August Starling protested that he supported the school system, that a petting zoo was a necessary part of any school system; and it therefore followed that a man in his position could only be accused of beneficence when making a contribution in behalf of children . . .

"Why are you chirping?" Joel-Andrew asked. "The hell-born carry a lot of dark knowledge. Are you a fake?"

"I'm a realist," Starling said. "You're confused. If you take your confused head from the sand and look around you, you'll know why I chirp."

"He has a point," Kune muttered. "Television news anchors," he explained.

"I like your kid," Starling said to Joel-Andrew about Kune. "I chirp because chirps are mindless. Remember, this is the twentieth century."

Joel-Andrew almost understood, but dared not show he was the least confused. "Maybe so," Joel-Andrew said, "but between us we can play with older rules." Joel-Andrew pointed a finger at the cages. A bird screamed, high wailing, a flurry of feathers. Bird and cage imploded, turning into a red and disappearing hole in the night. A rabbit wailed, then vanished.

"That's a scruffy-looking lot of demons," Joel-Andrew said. "Scabby. That act wouldn't even play in San Francisco."

"They actually *came* from San Francisco," August Starling admitted. "I have my own timetable. Sometimes you have to work with what you can get." August Starling no longer chirped.

"This town has enough demons of its own," Joel-Andrew said. "You'll understand why I won't allow imports." A cage disappeared. A bird, very much like a vulture, rose on night wings. It tumbled, squalling, gasping, torn, and fell—a dark bundle of feathers—back to the pier. It disappeared.

"If that is how it must be," August Starling said, and his voice was pleasant, "I'll work with the local commodity. Meanwhile we may as well both enjoy this." He turned to the cages, flicked his hand—screams of anguish—torment—squalls of horror. Suffering lived like flame in the light, lived lie the quick heat of nitro beneath the darkness of sky and Strait. The cages and the beasts became darkness, and then the darkness fled on the scream of the goat.

"Why do you keep it up?" Joel-Andrew asked. "Century after century. Sooner or later you always lose."

"I lose battles, but I win the war," August Starling's voice sounded almost cordial. "Because I always win the aftermath. The powers in my present incarnation have not yet come to full term."

"I doubt they'll come to term," Joel-Andrew told him. "Not if you continue to act so silly."

"You've learned nothing from history," Starling said. "When my powers do come to full term, I trust you will still be in the neighborhood."

"Count on it," Joel-Andrew told him. He turned to Kune. "The problem with Evil," he explained, "is that it tries to haul you down to its level. Don't make the mistake of taking August Starling personal."

"I'm a physician," Kune muttered, "and unless there is a neurological explanation for this, I'm a physician in trouble." In the distance, but not far off, familiar bells began to chime. Kune shook his head. "It's The Parsonage. Point Vestal is a very strange place."

"No different from Seattle," Joel-Andrew reminded him. "You told me that yourself."

"We can have but few secrets from each other," August Starling said to Joel-Andrew. "I suppose you know why I chose Point Vestal?"

"Because you figure it's a pushover," Joel-Andrew said. "Plus, of course, there's the tourist business. No need to waste strength in Seattle if you can get the marks to come to you."

"I wish Maggie were here," Kune muttered. "It is an absolute shame she is missing this."

August Starling's preacher harrumphed, and steepled his hands. "Indulgences," he said, as if explaining. "Missionaries to the Vatican. Crusades against the Turk. Conversion of the wily Jew. Fathers to— and keepers of—the darker races."

"You did a capable job on that one," Joel-Andrew said to August Starling. "Are you going to snuff it, or shall I?"

"Be my guest," August Starling said, "but be warned it's not a demon."

The energy of love projected from Joel-Andrew. Celestial light did not grow, but became more focused. Joel-Andrew gasped. Somewhere inside the preacher he felt the vacuum that once held a soul.

"You cut a deal with him," Joel-Andrew said to August Starling. "Which means I can doubtless set him free."

August Starling once more looked boylike. He stood young, supple, his narrow shoulders nicely padded in his expensive business suit. "No deal," he said. "This gentleman schooled himself." August Starling looked like a teacher taking pride in a prize student. "His business is called an 'electronic ministry.' You may have received some mailings . . ."

"The sacred cause," the preacher intoned. "Avoid inheritance taxes. We convert stocks, bonds, real estate on behalf of the heathen. Do not send trading stamps, discount grocery coupons; there is a twenty-dollar charge on all returned checks. We welcome credit cards."

Kune was relieved. "It's only a TV preacher."

August Starling looked at his preacher, then at Kune, then at Joel-Andrew. "For dependability," he said dryly to Joel-Andrew, "I'll take my boy over yours."

"He's not my boy," Joel-Andrew said. "He can handle himself. Meanwhile, I'll see you in court." Joel-Andrew released the celestial light. Darkness came so quickly, it was blinding. "Let's walk out of here," Joel-Andrew told Kune. "If you can't see, take my hand."

Heavy mist frosted the ground with black ice. Weeds and shrubs along the roadside made the surroundings like little landscapes, little towns. Kune shivered and trembled, his long blond hair stiff with ice.

"We'll get to The Parsonage," Joel-Andrew murmured. "We'll get you warm."

"I've walked in every kind of weather. I'm not trembling from the cold." Kune tried to force a grin. "This stuff is not very scientific."

"Science is still in its infancy," Joel-Andrew explained. "It will remain so until it stops denying evidence."

Kune trudged, deep in thought. "Denying evidence," he said, "is that what I've been doing?"

"When your lady friend, Shirley, became ill, and you could not help her, I expect you denied everything." Joel-Andrew's heart was glad. It was nearly worth the tussle with August Starling if Kune emerged from his self-imposed darkness. "And, yes," Joel-Andrew said, "you've been trained to deny evidence. If you cannot duplicate phenomena in a lab, you're trained to deny it exists." Bells from The Parsonage tinkled across the ice. The bells sounded joyous and a little deranged.

"Then miracles may exist?" Kune's voice was reluctant, but he obviously strove for an open mind.

"The Parsonage seems to be over that way," Joel-Andrew said, and pointed in the general direction of August Starling's burger franchise. He took Kune's elbow. The two men stepped gingerly over water-slick ice. "Miracles are only sprinkles on the doughnuts. The important thing is that Good and Evil exist. You just met one incarnation of evil."

"Then August Starling really isn't August Starling? August Starling is Evil in the shape of August Starling?"

"It is almost that simple," Joel-Andrew told him. Through freezing mist, blanketing clouds, tenuous footing, Joel-Andrew steered Kune toward the sound of bells. When nearly at the doorway of The Parsonage, they realized that something peculiar had been going on.

Kune giggled. Gurked. Snorted. "Oh, my," he said, "we seem to be short a burger franchise."

The all-seeing tower rose into the ice-ridden night, and The Parsonage sat squarely on the lot once occupied by the burger franchise. Both men paused.

"I see how it was done," Kune murmured, "but where did the burger building go?" He peered into the darkness. From the susurrous waters of the Strait came an interrupted murmur, as cold wavelets broke in slightly different patterns. "Dumped it in the Strait," Kune giggled. "The Parsonage sure had its dander up."

Joel-Andrew had not figured on a major confrontation just yet. "It must have looked like hopscotch," he murmured.

And, no doubt, it *had* looked like hopscotch. The Parsonage set its lot (150 x 200 feet, one maple, three apples, a pear and two cherries) on the lot of the burger franchise. The burger franchise was forced to move over. The Parsonage moved again. The burger franchise moved. Joel-Andrew figured The Parsonage must have moved four or five times before it finally got the burger franchise nudged into the Strait.

Chapter 26

GRAY-FINGERED DAWNS FOLLOWED GRAY-FINGERED DAWNS. TIME came and went, tick-tocking, sometimes tock-tocking. Winds of evil blew through our streets. Joel-Andrew visited members of the ministerial association and tried to persuade them to confront August Starling. The ministerial association also felt dark winds, but could make no decisions. The IWW man organized his strike, and the Victorians picketed. Joel-Andrew stood alone.

On the morning after the big blowout at Janie's Tavern, Gerald had a crawful, and rousted the Victorians from the tavern. The all-seeing tower watched as Gerald herded rumpled Victorians into the custody of The Parsonage. The Victorians were hung over, guilt ridden; and articles of clothing raggled and taggled in rumpled memory of an orgy that would supply copy for every pulpit in Point Vestal—and that copy would be good for an extra long month of sermons. The sermons were doubtless delivered, but time was about to become crisscross, so none of us remember.

On the Strait, nothing could be seen, except, rising above the waves, a forlorn plastic sign depicting a giggly hamburger. When the IWW man tacked the "Strike Headquarters" sign across the front of The Parsonage, The Parsonage felt proud.

And the all-seeing tower—knowing as it did, the state of all minds and hearts—understood that Gerald had made a wise move. Enough ghostly preachers walked stairs and corridors of The Parsonage to ensure that the Victorians would keep their braces snapped. It would be a cinch for Gerald to control the crew in The Parsonage. Plus, of course, The Sailor and the morose cop worked with Gerald, sort of.

Controlling the rest of the town proved less easy. The merchants' association, the Chamber of Commerce, the mayor and city council stonewalled. They knew they were rued, whooed, screwed, and tattooed. If the ghosts stayed on strike, everybody could kiss a tourist season on the hem of its departing skirt. In its awful need, the town turned to the man of the hour—and Starling, as surefooted as a mouse on Swiss cheese—scampered toward the pinnacle of his grand scheme. He promised to lead Point Vestal to its inevitable destiny—the center of the map.

"For indeed," August Starling explained with sweet reason, "when we combine blessed immortality with indulgences and Victorian charm, the town could hardly become less than the center of the map." August Starling opened negotiations with the strikers. He kept six Sicilians with their machine guns in the background.

Meanwhile, Joel-Andrew made quiet moves. He respectfully confronted the mayor and members of city council. He contacted Jerome, and issued a challenge to open debate with August Starling. He preached before The Fisherman's Café careful to stay on rational grounds. Perhaps he was too conservative. Recall, though, that Joel-Andrew had experienced enough busts on the charge of being a fruitcake.

Starling's hired preacher, the Reverend Thaddeus Goodman (Goody) Friendship, spoke of the sin-absolving power of cash. Joel-Andrew challenged Goody to a preach-in; no holds barred. Goody yawned. Joel-Andrew spoke of love and life. Goody responded with "life everlasting." The chess game, with the soul of Point Vestal as prize, opened beneath those cold, and icy, and gray-fingered dawns. The all-seeing tower watched.

"Because," Joel-Andrew explained to Kune on a rare evening in the basement of The Parsonage, "the all-seeing tower is arriving at a higher state of grace. Are you familiar with the philosophic idea of the 'Witness?'"

"They come to the doorway of The Parsonage sometimes," Kune murmured. "I have tracts. But tracts or not, I happen to know Point Vestal is not the whole world. I am taking my evidence to

Seattle. I'll talk to attorney generals and the CIA, FBI, Department of Immigration, plus district attorneys. I'm going to contact every legalized legbreaker until one of them takes action against August Starling. Maybe I can get the system to work." Kune's face seemed far more relaxed in the dusty light of the basement.

"A Witness," Joel-Andrew murmured, "would never give out tracts." Then Joel-Andrew explained that a true Witness watched, and said nothing. "The whole idea," Joel-Andrew explained, "is that when an immoral man knows he is watched, he will accuse *himself* and clean up his act. All a Witness has to do is watch. The minute the Witness says anything, the effect is spoiled."

=

Days foundered and stumbled. Time lay like a landscape above which the all-seeing tower peered. The all-seeing tower watched Samuel canter back into town. It watched Samuel's wrath, as Samuel consulted with Bev and learned of recent events. When time jumps increased, and our streets filled momentarily with Indians and Chinamen, the all-seeing tower stood mute. It watched children stand puzzled and fearful before darkly lighted Christmas trees. It watched the ministerial association form ranks behind Samuel. It watched the Reverend Thaddeus Goodman (Goody) Friendship cruise Main Street like a '47 Buick.

The all-seeing tower watched Collette—attended by the Irish cop—as she left the bookstore basement and once more opened her antique store. The Irish cop threw away boxes of dead roses while Collette still shivered. August Starling had mentioned, often enough, that his wife would soon join him from Boston.

Kune prepared to depart for Seattle. His long hair flowed washed and glowing. He confided to Joel-Andrew that he felt few fears and no expectations. At the same time, he had to give the system a chance. When Kune departed for Seattle, he was shadowed by a narc, who was shadowed by another narc. The all-seeing tower watched.

Time flowed, horsed around, turned back on itself. Sometimes the clock at The Fisherman's Café became confused. The tide tables stuttered quietly among their pages, and even clams on the beach were befuddled. Sea gulls avoided the town, but the number of ducks increased in the saltwater swamp. Orca and gray whales cruised the Strait. Their rolling backs, their shearwater fins, and the spouts of the grays became sights as familiar as the black and icy streets. Dolphins, seals, sea lions snorted, burped, glugged. The beasts did not approach the town, but seemed, themselves, to be Witnesses. The situation did not really get loathsome until two days before Christmas.

=

"August Starling's actions make no sense." Joel-Andrew sat among Christmas decorations in Janie's Tavern as he talked to Maggie. Maggie looked into black streets. A parade of horse drawn ebony hearses tiptoed past, gorgeously decorated in red, white, and blue bunting. Spans of perfectly matched black horses bowed their heads beneath icy rain and the weight of the hearses.

"This is opening day of the August Starling Layaway Plan," Maggie said. "At his new business address. Will you be joining the cheering boosters?"

"Count on it," Joel-Andrew said. "I'm going to go one-on-one with a TV preacher who's playing like he's John the Baptist." Joel-Andrew cultivated calm, because wrath wasn't going to make it with this particular house. "The Reverend Thaddeus Goodman Friendship has been passing gas," Joel-Andrew told Maggie. "He says a savior is headed for Point Vestal. You would think a savior would be scheduled to show up at Christmas. Goody insists that everyone repent."

"August Starling has a timetable," Maggie said. She looked down the nearly barren bar. Happy hour was no longer held at Janie's Tavern. Three drunken loggers, two drunken fishermen, and one member of the Loyal Order of Beagles brooded, sad and silent. Frank's tummy seemed smaller, and his whiskers looked like wilting ferns. Black lights replaced the once colorful neon, and the jukebox played a dirge. Joel-Andrew no longer had a job. He owned fourteen dollars and eighty-three cents, plus a nearly full jar of peanut butter. He did not think of himself as wealthy, but he was in pretty good shape.

"You might help your cause," Maggie said, "by asking our crowd a simple question. If they are so blamed *right*, then why aren't they happy?" Maggie stared dismally at steamy horse droppings sizzling on the icy street. "What's to be repented?"

"People spend money on food and shelter," Joel-Andrew explained. "Money that should go into the tourist business."

"Don't sit there trying to pass foolishness off on your elders."— Maggie sipped white wine, belched genteelly—"or your betters."

"It's a problem I have," Joel-Andrew admitted. "When things get crucial, I kind of hide behind words. I've been doing it since my ministry in San Francisco." Joel-Andrew looked at Maggie and responded to her honesty. "The Lord trusts me," he said, "and I'm scared silly of my anger. If my anger ever gets loose, and starts to wield the Lord's power . . ." Joel-Andrew looked toward The Fisherman's Café. In darkly lighted windows, a large poster offered a free funeral to the first volunteer to cast off this earthly veil for purposes of advertising. No one had yet stepped forward, but the Chamber of Commerce was optimistic. "You see what I mean," Joel-Andrew said.

"Use your mother wit," Maggie said. "Focus only on Starling. The reason August Starling is not bringing his messiah to town on Christmas is because people stay home on Christmas. They don't go touristing. August Starling has not begun to sell anything, except in Point Vestal."

"I'm not losing the battle yet," Joel-Andrew told her. "But I'm not winning, either." He sighed, his fatigue both great and evident. "In the old days, a prophet knew exactly what to do. He rode into town yelling 'Repent.' He preached in the streets. He promised destruction before the winds of heaven. But now, Goody plays the act. Plus, everybody has ignored stuff like that for centuries."

"You're not winning because you miss motives," Maggie explained. "The funeral business will turn reams of cash, but it's really a cover for the drug trade."

"I'm not missing that. Starling wants Point Vestal, and he's not far from getting it." Joel-Andrew pointed toward Frank, toward the drunken loggers and fishermen and the man from the Beagles. "The whole town deals drugs by default. If I take that message out there, I'll whip myself. If I even think about it too long, I'll fall into wrath and misuse power. Today I'm going to make August Starling take a fall. That may stave off a bad confrontation." Joel-Andrew looked sadly at the poster. The poster began: "Point Vestal Wants You," and it promised a funeral heretofore reserved for royalty. "You can speak truth to power," Joel-Andrew explained, "but when you speak truth to weakness, weakness gets mad and queasy. It accuses you of its own insecurity."

=

Sometimes time waffled. Sometimes a day passed in normal manner. On other days it remained noon—or three o'clock— forever. Some Tuesdays would fade into night, and when the black and icy day returned it was still Tuesday. On that 23rd of December, 1973—when August Starling opened for business, and when the forces of Good and Evil first joined: and Joel-Andrew and Obed got in a few licks—it seemed the day would never end.

When Gerald herded impeccably dressed Victorians toward downtown, it was about 11:30 AM. The Victorians were accompanied by Suffragettes carrying strike signs painted in red. The man from the IWW marched tall and proud, although weaponless, because Gerald made him give up his grub hoe handle.

The Victorians remained defensive after their debauch, which accounts for steely gazes, proper stances, their air of detachment, their dutiful calm. That they held the whip hand in strike negotiations did not hurt their detachment, either. When the Victorians passed the drowned burger franchise, they gave little sniffs of scorn. At their backs, and higher up the hill, the pharmaceutical company raised turrets into a black sky.

To the Victorians, Point Vestal had transformed. The pinks, purples, blues, and greens of former days were painted away. Storefronts gleamed black and glossy, like wet hides of matched horses pulling hearses. Black satin drapes hugged merchandise displayed upon black velvet: funerary urns, stitched hankies reading "farewell," ebony-tinted condoms, teddy bears with the very darkest fur, and with mournful faces.

August Starling stood before his renovated commercial building, surrounded by the GAR, the Martha Washington Brigade, the

Mothers Against Transgression and Sensuality (MATS). August Starling's building rose darkly. In front of the building, horses stamped, steamed, stood in their traces before gorgeous hearses. The black horses wore black saddle blankets with gold stitching—"August Starling Enterprises," "Point Vestal Immortality Company"—and the horses snorted, pawed, and sneezed foam.

"Bit of a show, eh, mate," The Sailor whispered to the morose cop. "But a sight too gay for an honest sailor." The Sailor, recovered from his hangover, thirsted for another.

"It isn't a bit gay," the morose cop said. "It's August Starling at his worst."

In the modest hotel beside the building, black wicker furniture stood on blood-red carpet. Lace twirled phantasmic, brocade positive as a commandment.

"The August Starling layaway plan," the morose cop said. "I expect we'll all be laid away before the day is out."

"The upper chambers," The Sailor whispered, "are filled with Chinese and Indians. The bloody heathen are curious."

"In Point Vestal you never look above the first story of any building," the morose cop said. "Chinese and Indians are there?"

"And whales upon the Strait." The Sailor glanced at the blackened front of Janie's Tavern. "But for a bit of coin . . ."

"I could use a drink," the morose cop admitted.

August Starling stood before his renovated building. He was young, optimistic, darkly handsome; like a friendly lawyer, or a solicitous used car salesman. He chirped, addressing people as "neighbor," "friend," "colleague," "pard," and "bro." At his right hand, Goody Friendship intoned, "We pray for the heathen." Goody turned from prayer to display lapel buttons proclaiming Point Vestal as the new Eden.

"Starling passes it around that The Parsonage did him a favor when it drowned his burger place," the morose cop said. "Something to do with tax write-offs. Starling loved the television news report. Says that 'advertisingwise, it attentionizes the market audiencewise.' A man has to wonder what that means."

"A bloody curious century," The Sailor admitted. "But picking pockets no longer gets a poor lad hanged." The Sailor mixed in the crowd before August Starling's renovated building. He casually bumped a gentleman who adjusted his watch. He eased back toward the morose cop. "A few quid," he muttered, "but enough to entertain two jolly fellows."

The morose cop stepped backward, tsked-tsked, no longer looked morose. "We must play the hand we're dealt," he whispered. "We must stay here, at least for a little while. Otherwise it becomes too obvious."

"Gerald?"

"Gerald is busy overseeing this crowd," the morose cop said. "My old pal, the Irish cop, is staked out in yonder building. I expect he saw you pinch that wallet, but doesn't care. I shouldn't wonder but that Obed is back there in the shadows."

"Cats and Irishmen," The Sailor whispered. "Aboard ship a cat is held a lucky creature. Irishmen, however . . ."

"August Starling is announcing a tour of his layaway facilities," the morose cop whispered. "Does it strike you that this day seems to be lingering?"

"That," The Sailor explained, "is why that toff I bumped keeps adjusting his bloody watch. I make it as about ten in the morning."

"We're headed backward," the morose cop complained. "Before long 'twill be sunrise. Janie's Tavern will not even be open."

The crowd flowed into August Starling's display room with small gasps, murmurs of desire, an occasional "oof" of amazement.

Coffins on the right of them, coffins on the left of them, stately coffins before them, coffins standing, lying; ranks of coffins like dominoes, like gun carriages. Coffins potent as artillery.

Coffins enameled red, enameled ebony. Coffins ornamented with gold leaf. Coffins in football brown, navy blue. Coffins padded with velvet, chintz, serge; padded with duck down, kapok. Coffins with reading lamps and magazine racks. Coffins sporting wet bars, AM/FM radios, televisions, kitchenettes, microwave ovens, electric beer bottle openers. Coffins fitted as recreational vehicles, fitted as fiberglass boats. Coffins carrying double beds, bidets.

"A bloody curious century," The Sailor muttered again as the crowd flowed among the coffins. A sort of buyer's frenzy lay below the subdued actions. Victorians' flickering faces carried memories of plain pine boxes, memories of soaking rains. Faces of townspeople seemed thinking of bank balances, trying to calculate finance charges.

Coffins decorated in Day-Glo colors, hermetically sealed, plastic. Gray steel coffins for the businessman, replete with calculators, pie charts, maps detailing natural resources. Coffins for young moderns, with saunas, morning-after pills, nylon jockstraps patterned with pansies.

The children's line, decorated with bunny rabbits, fire trucks, cartoons of smiling worms, happy snails. Coffins for the young set, with dashboards, stick shifts, folding seats. Coffins for the family, and coffins for special-interest groups ornamented with posters of bicycle racers, mountain climbers, and photographs from topless bars. Coffins with religious motifs; candelabra, stained glass covers, and whole-wheat communion wafers.

Whispers ran through the crowd. "Impressive." "Magnificent." "A tour de force." Desire muttered. "Look at that beauty, Marge. A pad. A shack." Low mutters. "Fruits of technology." "Beyond the mainstream." "The sound of a different drummer." "And look at the vaults. You'd naturally want a vault."

The crowd lingered among the vaults. Marble, granite, an economy line of limestone. The crowd stood awed before grave markers; sculpted cherubs, sculpted sports cars, massive marble scrolls carrying poetry by James Whitcomb Riley, Rod McKuen, and sayings of Kahlil Gibran.

Buyer's lust shone on the faces of the wealthy, and envy on the faces of the broke and despondent. The crowd gently elbowed aside those who were starry-eyed and overextended. It was then that crashing organ music heralded an address by Goody Friendship. The crowd turned toward the back of the building, toward a stage, and saw an organ with pipes rising twenty feet above the vaults. The real estate lady played. She wore an open choir robe, high heels, a bikini. The real estate lady brushed the folds of the robe away as she pedaled the organ. The crowd gasped. The lady owned a world-class pair of legs.

Organ music died. Goody Friendship, darkly dressed, stepped forward to a gravestone pulpit depicting a joyful figure rising from the earth. The gravestone stood draped in purple velvet robes. The portrayed figure was probably human, but no one could call it male, female; although anyone could call it vague.

"Dearly beloved," Goody began, and his nearly plausible eyes seemed to examine the heart of each member of the crowd. "We gather on this occasion which should bring such joy . . ."

A professional mourner (one of the Sicilians with machine guns) moaned. The lady who sold stocks and bonds dabbed at her nose with a hanky, and openly wept. The lady did not have world-class legs, but she had a perky little nose. She showed plenty of grief and cleavage.

"However," said Goody, "our joy is bounded by misunderstanding, a failure of charity." Goody explained that unless the strike could be settled, there would be no tourist season. Everything the crowd now saw would fade away. Goody was smooth, politic, and did not accuse. He hoped for bright tomorrows, and he spoke of right behavior, pride, and blessed duty. August Starling blinked and sniffed.

"For, as man is a poor worm," Goody explained with sincerity, "thus spiritually depraved . . ." Goody turned, gave August Starling a look that was stern but compassionate, as Goody fed Starling his cue. "So even the most noble of men may sink into the pit of error . . ."

August Starling confessed. He spoke of his sin of pride in Point Vestal. He spoke quietly, in control of his emotions. August Starling became a mourner; and he pled guilty to lusting for a proud tourist season that would benefit everybody—both the quick and the dead—and guilty of coveting all that was best for this prince among towns. He sniffed, snuffed, sneezled, snorked, and blinked back tears. He stood erect and manly in his dark business suit, and he admitted to gluttonous longings which asked that Point Vestal become the premier tourist town in the universe.

"Give the blighters their due," The Sailor whispered to the morose cop. "They've made this lot feel guilty from keel to tops'l. A guilty Victorian is a dutiful Victorian. I believe it's known as strikebreaking."

Janie sniffled. Her bouncer wept openly. Victorian gentlemen controlled trembling lips, and Victorian ladies hid their shame behind shawls and fans. Organ music groaned, sobbed, throbbed. The IWW man saw his strike fading. Suffragettes stood perplexed, and their redly painted signs began to turn pale pink. Somewhere back in the crowd, Jerome took methodical notes.

"It's a clear win for August Starling," the morose cop muttered. "The strike is busted. Let's ease on over to Janie's Tavern. This crew is now a dollar short and a day late."

"I make it to be 1:30 PM," The Sailor whispered. "We've yet a bit of time." The Sailor motioned toward the stage on which sat the organ. "Cast your beamers on that, mate. This race is not completely run."

A small glow of light appeared in the gloom. It was laughing light, like sunbeams playing between leaves. Amusing light, like light chuckling to itself as it danced over a playground; streaming down sliding boards, romping in the spray of fountains. Light with a sense of humor.

From stage rear, shrouded by ebony drapes, sounded the clear voice of a violin. The drapes moved backward, as the violin player stood not in darkness but in something that resembled dawn—or maybe it resembled dusk. At any rate, Joel-Andrew played.

"That's the good chap," The Sailor muttered. "A stout breeze in a fair quarter."

"I only regret," the morose cop said, "that the Irish cop misses this. For I do believe it's a violin-and-cat act."

"This comes a cropper for Gerald," The Sailor said. "Gerald can scarcely avoid making an arrest. All the while, though, that's Gerald's undercover cat."

Satiric Obed danced light as butterflies. Obed twirled, his white tail fluffy as Scotch broom in wind. Obed jumped like popping seedpods, in long leaps graceful as running vines of melons, in hops plump as strawberries.

"You'll notice," the morose cop mentioned, "the organ lady is nicely occupied. I judge we'll be hearing exactly nothing from the organ."

Cats surrounded the organ lady, propounding to her in English, Greek, ancient Mesopotamian. The organ lady sat silent. Attentive. Leggy. Gray cats with white tail tips. White cats with gray tail tips. Cats with all white tails. Cats with all gray tails. Cats with fluff, and cats smooth-furred. Cats more-or-less operatic. Cats coy, cats conversing in Spanish.

"It's a heist," the morose cop murmured, "but gorgeous nonetheless. I ain't seen such elegant derangement since Isadora Duncan."

Satiric Obed twirled, tail aspin. Obed tripped light as forest breezes, light as hatched shells of sparrows, larks, bluebirds. Obed performed a rite of spring, a dance optimistic as a seed catalog. Music followed Obed, admired Obed; music filled with life and filled with love—with fecundity—with hope. The music trilled above the heads of the congregation. It touched a sourpuss here, a confused Victorian there. It chortled before the dour face of Goody Friendship, then skipped happily past August Starling as it darted birdlike before Janie and her bouncer. The music was inviting. You could dance to it.

The music returned to flutter before August Starling, and momentarily the young face of August Starling was nothing but a flickering mask before a dry and clacking skull. The crowd gasped in admiration. This was showmanship. This was consistency in the theme of resurrection. The young mask of August Starling flickered. The dry skull clacked. Victorians exchanged shocked glances. They gasped and were sad. The Victorians understood that only the skull was real, the young mask of August Starling a facade. The crowd cheered.

"I have strained hump in half the ports of the world," The Sailor whispered, "and I've seen a gypsy circus. But I bleeding well never saw a troupe of cats."

"Isadora Duncan was very, very good," the morose cop explained. "I regret she isn't here. She could meet the artistic director."

A cacophony of cats. A chorus of cats. Cats singing a Ukrainian love song. Cats scattered across the stage like sprinkles of spice. Dancing. Leaping. Tails aflip. Talented Obed danced sparkly with spring. The music lay across the congregation, tugged at the corners of mouths, brought involuntary smiles.

For some it brought sadness. The music celebrated life. Janie's bouncer touched Janie's hand, the two remembering life. Flickering figures sighed, hungered for a second chance, or hungered for oblivion. Memories of a century of cold, of whooing and rueing in frigid garrets and cellars, memories of life; memories of the freezing antics of death. The Sailor looked at the morose cop, remembered, no doubt, a century spent together in a Victorian cell. The morose cop hawked, spat, turned.

"Maybe I've got to bear this," he muttered, "but I don't have to bear it sober."

"August Starling's ruse founders," The Sailor said. "View our people." He pointed to the Victorians.

The Victorians stood cast in darkness, cast in memory. The Victorians regretted death, and were somber before the joy of life. They flickered.

"And look at the Point Vestal people."

The citizens of Point Vestal stood confused, while the city council stood perplexed. The mayor dreamed of sewage rates, possibly of stained glass coffins. Tourism. Economics. Sex. Publicity. The Chamber of Commerce stood sensual as young toads, and responsive as saltpeter. The man from the IWW began to make his move, beginning to renew his strike.

"It is a fraud," a Victorian voice said, the voice firm and dutiful. He spoke to the living citizens of Point Vestal. "You citizens may not understand, but I trust you will someday. Someday you will die."

The Victorian speaker stepped forward. He was not tall, but he moved with dignity that made him seem tall. The Victorian gentleman might have once been a merchant—or a preacher— or possibly a politician. Now he looked like a man sustained by integrity learned from experience. He turned from the people of Point Vestal and addressed the Victorians. "There are many things I did during my lifetime which I repent," he said. "I was not the most pleasant gentleman. I most deeply repent, however, some lovely and loving things I did not do. The music reminds me of them."

The Victorian gentleman turned away from the Point Vestal crowd, away from his fellow Victorians, away from the music; turned his back from the lighted stage and faced the black and icy street. He gently but firmly thrust the IWW man aside. "Our affairs are not yours," he told the IWW man. "No doubt your motives were of the highest."

"We had hopes," Janie murmured. "Hopes of returning to life. It is just terrible when hope dies." Janie did not even try to stop flickering. Her shoulders slumped. Her bouncer half supported her.

"Let us take the high moral ground in this matter," the Victorian gentleman replied to Janie. "I trust it will not be interpreted as sour grapes should I note that I would not wish to return to *this*." The Victorian gentleman looked toward August Starling. "You have your wish, my man. The strike is broken. We retreat to The Parsonage, which will no longer be strike headquarters, but sanctuary. If you negotiate with us, it will be as one doomed man to another. If we must spend eternity in The Parsonage, so be it. I, at least, will endorse no part of your scheme."

"I, at least, will be a part of my own scheme," the morose cop whispered. "I'm headed for Janie's Tavern."

"A bottle of stout," The Sailor agreed. The Sailor watched a silent crowd of Victorians move deliberately into the black and icy street. If their minds were ablaze with loss, their fears regulated by duty, no citizen of Point Vestal could tell.

"Arrest that cat," Goody Friendship roared above the crowd. "This is trespass." Goody searched the crowd for Gerald, but Gerald simply shrugged. He watched the Victorians trudge hopelessly back to The Parsonage.

Murmurs of "trespass" ran through the confused crowd. An important message seemed to have been delivered, but the crowd saw only a group of cats dancing. Murmurs of "It's too deep for me" mingled with murmurs of "Victorian cop-out" and a ground-swell of whispers of "August Starling for President."

Gerald eased forward. "It does not constitute trespass." Gerald had aged. His lantern jaw seemed thinner. His mouth formed a thin line, his eyes sad. He did not flicker, not much. He tipped his cop's hat to the back of his head, and viewed August Starling with curiosity, Goody Friendship with contempt. He looked at the leaders of Point Vestal and viewed them with indifferent calm. The leaders squirmed and looked confused. Gerald had never behaved this way before. "You advertised open house," Gerald explained to no one in particular. "Be pretty hard to make a charge of trespass stick."

"Vag him," August Starling murmured. "It's a small and inconsequential matter."

"He's an employed cat," Gerald said. "He works for me." Gerald looked at the crowd like a father viewing children he has cared for through the years of their growing up. "At least," Gerald said, "Obed *used* to work for me. Back when *I* worked for you." He unpinned his badge and tossed it to the mayor. He looked at August Starling. "You've got your wish, mister. My retirement address will be The Parsonage. Don't call." Gerald squared his cop's hat, looked over the faces of the crowd. "I expected better from you," he said softly. "I really hoped for better."

Chapter 27

CHRISTMAS AVOIDED POINT VESTAL. TIME CHURNED, CAUSED VAGUE confusion. A few people, perhaps, understood that August Starling took some lumps. Even fewer understood that powerful forces ran through our streets. Our people—having never pondered the nature of Evil—festered in general agreement that Good is better than bad because it's nicer. The ministerial association felt the force of Evil and responded by fearing Joel-Andrew. The ministerial association had a growing sense that things were terribly out of whack, but it took time to sort the situation.

Time yerked, yorked, yanked. Well into December, somewhere around the 29th, we found it was still the 23rd. The only way to estimate the date was to measure the amount of black light which faded toward the end of the month. We had Christmas in there someplace, because children played with new toys. The toys were ugly—cemetery games, plastic dolls fitted with genitals and with veins for embalming fluid, lead soldiers lying in realistic positions—and the children were not the only ones confused.

"It's a genuine blessing," August Starling explained about the way time stalled. "How fairly smiles each dark and icy morn, where stern and beauteous duty stands free to play some catch-up ball." August Starling's comprehension of the twentieth century improved. He fitted out second and third floors of downtown buildings, and he was busy, busy, busy. Harlots must be recruited from Seattle, basements waterproofed and painted, opium obtained. The pharmaceutical company geared up. People hoped, spread paint, took lessons in how to smile through sorrow, took lessons in how to deal blackjack. They chatted about the rumor of a coming messiah. Would he be tall and blond, short and blond, chubby? Would his name be Olaf, Nickolas, Chester?

=

We sit in The Fisherman's Café and it is January, near the end of the century. We think about the past, and dread telling what happened after Gerald turned in his badge. It would be easy if we could simply write that all hell broke loose, but that would only cover part of action.

When Gerald retired, and was awarded the '39 LaSalle instead of a watch, the town policeman's job was up for grabs. No one grabbed. Even after August Starling bought the new police van—the one with two dozen colored lights, heat, seeking missiles and a flamethrower—hardly anyone wanted the job. It came down to a choice between a Sicilian gunman, the Irish cop, or the morose cop. An Irishman was a tacky choice, the Sicilian gunman worse. The job went to the morose cop, who appointed The Sailor his deputy.

"Someone should have taught him to drive," Frank sniffs. "Someone capable."

We sit and regret. Back there in 1973 everyone was busy. The only driving instructor was a logging truck operator. That accounts for at least two percent of what happened on Chinese New Year.

The Strait is calm today. Above the San Juan Islands light gleams silver from a remote dawn. On the coast whales play, but on the Strait not even a salmon roils the surface. The morning air is stenchy from the tide flats.

"And yet, we can't blame it all on the morose cop," Frank says. "Joel-Andrew and Kune and The Parsonage . . ." He blinks back a tear. Of the lot of us, Frank is least changed; occasionally his Victorian control slips, but his tummy has grown back.

"It was the most innocuous form of evil," Bev says. "Because everybody did what everybody does anyway. Except everything was tainted. You could feel August Starling's power growing."

"Let us do a summation," Jerome says. "Many things were happening."

"As long as we don't sum too quickly," Bev tells him. "When we began writing the book, you were the one who worried about the unities."

"And cows don't whistle," Collette murmurs, "'cause cows have got moo flues."

"It wasn't cows. It was cats." Jerome snuffles and tugs at his green eyeshade. "August Starling suffered a reverse, but Joel-Andrew suffered reverses as well. The Martha Washington Brigade named Joel-Andrew a Communist. The Loyal Order of Beagles said Obed was an incendiary. Mothers Against Transgression and Sensuality denounced violins as instruments of moral degeneration. Kune was already censured. You'll also recall that Kune went to Seattle to try to make the system work. When he returned from his visit, people threw rotting vegetables at him. People were sad, and afraid, and mad, and did not know why. The town council finally reacted."

"The Whip and Cat Act," Frank says, and with some satisfaction.

Jerome consults his notes: "All cats off the street by 7:00 PM or suffer flogging. All cats licensed, tranquilized, perpetually leashed. Cats to be banded, as well as branded with the name of the owner. No fraternization between cats until the cat sterilization plan was implemented. No assembly of more than two cats, public or private. An exorbitant tax placed on cat food . . ." Jerome raises his eyes from the page. He looks at us with cynical and journalistic gaze. "Politics is the lowest form of human endeavor."

As this book continues, Jerome becomes more generous. He is not intellectually flabby, but he forgives some things he does not understand. "I have to assume," he says kindly, "that in any given population, a certain percent is born stupid and graceless. The worst of them go into politics."

"It wasn't all bad," Frank explains. "It gave the Grand Army of the Republic a reason for being vigilant."

"They became vigilantes," Bev sighs. "The GAR teamed up with those government people who followed Kune into town." Jerome consults his notes: "Two narcs, the CIA, FBI, Internal Security, Internal Intelligence, IRS, Marine-Navy-Army and Air Force Intelligence, Forest Service, Immigration people . . ." Jerome shakes his head at the length of the list. "Just say no agency legally empowered to engage in criminal activities was absent."

"For a while," Samuel muses, "it seemed August Starling would face a federal charge. As it developed, the agencies checked on each other. So many dragnets spread through town that the nets got tangled." Samuel looks nearly churlish. "As I recall, the only charge filed was against the ministerial association. The IRS wanted an amusement tax on church services."

"At least the Whip and Cat Act solved the cat problem," Frank points out.

"It drove the cats underground," Collette tells him. "You can't say you cured a problem just because you no longer see it."

"It is a very good place to start," Frank tells her.

Jerome flips pages. "There is so much material. Perhaps we should make a calendar."

Bev agrees a calendar is a good idea. "Begin with January 13, 1974," she tells Jerome. "The day Kune returned from Seattle."

CALENDAR

January 13, 1974. Kune returns from Seattle. He gets hit with rotten cabbage, tomatoes, and limburger cheese. Kune is shadowed by a great many people. The morose cop has first driving lesson. Misses shift on a gear, and accidentally hits the flamethrower button. Burns down an outhouse.

January 14, 1974. Samuel departs town. Samuel puts together a plan.

"If you'd given us a hint of what you were doing, we would have been better prepared," Collette whispers, her voice low and conspiratorial. "We could have made doughnuts or cooked up chickens."

"It could not be told," Samuel whispers back. "Too much depended on the element of surprise."

"The calendar," Bev whispers. "Stick to the calendar." Then Bev sits up straight and looks puzzled. "Why are we whispering?"

January 15, 1974. August Starling cuts provisional deal with ghosts. Morose cop's second driving lesson. Morose cop gets befuddled, and heat-seeking missile explodes three tons of burning garbage at the dump.

Jerome pauses. "The deal Starling cut was ugly, although it promised to work, more or less. We should note the terms, which were simple." Jerome's normally objective voice layers with sadness.

"After the Victorians' resolution to withdraw to The Parsonage," Samuel points out, "it's a wonder there was any deal at all."

"They were trapped," Frank chuckles. "They talked big. Then they realized they were setting themselves up to spend eternity in The Parsonage. The Parsonage was loaded with ghosts of preachers. August Starling had them in a mousetrap."

"We knew when we began there would be terrible parts to this book," Collette says. "When Joel-Andrew stood up for the rights of the Victorians, he made his own situation worse. That's when the ministerial association stopped speaking to him." Her sadness is even deeper than Jerome's. "I just hate this part," she tells Bev.

"It was really quite simple," Jerome says. "What Starling could guarantee was warmth." Jerome tilts his green eyeshade and glances around the warm interior of The Fisherman's Café. "The five of us," he suggests, "have never known what it is to be perpetually cold. For a hundred years most of those Victorians had shivered in garrets, basements, doorways, even outside. At the time Starling cut his deal, the Victorians were all camped in The Parsonage. The Parsonage is not a cozy place in January."

"The deal," Samuel mutters to Jerome. "Just record the deal, and let's get on with this."

Jerome consults his notes. "The ghosts were to receive pardons for all sins, as well as for crimes against the community. That did not include The Sailor or Gerald or the morose cop. Those three spirits would not play ball with August Starling. It did not include the Irish cop, who was never a real ghost, only pickled." Jerome checks his notes. "In addition, the ghosts received new job descriptions. For example, the Crocker twins no longer took turns jumping off the bluff. They wailed from second-floor bedroom windows. Ghosts attending birthday parties no longer had to consume punch and cupcakes. The gentleman who used to hang staked on an iron picket fence got to rest in the Irish cop's old coffin at Janie's Tavern." Jerome shakes his head. "It is strange how Evil can sometimes cause remission of ugliness. The ghosts were not well off, but, technically, they were better off."

"The important thing was visibility," Frank explains to Bev and Collette. "Happy ghosts might make Starling's Immortality Company even more attractive to tourists."

Frank misses the satanic cruelty of August Starling. The ghosts had suffered a hundred years of hopelessness. Then, a spark of hope arrived with August Starling. Then, accepting Starling's deal, the ghosts were not really better off; because acceptance meant acquiescence to an eternity of hopelessness. Such matters are too subtle for Frank, and in a way, Frank is lucky. Eternity may not be such a hot idea.

"The real issue was warmth," Samuel mutters. "Starling's deal sheltered the Victorians from the cold."

"The lowest levels of hell are cold," Collette murmurs to Frank. "I read that somewhere."

Beyond the windows of The Fisherman's Café frost and flakes of ice rime the beaches. We wish Collette could find some other way to make her point.

> January 16, 1974. Morose cop has third driving lesson. Backs through the front of Janie's Tavern. He nearly runs over two drunken loggers and three drunken fishermen. The whole front of the Tavern is knocked to flinders. Bricks and glass and wood and rubbish lie everywhere. Maggie is delighted. Claims she has waited years to see look on Frank's face. Meanwhile, the Victorians show reluctance to leave The Parsonage and rehearse their new jobs. Victorians mutter among themselves and no one can figure the cause.

"August Starling counted on the Victorians," Frank sighs. "He assumed that when duty called, Victorians would respond."

"And so they did," Bev chortles. "Meanwhile, that was a jerry-built job you did repairing the front of the Tavern."

"I could not get competent help," Frank told her. "Every carpenter, boat builder, and cabinetmaker in town was fitting out opium dens." Frank's feelings are hurt, and we find ourselves feeling a bit sorry for him. A teeny bit. "It was a flimsy piece of work," he admits.

> January 17, 1974. Agatha joins crowd of ghosts at The Parsonage. Agatha was the woman Starling killed, then danced with, back in 1888. Sicilian gunmen move into pharmaceutical company, spend time peering at the FBI through gun ports. Collette receives six black roses and seven white ones, delivered by a Chinaman. The news anchor from the television station arrives back in town. She is accompanied by her cameraman, a helicopter, and three enormous camper vans loaded with equipment.

"August Starling was delighted with those network people," Jerome snuffles. "He failed to obtain free advertising in the newspaper, but he managed to get network coverage. Fifty percent is not bad."

"In terms of circulation," Samuel mutters, "it was a tad bit over fifty percent."

"You people are unintentionally cruel," Bev tells Samuel. She reaches to cover Collette's hand, which trembles, as does Collette's cute little Irish mouth. "It is going to be all right," she assures Collette. "It will take a few more years to wear off."

Many long years have passed, and Collette still trembles over the awful events of January 23, 1974. Collette claims she wants a man. Anyone as pretty as Collette could get most any man she wanted, years ago. We feel real bad. Maybe Bev is wrong. Maybe things will never be all right for Collette, ever again.

"It was like being a convict waiting for execution," Collette whispers. "From January 17th to January 23rd, roses arrived every day. On the 18th there were seven black roses and six white ones. On the 19th there were eight black roses and five white ones." She looks down at the table, unable to meet our eyes. "On the 23rd," she says, "there were thirteen black roses. Of course, I don't remember . . . I have to take my grandfather's word."

Collette does not remember, because by January 23 Collette lay in a coffin concealed at the pharmaceutical company. Her grandfather, the Irish cop, nearly went mad until he rescued her.

"It was a fancy coffin." Collette trembles while Bev holds her like a mother holding a young daughter.

We all remember how fancy it was. Brocade and plastic, with a bed styled in early Victorian. Color TV. A mirrored ceiling.

January 18, 1974. Time flickers around the boat basin. Chinamen appear, then fade. The Strait heaves and burps. Lots of whales. Lots of ducks overhead. The GAR raids a basement and apprehends two kittens, locks them in the basement of City Hall. The Sailor releases them back on the street in ten minutes. Ministerial associ ation endorses motherhood. Morose cop has fourth driving lesson. Hits master switch and town is flooded with two dozen colored lights, tracers, parachute flares, signal rockets. The lights are blue, orange, red, green, and white. TV news anchor, convinced she experiences explosion of a nuclear bomb, is dragged from an opium den. Her cameraman is sobbing.

January 19, 1974. Kune challenges Goody Friendship to public debate on the topic: "Faith or Science in the Modern World." Goody answers by trying to spread Kune with peanut butter. Goody displays embossed indulgence forms for public admiration. Indians do not exactly return to town, but they visit during daylight hours. They consult with Maggie. Maggie seems robust, a little younger. She no longer flickers. Frank worries for her health.

"Because," Frank explains, "Maggie was an old friend. Also, tradition was at stake."

"Uh-huh," Collette whimpers, "because Maggie was always at Janie's Tavern, the same way my grandfather was always kept in a cheap coffin for Halloween display." Collette stops whimpering and begins to get angry. "I don't think anyone learned *anything* from the whole affair." Her voice is bitter.

"Some of us did," Samuel says, his fatigue great but his voice soothing. "We learned we had spent our lives living by dogma. We had patterns, but we had lost the knowledge on which those patterns were based. We forgot that Evil exists, and there is nothing relative about it." He looks at Bev, as if pleased with her—or with himself—or with both of them. "Nineveh," Samuel chuckles. "My dear, we were at least partly correct."

"The town still stands," Bev admits. "Most of it."

January 20, 1974 (Sunday). The ministerial association finally decides to take staunch action. August Starling is condemned from eighteen pulpits. FBI opens a file on every preacher in Point Vestal. August Starling is denounced as a drug dealer from eighteen pulpits. The Department of the Interior opens a file on every preacher in Point Vestal. The Lord is praised from eighteen pulpits. The CIA opens a file on every preacher in Point Vestal. Catholics, Lutherans, Presbyterians, Quakers, and Baptists open cat sanctuaries. Department of State and Department of Immigration set up barbed wire perimeters around the churches. Two Navy missile frigates arrive and cruise on the Strait.

January 21, 1974. Tourists begin to arrive. The town has never seen so many tourists. Better yet, the town has never seen so many *rich* tourists. The tourists arrive in cars, buses, yachts. The weather is rain and ice, so tourists cluster in cathouses, and in gambling parlors. The tourists have nothing to do but spend money until the opening day of Starling's Immortality Company. The indulgence business skyrockets. Tourists are not waiting for opening day to start sinning. The ghosts sullenly take their stations, but they put in only eight-hour days, then return to The Parsonage. The ghosts meet their contracts minimally. They gather in groups and mutter. Some people say the Victorians lay plots. Tourists strain our accommodations. There is not an unrented spare room in town. Hoovervilles, constructed of corrugated boxes and RVs, spring up on the outskirts. As the cathouses and opium dens boom, August Starling fills out, grows slightly plumpish. He is everywhere greeted as a hero. August Starling is still clean-shaven, except for a little pencil line mustache. August Starling chirps. He still seems very young, but is far more muscular. In addition, TV anchor and her cameraman catch Goody Friendship in the sack with the real estate lady. Anchor files unedited report for network evening news. Goody Friendship is awarded town medal for best symbolic performance embodying theme of Point Vestal renaissance. Real estate lady's sales quadruple. Joel-Andrew and Kune retreat to the basement of The Parsonage. Irish cop joins them. Gerald joins them.

January 22, 1974 . . .

"Whoa," Bev says, and halts Jerome. "If you don't protect the unities, I must. We can't just sum up the events of those last two days. We have to tell about them. January 23 was the official grand opening. The parade, the dancing ducks, all of it."

"When we finish this history," Samuel says to Bev, "let us get away from Point Vestal and everyone we know. Let us promise ourselves at least two weeks." It is a little frightening to see a powerful man like Samuel shudder.

Bev nods, more angry than shuddery. "We'll get through this," she tells Jerome and Frank. "Then it is simply ta-ta for a while. Don't call. Don't write." To Jerome, Bev says, "Let's pick up Joel-Andrew on the morning of January 22. That would be the day before Chinese New Year. In fact, it was the day of Chinese New Year's Eve. You'll remember Joel-Andrew was exhausted. He walked the beach early that morning. Almost as if he had a premonition."

Chapter 28

NORTH BEACH IS A BEACH OF ROCKS; MOSTLY DARK VOLCANIC shades, worn smooth when glaciers splintered the land. Glaciers carved passes, canals, shaved tops from low mountains and girdled sides of taller mountain ranges. North Beach holds mussels, tide pools, memories of shipwrecks and drowned bodies. It is a lonely stretch, relieved only by the lighthouse on a little hook several miles from town. Anyone walking the beach can be seen from great distance. If the walker is also sensitive, the beach appears as a dark seam edging the fabric of the land.

On this January 22, 1974, two people had occasion to walk. Shades of silver and black moved over the face of the Strait. Clouds drifted like layers of licorice, and Joel-Andrew, stepping alone, could not figure why clouds drifted when there was no wind. He shivered, partly from fatigue, partly because his wardrobe included only a light sweater.

On the Strait two missile frigates searched for small boats containing refugee Chinamen or refugee cats. A couple of fishing vessels passed beneath the frigates' protective guns, as the fishermen headed home from a rendezvous with a Panamanian freighter.

"Lord," Joel-Andrew prayed, "I'm failing the task. I'm supposed to be furious and strong, but I still keep myself on a leash." Joel-Andrew's gray-green eyes were downcast, his slight form slumped. His fingers plucked nervously at his pant legs. A hundred yards away, Bev trudged carefully over rocky ground. She held a lumpy package. Joel-Andrew looked about for any response from the Lord. He saw no burning bush.

"The people are confused," Joel-Andrew explained to the Lord. "They are angry because on Sunday the ministerial association spoke the truth about August Starling. I thought when their preachers put the finger on evil, the people would respond." Joel-Andrew felt the dizziness of fatigue and sadness. He had not slept for thirty hours. He preached on the streets, preached in buildings, and—when he tried to testify for the Lord among swirling fumes of opium—got bounced on the charge of being a secular humanist. He no longer hoped for a burning bush. A talking clam would do. "Lord," Joel-Andrew said, "I hope You've not chosen a coward. Ever since my ministry in San Francisco, I've been on defense."

At his back, along the wide main street of Point Vestal, Goody Friendship and the real estate lady cruised in a '47 Buick. The Buick gave a chromed and toothy smile. The real estate lady wore a bikini and a flowered garter. Goody Friendship waved. The street clogged with tourists. Bumper stickers proudly proclaimed "Point Vestal—The Living End," while a rock group named Josh and the Resurrection Sutra played an upbeat dirge.

"Because," Joel-Andrew explained to the Lord, "I figured I knew everything about Evil. Evil isn't worth all this fanfare."

Low on the horizon, like a flight of fighter planes, a multiplicity of ducks formed vees, triangles, circles, squares. They stunted and caromed off dark clouds. The perspective was such that the ducks were a constantly changing halo behind Bev as she approached.

"I've got it all on the line here, Lord," Joel-Andrew murmured, "but I don't know what to do. Appeals to reason do not work." He watched as the TV news helicopter chipped, chipped, chipped, overhead. Cameras pointed at the changing patterns of stunt-flying ducks. Cameras picked up Bev as she approached within earshot.

"Of course," Joel-Andrew said, "I'm hardly a theologian; but even a theologian would know the *results* of Evil are more ugly than evil itself. You can't get people to fight Evil, but sometimes they'll fight the results."

"Total nonsense." Bev greeted him, and she seemed looking forward to a talk. It was a nice change for Joel-Andrew, because everywhere he went he was scorned.

"Evil exists on a lot of levels," Bev told him. "You prophets try to make things too simple." Bev dressed worse than a tourist. She wore nice wool trousers, wool shirt, a down parka. She carried a rolled jacket beneath one arm. Her long hair was tucked beneath a colorful sock hat. She stood warm and cozy and did not look Victorian at all.

"You'll freeze your brisket." She passed him the jacket. "You get so distracted, you forget prophets can freeze the same as folks."

Joel-Andrew pointed toward the missile frigates and the helicopter. "Are those evil?"

"Nope," Bev said, "they are machines." She shook her head, smiled her wide and warm smile. She looked schoolteachery. "I'm going to tell you all about Evil. Then we go to The Fisherman's Café for a decent meal. Then you go to The Parsonage and get some rest. Tomorrow there's going to be a confrontation. You'll need your strength." Bev's motherly concern sounded positive as a dictator. It made Joel-Andrew feel loved.

"What confrontation?"

"It's a surprise," Bev giggled. "Just say I've received another message from Samuel. He figures you'll play at least a small part." Bev looked toward the helicopter. "I wonder if those people read lips." Then she returned to her subject. "There is no such thing as original sin, but there is an original state. We are all born unto ignorance."

"I wish I had Samuel's wrath," Joel-Andrew admitted.

"You're a sweetie pie," Bev said, and sighed as she goaded Joel-Andrew. "As a martyr, you'd be great."

Along Main Street, Disney characters gave out hugs and black balloons. The Marine Band played a strident march. Singers wearing cowboy outfits and carrying guitars mingled with noted revivalists, comedians, politicians.

"Evil is a force rising in history," Bev explained. "It comes from weakness, from intellectual decay. It rises when things get too sloppy."

"There is ancient evil," Joel-Andrew murmured. "August Starling is old as time."

"August Starling is a twerp," Bev explained. "I don't care if he's ancient, he's still a twerp."

"He's a twerp with the souls of Point Vestal in his pocket," Joel-Andrew admitted sadly. "As a prophet, I'm supposed to save folks from August Starling." From the Strait a porpoise stood straight up in the water, the porpoise's smile sarcastic.

"That may be the sin of Pride, because they have to save themselves. I'll give you a tad bit of advice." Bev's voice was kind. "Save the ones who want to be saved. If you try saving them all, you won't net any."

"What does Samuel want me to do?"

"We're not finished with Evil yet." Bev remained teacherly. "Evil is a force generated by ignorance. It is a totally powerful force that through history has used some ugly tricks. Evil is not weak."

"Yet you say August Starling is a twerp." Joel-Andrew felt himself warming up in the soft clasp of the jacket. He looked forward to a nice discussion.

"The twerps start it," Bev sighed, "but the twerps are only twerps. It is the force of Evil that builds and becomes something." She touched Joel-Andrew on the shoulder, turned him toward the Strait, where missile frigates blinked code to a shorebound intelligence unit. The frigates received a message and began cruising in reckless little circles. "As it builds," Bev said, "people take it serious. Then the twerps feel like great big boys, but they're still twerps." She was sad, and turned toward Main Street. "The mind of the Middle Ages is not dead." She turned back to Joel-Andrew. "Don't you *ever* get angry?"

"Only at myself," Joel-Andrew said miserably. "What does Samuel want me to do?"

"There will be a parade," Bev told him. "Samuel wants you at the parade."

"Doing what?"

"I don't know," Bev told him. "Just be there. The parade starts by the cliffs where the pharmaceutical company sits. It winds three miles down past the saltwater swamp and the boat basin."

In the far distance, like the rattle of small-arms fire, pops and cracks and explosions sounded from the boat basin. Explosions puffed hard against the black and silver sky.

"Chinese New Year," Bev explained. "Lots of firecrackers. The Chinese start early this year. They don't usually come ashore until late afternoon of Chinese New Year's Eve."

Joel-Andrew looked worried. "The Parsonage sits very near the boat basin," he said. "I hope the Chinese are judicious."

"If the situation gets irksome or dangerous, The Parsonage will simply move." Bev had seen The Parsonage take care of itself for more years than she cared to remember. She looked to the horizon, at the stunt-flying ducks. "I wish Maggie were here," she murmured. "It is a shame for Maggie to miss a show like that." On the Strait a pod of orca whales looped across the surface. They chuckled as they passed the missile frigates. "Come with me," Bev told Joel-Andrew. "Samuel is paying for your breakfast, even if he doesn't know it."

"I'm not rich," Joel-Andrew protested, "but I'm not broke."

"This one is on the Methodists." Bev firmly guided Joel-Andrew by the elbow.

Tourists plugged every cranny of The Fisherman's Café. Tourists stood in long lines excitedly discussing virtues of hookers named Bambi and Lance and Fawn and Dirk and Lollipop. Tourists waved gilt-edged certificates of indulgence, and they burbled happily of orgasm, immortality, resurrection. The poster on the front of The Fisherman's Café still proclaimed "Point Vestal Wants You," but now the poster carried an artist's rendition of the real estate lady's legs. Graffiti surrounded the drawing.

"No one has yet stepped forward to claim that free funeral," Joel-Andrew muttered to Bev. "Perhaps August Starling's parade will fail because he lacks a corpse."

"You know better than that," Bev said, and she was grim. "If Starling is short a corpse, he'll make one." She looked at Joel-Andrew. "It won't be you, although in many ways you have a lot of appeal."

"We must stop him from committing another murder."

"Forget that and do your job," Bev told him. "Gerald, and the Irish cop, and the morose cop, and The Sailor are working on the murder angle." She led Joel-Andrew to the back door of The

Fisherman's Café. They ate breakfast in the warm kitchen. Bev finished first. "Get some rest," she said, and departed to open her bookstore.

When he finished eating, Joel-Andrew walked toward The Parsonage. He felt despair because he could not see any difference between Main Street and San Francisco. He paused and watched the boat basin. It was interesting to see Chinese come ashore.

Chinese emerged dripping, seaweed flowing as long as their plaited hair. They bowed to those of their tribe who were ancient. Seaweed fell away, and as clothing dried, Chinese faces became inscrutable. Younger members blasted away with firecrackers. Elderly Chinese sat in meditation or conversed quietly. A white tail flicked among the Chinese. Obed was too busy to wave toward Joel-Andrew, and that made Joel-Andrew feel lonely. Obed sat respectfully in a circle of old men.

Joel-Andrew looked toward the saltwater swamp, then looked again at the Chinese. They were naked to the waist, wore baggy trousers, were slight but muscular. He estimated there were as many present as one would find at a well-advertised rock concert. The Chinese flowed, flickered; and a framework rising in the center of their group was not, after all, the keel of a new boat. It looked like the skeletons of dinosaurs seen in museums. Joel-Andrew recognized that the Chinese were constructing: a dragon.

Joel-Andrew turned toward The Parsonage. A bell in the octagonal tower clinked a tiny welcome. The Parsonage stood deserted, the Victorians in town working, or possibly laying plots. He realized Bev was correct, because he was as tired as he had ever been. The all-seeing tower watched him head for the basement, then turned its attention elsewhere.

The all-seeing tower briefly noted a lavish tour ship at some distance up the Strait. It moved slowly, looking for solid ground to ride at anchor until the following day. A dance orchestra aboard ship performed for tourists, and for a man in a glowing black robe. The man carried a battery pack beneath the robe. Above his head, light from the pack formed a hologram, a purple halo. The all-seeing tower puzzled to itself, then watched Collette's antique store as Collette opened one more box of roses. There were twelve black roses and one white one. The all-seeing tower watched

Collette flee, followed by six Sicilian gunmen. The all-seeing tower trembled. The Parsonage flexed its timbers.

In surrounding forests, thousands of shadows moved beneath the black and silver sky; shadows like men, and shadows like animals. At the boat basin fireworks still popped, while along the main street of Point Vestal cash registers chugged, tinkled, spat receipts. In upstairs rooms, Dawns and Dirks and Bambis were hard at work. In Janie's Tavern Frank tapped another keg, and Maggie muttered maledictions and predicted storms. Jerome took meticulous notes from his observation post beside City Hall, while Bev steered customers to the section of books on theology. Kune leaned against the counter of the drugstore as he put together a small medical kit. The sweet smell of opium drifted toward the boat basin. The all-seeing tower searched everywhere for Samuel and his horse, finally spotting them in the forest. The Parsonage continued to flex its timbers; and, while all of this was going on, Joel-Andrew snored the sleep of an exhausted man.

The all-seeing tower was fascinated, but turned away to watch the loading dock at the pharmaceutical company. A gorgeous ebony coffin, big as a bedroom, sat on the freight elevator.

Chapter 29

Dreams came and went, and sweat burst across Joel-Andrew like erupting pustules. Sometimes he thought he was awake, and sometimes he dreamed he was dreaming. He jerked into wakefulness, then—as if dragged by a claw or hook—sank back into the chasm of sleep. He mumbled and heard ancient prophecies. Pictures of seven golden chalices, of seven fatted cattle, of seven bronze trumpets flared. He saw pictures of nomadic armies; men wearing crude leather helmets, carrying spears and slings and flags—the men followed by tribe after tribe of women, children, and the old. He saw rivers flowing, saw opposing armies of peoples camped in colorful tents on opposite banks of steaming rivers. He saw processions of camels, giraffes, ostriches, gorgeously ornamented and draped with painted robes, stepping along sandy beaches. He heard the voices of black Kings, of white Kings. He heard ancient prophets, and the murmurs of a thousand Gods. He heard the horns of Joshua, the horns of Gideon, the young and petulant voice of Jonah.

Sodom. Gomorrah. San Francisco. Nineveh.

He heard the voices of Gerald, of the Irish cop, of The Sailor. The morose cop spoke while Kune diagnosed a situation. Joel-Andrew clawed toward wakefulness, dreamed of his great responsibility, and the bronze trumpets became rams' horns, bugles, the sound of storming winds.

"Let the poor bloke sleep," The Sailor said as he entered the basement. "He's of no help in this bloody business anyway." The Sailor's voice just missed being hoarse with emotion.

Kune lighted a lamp. Above them, whispery footsteps sounded as Victorians returned from downtown. The Victorians did not chat, exclaim, recite poetry. The footsteps sounded weary.

In the near distance, fireworks exploded around the boat basin, and from Main Street came the snort of a calliope. The Irish cop entered the basement, restrained by Gerald.

"You have one of two options." Gerald threatened the Irish cop. "Either get yourself in control, or I call a priest." Gerald's was a cop's voice. "You were outnumbered. You couldn't have done much against six Sicilians with machine guns."

The Irish cop struggled to pull free. His face twisted with anger and pain. Gerald's hawkish face, his jaw lanternlike, his scarred hands, exerted steadying force over the Irish cop. The morose cop stood silent and attentive. Ripples of Chinese expostulations came from the boat basin.

"I'll take them out with a shillelagh," the Irish cop said, his voice frantic. "'Tis me own fault Collette is stole, but August Starling distracted everyone's attention. He announced I was the man resurrected after sixty years. A mob surrounded me. They wanted autographs." The Irish cop buried his face in his hands. "They spirited her away before me very eyes. She's dead by now. By all that's holy, and all that isn't, I'll get revenge." The Irish cop sobbed.

"She isn't dead," Kune said quietly.

"And a goose don't whistle," the morose cop paraphrased Collette, "'cause a goose got a hisser-kisser."

"Place your lips together tightly," Kune told the morose cop. "Keep them rigidly in place. Doctor's orders." Kune turned to Gerald. "Give me two minutes of silence while I diagnose this mess."

Gerald nodded. At Gerald's back, asleep on an old mattress, Joel-Andrew's body shook. Perspiration stood on his forehead. The Sailor watched him. "Been a bit overlong on watch," The Sailor murmured. "I recall such nights."

"Button it," Gerald whispered.

Silence was punctuated by firecrackers, by whispers from upstairs rooms where Victorians complained or plotted. Silence was soothed by the sigh of a silver wind around the all-seeing tower.

"Collette is not dead," Kune said finally. "It works out this way . . . she is drugged. The drug is carefully timed. Collette will be in the coffin and the coffin will be in the parade. August Starling figures to open that coffin just before Collette comes out of a drugged sleep . . . and at the same time the new messiah arrives. It is set up to look like a resurrection."

"Mother of God," the Irish cop said. "Be praised there's still hope." The Irish cop popped his knuckles, looked for something that could be used as a club.

"This bloke's a flaming genius," The Sailor said to Gerald, and he talked about Kune. The Sailor's voice no longer sounded hoarse. Of Kune he asked, "Where is the lass kept?"

"That's the easy part," Kune told them, his yellow hair white in the lamplight. His face, which had once been so filled with old grief, was now lined with concentration. He looked like a man about to jump into a fight he knows he can win. "Collette is stashed in a coffin on the loading dock of the pharmaceutical company. Six Sicilians with machine guns guard the place."

The Sailor walked toward the door, pleased with the chance to rescue Collette. His shoulders squared. His shaggy black hair and shaggy black beard looked nearly alive. Gerald restrained him. "We need a plan," Gerald said.

"I have died more than five thousand times," The Sailor told him, and The Sailor's voice held dignity. "One more time? What odds?" If The Sailor was mortally angered, no one could tell.

"It's a hostage situation," Gerald explained. He turned to the morose cop. "Is that fancy police van working? We need a diversion."

The morose cop straightened his skinny frame. He spit accurately into a cuspidor no more than fifteen feet away. "I know the workings of every button on that honker," he told Gerald in CB language. "Plus, the rig itself ain't hardly even got any dents."

"I see it this way," Kune diagnosed. "The morose cop parks the van a hundred yards from the pharmaceutical company, on the side away from the loading dock. He sets off lights and rockets. He lays down fire with his flamethrower. When the building is burning nicely, he lets off his heat seeking missiles." Kune's voice saddened. "I hate this next part. We're going to kill some Sicilians."

"We'll take 'em alive," Gerald said. "Set off the lights and rockets. Don't fire the missiles. I'll set off firecrackers to the left. The Irish cop lights off firecrackers to the right. They will be mistaken for small-arms fire. The Sailor circles the building and comes in sneaky from their blind side. The Sailor steals Collette."

"You got it wrong," the Irish cop said. "The Irishman comes in like Brian Boru. The Irishman takes back his own. He sneaks not, nor does he steal."

"If that's the way it must be." Gerald looked at the Irish cop who was his friend. "Take care," Gerald said. "You've been pickled, but you've never died. It isn't the least bit fun."

"Irishman or not, the lad deserves his chance. The lass is his granddaughter." The Sailor pointed upward, where Victorians whispered or plotted. He chuckled. "Another interested party resides upstairs."

"Yes," Kune diagnosed. "I believe we might ask Agatha if she would take Collette's place in that coffin. After a century, Agatha deserves a shot at August Starling. It will make a nice surprise when that little priss opens the box expecting to see Collette, and finds the woman he danced with nearly a hundred years ago."

"This situation jolly well gets nastier and nastier." The Sailor chuckled.

"I'll ride with the morose cop," Kune said.

"You'll keep your medical self right here," Gerald told him. "We're bringing a woman back who'll need a doctor." Kune was about to protest. "That's final," Gerald said. "You stay here with the preacher."

"Leg over leg . . ." The Sailor said, "the old dog got to Dover." He led the other men through the doorway and into the silver night.

Kune silenced. Joel-Andrew dreaming.

The dreams refashioned themselves, played over and over; changed from graphic to impressionist; changed from prediction to prophesy; changed finally to memory—and a memory, suppressed through too many years on the streets—returned and captured him. He allowed himself to know that the year had been 1966. He heard the clear voice of the Lord saying, "Go to San Francisco."

So he left Rhode Island, riding a bus across the Lord's Creation. He went to San Francisco, and saw things strange and beautiful, and, most of all, ugly. He saw a drugged girl standing nearly naked in an alley. She fled screaming.

Joel-Andrew pushed the dream away. He allowed himself to dream of a slightly later time. He had been in the Haight nearly a year before he was excommunicated for performing unauthorized miracles, and for molesting a violin. The excommunication was not flamboyant. It was, in fact, a bit dull.

The Archbishop wore a nicely tailored business suit. He was stout but not chubby, his eyes reflective, his nostrils experienced. He was a man who knew about empires, dark brethren, tsetse flies, and novels by Rudyard Kipling. He put his feet on his desk and puffed on a pipe. Bookcases were lined with Bibles and bound copies of 1940s *Esquire* magazines. The Archbishop did not wave a censer, he did not say "*Apage, Satanas,*" and when he raised a pink and chubby hand it did not turn into a claw. The Archbishop's voice was not hooded like an Inquisitor.

"You're out," the Archbishop had said. "Take off the collar."

Joel-Andrew admired the ploy. "It's my collar. Bought and paid for."

"It's *my* church."

"The First Amendment to the Constitution," Joel-Andrew said. "Freedom of religion, freedom of assembly. Thomas Jefferson."

"Beat it, bum," the Archbishop said. "And get a haircut."

"Roger Williams," Joel-Andrew said. "Anne Hutchinson. John Woolman."

"And take a bath," the Archbishop told him kindly. "But *after* you get your kiester out of my office."

And that was all there was to it. Joel-Andrew issued forth stripped of ecclesiastical authority. He went back on the San Francisco streets.

The dreams insisted. Joel-Andrew lay finally helpless before the dreams. His teeth clashed. His muscles knotted with tension. The one memory he really could not bear returned in a dream.

He had seen the girl again. She reappeared on the night of his second day in San Francisco. Gay and twinkly lights illuminated the street. A rock group called The Apothecary Weekly slapped the night air with driving drumbeats. Bells tinkled along the Haight, and incense wove little currents through which Joel-Andrew walked. Because he had just arrived in San Francisco, his clerical clothing was intact. His shoes were shined. Policeman waved to him and smiled. Freaks offered him a toke. For the entire day Joel-Andrew watched everything and everyone. He tried to understand the will of the Lord.

"Like, man," a young voice drawled, "like man, there's a chick back there doin' a real, real downer." A kid no more than fifteen pointed down an alley. The alley lay black as the innards of hell. The kid's hair tangled, his eyes bright and speedy. "Bum trip," he said. "But this is where it's at," he said, vague but enthusiastic. He bopped away.

Joel-Andrew entered the alley. He found her dead, naked, and being eaten by rats. There was very little blood. He sat beside her all night. Weeping. Praying. Powerless. Trying to understand the will of the Lord. He kept the rats away. When dawn arrived he wrapped her in his coat and carried her into the deserted street. Rigor mortis locked the body. The coat fell awkwardly away from soft places where flesh was bitten and gone. A police car cruised toward him. The cop called a meat wagon.

"You're being too good to these people, Father. You got to get tough." The cop drove off.

That was the first soul he lost, the first one that lay beyond the power of the Lord—and that soul lay beyond the power of the Lord, because all the Lord had in that situation was Joel-Andrew. All the Lord could do was keep the rats away.

Joel-Andrew's body shook beneath the dream. His mind shook. Then he realized someone's hand was shaking him. It was Kune, and Joel-Andrew was pulled from San Francisco to Point Vestal beneath Kune's gentle hand.

"I need the mattress," Kune explained apologetically. He turned, speaking to someone behind him. "Put her here," he told the Irish cop.

Joel-Andrew sat up. He leaned against a dusty wall in the dusty basement. He wiggled his toes, found his legs still worked. He stood as the Irish cop lowered Collette to the mattress. Kune bent over her.

Whistles and screams came from the distance. Machine-gun fire. Thumps of explosions sounded from the forest.

"Will she be all right?"

"It's touch and go," Kune said. "A matter of metabolism." He took Collette's pulse.

"What is happening?" Joel-Andrew still felt slugged with sleep. He could not connect what he saw with what he heard. The dream still pulsed. His anger grew. The Parsonage trembled. Joel-Andrew was becoming furious.

"How can I help?" The Irish cop banged a fist against an open hand.

"Just stay in control," Kune told him. "I'm pretty good at what I do."

"What is happening?" Joel-Andrew asked again.

"We take a bit of a drubbing," the Irish cop said, "although we give a thump or two in return."

"Those aren't firecrackers," Kune said.

"Mistakes have been made," the Irish cop told him. "We be presently brawling with the Navy." The Irish cop headed for the doorway. "I'm bleeding well on my bloody way." He sarcastically mimicked The Sailor. "The Irish will na' allow the flaming Limeys a monopoly on this entertainment."

Chapter 30

SILVER CLOUDS DRIFTED ACROSS THE NIGHT SKY. MISSILES ARCED, pooted, spit, fuzzled, screamed. Missiles rose from frigates and whooshed above the boat basin where gratified Chinamen took pleasure because the Navy joined their New Year's celebration. Along Main Street tourists watched, yelled patriotic slogans, judged this an extravaganza second only to the Super Bowl. Tourists saw multicolored lights, signal flares, rockets flaming high from a site near the pharmaceutical company. As colors intensified—green, red, blue, purple, orange—normally inscrutable Chinese gave a massive cheer.

The beginning of the affair may be laid to the morose cop who touched off the battle through awakening enthusiasm. His life and death had, to that point, been unsatisfactory. He was melancholic by nature, never lucky. He had chain-whipped his pal, The Sailor, more than five thousand times. He was wise about the worthlessness of power.

Following Gerald's instructions, the morose cop pulled the police van within a hundred yards of the pharmaceutical company. Gerald and The Sailor took up appointed positions. The morose cop switched on the many-colored lights, and the lights looked like Saturday night in Seattle, or like the last throes of a used-car dealership. Lights silhouetted the seven-story pharmaceutical company which looked like opening night at a porno flick.

From the Strait where the missile frigates cruised, the pharmaceutical company shone as visible as the center circle on a target. Machine-gun fire rattled from the pharmaceutical company as Sicilian gunmen hosed the brush, the forest, the rocky ground. The Sicilian gunmen were good at what they did. They put down a cover of fire beneath which no man could move. Being Sicilian, however, and thus emotional, they were long on anxiety and short on tactics. It was no great job for the Irish cop, accompanied by Agatha, to sneak to the rear of the pharmaceutical company and rescue Collette.

The morose cop, pinned by enfilading machine guns, but happy, fired distress flares. Flares shot high above the pharmaceutical company, then drifted on lacy parachutes. They were red and white and blue, spelling anxiousness to every horizon. Fluttering sounds of a helicopter came from a downtown roof. The TV network chopper hove skyward. Above the grand panorama of Strait and silver sky, the TV helicopter looked like a ladybug with a case of the hots.

The morose cop fired signal rockets. Rockets arced above the pharmaceutical company, lighting stained glass windows like incandescent suns. The Sicilians, blinded, fired until gun barrels melted. Sounds of the helicopter closed; then the shadow of the helicopter hovered before the pharmaceutical company. Above the whoosh of rockets, the news anchor's voice gave an in-depth analysis of sexual misconduct in Congress. The situation heated up. It would take only one little mistake, and surely the Navy would chip in and help.

The morose cop made that mistake. He fumbled his gears, and the police van rose on its hind tires like a rearing stallion. It snorted—flashing lights of blue, green, purple. The police van scorched through the field of fire. The morose cop barely jumped from the speeding vehicle as it hesitated on the edge of the cliff; flashed, fooled around, spinning its wheels and making decisions, then tumbled flashing over the cliff. Meteoric. When it struck rock, three hundred feet below, heat-seeking missiles exploded.

The roar tickled onlooking Chinese, but the missiles nearly concussed a school of minnows. The missiles destroyed the secret passage and the elevator shaft leading from the pharmaceutical company. Boulders flew high in the air, and, as small rocks sprayed into the Strait, the sky filled with grapeshot. One or more pebbles struck the missile frigates.

The all-seeing tower, intrigued, watched the minnows shake their tails, gather themselves, and groggily head seaward. Clams dug deeper into the beach. The all-seeing tower saw the morose cop roll away from the edge of the cliff. He took cover behind unthrifty shrubbery. The helicopter chip-chipped, cast a shadow. The news anchor's voice chattered an in-depth discussion of perverse practices among South American male sand fleas.

Missiles from the frigates rose above the dark Strait. In diminished but still-bright light, six Sicilians broke from the sanctuary of the pharmaceutical company. They fled to their limo. There followed a great squealing of tires. The Sailor and the Irish cop pelted them with cherry bombs, but by the time the first naval fire arrived, the Sicilians were a rapidly diminishing dot on the road leading out of town.

The first cluster of missiles hit a drifting flare. The silver sky turned white. Downward concussion pressed the helicopter toward the ground, and newsy voices tensed until the helicopter gained altitude. The chopper sat high above the second cluster of missiles when they hit the dying site of the first cluster. The helicopter was blown skyward. It zoomed back and forth, back and forth as the cameraman rigged a telephoto lens. The third cluster of missiles fell in the nearby forest. They chipped bark from an ancient cedar, and frightened a family of mice. The all-seeing tower watched as the cedar mumbled in slicky-cedar language, and dug deeper with its roots.

The fourth cluster of missiles landed in a pasture. They startled a cow. She gave no milk for three days.

As the Navy found its range, the fifth cluster of missiles bracketed the pharmaceutical company. The missiles finally landed in an auto-wrecking yard, busting the windshield in an 1895 Daimler.

The sixth cluster slammed into a distant mountaintop. It chipped ice from a glacier.

The seventh cluster chased a snowy owl across fencerows, the owl only escaping because the missiles diverted to strike empty wine bottles in a drainage ditch.

Above the pharmaceutical company, the helicopter chugged, then choked. The eighth cluster of missiles cruised beneath the copter, the missiles eventually exploding above the forest. The explosion so perturbed two Sasquatch that they hid in a cave and cuddled up to a snoozing bear.

The all-seeing tower watched as three parachutes bloomed from the helicopter, and it watched as the helicopter tumbled and whirled from the sky. The all-seeing tower watched the helicopter smash into the roof of the pharmaceutical company where it exploded; and while—as all of this was happening—Gerald waited as the parachutes descended. Gerald rescued the news anchor, her cameraman, and pilot. He herded the three into the '39 LaSalle and drove them to their hotel.

The Navy fired until dawn, while the shattered top of the pharmaceutical company flamed. After three hours, the pharmaceutical inferno, feeling ignored, called it "half a day" and put itself out. The pharmaceutical company now stood only six stories tall, raggedly, one side blown away by the busted helicopter. Missiles sped overhead. Cannon fire stained the landscape black. No fatalities occurred, no injuries, but a couple of forest trees bent slaunchwise. A member of the Martha Washington Brigade, at the tender age of eighty-one, listened to the cannon fire and experienced her first bout with sexual arousal.

=

The silver night proved sleepless for many in Point Vestal, although a few people sought rest. Hookers worked until midnight, then caught a few winks. Janie's Tavern closed at 12:30; The Fisherman's Café gazed with darkened windows into the street. Tourists began snoring by 1:00 AM. The bookstore's unlighted windows displayed an illuminated text from Josephus. Mice slumbered in uptown basements, but cats did not.

An infiltration of cats moved silent through the black and silver streets. Cats erupted noiseless from behind garbage cans, or shimmied down trees. Cats shadowed patrolling members of the CIA and the Grand Army of the Republic, cats flipping white tails, then disappearing around corners to the confusion of the FBI and the Forest Service. A strike force of cats seemed nearly suicidal as it dashed from an opium den. The strike force singled out two narcs, surrounded them. The cats rubbed against the narcs' legs, purred, pretended favoritism. Immigration agents arrested the narcs on a charge of conspiracy, while the cats melted into the shadows. The cats' gray fur and white tails were perfect camouflage in the black and silver night.

The strike force established (and in fewer than three hours) one of the highest records of bravery in the annals of cat history. The trick worked, and the strike force played it over, and over, and over again. The victims did not catch on. Government cops arrested each other. The Grand Army of the Republic declared itself betrayed by its leadership. Government cops hissed, whispered, resisted silently as covers were blown. Well before dawn, while Navy missiles still fizzed above the busted pharmaceutical company, every Fed in town—except the WPA foreman who had designed and built the 307-step staircase—moldered in cells beneath City Hall. Cats dispersed to quiet corners where they took catnaps, or prepared for the big parade.

At the boat basin, firecrackers ceased at midnight, but the Chinese were unsleeping. As Chinese New Year arrived, chaos once more departed from the Chinese world. For five days the lunar calendar had been playing catch-up ball: because, on the lunar calendar, each year contains five days when all bets are off. To the wily Oriental mind, chaos rules the universe during those five days.

But now it was the Year of the Tiger. Customs, forms, obligations and proper behavior reigned. The Chinese, on foreign soil and surrounded by round-eyed devils, wanted only to see their bones resting in their native land. At the boat basin, through the rest of the night, small campfires illuminated the serpentine form of an enormous dragon. The dragon stood on wheels, like a float for a parade.

The all-seeing tower watched through the silver and exploding night. When it saw that Joel-Andrew had still not worked up a case of wrath, it turned from him. It did not watch Joel-Andrew when he entered into silent communion with The Parsonage.

Joel-Andrew carried no wrath because Joel-Andrew felt that wrath belonged to the Lord. What Joel-Andrew owned was fury.

The memory of a girl dead in a garbage-strewn alley finally cleansed his mouth of equivocation. The suppressed memory, which had once rendered him wordless, flew forth. To Joel-Andrew, the figure of August Starling, the customs of Point Vestal, the smoggy shapes of Seattle, came together in the memory of that doomed girl. As Kune hovered above the drugged form of Collette—Kune practicing medicine—Joel-Andrew readied himself for work. He understood why the Lord had chosen him for the solitary life of a prophet. When the offenses of men became too great, most people cowered or fled; they changed their names or dug foxholes. When they figured they had too much to lose, they spoke of compromise. The Lord did not need a relativist.

Because Joel-Andrew knew that in this world some things eternally *ought* to be, regardless of cost or consequences. And, in this world, some things eternally ought *never* to be. Regardless of cost or consequences. Never.

Chapter 31

PICTURE IT HAPPENING. IN LIGHT RAIN, BLACK AND SILVER DAWN nudges over the San Juan Islands. Point Vestal dozes. Wood smoke rises from brick chimneys, crows fly cawing and contentious, ravens croak and flutter. Massive Victorian houses stand silver-roofed with mist and rain.

On the hill beside the cliffs, the shattered pharmaceutical company stands like a broken remnant of an obscene cathedral. Brickwork is black with footprints of explosion. Windows stand blown and agape. On the loading dock an enormous ebony coffin, like an unblinking eye of darkness, awaits transportation.

Movement begins, and for the most part is jolly. Darkly stumbling men sip coffee from paper cups, hack lungers, talk softly to team after team of black horses. Horses nicker, whinny, snort, and go clop-clop. Hostlers prepare spans of animals, harnessing them with black leather, backing them into traces of ebony hearses. Hostlers kneel before the horses, giving each hoof a shine of jetty black shoe polish. The horses breathe steam, the steam interpenetrating with swirling steam from the coffee. Since horses and hearses are the big feature in the parade, they must be on location early. The parade route begins at the top of the hill. It ends at the reviewing stand before August Starling's commercial building.

As daylight increases, so does movement. On the Strait, missile frigates cruise with shot wads, while an occasional porpoise giggles. The Navy has no more missiles. Signal flags bloom in colorful confusion among halyards. Shouts of protest rise dimly from the basement of City Hall, where federal cops lie neutered. The CIA does not care that Point Vestal is without a police van. The FBI does not care that government is helpless. The IRS wants breakfast. Federal cops run tongues across unbrushed and fuzzy teeth, blush, have old memories of being spanked by their mothers. Entering the boat basin a tour ship toots, runs ahead-slow, carrying the new messiah.

Elsewhere, happiness or determination greet the day, depending on whether one is a ghost or a cat. The cats of Point Vestal promenade the morning street. They hum inappropriate music, mostly Gershwin, King Oliver, Donizetti. Mice creep from uptown basements and peer timidly over the bluff as they watch cats walk a hundred feet below. The mice, who have not seen a newspaper in days, remain puzzled. The cats are bawdy. Some are attired in red ribbons, and wear captured federal ID, the silver badges blinking beneath a black and silver sky.

Victorians attend to toilettes. Starchy collars are pressed, wool jackets dusted. Victorian ladies have spent the night fixing each other's hair. Pink pleats, crimson tucks, pastel blue hems are pressed with flatirons. Undergarments gleam the whiteness of purity, while boots and slippers glow. It is a fine show, a gorgeous show, a heart-stopper. In addition, it is a tough act because the Victorians have nary an Irish servant. The Victorians glance at each other, give tight but dutiful smiles.

Beside the boat basin, and not far from The Parsonage, Chinese seem equally determined. The Chinese only want to go home. Since that is impossible, the Chinese want revenge. Elders advise caution. Young hotheads advise storming The Parsonage and taking the Victorians hostage. The huge dragon is red and yellow and orange and emerald and black. It gazes, enameled and gorgeous, across the road, and across the saltwater swamp.

Goody Friendship and the real estate lady cruise past in a '47 Buick, heading for doughnuts at The Fisherman's Café. Goody fondles the real estate lady's knee as he makes notes for a sermon on the Yellow Peril.

And, along the road, the first segments of the parade arrive. A drum-and-bugle corps from Seattle blinks in the light rain.

Members wear spiffy uniforms of purple and gold. Misting rain chews at covers on drum heads. Nearby, another band of sleepy-eyed high schoolers, their instruments dangling, stumble with hangovers to their appointed meeting place. Their uniforms are black with stripes of crimson. They pass the Marine band, the Army band, the Navy band and are vaguely impressed. A dark gray bulk stands at the top of the hill—waves its trunk—for someone has brought an elephant. The elephant's gray hide matches the gray mist, but it wears robes of red and yellow. Rumors circulate about an air show; and, in fact, above the horizon a snow-white blimp heads toward town. Its flashing signs advertise indulgences, slivers of wood from the True Cross, and holy water.

The Sailor and the morose cop hold conference on the sidewalk before Janie's Tavern. They do not flicker much, but they yawn and stretch after a long night.

"Something smells jolly well filthy about this day." The Sailor pulls at his black beard, watches Goody and the real estate lady enter The Fisherman's Café.

"Gunpowder." The morose cop sniffs air sharp with cordite and the acrid scent of black powder. "There'll be so many throbbing heads, things may proceed slowly." The morose cop spits accurately at a discarded beer can. The beer can tinkles as it rolls in the gutter, like the tentative voice of a child who suspects it is lost. Along the street horses and hearses plod toward the top of the hill. Wheels rumble like tumbrels as horses hoof it with methodical pace. Steam rises in chill rain, while in the street and on rooftops TV crewmen set up cameras. The news anchor directs her cameraman to shoot at this—at that—at the other; and fine footage is taken of the broad beams of horses.

"Some days are born ugly." The Sailor turns to look through the windows of Janie's Tavern. "Maggie is up and stirring. Seems in a bit of a snit. Frank looks dutiful." The Sailor looks toward the hill where the pharmaceutical company stands in crumbles. The Sailor chuckles with satisfaction, while the morose cop shows a thin smile. "Crowds already gather there. I suppose Gerald is stationed up that way." The Sailor watches the blimp hover above the boat basin, where crowds of sleepy tourists stand in admiration of the

Chinese and their dragon. A Chinese gong sounds, then sounds again.

"Maggie is not just having a snit," the morose cop mutters. "Maggie is so mad she isn't even flickering." The morose cop steps away from the tavern because the entire front seems about to collapse.

On top of the hill the parade assembles. There is a chowder-and-marching society in green derbies, a pet contingent—children with dogs and gerbils—a number of Army tanks. Clowns bounce and flounce and mingle around floats. The floats—some fifty of them—carry pretty girls in long gowns, and the floats celebrate Miss Water Softener, The Irrigation Queen, and queens of truck stops, underground transit and bus barns. Motorcycle gangs cruise back and forth, their bikes popping among Disney characters; and majorettes already twirl silver batons before groups of country singers. Banjos plink as black balloons dance above the crowd. Everywhere flowers wilt in the cold as colleagues of Goody Friendship pass collection plates and pray for the heathen. The Martha Washington Brigade mounts its float. The tires on the float flatten. The Mothers Against Transgression and Sensuality do the same. The Loyal Order of Beagles dons doggie hats. A few stragglers from the Grand Army of the Republic adjust forage caps. The mayor and city council wave from a pink '29 Duesenberg.

"The stage is set most rapidly," The Sailor says as he peers toward the hill. "Yet I feel movement behind me." The Sailor peers in the other direction. All is silent there. "Something is happening, mate." The Sailor peers upward at the bluff. Mice move up there, but behind the mice is other shadowy movement.

"Probably only tourists," the morose cop assures him. "Trying to find a grandstand seat."

And it may well be tourists, for tourists flow from everywhere. They step yawning and rubbing their crotches from hotel rooms and camper vans, or creakily from the backseats of cars. Tourists rise blinking from opium dens, cathouses; even basements where they have sought shelter. Sidewalks overflow. The Fisherman's Café serves coffee, passes out doughnuts with black and silver sprinkles. The Fisherman's Café cannot accommodate everyone. People crowd around Janie's Tavern where Frank, accepting the inevitable, serves pick-me-ups and potato chips. The tourists chat and check their zippers.

"There's that preacher." The morose cop points toward the small but approaching figure of Joel-Andrew, sandals aflap, making his way through the crowds. "I see Obed is with him."

The Sailor watches the pair approach. "The cat can be trusted," The Sailor mutters. "The preacher, though, is sometimes flighty." The Sailor seems lost in reminiscence. "I recall the day that preacher and I first met. We had a nice talk."

"He seems different, somehow." The morose cop is not optimistic, but is interested. He looks toward the hill and pharmaceutical company. "The hostlers load the coffin on the hearse. Goody Friendship and the real estate lady depart for the boat basin. I reckon they are picking up the new messiah. The parade will soon start."

Chapter 32

LITTLE SCATTERS OF DARKNESS SPATTED THROUGH THE SKY LIKE latitudinal rain. Clusters of the stuff framed shapes of faces and shapes of things. The TV news anchor's nose smudged with darkness. She gave an in-depth analysis of safe sex practices that depended on dildos fashioned after the faces of world leaders. Darkness made little frames around Goody Friendship, around the real estate lady, and it made an ornate Victorian frame around the figure of the new messiah as he stepped from the gorgeous tour ship.

The messiah threw back his hood and tourists gasped with awe. No one—no, not a single tourist anywhere—or anyone else, anywhere—had dreamed the messiah would be Beauregard Shooter, world-famous basketball star. The elephant trumpeted, heralded, and stomped its great feet. The messiah dribbled, then clasped his hands above his head like a winning fighter.

Many people were impressed, but, in memory, no one really knew anything was skewed. Then things happened quickly. A screaming Chinese mob, with skirmishers in baggy pantaloons, and companies of club-wielding foot soldiers, mounted an attack on The Parsonage. The Chinese carried smudge pots and buckets of boiling tar. Things were getting tacky.

The Parsonage did not try to stand its ground. Instead, it took the all-seeing tower and Victorians for a ride. When we (and everyone else in Land's End) looked to the morning sky in admiration of the approaching blimp, what we saw was the airborne form of The Parsonage cruising away from the frustrated cries of the Chinese.

In the past, when The Parsonage moved, it did so quickly and silently. There would be a little burst in the atmosphere. Leaves trembled on trees. The Parsonage would shrug its way onto one lot or another, shove one or another Victorian house aside. The Parsonage had never before shown a propensity for aerobatics.

The Parsonage—which still proudly wore its red-lettered "Strike Headquarters" sign—hung in the sky and slowly circled the blimp, while beneath both blimp and Parsonage Navy frigates cruised in tight circles of hard-helmed confusion. The huge lot of The Parsonage, sporting maple and cherries and apples and pears, was a small patch of winter landscape above the Strait. The trees were leafless, but chimneys in The Parsonage sent streams of wood smoke across the sky. When The Parsonage moved, the wood smoke looked like exhaust from mighty engines. What with the deranged clanking and pealing of bells from the octagonal tower, The Parsonage gave every evidence of being the first engine in a celestial train. Starched Victorians leaned from windows of The Parsonage. A few of the ladies screamed, but the screams were only for show.

The Victorians, now riding in The Parsonage, had planned the capture of August Starling at the opening of the coffin. Agatha was to arise and dance with Starling. When she had him close to the coffin, Victorian gentlemen would shove him in and lock the lid. The Victorians' grand plan now lay in tatters; but, knowing The Parsonage as they did, they suspected they were not yet out of action. Meanwhile, in the basement of The Parsonage, Kune still attended Collette.

Darkness followed the tail of the parade. One felt (and so it would develop) that when entering that darkness to the depth of two inches, one would be blind as if cast inside a slab of black marble. The darkness was like a tombstone rising into the firmament. Joel-Andrew, who stood alone except for Obed—and also, no doubt—Samuel and the ministerial association, who at the time were in concealment—recognized the true nature of the darkness. It was medieval, the stuff of witchcraft, of Inquisitions, of bigotry and intolerance. It was positive as the ebony face of history, the blackly laughing face of dogma and theocracy, the nighttime shine of satanic worship. A coven of witches might hope to create a small patch of such darkness, but no witch or warlock who ever walked could pull forth such saturating night.

The parade, however, remained joyous. Before the enormous ebony coffin, the stately carriage of the grand marshal, August Starling, moved with the certainty of a capital ship. For the occasion, August Starling dressed in a mourning suit of deepest black. His boyish face displayed woe, but boyish charm also crossed his face in flickers of friendliness and compassion. August Starling looked like the confused dreams of gently but firmly raped children. He looked like the hoary reminiscences of aging burlesque queens.

In the carriage with August Starling sat Beauregard Shooter, the new messiah, and the lady who sold stocks and bonds. The messiah waved. He scattered coupons and indulgences. The lady who sold stocks and bonds wept copiously. She wore an elegant black gown with a plunging neckline that tickled her navel. The lady mourned the passing of the dear departed, showed cleavage, was so sincere the roadway got slicky-slick with frozen tears as horses, people, the elephant and the Grand Army of the Republic joined in.

Meanwhile, The Parsonage jived with the Navy. The Parsonage clanked its bells and flew in precise angles so that naval action would take out the blimp, or part of the parade. The missile frigates tracked The Parsonage with pom-poms, so busy aiming at The Parsonage that it did not notice a flotilla of tiny specks distantly approaching down the Strait. Waters of the Strait boiled, as if expressing school after school of five-ton sardines. The frigates founded themselves surrounded by at least half of the world's remaining whales.

The parade thumped along. As it passed the boat basin, the Chinese dragon rolled into the parade route where it snorted smoke to the bonging of gongs. Gongs sounded broad and stately in the midst of farewell music by a choir of porn queens. The dragon looked alarmingly lifelike, but surely the smoke came from smoke pots concealed beneath its framework. At the head of the parade, August Starling waved. A black and silver shadow passed over the parade, blimpish; a houselike shadow followed. Drums rolled, while clarinets squealed like impassioned piglets. The

Parsonage cruised low and slow above the parade, its chimneys streaming smoke. The Chinese dragon snorted smoke in return. Nearly naked Chinese turned taunting faces upward, and roared Chinese curses. Victorians leaned from windows of The Parsonage. They stuck out their tongues and went, "N'yah n'yah." Giddy and un-Victorian Bronx cheers trailed away as The Parsonage headed for the Strait and a showdown with the Navy.

"I must know where everyone is placed," Joel-Andrew confided to Obed as they watched the approaching parade. "We must protect those who cannot protect themselves." Joel-Andrew and Obed stood before August Starling's restored commercial building. The street seemed deserted, except high on ledges where cats wove dancing ribbons of gray and white. A rumpus progressed behind the doors of The Fisherman's Café. From the boat basin came a desperate whistle as the tour ship signaled distress. Fleeing sailors and officers tumbled down the gangway, as the tour ship was abandoned to an attack force of cats.

"Cats have captured the tour ship and The Fisherman's Café," Joel-Andrew told Obed. "I hope it is not a foolish move."

Obed smiled. He did not tell Joel-Andrew of the cats' primitive plans and methods. He said nothing of tails wrapped in garlic, of claws tipped with silver.

Obed turned to check the street. Maggie stood unflickering behind the window of Janie's Tavern, while Frank polished the bar. Maggie's eyes glowed dark as the eyes of storm. It seemed that Bev, together with the Suffragettes, the IWW and the World War I vet, hid in the bookstore. Jerome snubbed several TV cameramen as he made methodical notes from a third-floor vantage point.

"O Lord," Joel-Andrew prayed, "not one of us is innocent of very much, especially Your humble servant. But Lord, may we be given light to battle darkness?" Joel-Andrew, now carried by the decisions of fury, stood ready to wield the power of the Lord.

Obed advised that Gerald engaged with the Chinese, while The Sailor and the Irish cop kept eyes on the dragon and the elephant. The morose cop monitored August Starling. Townspeople showed off new wardrobes, while tourists formed a great wave following the coffin. In addition, Obed pointed out with interest, a number of time jumps were appearing. At least, Obed pointed out, he *hoped* they were time jumps. In addition, Obed further pointed out as he hit the deck, there was a concerted beating of wings.

More than a hundred squadrons of ducks swept overhead. The ducks quacked wonderfully as they headed toward the conflict developing on the Strait. The ducks showed off. That was especially true of the mergansers, who flew on their backs.

Subtleties of light began to ascend. "O Lord," Joel-Andrew prayed, "there is only one enemy. I beg You do not smite the multitude." On the Strait, The Parsonage flashed only a foot or two above the waves. The Parsonage moved at enormous speed, accompanied by ducks. Shakes blew from its roof, cracks appeared in windowpanes. The Parsonage took some wounds.

Light grew slowly; a theater of light, a concatenation. A helix of rainbows stood overhead as ball lightning and chain lightning dwelt above distant islands. Silver and blue light danced along edges of the helix. Three suns stood in the sky, while against August Starling's backdrop of darkness beat the brilliant wings of angels.

Angels cannot be viewed directly, for the human mind and eye become stunned. The wings spanned distances far greater than the wings of any aircraft; and although the TV news anchor reported them as northern lights, the report was in error. The crowd knew northern lights when it saw them, and these were not they.

When cherubs occupied the ledges of downtown buildings, even cats ceased their dance. On the Strait, ducks strafed the Navy, the frigates turning gleaming white beneath great burdens of guano. The Parsonage cruised inches above the masts of fleeing ships, as Victorians pelted the Navy with sachet-scented hankies. The Victorians expended ammunition wantonly. Paintings of Presbyterian preachers crashed on flying bridges. Victorian loveseats exploded against cannons. As the ships fled, they passed the growing fleet of specks progressing down the Strait. Whales banged against the fleeing frigates, the ships bouncing like plastic toys in a bathtub.

"I would tell people to repent," Joel-Andrew explained to the Lord. "The problem is they pay no attention. That means I'll have to use graphics, because they are unsure of what should be repented. It's that sort of time in history, Lord."

Voices of tourists and townspeople chattered. "I knew August Starling was just *super-duper*," a member of the Martha Washington Brigade confided coquettishly to a member of the Loyal Order of Beagles, "but I never dreamed he was *this* good."

Light rose beneath the beating of mighty and angelic wings as August Starling's parade bumped forward. The hearts of tourists gladdened. This was a display of American might, and God was on the side of the Just. God was a winning quarterback, a colonel of infantry.

The sky opened in the form of a rose window. Beams of stained glass-flavored sunlight, red, gold, orange, purple, blue poured onto the street. Cherubs sang in reedy voices. Broad sounds of Chinese gongs seemed no more than tiny punctuations to the controlled pianissimo of a heavenly choir.

At Joel-Andrew's back, time jumps intensified, and while the time jumps were colorfully macabre, they were not unbeautiful before the music of the choir. The crowd watched, and it seemed there was very little to repent. Asian women wept above emaciated babies, while children lay with blackened hands and faces beneath the scorching scent of napalm. Street kids rapped, gave each other high fives, or lay stoned and dying in doorways. Disemboweled grandmothers, dressed in gaudy South American costumes, lay beside starved bodies of Africans, while oil rigs hovered in the far distance; and a babble of Middle Eastern languages argued above purring engines of Mercedes and Lincolns, above the exasperating cough of lungs burned by mustard gas.

"These, too, are my beloved," Joel-Andrew confided to Obed. "There has been a lot of dancing going on."

Presidents strode proudly, and a garrulousness of flags snapped above the distant oil rigs. Statesmen swapped naked concubines. Chain saws roared, great trees fell, and bulldozers moved across the sky; the bulldozers ridden by white men and yellow men and black men—the men in business suits—as machinery of every kind—and cleverly designed to fail—fell apart like unfulfilled scrap metal. Banners, denoting efficiency, flew above ghettos. Credit cards rained from tiny puffs of storm clouds, whispering in plastic voices; and the TV news anchor yammered. "At no time in history," the news anchor proudly proclaimed, "has this network reported such evidence of systems endorsement. We will attempt to interview a cherub after this important commercial break."

August Starling's parade thumped to a halt. The enormous ebony coffin stood behind spans of black horses; the coffin decorated with white ribbons of virgin purity. Darkness stood at the back of the parade, while heavenly light stood in front. About fifty yards of normal daylight separated the head of the parade from celestial light.

The new messiah descended from the carriage, and August Starling descended as well. The messiah grunted to the crowd, "Yuh know, a big bad miracle. A real mutha. We gonna have a miracle, yuh know." The new messiah's seven-foot-six-inch height hovered above the slight and chirping figure of August Starling. The messiah looked downward and deeply, into cleavage of the lady who sold stock and bonds. The messiah scratched his crotch, seemed puzzled. "It's a matter of defensement," he explained kindly to the crowd. "Defense 'em good and put on a full court press . . ." The messiah's message was drowned beneath applause.

Joel-Andrew stepped forward. The elephant gave a raspberry. The dragon looked puzzled. Angel wings churned wind in the high heaven. Above the Strait, The Parsonage was heavily buffeted as it returned—bells aclank—from its skirmish with the Navy. Bare rafters appeared here and there on The Parsonage, which had lost about half of its roof. Its "Strike Headquarters" sign flapped in tatters. The Parsonage rose—accompanied by ducks—toward a dogfight with the blimp. Victorians cheered, and Victorian ladies unsheathed hatpins. Obed scampered forward, conferred in a low voice with the dragon. The dragon looked surprised. Its enameled hide no longer looked enameled. Its tail switched, rose high, and, as Obed continued the conversation the dragon's eyes showed that it understood the situation.

"Matters proceed apace," August Starling said, and perhaps he spoke to Joel-Andrew. "I've not been so pleased with anything since the creation of fire." His pencil line mustache twisted, curled; his lips vital. August Starling looked about him, looked at the fantastic congregation of souls, and he forgot to chirp. He licked his lips.

"You are missing some members of your crew," Joel-Andrew observed quietly. "My anger is for all of you. I don't see your imitation preacher or the real estate lady." His eyes, usually so gentle, now flashed with anger.

"They engage in a symbolic act," Starling chuckled. "In the backseat of the carriage." Starling looked to the sky, looked toward the Strait boiling with whales. "Their *last* symbolic act," Starling chuckled. "Goody has no soul, and hers won't assay very high; but a few pennies here, a few pennies there. It adds up." August Starling put on a wonderful show for his audience, but his eyes at first seemed dead, then momentarily fearful. "I had you figured for another fruitcake," August Starling said. "Now I'm impressed. Who are you? I thought all the men like you were dead."

"You're not dealing with me," Joel-Andrew said serenely. "You deal once more with the Lord."

"Don't try to run a number," August Starling said. "The Lord and I go back a long way. The Lord is only as strong as His servants." August Starling seemed ruminative, then seemed nearly fatalistic. "Up till now," he said, "I've had a most enjoyable century."

"Evil makes no sense," Joel-Andrew said. "Why not do something else?"

"You think Evil is senseless? So, go and explain Good," August Starling said. "Meanwhile, this is going to be a real shootout." August Starling pretended unconcern. "I haven't been in one like this since the 1740s."

"You has to maintain a good protein balance if you gonna be a jockstrapper." The messiah's voice sounded in the background as he gave serious explanations to the crowd. "You also gotta know your dealer better'n you know your brotha."

"As a matter of curiosity," Joel-Andrew said, "what do you do with folks after you get them? Pitchforks and everlasting fire? It doesn't seem like much fun." Joel-Andrew's voice remained nicely controlled, but his eyes were afire in a concentration of fury.

"It's a different time in history," August Starling said. "The ones like Goody we simply render into tinned meat, sandwich spreads, that sort of thing. The women, of course, we use." August Starling looked sadly at the Martha Washington Brigade. "Some are unusable. We put those to sweeping up charnel houses, or transform them into social workers. The transformation takes a very small investment, and we enjoy quite sizable returns."

August Starling looked fondly at his parade, gasped as the dragon left the ground in a roar of flame and smoke and Chinese cheers. "Dirty pool," August Starling said. "Who breathed life into the dragon?" August Starling looked at Joel-Andrew, looked at the brilliantly lighted heavens, then looked toward Janie's Tavern, where Maggie sneered at him and waved.

"You better get on with your show," Joel-Andrew said. The dragon thundered Chinese curses as it flew—clumsily at first, in fact almost puppylike—toward time jumps of gunboats and diplomats and sweatshops. "That particular dragon is not a Buddhist," Joel-Andrew said.

And, in fact, Joel-Andrew was correct. There seemed nothing contemplative about the dragon. As its wingbeat stiffened, as it became more accurate in flight, it was joined in its attacks by platoons of muscovy and wood ducks. Across the great and angel-filled sky, beneath the gorgeous stained glass rose window, the dragon flew like a green and crimson flash. When it paused from breathing smoke and flame, it sang wailing music based on flatted fifths and Oriental progressions. It flung its fire at incredible speeds from incredible heights. Japanese businessmen fled, while transistors crackled and died. Old scores were apparently being settled, and—while the ducks had no agenda—they were carried by the excitement of a major win. The ducks quacked and splat. From inside Janie's Tavern, Maggie cheered.

"Let's get it over," Joel-Andrew said. "I won't make a full move until you take your best shot." Joel-Andrew looked at the three-mile parade, the great throng of people, and at the Chinese mob which now yelled and cheered as the dragon did a series of intricate loops accompanied by widgeons.

"And, incidentally," Joel-Andrew said to August Starling, "if you step forward into the Lord's light, you know what will happen."

"I always hate this part," August Starling admitted. "On the other hand, I always win the aftermath. In addition, simple statistics say a certain number of wins are inevitable; and odds on this one look good."

Above the Strait, the blimp seemed thinner. Its flashing signs stuttered. Bells from the octagonal tower of The Parsonage clanked in celebration, mixing with songs of cherubs and the high-keening call of the dragon. The dragon took tips from the ducks. It barrel-rolled, then headed toward the sky above the busted pharmaceutical company. The blimp hovered there, and both blimp and Parsonage had suffered harm. The blimp looked like a punctured tire. The Parsonage had scarcely a shake or shingle left. August Starling motioned toward his messiah. Then he motioned to hostlers to open the elaborate ebony coffin.

A coffin so huge must surely contain mechanical mysteries, and indeed this coffin did. The opening movements were like the slowly paced opening of an ebony flower. Cleverly concealed hydraulic shafts slowly lifted the lid, lowered the front and the ends. Members of an Air Force drill team presented drawn sabers as the Marine band played Wagner, Wagner taking another loss.

"It moves so slowly," a member of The Martha Washington Brigade confided to a member of the Loyal Order of Beagles. "As a true American girl, I used to enjoy slow and rhythmic motion." The lady giggled and blushed, as the gentleman cast a desperate gaze about, looking for an escape route.

"You stand here," August Starling whispered to his messiah. "The lady in the coffin is named Collette. The moment she stirs, give an incantation. Then raise your hands to the sky. Can your brains handle all that?" August Starling faced the crowd like an orchestra conductor leading the congregated weeping. He faced a sea of hankies, honking noses, tearful eyes. At his back, time jumps stood above the islands. The blimp—or what was left of it—hung draped like a squeezed bar rag over the ruins of the pharmaceutical company. From the gondola of the blimp, crewmembers dropped a rope ladder and escaped. Victorian cheers sounded faint in the distance.

The ebony flower of the coffin spread its petals wide, and the first things visible were the tall and ornately carved roses of a Victorian bed. The bed stood curtained, but front draperies opened to reveal remains of the dear departed. At first the dear departed could not be seen, for the walls moved so slowly. From the Grand Marshal's carriage, Goody and the real estate lady descended. Goody checked his fly, as the real estate lady faked a satisfied look. The new messiah faced the coffin muttering incantations. "Stock options," the messiah muttered. "Ya' gotta trust ya' agent." The messiah's voice rose firmly. "Man-to-man defense," he proclaimed, "must-a play 'em tough inside. Press 'em into zone."

Small gasps ran through the crowd of Point Vestal residents as the coffin opened farther. The crowd had not known who the dear departed was going to be, but the crowd knew Agatha when it saw her. Had they seen Collette, they would have been impressed. But Agatha was only a ghost. The crowd could not know that Agatha was part of a Victorian scheme to capture August Starling. What the crowd also could not see was the confusion going on in Agatha's mind.

She was—and for that matter—remains, a country girl. She became nervous, and the more nervous she got, the more rapidly she flickered.

"Contract violation," the new messiah chanted in the direction of August Starling. "Hey, coach, this is one screwy-looking bimbo."

Chapter 33

AUGUST STARLING'S FACE AGED. FOR A MOMENT IT BECAME A shadowy mask before a dry and clacking skull. He slumped in his fine mourning suit, then corrected his demeanor.

"You may not amount to much after all," Starling hissed at Joel-Andrew. "If you and the Lord have to stoop to subterfuge, I've got you both on my level. On my level, I *always* win."

"It's your own mistake," Joel-Andrew told him. "You owe this one to Agatha and the Irish cop, to Gerald, the morose cop and The Sailor. You forgot that not everyone has volunteered to become trivial." Then Joel-Andrew blinked, and backed up a step. He was not having a revelation, only a realization. "That's the reason everyone around here has been dancing with the dead. That's the reason they are drug dealers by default. Their civilization is trivial."

"It isn't much of a crop," August Starling admitted. "But it's the twentieth century, and you take what you can get. Trust me. I've been in the business a long time." August Starling turned back to the crowd, and announced that resurrections were not accomplished instantly. To his messiah, he hissed, "Start dribbling while I put together a diversion." Starling turned back to Joel-Andrew. "Poker it is, then. I call your angels and raise you."

Splats of darkness crashed against the face of the bluff and ran like ink. Streaks of darkness became filaments above the parade, and strands of the stuff began to wave and weave. A gigantic dark net fashioned itself above the crowd. The TV anchor chattered,

240

giving an in-depth analysis of perverse mating practices among marsupials. Above the crowd, imps and demons climbed along the filaments, and the sky above the parade erupted with obscene laughter, or with perverse jokes of locker room and office. The TV anchor switched to an indepth analysis of social norms as reflected by graffiti.

Joel-Andrew moved his hand. At his back, flowers sprouted from the pavement. Daffodils, black-eyed Susans, a sea of nasturtiums; and Joel-Andrew stood in a field of flowers. The scent of flowers perfumed the winter air. Poppies bloomed orange, red, purple. Wisteria dripped from the fronts of buildings. Morning glory twined about stands of daisies. Shadows of cats and cherubs danced across the street of flowers.

"Thank You, Lord," Joel-Andrew said. He turned to Agatha. "This *thing* will never harm you again," he said, and he referred to Starling. "Just lie quietly, because it is almost over."

If August Starling was disconcerted, no one knew. His smile seemed genuine, although his sallow face aged rapidly. Light breezes blew flower petals toward him as he stepped backward and away. A floating petunia lodged in the cleavage of the lady who sold stocks and bonds. Starling spoke in gutturals.

Starling looked skyward, where in the distance the dragon and The Parsonage stunted with each other as they returned from a successful engagement. The wings of angels flashed. The dragon warbled. August Starling looked at the network of black, and flicked his hand. The network began transforming, drawing accurate and intricate lines. In the sky above the parade, a giant spider's web formed and began to vibrate before a cold and sulfurous breeze.

"People are going to die," Starling said happily. "I'll shock them into battle. I may not get them all, but I'll net the ones who actually maim and kill. We'll see who collects the remains." As the web formed, tiny red spiders began to rain onto the crowd. The spiders moaned in teeny voices. Spiders flung filaments of web, so that hair and clothing became sticky. At Joel-Andrew's back, olive trees sprouted, their silver-greenish leaves like wind-whispering darts. Columbine and sweet peas tangled among lilacs and cosmos and hollyhocks. The approaching figure of The Parsonage now had someone at the helm. A figure stood in the all-seeing tower, and as The Parsonage entered into sunlight Kune's long blond hair could be seen streaming in the wind.

The Parsonage moved like a rescuing hand as Kune issued confident orders to the Victorians. In the crowd, where he had been making explanations to the Chinese, Obed's voice raised the powerful notes of "Old One Hundred."

"My powers are at full term," August Starling said pleasantly, although his face aged by the second. "If past experience holds true, nothing frightens people more than darkness. However, let's spice up the darkness." He waved his hand, and across the web appeared the figure of a monster spider. The spider was yellow and black and red. It snarled. It spread wide as a shopping mall and had fangs dripping black and acidic drool.

August Starling sneered at Joel-Andrew, and at his messiah, at Goody, at all of his entourage. He raised his eyes above the parade, and motioned toward the trailing darkness. "Fear of darkness is in part preternatural," he sneered. "It is principally atavistic."

On Joel-Andrew's side the world lay agleam with sunshine. On Starling's side, night winds blew cold and cruel across the parade. Darkness deeper than a muffler of black velvet blanked the parade. Screams of Chinese terror echoed, intermixed with screams from tourists, townspeople, the elephant. The parade was about to stampede as terror increased beneath the wail of demons. August Starling turned to Joel-Andrew.

"They will fall upon each other in the darkness," August Starling said. "It's so dark in there, they cannot see your light. They cannot hear your voice, nor other sounds beyond the darkness. They cannot see the tips of their noses."

"The Lord would destroy you now," Joel-Andrew said, "but there's a lesson to be learned by the people of Point Vestal. You trick yourself with foolishness."

From the darkness came the roaring voice of the Irish cop as he fought for order. The elephant trumpeted. A magnificent splat came from somewhere, and the elephant gasped and fell silent. In the distance, Gerald's voice rose, commanding, and shrieks of frightened horses diminished beneath the morose cop's quiet voice; while screams from tourists and townspeople became ascendant. As its hissing became louder, the giant spider seemed lowering toward the mob. From darkness covering the parade, the news anchor's voice gave an in-depth analysis of reproductive practices among arachnids.

"Please do something," Agatha begged Joel-Andrew. "Those people suffer." Agatha flickered more slowly as fear turned to compassion.

"They suffer deeply," Joel-Andrew said. "They have not, however, yet suffered as you have suffered."

"I don't want that to happen to anyone," Agatha told him. "I was happy with a new husband, and then I was murdered. I had no children or grandchildren. I've been twenty years old for a hundred years—and all I can say"—and she broke into tears—"is please save them."

The shadow of a house hovered overhead. "I trust that torches will carry the day." A Victorian gentleman's voice was controlled. To August Starling, the voice said, "That is a dastardly trick. We will deal with you directly, sir." It was the same gentleman who had spoken at length during Starling's display of new coffins.

"Torches," Janie confided to her bouncer. "There are children and pets trapped in that darkness."

Obed's voice rose in a singsong of Chinese, and Obed was answered by the dragon who entered the darkness high above the parade. The dragon disappeared in a snort of smoke, and from its hide sparks of light showered like fireworks.

Some of the more adventurous Victorian gentlemen had doffed coats and hats. The gentlemen clung as lookouts in winter branches of trees. Other of the gentlemen rigged lifelines, and prepared the enormous lot of The Parsonage to accommodate refugees.

"We have light." Kune's voice sounded from the all-seeing tower. "We also have the honor to be doing something useful." From the all-seeing tower, a beam of light so pure that at it could only be the light of heaven pierced August Starling's darkness. The flashing tail of the dragon could be seen as the dragon flung itself toward the monster spider.

"What about the bloody heathen?" another Victorian gentleman asked about the Chinese. This gentleman was small and potbellied, but his voice sounded resolute. His sleeves were rolled in anticipation of the task, and his wrists looked capable. "I suppose one cannot, in good conscience, abandon the poor blighters."

"One cannot, of course," said yet another Victorian voice, a rather aged gentleman. "Although they meant to take us hostage, and certainly mean us harm."

"For beyond doubt," yet another gentleman said, and this voice had the clipped intonations of a businessman, "there are those of us who contributed to their unhappy state. We have a responsibility—nay, a duty—to their souls."

"Because we are Victorians," yet another voice said.

"Because we are Presbyterians," Janie told the lot of them.

To Kune, she yelled, "Let's *move* it up there, buddy."

=

Sobbing diminished, screams diminished as the Victorians and The Parsonage brought load after load of refugees from the darkness and into the street of flowers. Victorians kept stiff upper lips, remained calm; and some of their strength and calm affected the crowd. As Bev and the IWW and the Suffragettes and the WWI vet attended minor bruises, scrapes and hysteria, the darkness was gradually defeated. Joel-Andrew engaged in a struggle against darkness, but no one except Agatha had time to pay attention.

Forces of light and forces of darkness played across the heavens, and across the faces of Joel-Andrew and August Starling. They locked in struggle, like the struggle of mythical and titanic forms. Cracks in the pavement opened as fire and the yellow stench of sulfur rose clawing at Joel-Andrew's eyes. Joel-Andrew answered with a little whirlwind that carried the dangerous stuff into the atmosphere. In retrospect, Agatha feels the issue was never in serious doubt, although she remembers flashes of awful fear. There were moments when every soul in Point Vestal seemed forfeit.

August Starling stirred the earth, rumbled the earth, so the bluff shook in danger of avalanche. Soil and boulders hovered ready to fall on the hidden parade. Joel-Andrew answered with the winds of heaven and with the molding power of driven rain. Joel-Andrew cast forth sycamore, blackberry, and thickly netting roots of ivy. The bluff held. Joel-Andrew struck hard with the cries of birds, the crashing echoes of waterfalls, and with glancing light like sunlight hovering around fountains. Starling staggered, lost ground; and then Starling replied with the screams of tortured men, with the choking smell of cremation ovens and gas chambers. Through it all, Kune's voice, sounding firmly from above, directed the rescue operation. Obed and Gerald had the crowd under strong control. Obed's voice called from the darkness. Obed told jokes, or sardonic stories that were fabulous.

August Starling's face became drawn. It shriveled like paper, seemed flayed. His eyes turned dark black, then turned to red. Tiny whispers of flame dwelt about his lips. Joel-Andrew's gray-green eyes were alight with strain, and he stared, stared, stared at August Starling. Joel-Andrew seemed to fear risking so much as a single blink, and his slight form tensed until his shoulders shook. August Starling brought forth flame from the earth, and Joel-Andrew covered it with soft fingers of rapidly falling snow. Joel-Andrew shoved Starling's darkness backward, then paused to catch his breath. Starling brought the darkness forward, nearly to the edge of the field of flowers. It was then that the battle heated up.

Cracks appeared on the horizon. The line between sea and sky shattered, and from the awful void between sea and sky spewed creatures of hell, and of hell's imagination. A wave of fangs, claws and witchery spread above the waters of the Strait while heavenly light staggered beneath the molten glow of volcanic eruptions.

Warlocks rode high and grand, their long capes flying so the sky temporarily stood curtained in darkness. Witches ran the scale of satanic laughter, while demon bats stroked the skies with leathery wings. Trolls and werewolves and obscene giants walked a path above the water. Snakes as long as sea serpents cruised the surface of the Strait, but the snakes were met by pod after pod of killer whales. The snakes flailed, then disappeared in flashes of smoke as the whales struck, then struck again. Lightning cracked and thunder roared. As his forces massed, August Starling dropped every pretense of chirping. His slight form grew, his face became tense and lean. As the sky blackened, fire dwelt on August Starling's fingertips, and fire lived on each side of him; the fire coiling heavenward in twisting fountains.

Joel-Andrew answered with extravagant rainbows. The rainbows formed complete circles, like colored smoke rings in the sky. Rainbows spun loops through which no warlock could pass. Witches attempted to ride through the circles, and the witches and warlocks turned into clear air. Trolls tumbled and were torn by werewolves, while the werewolves—with long drawn howls—were absorbed by streaks of silver light. The void between sea and sky snapped shut as giants struggled in the mouth of the closing seam. The sky brightened a shade, and Joel-Andrew cast forth a rope of seasons. The beauty of winter twisted happily in a woven strand containing summer, spring, and autumn.

August Starling answered with ice, and it was clear that August Starling was as exhausted—or perhaps more exhausted—than Joel-Andrew. Ice cloaked the Strait where whales broke through a layer of salt ice in order to breathe. Icebergs bumped the shore, and ice fell into the darkness covering the parade. When The Parsonage emerged with yet another load of refugees, it moved ponderously beneath a great weight of ice. Ice fell upon Joel-Andrew, and his face turned into a mask of frost. He was forced to answer, forced to take his best shot.

"There is eternity, and there is life," Joel-Andrew whispered to Agatha, but he kept his eyes locked on August Starling. "Eternity can be just lovely. It is a little like life, but with more peaks and chasms." Joel-Andrew brought forth rack after rack of warm breezes. The breezes struck the ice and cooled. "On the other hand, you are a woman who never had a chance at life. If you could live once more, would you choose that?"

Agatha recalls that there was really no decision to be made. Yes, she would choose life. She recalls that she nodded dumbly.

"O Lord," Joel-Andrew prayed, "may thy humble servant Agatha once more enter unto Your beautiful world." Joel-Andrew's voice was hoarse, his frame shaken beneath ice and the blows of ice. His voice staggered with fatigue. Agatha heard him, and August Starling heard him; but, after all, they were close enough to Joel-Andrew, and they could hear the slightest whisper.

Agatha recalls the surge of heavenly light. She recalls the entry of life, of resurrection. She recalls her gladness as her arm raised and she felt its weight. She recalls the sweet and stenchy air that

246

first entered her lungs. Agatha stepped from the enormous ebony coffin, and Agatha was alive. It was then that August Starling stood in a pyre of flame and began to scream.

Starling's form extended, became taller, thinner, like a wisp of his own fire. The elegant suit fell away as flesh melted beneath flame. In moments, it seemed, only moments, a dry and clacking skeleton stood screaming in the flame. Then the skeleton became etched with blue fire, like a blueprint of death standing before its own darkness. The skeleton gradually lowered, began to crumble, and the crumbles screamed. The crumbles turned to dust, so that in moments August Starling was only a pile of dust lying before darkness. The dust screamed, and it uttered fragmentary and tiny screams as it was carried away before a flower-scented wind.

Saturating darkness turned deep gray, then lighter gray, as people escaped under their own power. It was quite a show, and the tourists were confused because they did not know if what they experienced was part of the planned program. As darkness turned to pale gray, the broken corpse of the spider dangled across the equally broken rack of web and sky. A gleam of sunlight touched the spider, and the hulk melted into steam. Confusion remained rife, but it appeared that, except for one enormous headache, and one set of badly bruised knuckles, no serious injuries were sustained. The headache belonged to the elephant, which had to be pulled back to this world with smelling salts. The knuckles belonged to the Irish cop, who had been forced to coldcock the elephant before it went on a frightened rampage.

Joel-Andrew knelt in a field of broken flowers. He began to give thanks to the Lord. His mouth moved, whispered, and while he did not mean to speak privately, his fatigue was too great. He tipped forward, then caught himself and rested on all fours.

Around the wreck of the parade, Chinese formed a frightened mob, while beside them the dragon gave tranquil snorts. Townspeople stood before The Fisherman's Café, and tourists huddled everywhere. Obed and The Sailor and the morose cop stood with the Chinese. Gerald dusted his hands, then announced he was headed for City Hall. With Starling defeated, Gerald looked forward to a jail delivery of federal cops. He looked forward to running every single one of them out of town. The Victorians stood on the huge lot of the broken and wounded Parsonage. Kune reigned in the all-seeing tower. The Victorians looked toward Joel-Andrew, and then they knelt in Presbyterian prayer. It was then the angels made their move, and Samuel made his.

Above the parade, high up there on the bluff beneath the celestial light of angels, shadowy figures took distinct forms as band after band and tribe after tribe of Indians rose in silence. They wore war paint, carried banners; and their horses—trained to battle—snorted. Every local tribe was represented, and there were visitors from the far outskirts of Seattle. Lances sported scalp locks; spears were adangle with feathers. The Indians looked toward the Strait, where a thousand war canoes glowed black and crimson, yellow and green. Banners flew from the Strait, banners flew from the bluff; while at the other end of the street—some two thousand yards away—and with stately calm, Samuel sat astride the dark horse Wesley—Samuel flanked by the ministerial association—Samuel backed by half the Tlingits and Haidas and Shimsians of north Seattle. The dragon puffed smoke. Oriental chatter welled and was punctuated with Oriental fear.

Because, what the Chinese did not know, and nobody else knew either, was that Samuel had not been fooling when he said there was a great awakening in the countryside. The Indians came to town in order to contain the original curse; the curse which said the sea would rise. If the curse were not contained, the sea would spread as far as a man could go in a day and a half. The ministerial association and Samuel formed ranks at the far end of Main Street. They formed other ranks on top of the bluff.

"O Lord," Joel-Andrew prayed, "there really *is* a peace that passes all understanding, and I thank You for it." Joel-Andrew's eyes were transcendent, although he breathed heavily, and remained on all fours.

The sky lighted with heavenly flame. Then came the whisper of gigantic wings as angels floated gently from the heavens. Bare-branched trees on the lot of The Parsonage burst into foliage and fruit. Grass turned from winter brown to a rush of spring green. Light became so concentrated that no one could look directly, but a few old-timers knew enough to turn their gaze aside and look from the corners of their eyes. They report that each angel took the hands of two Victorians, then rose skyward; and the Victorians sang with the unbounded joy of freedom. In an anthem of praise, Janie's voice rose in a firm contralto beside the raspy bass of her bouncer. Janie's red hair and purple gown looked like gorgeous ornaments against the purity of the angel's white gown. Other angels floated down silently; then the angels' wingbeats began as they rose, and flower-scented winds washed over the great crowd. Prayerful songs of joy rose from Victorian lips as angels stepped skyward on heaven-bound wings. The Victorians at last were free from the shabby bonds of harlotry, the shabbier bonds of meaningless duty. Their voices congregated in a grand doxology above the voices of departing cherubs, as the entire heavenly body disappeared through the rose window that now overflooded the sky. When we looked around us, the only ghosts left were Gerald and the morose cop and Maggie and The Sailor.

And we knew, all of us—at least all who cared—knew that Joel-Andrew may or may not have brought salvation to Point Vestal, but he certainly brought it to the Victorians. The entire town, The Parsonage, the tourists, even the surrounding tribes of Indians stood silent beneath the great rose window and watched Joel-Andrew's tired figure as he sank back on his heels and rested.

"Dad blast it anyway, Tammy," a chubby and aging tourist said to his chubby and aging wife. "I didn't see any resurrection, and now even the ghosts are gone." The tourist was affluent, his pockets stuffed with indulgences, and he wore casual clothing which carried all the correct labels. The tourist turned to his colleagues. "Mark you, I've been in one or another business all my life," he said, "and so I sure don't mind when folks try to make a buck." The tourist looked at the shattered parade, at the pharmaceutical company still cloaked with the limp figure of the blimp. "But when folks try to make a buck," the tourist said, "I expect some kind of show for my money. This is a Victorian con." He looked at the crowd of people from Point Vestal, his look not kindly. "This is just one more tourist trap," he said to the other tourists. To his wife he said, "C'mon, Tammy, we're taking our business somewhere else."

Murmurs of "Victorian con" and "tourist trap" ran through the largest congregation of rich tourists Point Vestal had ever seen. Murmurs of "lousy organization" mixed with querulous questions about the disappearance of ghosts, the disappearance of August Starling. Words such as "flimflam" and "overpriced" mingled with words such as "too commercialized." In only moments, the entire crowd of tourists sprinted to cars and motor homes and motorcycles. The road leading out of town rapidly filled with vehicles, as drivers honked in disgust.

Residents of Point Vestal stood before and beside The Fisherman's Café, or on the beach and by the Strait which laps at the back of The Fisherman's Café. They looked at each other, looked at blossoming store windows now crowded with unsalable merchandise. They looked at ebony storefronts, at embroidered silk hankies that read "Farewell." Our people were momentarily confused, for they could not figure out what had happened—or why it had happened—or who was to blame. They muttered and murmured and buzzed. They consulted. Stronger members supported others whose knees became weak. Our people watched the departing automobiles, the diminishing mob of disgusted tourists. It seemed for a moment there would be a town meeting. And then, of course, someone analyzed the situation and arrived at a conclusion.

=

No one knows who actually threw the first stone. Since it had to be someone without sin, we assume it was one of the Mothers Against Transgression and Sensuality. We do know that the first stone made little difference. The throw was tentative, the stone arcing blackly beneath a sunlit winter sky to fall among crushed flowers and roll to a halt three or four feet in front of Joel-Andrew. Joel-Andrew watched it, and at first he was puzzled. Then his face crossed with sadness.

"Get on it!" the TV anchor shrilled to her cameraman. "Stay on the target. This is classic footage." The TV anchor took a couple of deep breaths, then spoke rapidly into her mike. "The network, in an unprecedented piece of investigative journalism, brings you to the small town of Point Vestal where citizens engage in an ancient religious rite." The news anchor yammered, and, because she yammered, our people felt obligated to throw. From his third-floor perch in a building, Jerome tried to countermand the journalistic order, but stones arced beneath sunlight. From the all-seeing tower, Kune screamed, and from the far distance Samuel goaded his dark horse into a dead run. Gerald came from the basement of City Hall, as Obed and The Sailor and the morose cop broke from the mob of Chinese. All of them discovered that they shared a single problem.

It does not take very long to stone a man to death, not if you have enough stones and enough people throwing.

Joel-Andrew attempted to stand. His voice shook, but at least it was no longer a whisper. "Lord," he said, "they are hurt and confused. They are only making a mistake . . ." And then his teeth shattered as a rock cracked against his mouth. Joel-Andrew was silenced. Blood flowed from his lips as he forced himself to his feet. A sharp stone glanced from his forehead, and a second and sharper one pierced his right eye. His head fell forward as he clasped his eye, and a heavy stone caught him in the groin. Bones in his hand cracked and broke as he covered his face, and then one hand fell away as a forearm went limp. The deathblow was probably a rounded rock, weighty as a ball-peen hammer, that struck him in the temple. He did not fall immediately.

Loggers and fishermen showed the power of their arms. Rocks with flat trajectories smashed against Joel-Andrew's knees, and rocks with gleaming quartz crystals divided his ribs. It was a not a merciful death, but at least it was quick.

Patriotic cries came from the Martha Washington Brigade. The Loyal Order of Beagles woofed and howled. The Grand Army of the Republic raised rebel yells, while Mothers Against Transgression and Sensuality huffed and puffed as they threw. Older citizens of Point Vestal passed rocks to stronger and younger men. Permissive parents pressed rocks into the hands of their children.

Joel-Andrew crumpled amid a rain of rock deadly as shrapnel, and the rocks continued to fall although cats jumped screaming from ledges with claws bared; although Obed charged fearless toward the mayor and city council, who competed for the largest number of hits. The rocks rained down, and they drove to the ground the charging figures of The Sailor and the morose cop and the Irish cop. Gerald arrived only a second before Samuel, plus the ministerial association came at full gallop. Gerald and Samuel pushed the mob apart. The TV anchor yammered, while proud citizens of Point Vestal faced the cameras and yelled affectionate words to their mothers. Point Vestal flashed the V for victory sign, and Point Vestal proclaimed that it was Number One, Numero Uno. No one paid the least attention when the front of Janie's Tavern crashed forward, and Maggie stepped forth to brood silently and darkly on the scene.

And to us, who must record this, a sorry scene it was. Joel-Andrew's sandals were worn, his clerical collar frayed. His sandy hair with streaks of gray was clotted with blood. His face looked like a shocked child as Kune knelt above him and felt for a pulse. Kune's physician hands touched gently, but Kune's eyes could not hold the physician's objectivity. His washed yellow eyes held tears as he motioned Samuel toward him. Kune turned Joel-Andrew on his back, arranged Joel-Andrew's hands, and closed Joel-Andrew's broken eyes. Kune looked at the mob, and his own eyes held contempt.

"You love your stories and traditions? You brag about your virtue? You enjoy your dance?"

The crowd turned to each other, gave pleased smiles, bobbed heads nodding yes. It seemed to the crowd the first hopeful sign of a new ad campaign.

"You dance," Kune said, "and this man tried to show you how you dance." Kune's voice rose, a rumble of thunder. "*You have been dancing with the corpses of your Gods!*"

The crowd looked puzzled. Kune had never acted this way before. He had never looked this way before. His blond hair spread across his back, but some of it was colored with Joel-Andrew's blood. Kune knelt, but he still seemed taller than anyone else.

"You are censured," Kune hissed. "I give you the Judgment of the Lord. Live forever, because that means you will forever have to live with yourselves."

The mob recoiled, its collective gaze downcast. The mob moved in shamed silence. Censured. And then, as one person, the mob looked toward Maggie, who stood before the wreck of Janie's Tavern. Maggie no longer flickered, and Maggie was merciful. She could, if she wished, destroy the town as surely as if it were

Sodom. "I knew it was going to happen," Maggie said, "because I know everything. I knew it was going to be ugly. I tried to believe it would not be this ugly." She watched Samuel's tired figure as he knelt beside Joel-Andrew, as he took Joel-Andrew's hand. Samuel's broadcloth suit was dusty, flecked with lather from his aging horse.

"Indians can contain the curse," Maggie said, in the general direction of the mob. "It will not spread beyond the town. But I have something special saved for you." Maggie lifted her arms toward the horizon, and she spoke in language none could understand. Winds arose. The Strait churned. Rain began. Almost instantly the street overran with water, the water washing blood from Joel-Andrew, the rain and wind nearly obscuring Samuel's prayer. No one heard much. All we heard was Samuel's choked weeping and his fervent plea. "O Lord," Samuel prayed, "may Joel-Andrew, Thy humble servant, now depart in peace."

Chapter 34

IT RAINED FOR FORTY DAYS AND FORTY NIGHTS, WHICH IN THESE parts is normal weather in January and February. What was exceptional was the quantity. Rain washed down the mouth of the Strait, as if the Strait itself were a conduit for every storm on earth. Lightning became so common that people forgot to light coal oil lamps; and an eternity of rain crashed over Victorian roofs as water accumulated and covered the town. The wrecked tower of the pharmaceutical company stood in relief against a lightning-stricken sky. As the water level rose, whales and walrus and sea otters and seals played hopscotch around the tall facades of downtown buildings. Our people stood on the bluff, or at the top of the 307-step staircase. They watched the waters rise and keep rising. When the last flagpole on the last roof of downtown disappeared beneath the waves, our people fled to their houses and moved valuables to upstairs rooms.

Shy octopi made nests in The Fisherman's Café, and black cod rested and waved fins along the bar of Janie's Tavern. Beside the bluff whales cruised, and there was no kindness in the eyes of the whales. While ravens chortled in iambs, the whales sneered and slapped mighty flukes, as twice a day—and predictable as storm—tens of thousands of ducks flew over and whitewashed the town. Rain mixed and churned the whitewash, and the whitewash permeated bricks. To this day City Hall remains stained.

During the third week of rain, the waters of the Strait boiled over the bluff and spread through uptown. Whales and water carried away ornate wrought iron on which ghosts were once impaled. Sea lions washed through basements where ghosts once huddled, their teeth chattering with cold. Water flushed away reproduction Victorian gimcracks, while imitation stained glass melted plastically. Water seemed intent on flushing all that was sentimental and false. When the water would finally recede, the town would stand stark, and—if not honest—at least with overt phoniness washed away. However, the water did not recede for a long time, and people spoke of moving. Their problem was that they had no place to go except Seattle.

A few things happened which were remarkable. Chief among them was the tour ship that cruised past uptown houses at the height of the flood. People watched from attics and roofs as the enormous and gorgeous dragon hunkered in the bow like a mighty bowsprit. The dragon blew fire into the rain, and rain turned to a caldron of steam. The Chinese were going home, and this was the Chinese way of hooting goodbye. At the helm of the tour ship The Sailor stood, while the morose cop stood on the plates deep in the engine room—but perhaps this is getting ahead of our story.

Rain exempted the Indians and their war canoes. Indians dryly and mirthlessly paddled through the streets, or they bounded on horses around the perimeter of town, as they contained the curse. The Indians were sarcastic as the whales, and there was no kindness in the Indians. The Parsonage moved to high ground as Kune, transformed, directed rescue operations. Kune spoke to no one except Obed, and Obed gave orders. The very young, the aging, and the ill were protected.

The Starling House became the focus of the elements. Lightning crashed against its towers, and the darkest of all dark clouds hovered to rain on its turrets. Day after day and night after night, lightning struck, set fires, and the fires were washed away by the rain. The Starling House did not melt easily from the scene. It was broken apart, blown into microscopic cinders; as beneath the thunder of rain—and, while porpoises leaped and chuckled above the wreckage—people swore they could hear the cinders uttering small screams.

We understood, almost immediately, that a great depth of purpose was abroad, when, beneath the coiling waters of the Strait, August Starling's commercial building was carried away. The collapse released the ugly merchandise residing on its showroom floor. For three awful days and hideous nights, elaborate coffins floated through our streets. We were glad when they were singled out and exploded by lightning.

The town stood flooded and abandoned by the outside world. The elephant and horses, the federal cops and the television people, had long ago followed the road out of town, over which had traveled the tourists and the Sicilian gunmen and the crews of tour ship and blimp. The town never heard from them again, although in the following year we discovered that the news anchor cinched an Emmy for work done in Point Vestal. Goody and the new messiah and the real estate lady gave the glad news on their new morning TV talk show. The lady who sold stocks and bonds—and who had been hit in the cleavage by a heavenly flower—became a well-known proponent of astral religion. She is reputed to have made a bundle.

It was during the days of unending storm that Samuel and the ministerial association, together with the IWW, the WWI vet and the Suffragettes, embarked on the painful and slow task of healing the broken lives and property and spirits of Point Vestal. They ministered to the frightened and the guilty, even to a few who were repentant. The Irish cop might have helped, but he was too busy attending to the needs of Agatha, who had to make both practical and emotional adjustments. Both he and Agatha succeeded. This was made clear after several months of courtship. Theirs is a happy marriage.

As rains continued, the ministerial association put forth healing hands, and the cats volunteered to stay out of it. This was partly because of sarcasm, partly because the cats busied themselves hiding out in dry attics. The closest the cats could come to charity was to declare a moratorium on mice until the waters receded. After all, the poor mice did not cause the problem, but were forced to retreat to attics like everyone else.

If there was lack of charity (or perhaps a deeper understanding of justice), it was owned by Maggie and Gerald and The Parsonage.

They stayed away from the scene. Obed and The Parsonage were in mourning, while Kune nailed his evidence against August Starling, together with the evidence Collette had collected, to the door of The Parsonage. The evidence flapped in the wind and rain, but it did not melt.

Gerald spent his time keeping order and rebuilding the flooded engine of the '39 LaSalle. Maggie stayed busy orchestrating storms. At the end of forty days and forty nights, Maggie allowed the rains to cease. It was not until after the flood receded that true horror descended.

At first no one noticed anything. Everyone was too busy looking over damage to the town. Gay Victorian houses now stood stark and toneless. In the days when they were haunted, the Victorian houses echoed purpose and pride in heritage. Now they seemed lifeless as tract slums built by governments. The churches weathered pretty well, although none escaped damage. The churches raised steeples to the gray and misty sky, but the steeples now seemed a supplication and not a proclamation. The jail beneath City Hall filled with debris so caked in duck lime, it became cemented. The first act of city council was to float bonds for a new jail. Collette's antique store survived in fair shape, since most of the merchandise could be cleaned. The boat basin had to be rebuilt, although the saltwater swamp did just fine; but it is a lonely place now, where no Christian Scientist voice—or any other voice—echoes. Janie's Tavern had to be rebuilt, as did The Fisherman's Café. Bev's bookstore was a loss, of which more in only a moment, because we come to the final pages of this task.

=

We sit in the warmth of The Fisherman's Café, and it is April. Spring winds crash against the café. The tide smacks and slurps against bulkheads. Gray mist and rain flies before gray spring wind, as Mikey Daniels's milk truck staggers past. The truck looks like a sideways-standing domino deciding which way to tip. In the far distance, out there in the mist, the abandoned pharmaceutical company rises like a specter. Broken top stories are still marked with the heat of fire. This morning the doughnuts gleam goldy with warm brown sprinkles, like the spots of a giraffe. We all agree the doughnuts are very pretty, but no one is eating one.

"We have only two remaining tasks," Samuel proposes. "We have the theological explanation, and we must tell about Kune and Obed and Maggie and The Sailor and the morose cop. We must tell about Gerald." Samuel looks far less fatigued this morning, and his broadcloth suit is nicely brushed. "It is possible," he says, "that explanations about The Sailor and the morose cop and Gerald will say something about theology."

"And pigs don't whistle," Collette murmurs, "'cause pigs have got root-snoots."

"That may well be," Frank says to Collette, "but I don't know what it means." To Samuel he says, "We have *three* things left to accomplish. We must include information for tourists." Frank strokes his beard, looks at the pretty doughnuts; his eyes glazing while his mustache twitches.

"We have *four* tasks," Bev insists in a firm voice. "We are not going to dodge the issue. We have worked too hard and come too far. We will confront the horror that arrived as the waters receded."

We figure we could never have made it this far without the strong offices of Bev. Bev is very pretty this morning, almost girlish. Maybe seeing an end to this book causes her hair to be thicker, her eyes brighter. "Tell it," she says, "and get it over with."

So be it. After the waters receded, everyone stayed busy rebuilding the town. It was only after busy months turned into a full year that we began to fear the Lord's judgment. In a whole year, no one died, not even the very, very, very old people. No one even seemed to age. Some folks were glad, some shrugged it off, and a few began to worry. After the second year, more began to worry. Optimists claimed it was only a matter of time. Pessimists claimed that time was what they feared. After three years, even optimists got queasy. As years tumbled along, new people occasionally moved here from Seattle; and sometimes one of them passed away from illness or accident. Some of their spirits even manifested, but as ghosts they are uninteresting. They mostly enjoy standing in lines. One finds them at the grocery, or the movie, or the laundromat. When they cannot find a line, they make one. We see them forming ranks to view a sunrise.

The sum of it is that no citizen of Point Vestal who suffered the Lord's judgment has died. The sum of it seems to be that we are to live in Point Vestal, undying, for always. Always we will say the same good mornings to each other. Always we will know that city council will raise the sewage rates. Always and always the biggest news will be who wins the pool tournaments. Always we will experience the judgmental smiles of the Martha Washington Brigade and Mothers Against Transgression and Sensuality. The Loyal Order of Beagles will woof, and the Grand Army of the Republic will camp at Janie's Tavern and refight old wars. Fishermen will mutter about the weather. Loggers will hold drinking contests. We will see gray mist rise from the Strait, and the greatest point of interest will be which colored sprinkles decorate the doughnuts at The Fisherman's Café.

"A change may be coming," Jerome snuffles optimistically and consults his notes. "Kune and Joel-Andrew have been walking more of late. Joel-Andrew has been prophesying more of late. I'm pretty certain that means change."

Samuel looks at Bev. Their eyes meet, and in their eyes lie deep and awful understanding the rest of us find puzzling.

"When I cleaned out the bookstore, I experienced a revelation," Bev says. "Largely, I think, because, of all the sections in the bookstore, only the section on theology was an absolute and clotted mess. The rest of the inventory fell apart pretty easily." Bev explains her revelation. Then she explains that we would be wrong to make quick assumptions about Kune and Joel-Andrew.

"It may not be as easy as we think," Samuel says sadly. "Outline the actions of Kune and Obed and Maggie and The Parsonage. Think of The Sailor and the morose cop and Gerald."

"That is easy," Jerome says, and checks his notes. "The Parsonage stands unrepaired. When anyone attempts to put on a new roof, or glaze the windows, The Parsonage moves. It stands nearly roofless beneath the rain." Jerome's honest accounting makes us sad. The Parsonage understands both humility and pride. We do not. The Parsonage's plain walls stand streaked with rust from exposed nails. The all-seeing tower is battered, but not so battered that Maggie cannot live there.

"And Kune is also a silent witness," Jerome snuffles. "Kune walks our streets. Our people see him and know that they are censured. Kune witnesses our actions. If we knew what those actions should be, we would do them; but we do not know." Jerome smiles, his smile a little distant. "It has cut the crime rate one hundred percent." He waves his hand in a vague way. "An ill wind," he mutters.

"Kune and Obed live in the basement of The Parsonage," Frank says. "Nothing civilized about it. Downright frowsy. About what you'd expect, I suppose."

Frank misses something. On clear nights when the moon is full, Obed sits on the bare rafters of The Parsonage and sings. Sometimes the songs are beautiful and filled with hope. Obed has not given over to misery. Obed simply seems waiting for another journey with Joel-Andrew. We might say the same for Kune.

"The theological question," Collette begins.

"The *tourist* question," Frank interrupts.

Collette turns to Frank, and she has had it with Frank. We did not believe Collette capable of such depth of scorn. "To bloody blazes with your flaming tourists," she tells Frank. "And to blazes with you as well." Frank quivers and remains silent.

"The theological question, from a historical point of view, is this," Collette says. "Why did the Lord not send angels for the best of the ghosts? Maggie and Gerald and The Sailor and the morose cop? They were the only ones not taken into heaven."

"For a while now," Jerome admits, "I've been wondering if maybe Maggie actually *is* the Lord."

Samuel's reply is gentle, and although what he says is radical— at least radical for a Methodist—he is not embarrassed. "We may never know. But, we can know this. Truth may sometimes be spoken by the most lying tongues." Samuel turns to Collette. "I've thought and thought about this. August Starling told the truth when he said the Lord is only as strong as His servants. The Lord needed The Sailor and the morose cop to take the Chinese home. The Lord needed Gerald to keep the town from falling upon itself. The Lord needed Maggie, and not simply to orchestrate storms. Without Maggie and The Parsonage, Joel-Andrew's spirit might grow weak."

"Because," Bev explains about the ghosts, "all the Lord had was the ghosts. All He had was *them*. The Lord did not have us."

Collette looks ashamed. Jerome seems confused. Frank is huffy and defensive.

"So I do not think any good changes are coming to Point Vestal," Samuel says. "We have always reassured ourselves by saying, 'At least Joel-Andrew has not abandoned the town.' Now I think otherwise." He looks toward Bev. "My dear," he says, "we promised ourselves a bit of vacation after this book was finished." He reaches to touch Bev's hand. Frank blushes. "Because," Samuel says, "Joel-Andrew walks the beaches. He plays his violin for the gulls. I think Joel-Andrew has not had much to do with the town for a very long time. It seems that Joel-Andrew awaits the return of The Sailor and the morose cop."

"And when that comes to pass," Bev says, "then all of them will leave. Joel-Andrew and Obed and Gerald and Maggie and Kune and The Sailor and the morose cop and The Parsonage. When that happens, we will truly be on our own."

Gray waves crash against bulkheads behind The Fisherman's Café. Those waves have crashed on these beaches since the last ice age. Clouds sail in a weather pattern old as the ocean.

Forever and ever we will sit here as generations of gulls hatch, grow, nest, and die. Whales will cruise the Strait long after the clever ships have passed forever down the channel. The forests will grow, will be clear-cut, will grow again. We will read the newspaper with its weekly account of tricycle wrecks, new litters of kittens, the antics of the city council. Someday, perhaps, we will pray for more than mercy; because surely the day will come when we understand Bev's revelation not only with our minds but with our hearts. Maybe then, there will come another Joel-Andrew, although such men do not arrive in every century.

Bev realized that works without faith are nothing, and faith without works is even less.

And she realized that faith, itself, is shabby stuff. It is not even as strong as doubt. Perhaps we will understand that faith and doubt are only doorways to the kind of work and reverence that will open us to knowledge.

But meanwhile we will sit. The tides will come and go. Samuel and Bev will talk of vacation. They will touch hands and plan, but where will they visit? The land wears away slowly, perhaps an inch or two a year. We sit in The Fisherman's Café and think of time. There is no place to go. There is only here. And then, of course, there is Seattle. And that is all there is. And things have gotten to such a point that maybe that is all there ever will be, ever again. World without end.

Supplemental Material

On Writing the Ghost Story

APPROACH THE CATHEDRAL FROM THE SOUTH AND WALK AROUND *it three times. On the third time, stop before the second gargoyle from the southwest corner. Spin around seven times very slowly while repeating 'aroint ye, aroint ye, aroint ye,' and your warts will disappear.*

I

And, wouldn't you know, that ancient man followed instructions and his warts dried up. The happy results might have caused him to figure that time and expense going into cathedral construction was money well spent. He probably said as much to his neighbors. Word probably got back to the local priest, and the priest had to deal with it; just as we do, today.

The priest would have said, "Miracle," or at least, "Blessing." He would be quick to point out that it was Faith, or the presence of the cathedral that caused disappearing warts. It was not the gargoyle. Or, maybe he would have said something else. After all, it was a long time ago.

Today, we might say "coincidence," or "the placebo effect." We might say, "Quaint story, and isn't it wonderful how even the ancients could spread a certain amount of bull."

Having said that, we could dismiss the story and turn away. We could, in fact, make the same mistake that many have made since the rise of science and rationality in the 18th century. The mistake is best termed "denial of evidence." In its way, it is quite as serious as previous mistakes that denied all rationality and/or science. The universe, I fear, is rather more complicated than we might wish.

For that reason (complication) and because unseen matters sometimes compel me, I wish to spend a few moments giving a definition, and making distinctions. There are reasons to write what I call The Fantastic, and they have nothing to do with notoriety, fame, or money.

Definition: The Fantastic deals in those elements of human experience unexplainable by logic or reason. Such elements may exist within the human mind, or they may exist beyond it.

As we approach distinctions, let us first acknowledge that just because we name something doesn't mean we understand it. We generally understand bull, but not always, because it's an easy excuse for not thinking. We feel that we almost understand coincidence, but coincidence sometimes gets stretched to the breaking point. It gets just too blamed coincidental. If miracles occur, we understand either "faith" or "gee-whiz," and that's about it.

We haven't the foggiest notion about the placebo effect. Physicians know it exists, and physicians use it as standard medical doctrine, but they can't explain it. Nor can they define or explain death, although they can generally tell when it happens. They cannot define life, though science struggles mightily to create it; and, when successful, still won't be able to explain it: only how they made it come to pass. We give names to things, partly, it seems, so we can live comfortably beside matters beyond understanding.

At the same time, it would be the height of stupidity to deny the values of science and rationality. Science helps our understanding. Rationality helps. Logic helps. I stand amazed, sometimes, at the complexities that science reveals about the natural world, and about genetics, physics, astronomy. The trick is to understand that science and rationality are not geared to deal with every problem.

There's a problem of matters that exist "beyond all understanding," a religious phrase describing religious peace. If the phrase didn't go beyond religion, we could categorize it and feel comfortable. To our discomfort, though, "matters beyond all understanding" do not reduce to a single category. Some people have proclaimed this for a long time.

For example, back in the 19th century a social philosopher named Herbert Spencer claimed that we live with The Known, The Unknown, and the Unknowable. Spencer was often a pain-in-the-intellect. He was conceited beyond belief [1] but at least he acknowledged something that the 20th century, and now the 21st, seem to deny. Some things are unknowable, and we live with a little less comfort when we accept that notion.

On the other hand, I here aver that too much comfort is dangerous, anyway, and that is one reason why I explore and write The Fantastic. My other reason has to do with history, a subject to turn to later.

I first propose my discomfort. I do not know why a secondary power station in San Jose holds, for me, a sense of evil and dread. It's not the invisible strength that comes from the transfer of electricity, because no other power station causes such sensations. I do not know why I feel surrounded by peace and enormous power when entering a Tlingit cemetery in Sitka. I do not know why the late night roads through mountains or beside rivers offer sights more slippery than hallucinations; because hallucinations are positive things. I don't know why the voice of a father or brother suddenly sounds from the inner part of my mind, and saves me from being hit by a drunken driver. And, intuition remains a mystery, though I use it successfully in writing and in other forms of living.

I do know that intuition can be trained. In other days when I drove truck long distance, my intuition rose to the task as thousands and thousands of miles piled up. There came a time when, while pulling up the back side of a hill, I knew that trouble lay ahead: a wreck, a cop car, a washed bridge, a tree in the road . . . and I didn't "think" it or "feel" it. I knew it. This, despite the absence of clues. There were no lights in the sky, no sounds, and nothing unusual about the road.

I also know of an invisible world that some folks try to explain. The explainers speak of parallel universes, or past lives, or spirits. Perhaps one or more of their notions is correct. Perhaps all three are a crock, because plenty of flummery surrounds these notions.

Phony mystics sell cheap tricks to the gullible: séances, mysterious rappings on tables, or flying saucer rings in hayfields. There's no end to the clap-trap.

And yet . . . there is evidence, centuries of it. Things Unknowable go on in the universe, but they also go on in the human mind. When rationality is applied to that Something, rationality generally ends up sounding silly.

For example, some who have had a near-death experience report seeing a tunnel of light. The rational explanation for this is offered as: "Your endorphins were kicking in. No wonder you felt wonderful."

It's a questionable analysis, and probably silly. When a person is dying, there's no evolutionary survival-reason for endorphins. That is especially true if one is dying without pain. As explanation, the use of endorphins seems an assertion of faith about biological fact. It is no better than tripe purveyed by the average faith healer.

There are at least four fields of evidence that rise among humans: religious, observational, luck, and creativity. Perhaps one or more are connected, perhaps not.

The first body of evidence concerns the religious and miraculous: the appearance of apparitions, or guidance by an unseen hand. The centuries are filled with reports of healings (Lourdes a modern example), visions, Joan of Arc, Joseph Smith, Mary Baker Eddy; and among contemporaries, the reported appearance of the Virgin Mary at Medjugorje. Such appearances are generally accompanied by revelations.

Guidance by an unseen hand has been reported so often in the history of America that it is practically a rib in our body politic. Many, perhaps most, substantial reports come from Puritans and Quakers in the 17th century. We have records of ships blown so far off course that death from starvation was inevitable; yet a sign in the heavens, and a correcting wind saved them.

One must approach such evidence with skepticism, but also with an open mind. After all, we have records of such evidence (in the western world) for over two thousand years. The odds on all of it being meaningless are impossibly long. There's just too much of it. We can't explain it. Perhaps we can't understand it, but it is the height of folly to deny that it exists.

Further, it is just plain impotent to say that if evidence cannot be duplicated, and thus subject to scientific method, it does not constitute evidence. There's no scientific way to explain sources of religious revelation. Yet, religious revelation happens over and over in history.

The second body of evidence is generally dismissed as illusory, or coincidental, or fabrications by unsettled minds. It includes ghostly sightings, flying saucers, possession by the Devil (or something equally nasty) and communications from the dead.

The standard responses to such evidence is generally, "It's a damnable lie," or, "Oh, lordy, I believe." Very few responses say, "I wonder?" or, "Let's examine the evidence."

If we do, we find that it is almost always intensely personal. While the first body of evidence is sometimes communal, this second sort is singular. Groups of people hardly ever see ghosts. Flying saucers, or lights in the sky, may be seen by large groups; but encounters with flying saucers are almost exclusively reported by individuals or couples. Possession by evil is generally one-on-one (although when we arrive at a discussion of creativity we'll see it happen to groups), and messages from the dead are exclusively reported by individuals. (Group séances may well be unrepresentative because of a long record of charlatanism.)

This second body of evidence can be subject to both psychological and physical examination. Some people are amazingly neurotic. Some are insane. Some are physically unbalanced. And for some, there seems no help. It is as if some genetic flaw, some "bad seed" compels them. Physicians can measure brain waves and chemical imbalances. Psychiatrists can exert their skills. Between medicine and psychiatry many are helped and some are healed.

If we set aside all evidence given by those who are emotionally or physically injured, we are still confronted by countless reports from people who are as sensible as salt. They are not famous liars. Some of them are beyond reproof or reproach. They are not lying, and have no record of hallucinations. For them, at least, something happened. They can't prove it. Yet, because of who they are, and because of their great numbers through the ages, their testimony constitutes valid evidence. I would, for example, no more argue with the mystical knowledge of some American Indians, than I would argue with the sun.

Good luck constitutes a third body of evidence. It sometimes happens beyond all statistical probability. It is with luck of gamblers that we see evidence of something "going on" that cannot be rationally explained. It is probably statistically impossible to make seventeen or eighteen successful passes with dice, yet it occasionally happens. I have seen three royal flushes in a night of poker. The winning hands were held by different people. No one in the game had sufficient skill to cheat, and the cards were not marked. And, we were playing for pennies, thus with no great motive to cheat. Three such hands in one night (with no wild cards) are statistically impossible. Gamblers speak of "lucky streaks," and "hot dice." One branch of psychology speaks of "extra sensory perception."[2]

Bad luck is practically impossible to demonstrate, but scarcely anyone over age twenty-five has not experienced a year in which a series of major bad things happened. I'm sure we've all heard someone speak to the effect, "I wouldn't live 1988 (or some other year) over again for all the money in the world."

A fourth body of evidence is creativity, and of all mysterious evidence, creativity is the kind most studied by thinkers and psychologists. The creative process has been examined and documented. It is so commonly demonstrated that it appears in college freshman textbooks. It is described almost perfectly, and not a soul who describes the process understands it.

Nor do artists, writers, theoreticians, physicists, architects, musicians, dancers, or actors. In general, the solitary artist; i.e. the writer or painter or sculptor, will report that "There are times when it's all coming together, like somebody or something runs the show." The writer will say, "Thus, I'm not writing, I'm typing. Later, I clean up the language, but when the story is coming, it comes from somewhere else." Painters tell us that their hand knows what to do, even when they don't. Sculptors the same. I doubt if there is a single worker in the solitary arts who will not make such a report.

Group creativity is something else. The creativity of groups has received small interest from thinkers and psychologists. They speak of "mob psychology," but rarely go beyond the mob. And yet, the idea has been around for a hundred and fifty years.

Back in the 19th century the French social thinker, August Compte, postulated the notion of The Group Mind. He tried to apply it to small groups and to nations. His ideas did not fly. He could not get his fellow thinkers, including Herbert Spencer, to buy into the idea. It would be wonderful if Compte were alive today, because his thought might now be valued.

I doubt if there is a theater group, a dance troupe, or a jazz band anywhere in this country that will not attest that at some point in a play or a performance, the group takes over. There isn't a symphonic musician anywhere who will not tell you that at some point the entire symphony pulls into a single mind and expresses the statement of the composer, and the symphony.

With the positive creation of art and music, I have little to think about. It operates so commonly in my life, and in the lives of my friends, that it gets taken for granted. It is negative creation by groups that I find worth examination.

I first stumbled on this when reading depositions of the Salem Witch Trials. I did not come unprepared to the reading. The 17th century was so fascinating that I'd studied somewhat of its writing, society, and culture. I was not an able historian, but was an able student.

Revelations abounded. It became evident that through circumstances (some beyond its control) Salem had gotten itself tied in a Gordian knot it could not slice. It was surrounded by other religionists (mostly Quakers) who held ideas that Salem considered evil. It had Indian problems. It had a tax rate as high as any in American history. It was isolated by weather for at least five months a year. Social control was held by the preacher. The educational level was nowhere near as high as in Boston. The town was filled with bickerings, some petty, some substantial. Any deviation from the accepted way of "doing things" constituted a terrible threat. As I have written elsewhere, Salem, when it self-destructed, did not explode. It imploded.

In consequence, Salem created hell, and the Devil walked the streets of Salem. One preacher couldn't have done it, although through history plenty of preachers have tried. One politician couldn't have done it, nor could one farmer; or one of anybody else. It took the mind of the entire town to create hell, because in the creation, dissent was at first silent. It was not mob psychology in any sense that we understand. It was genuine creation.

Once the proposition of group creation is accepted, it's easy to find all through history. The Nazis, for example, could not have gone so far, and so fast, had not Hitler been of the maniac quality that would build the group mind. An American historical example can be drawn from the witch hunts of Senator Joe McCarthy during the 1950s. A mob mentality did develop. Beyond that mentality, though, was a creative quality that produced a spirit of evil. We, who are old enough to have experienced it, will attest that something awful overran the mind of the nation. National insanity only faltered after McCarthy became so extreme that he became ridiculous.

The four bodies of evidence are simply that: evidence. They are not proof. Such evidence causes discomfort, and a certain amount of discomfort makes some people want to think things through. A lot of those people are writers.

Having accepted the fact of an invisible world, the writer may rightly ask: Is it my cup of tea? What can I do with it? Is it worth my time? How do I get a handle on it? Isn't reality difficult enough, without messing around in surreality? Is there something constructive about fantastical writing? Is it a valid part of the human experience, or is it only amusement?

Writers always find individual answers, because the task is individual. Some answer questions by saying: "It's amusement, and easy to sell." Others answer, "There's something going on and I need to examine it, because it needs come to the reader's attention." Such writers are usually worrywarts, or at least have some kind of mental warts. Writers who deal with the Unknowable, and with the power of the Unknowable—be it in the universe or in the human mind—tend to swing between practicality and downright mysticism. It takes immense courage, or immense stupidity, to mess with metaphoric gargoyles.

Writers choose fantasy, or magic realism, or science fiction. Others deal in horror, or allegory (as for example, *Watership Down* with its lovely thinking rabbits). For my own part, I am more than a little fond of ghosts.

II

One of the finest ghost stories I have read in many years is Peter Beagle's *Tamsin*. It contains everything that lies within the realm of a ghost story: character, situation, suspense, evil vs. good, innocence, heroism, and history.

The beauty of a ghost story is that it's almost impossible to write one without resorting to history. After all, if you've got a ghost, that ghost has ordinarily come from time past. (There are ghosts of the future, as in *A Christmas Carol*.)

As a fiction writer I think of myself as a historian. My history is not the pulling-together of a massive number of details, and the objective reporting and analysis of facts. I don't have that kind of ability, though capable historians are among the people whom I most admire.

A story is a different kind of history. It gives a feel of time(s), place(s), and event(s). The skilled writer can take us into a world we would never, otherwise, know. While there are many places I cannot take you, I can take you to a small ship on the North Atlantic, to a mist-ridden hollow in Kentucky or North Carolina, and to the Washington rainforest. I can take you along empty roads, or to the top of tall trees, or to the bays and snows of southeast Alaska; and I can tell you how things look and feel. What is more, in the process of taking you there, I discover feelings and sights and whole landscapes that even I did not consciously know existed.

Thus, when events in the story happen, they happen in the context of what I know and report, but also of what I discover. If I were indifferent, and reported a context I did not know (for example, flying a sailplane) the context would be no good. With a sour context, events in the story would have no meaning in the life of characters; and thus the story would have no meaning.

But, if I stick with what I know and one of my characters is a ghost, I can give the reader the feeling of what is, and what used to be; and I can do it at the same time.

I, and you, when you think about it, can tell whether the writer of a ghost story actually believes in ghosts. Most don't, and that is one reason why there are so many lousy ghost stories. If a writer doesn't believe in ghosts, then he or she will have a terrible time suspending disbelief. The story becomes an exercise in special effects, only.

Knowledge of ghosts is not something one acquires through simple faith. Or, if one does acquire it that way, then one is intellectually stuck before a campfire warming his frontside, while getting chilled along his spine by spooky stories. Simple faith, without reason for owning it, seems pretty adolescent.

Knowledge generally arrives through experience, reading, and observation. By observation, I mean more than simply looking at events or the world. Observation requires thought.

Here is a simple example: I used to teach at a small university that boasts a magnificent campus. Old and new buildings are surrounded by huge fir trees that tower over rooftops. It is easy to walk across campus and say things like, "Wow!" The trees offer greater meaning, though, if one knows that the university was a hundred years old in 1990.

The university is in Tacoma, Washington, and Tacoma was once a lumber town. During the 19th century forests were chopped like grass before a lawnmower. There was no clear-cutting, though, because there were no chainsaws. Unmarketable trees were left standing. These would have been trees younger than thirty years.

When land was cleared to build a college, marketable trees went. The young trees remained. After one hundred years, it was a fair guess that the giant trees on campus were, give-or-take, a hundred thirty years old.

I could look out my classroom windows and feel the presence of those old lumbermen. I could see their tools: the steam donkey (a yarder for moving logs), their two-man crosscut saws, their axes, their teams of horses or mules hauling logs to mills, or to a steam railway that ran to the harbor. I could imagine them working through summer heat or winter rain in this wet northwest.

I could do all this because reading combined with experience. As a student of history, my reading about the northwest prepared me for a one-hundred-year-old scene. My work experience had once been in trees when I worked for a tree company in Arlington, Massachusetts. (There was time when I claimed a Harvard education on the grounds that I had climbed every tree on the Harvard campus. It was a bit of a stretch. There are a zillion trees on the Harvard campus.)

With that background there was no problem understanding ghosts. In my mind those old lumbermen busied themselves around that campus every day, and students walked among them. Just because no one could see them didn't mean they weren't there.

"Lordy," you say, "I'm reading the words of a maniac."

It's a possibility. On the other hand, we may be onto something. Suppose that our usual ways of looking at time and history are flawed. We think that Monday comes ahead of Tuesday, and when Monday is over we won't see another Monday until next week. That seems a real limit on consciousness.

If we admit, though, that the past operates with great force in our Monday lives, as well as Tuesday, and the rest, maybe we can step beyond the limits. In some ways, at least, we may live a series of Mondays. At least we live according to ways that are laid down by the past, and not by a succession of days.

Virtually everything we know and do steps toward us from the past. Let us look at only a very few examples:

Family. We may, through thought and experience, eventually create original forms. No one starts that way. Almost everything we accept or reject about human relationships began as learning in some kind of family group, even if that group was an orphan's home.

We are raised by people (usually parents) who were raised by parents who were raised by parents, etc. If one's grandfather was a farmer, then his son will know things about farming even if the son lives in a city. He'll know them because his dad tells tales, and the family sometimes visits grandpa.

Let's say the city-son hates farms. The grandson will also have an attitude toward farms. He's either going to embrace cows in order to offend his dad, or else he'll think ill of milking-time because "that's what pop told me."

Law: Our entire system of laws derive from English law and philosophy that reach far back beyond the Magna Carta. And, the

Magna Carta has roots all the way back to the Code of Hammurabi. Six thousand years, give or take.

Society: We boast a diverse society made up of many people with different customs. Virtually all of those customs step right out of the past. A few, such as watching too much television, are fairly recent.

Religion: People who take it seriously, be they Christian or Jew or Muslim, have to take the historical Moses seriously. People who do not give a snip for religion still live in a world that does, so even an atheist has roots in the doings of Moses.

Even superficial matters like dress have already been decided. Contemporary men and women generally own pants, not caftans. Styles come and go, but only a very small percentage of us own kilts. This has been so in the western world since the peasant frock, and the Roman toga, hit the rag pile some centuries back. In a very real way, the past is right here with us, hanging off of our suspenders.

Briefly put, at least ninety percent of the way we live our lives comes directly from the past. To me it follows, then, that just because I can't see things invisible, does not mean they aren't there. The creative eye learns to see them because the creative eye trains itself to look.

The challenge for the creative writer, and the creative reader, is the same as the challenge for painter and sculptor and musician. In order to dwell with ghosts, we need to learn how to feel the joy and pain of the past. Otherwise, no spirit rises from the pages, or canvas, or stone. Compassion is wanting.

As this essay is being written, I'm reading *The Tide At Sunrise*, a history of the Russo-Japanese war at the beginning of the 20th century. If I had not read a lot, and been around quite a bit, the history would seem fairly objective and cold. Not a single ghost would be present.

But, I have read, and I have been around. I remember Pearl Harbor. I have read *Shogun* and *Sayonara* and *Fires on the Plain*. The overwhelming devotion of the Japanese to their emperor during the Russo-Japanese war does not surprise me, and I expect to find it where I do find it; in the joy of soldiers marching to certain death. I mourn those soldiers, but I also understand something of their joy.

And, I have read Karl Marx and *The Communist Manifesto*. I have read a history, *The Fall of the Great Powers* which, among other matters, tells of the arrogance and violence of Czars Nicholas I and Nicholas II. I have read the humorless Solzenitzen and the gentle Abram Tertz, both of whom did time in Soviet prison camps. I know the state of the Russian people as the 20th century opened. Thus, do I understand the dogged determination of Russian soldiers and sailors even though their situations were doomed. I can feel their fear, and how they longed for a home they knew they would never see again.

Spirits rise from the pages. I'm not dealing with dry fact, but with human hopes and fears and dreams. Does it seem strange to mourn Japanese soldiers now dead these hundred years? Or, does it seem strange to mourn the same for Russians who were so badly led, and so heartily defeated? If it did seem strange, I would have no right to be a writer, and no right at all to tell ghost stories.

But, if the writer and reader do understand that men marched to their deaths en masse, but died individually, then writer and reader are ready to understand the presence of ghosts.

Ghosts are, first of all, a metaphor for history. The metaphor becomes strong as the ghost becomes strong. When the ghost is an actual character, as in *Tamsin*, the past rises and mixes with the present. The reason so many good ghost stories cause uneasiness is not because they scare the reader (although some do), but because they take the reader into two dimensions at the same time.

It is this dual quality that causes a ghost story to succeed. For that reason, one can write a ghostly tale and not scare anyone. If a ghost is a metaphor, in addition to being a character, then the ghost is in the happy position of being able to help the living. We have a friendly ghost, and I don't mean Casper.

Let's look at it this way: The ghost is someone (or, as we'll soon see, something) manifesting a spectral life after death. The ghost became dead for any number of reasons, including its own screw-ups. If, for example, it died while trying to drive a fifty-mile-an-hour curve at eighty, and if it appears five hundred yards before that curve on late Saturday nights, there's not a message of threat, but one of salvation.

Equally, ghosts bearing messages need not be people. They need not even be animals. They can be mountains and cars and ships and trees. Creatures or objects of the past gain fantastic reality when they become ghosts in a ghost story.

I am absolutely sure, for example, that if one has lived in the American Southeast, and not seen ghostly soldiers and horses moving silent through mist, than one has not been paying attention. I am positive that if one climbs a one-hundred-foot tree, and while resting, does not feel a presence; danger increases. It increases because the climber does not have enough respect for who he's with.

If climbing tall trees is too scary, try walking through an auto graveyard where wrecks have been sitting for so long that weeds grow through floorboards. Be there sun or mist, watch what's happening.

Thus can we understand that ghosts of people, and sometimes ghosts of machines, are there to help the living. If, for example, generals of WWI had turned back to study the Russo-Japanese war, and acknowledged the hundreds of thousands of men who died, those generals would not have then destroyed an entire generation of English and European men.

The generals may have read the casualty figures of the Russo-Japanese war. They may have nodded their heads with pretended wisdom when they thought of assault against mountainous or dug-in positions, or defense of those positions. They may have read the record.

What they didn't read were the spirits who rose from the record, and those spirits were twofold:

The combatants on both sides were going through the first war with truly modern weapons. Their ghosts would have explained that nothing anyone ever knew about war applied. Something different was happening. Something awful.

The other ghostly, and ghastly spirit would have been a weapon, a machine gun. Had it rattled its voice in the ears of WWI generals as they marched their troops to war, a half a million men might not have died. But, then, generals do not believe in ghosts. They did not learn from a ghost that a single weapon had changed war forever.

Thus, are ghosts among us bringing messages. I have discovered that they exist, more often than not, to offer aid instead of fear. I have grown fond of them because they have so much to teach.

Notes

1. In his old age he practiced what he called "Cerebral Hygiene" which meant that he read no books except the ones he had written.

2. As a young man during the '50s I recall resistance to the whole business of extra sensory perception. A favorite story of the time, and one that was probably true, said that the President of the American Psychological Association was on record: "If there was a tenth this much evidence to prove something else, I would believe it. If there was ten times the evidence to prove this, I still wouldn't believe it."

Jack Cady (1932-2004) won the Atlantic Monthly "First" award in 1965 for his story, "The Burning." He continued writing and authored nearly a dozen novels, one book of critical analysis of American literature, and more than fifty short stories. Over the course of his literary career, he won the Iowa Prize for Short Fiction, the National Literary Anthology Award, the Washington State Governor's Award, the Nebula Award, the Bram Stoker Award, and the World Fantasy Award.

Prior to a lengthy career in education, Jack worked as a tree high climber, a Coast Guard seaman, an auctioneer, and a long-distance truck driver. He held teaching positions at the University of Washington, Clarion College, Knox College, the University of Alaska at Sitka, and Pacific Lutheran University. He spent many years living in Port Townsend, Washington.

Resurrection House, through its Underland Press imprint, is publishing a comprehensive retrospective of his work in a project called *The Cady Collection*.

Gordon Van Gelder was an editor for St. Martin's Press for twelve years and was the editor of *The Magazine of Fantasy & Science Fiction* from 1997 through 2014. He has been honored twice with the Hugo Award and he has also won the World Fantasy Award twice. He lives in New Jersey, where he works as the publisher of *F&SF*.